WARP SPEED CHARLIE

THE DRAGON MAGE BOOK 8

SCOTT BARON

"He moved on, in the centre of a widening circle. He wasn't an enemy, he was a nemesis."
— Terry Pratchett

CHAPTER ONE

He didn't know what hit him, but Charlie found himself flying through the air, his arms and legs akimbo as he tumbled end over end before hitting the ground.

Hard.

"Okay, okay, hang on a minute. That's just not fair," Charlie griped, slowly pushing himself up to his elbows on the dusty patch of reddish turf, where he'd been unceremoniously thrown yet again.

"There is no 'fair' in combat," Kort replied, the master assassin smiling with a hint of amusement. "There is merely living or dead."

"I could not have said it better myself," Bawb added, reaching down to help his human friend to his feet.

Farmatta, the deadly assassin who just so happened to also be an old woman—in appearance and age, though certainly not skill and energy—laughed with glee. She had been the one to upend the human this time, and had taken great pleasure in doing so.

"Call it what you will, but four on one isn't exactly an

example of reasonable odds, is all I'm saying," Charlie said, dusting himself off.

"*Three* on one. I did not lay a finger on you," Pimbrak said, the dapper Wampeh Ghalian master's clothing untainted by sweat, blood, or dust.

"No, but you *might* have," Charlie grumbled. "You were just *lurking*. And with Wampeh Ghalian, that's just as good."

Pimbrak laughed. "And you were paying attention to the man *not* engaging you. Very good. A lesson far too many have learned the hard way."

"If by 'learned' you mean died a quick death at your hands, that is," Charlie corrected.

His four adversaries shared amused looks, but only Bawb felt any pang of sympathy for the human test dummy. Training was pain, more often than not, and the more you sweat in training, the less you bleed in combat. But Charlie was his friend, and he did wish the best outcome for him.

The others, however, simply took this for what it was. Namely, another teaching moment. One that might help the poor human keep his head attached to his shoulders should he find himself faced with opponents *truly* trying to kill him.

Henchmen and guards they had no doubt he could easily handle. In fact, for someone who had only been training with the Geist a relatively short while, they were all impressed with his martial prowess. Of. course they'd never admit as much out loud.

But Charlie had managed to earn a modicum of respect from the band of elite assassins, who normally wouldn't have so much as looked at him twice, let alone provided any training. Having the Geist vouch for him didn't hurt.

They'd only just met their long-lost brother, but Bawb and the Wampeh Ghalian masters were already thick as thieves––or assassins, as the case may be. For Bawb, being with members of his order again after so long was a refreshing breath of familiar air.

For them, having the legendary Geist in their midst was an unexpected and quite welcome surprise as well. More so for the fact that Bawb was the sole living Wampeh Ghalian to know the location of the order's secret cache of wealth, weapons, and no one knew what else beyond legends and rumors.

No one but Bawb, that is.

As the sole surviving member of The Three––the other two having perished hundreds of years prior, just as he went missing when he was thrown through time and space to ancient Earth by a collision of spells gone wrong––Bawb alone could lead his brothers and sisters to reclaim their rightful property, hidden and untouchable for centuries.

His return to them would have been a fortuitous turn of events in any case, but with what was shaping up to be an all-out war against the mysterious Visla Dominus on their hands, his reappearance was even more so. And from what they'd seen of the visla's powers thus far, it looked as if they'd likely need every last bit of whatever resources were secreted there.

"Might I join?" Hunze asked from her seat on the periphery of the training ground.

"Of course," Kort said, stepping aside with a little bow.

"You sure you want to do this?" Charlie asked.

Hunze smiled brightly, her cheerful good nature radiating almost as brightly as her golden hair. "Why wouldn't I, Charlie? It's important to practice."

"I know. It's just that––"

A quick kick to his head sent him staggering backward. "Hey! We didn't say go!"

"Go!" Hunze said with a chuckle, her next flurry of attacks already underway.

Charlie quickly put his shock aside as he engaged with his until recently pacifist friend in a fierce exchange of attacks and defenses, both physical and magical. Hunze was not just good, she was in possession of the Geist's martial skills, the result of a neuro-stim transfer drip fed into her mind over their months together on modern Earth.

The technology had seemed strange to the magic-using man at first, but, ever one to seize upon any advantage available to him, Bawb had quickly adopted the device's use and had Cal, the massive AI running Los Angeles, adjust and tune it for him and his lady love.

It hadn't worked, though. That is, not until he cast an ancient, arcane spell, granting her power back to her. And with that, there was an unexpected result.

Not only had Hunze abruptly gained control of her own magically charged hair, as he had hoped, but all of the knowledge that had, for all intents and purposes, appeared not to be sticking despite the neuro-stim's best efforts suddenly clicked and fell into place.

Hunze now knew the ways of the Wampeh Ghalian, and that made her one of the deadliest women in the galaxy.

But for the moment, she was enjoying some good-natured sparring with her dear friend. Their relationship didn't stop her from laying him out repeatedly, however.

"Charlie, you need to guard your weak side better," Bawb said from the sidelines as yet another kick landed.

"What do you think I'm trying to do, Bob? It's not like she's some scrub wildly throwing kicks, here. It's like fighting you, only she's better looking," Charlie said with a chuckle.

"On that point, I would not argue," the pale assassin replied, flashing a warm smile to his Ootaki lover. "Dearest, would you please make my point for me?"

"Of course, love," she replied, then flashed out yet another kick, pulling back at the last minute.

It was fun beating on Charlie, in a playful way, that is, but she didn't want to leave him black and blue. At least, not any more than he usually was from training. Leila wouldn't like it if her king was returned to her covered in bruises.

But she was not here. In fact, she was nowhere to be found. Leila was *somewhere* in this strange, magical galaxy, but Charlie and his friends had no idea where. Not yet, anyway. All they knew was that she was somehow with Visla Palmarian's men, but precisely how or why remained a mystery.

But this was not the time to think about that. No one in this time or place knew who she was, so she was safe. And this was the time to train, not miss your loved ones. There was plenty of time for those worries later.

The other Wampeh Ghalian stepped forward, each ready to impart another lesson to their human pupil. It would hurt, and Charlie would be quite sore, but at the end of the day he was grateful. The little adjustments made to his techniques in sessions like these could very well mean the difference between life and death. And Charlie was very much a fan of the former over the latter.

CHAPTER TWO

"You've really improved your slaap defenses," Bawb said as he took a seat beside his aching friend as he held a cool compress to his jaw.

More than a few blows had landed with a little more force than he'd have liked, but the pain of the impacts did more to drive home the lesson than any text or static practice form could.

"Let's say I'm quite motivated, Bob. But seriously, it really means a lot that the others are willing to take the time to work with me. I know they're making an exception, and a big one at that."

"True, you are not a Wampeh Ghalian, but we fight toward the same objective, and you have more than proven yourself worthy of this knowledge. In fact, if you were to dedicate the next ten or fifteen years, I think you could even make a fine assassin," Bawb said with a wry grin.

"Ha-ha. Very funny. And it wouldn't take me fifteen years. I like to think I can handle myself okay."

"True, you can. And seeing as you did kill all the Tslavars in a system—albeit by accident—I think your body count may even surpass that of many in my order."

That had been something of a sore spot for Charlie, and Bawb was trying to help him get over it. He had lashed out with his magic to stop a deadly attack from which they had little chance of survival, tying his own magic to the strange, other-galaxy power flowing through Rika, but it had gone a bit awry, killing hundreds.

The violent effect had been partly due to the almost translucent white magical pigment inked into Rika's skin, which gave her great power. That, combined with the magical energy of the black sun she'd been exposed to, added to her own strength, making her spells able to cut through the enemy defenses.

Ara's Zomoki power, and the magic of the locks of Hunze's hair, wielded by Bawb, were also tied to his power, feeding it as it grew, but this was something more. And Rika had been the key.

She was what had provided him the break in the Tslavar shielding, but Charlie alone had done the killing. Given the strength of the enemy's defensive spells, he'd used all of his continually growing power, hoping to stop the attack before it was too late.

Instead, his spell blew through their enemies' defenses—thanks to Rika's magic—and in an instant, every Tslavar combatant in the system was dead. And with them, Charlie's friends had inherited over a dozen powerful warships, each of them drifting in space as their crews lay motionless on their decks.

Once the elation of realizing they weren't going to die had passed, Charlie was horrified. Horrified, but amazed at his own power. And here he was, unable to utilize any of it to find his queen.

"I'm going to go after her," Charlie said, removing the

compress from his cheek. "Leila's out there somewhere, and on one of Visla Palmarian's ships."

"You know you cannot go chasing after every ship in the galaxy, hoping to stumble across her."

"It's a Palmarian ship."

"Fine. You cannot go chasing every Palmarian ship in hopes of finding her."

"But there's something fishy with this Visla Palmarian guy, Bob. And everything keeps coming back to Slafara, which quite conveniently happens to be his home planet. You can't tell me you don't see the writing on the wall."

"Of course I am aware of these irregularities. And I agree, they need to be looked into. But we need a plan, Charlie. You cannot go running off into a situation like this without intel, and a lot of it."

Charlie grumbled, but he knew his friend was right. "It's just hard sitting by and waiting. I mean, if Palmarian really is tied up in this whole mess, then what if someone figures out who she is?"

"Why would anyone have reason to suspect her of being in conflict with Visla Dominus? Remember, Charlie, she is from *this* galaxy. The fleet is targeting *yours*. Leila should slide by without notice."

"I hope you're right," Charlie said. "But I can't just wait idly for something to happen."

"I know it is difficult, my friend," Bawb said, eyeing Hunze as she spoke with the other Ghalian masters not far away. "We will find her. But we will do it the smart way. I shall have one of the order sent to infiltrate the staff under Visla Palmarian's employ. It will take a little time, but they will gather intelligence, as well as observing goings-on and rumors within the ranks. They should be able to discern where she is. If she is still with the visla's ships, that is."

Reluctantly, Charlie let his emotions calm to a simmer. "It's hard not doing anything, Bob."

"I know. But she will be all right. And we *will* find her."

"Thanks, man," Charlie said, his thoughts drifting to their other friends. The ones who were no longer in this galaxy.

A sizable group of them had crossed over in the recent fight, fleeing the deadly onslaught from Visla Dominus's fleet as it tried to reclaim the portal. Not only had Rika and Marban slipped into the distant realm, but their new allies, Daisy and Korbin, had as well.

"I hope the others are doing okay," Charlie said.

"We know Rika is safe and sound," Bawb replied. "The portal is already functioning on its new timing, so she and Jo obviously made it without issue. And she was flying with Marban, so unless he was targeted by our ships, he should be fine as well. I think it is safe to assume the others fared equally as well, so once we have a proper plan in place, we should be capable of effecting efficient and relatively safe crossings of the portal with the new timing."

"And in the meantime, we'll keep popping in relatively close to check the little spy satellite Zed sent through. As long as it keeps functioning, we've got a way to talk to the other side during those brief open sequences."

"Precisely. Now, shouldn't you be preparing another of those burst transmissions to embed in the device? We want to be ready when it next opens. When is that, exactly?" Bawb asked, though he already knew the answer.

"Twenty-three hours," was the reply. "You're right, I should put together that transmission packet. I'm sure they'll be glad to hear our numbers are slowly growing. Who knows? We might have an actual fleet pretty soon if things keep going at this rate."

"I hope so, my friend. For we shall most certainly need it."

CHAPTER THREE

Daisy was pacing the vast war room aboard Zed's expansive command ship in orbit above Earth. Freya and the other craft ferrying the additional participants in the confab were safely tucked away in his massive hangar network.

It was taking some time for all of the leaders of the allied systems to make their way to the meeting, some having to make warps spanning a great many solar systems on their way to the blue-green orb third from the sun.

The wait was driving one particularly on-edge woman batty.

"Stop pacing, Daze," Sarah said inside her sister's head. *"You're gonna wear a hole in the deck."*

"Yeah, what I said," Sarah added.

"Oh my God, will you two stop?" Daisy grumbled.

It was tough enough having the neural clone of her formerly dead sister riding around in her brain, opining about all things big and small, but now that the living iteration of her dead-not-dead sister was there as well, the chatter of the two of them could be more than a little grating at times, no matter how much she loved her. Both copies.

She could have simply removed the small neuro link patch

she had stuck to the skin behind her ear, but no matter how she might want to at times, that would be rude. Besides, Freya had spent a long time devising the tiny device. It wouldn't work for long distances, but up close like this, it was just as efficient as the slender headband aboard Freya, and it allowed the two Sarahs to communicate with one another.

The injuries that Sarah—living Sarah, that is—had suffered nearly two decades earlier when she was killed-not-killed had left her minus an arm, and with massive internal damage. Freya's heroic attempt to save her had required the use of not only a powerful stasis chamber to hold her at the edge of life and death, but also a massive reconstruction of her damaged body with the AI's experimental nanite technology.

Freya had devised the little machines and integrated them into her own hull and systems, but whether or not they'd be able to save a flesh-and-blood woman was another matter entirely. It took time, and a lot of adjusting after the fact, but Sarah was made whole again, her arm replaced by a perfect replica, courtesy of her nanite swarm.

Even the flesh coloring of the arm was correct, the tiny machines tapping into her mind's image of herself and shifting to her will. A great many organs, including her ruptured lungs, were also rebuilt by the little machines. Time spent in the void of space sans space suit does terrible things to a body.

But Sarah was alive, and that was all that mattered.

"Daisy, stop!" she groaned, as her sister once more began pacing back and forth.

"This waiting is killing me. We need to act, and I mean *yesterday*. You know what those bastards did. What they're capable of."

"I know you want payback, but—"

"You're goddamn right I want payback. It's the only way I can keep my family safe, Sarah. That includes you."

"Hey, I'm not exactly a defenseless waif, you know," she said, her nanite swarm hand abruptly snapping into the shape of a deadly spike with a single thought.

"*Yeah. We're kind of badass, Daze,*" Sarah agreed. "*What you need to do now is chill and focus on the meeting. After that you can rage all you want, okay?*"

"Fine," Daisy grumbled. "But some magical alien asses are in serious need of kicking."

It only took an hour for the remainder of the key leaders of the allied forces to arrive and make their way to the war room. Cal, the greater AI representing Earth, was present, as was Sid, the AI mind overseeing Dark Side moon base. Freya was there with Daisy, naturally. Freya's partner, Joshua, the former mind behind NORAD and hands-down the greatest AI military strategist Earth had ever known, was there as well.

Representatives of the most recent race to join the alliance, the Uroks, were on hand, as were the Chithiid representatives from Earth. Their main leadership had not made the hasty journey to Earth yet, but their local reps were more than capable. Even the Kathiri had sent an envoy.

"I'm glad you all could make it on such short notice," Admiral Celeste Harkaway said.

The silver-haired woman's greeting silenced the room. All had the utmost respect for her and what she'd done before, during, and after the Great War. Her husband, Lars Harkaway, the gruff and ready captain of the *Váli*, stood against the far wall, watching with an appreciative eye. His wife was a thing of wonder to him, even to this day. After all they'd been through, and despite the decades, he still found himself smitten.

"Admiral, it is a great pleasure to see you again," an orange-skinned Urok by the name of Grand Marshal Fott said.

"I'm sorry it's so soon, and not for a more pleasant reason," Admiral Harkaway replied. "The Urok have only just become allies, and, yet, here we are, drawn into a conflict together after such a short time."

"Yet it was a conflict caused by these same adversaries that brought us together in the first place. For that, at least, we have them to thank. But it would seem this new threat is even greater than before, if I am not mistaken."

"You're correct," she replied. "Things have changed. When Rika Gaspari crossed back from the other galaxy, she brought with her not only valuable intelligence, but also a new means to control the portal. Given what so recently happened with our failed attempt to send a force across, her revelations are quite astounding."

"How so?"

"Rika, would you mind?"

"Of course, Admiral," she replied. "While I was in the other galaxy, I discovered more about the nature of the fleet that had formed to invade our world. It's far, far larger than we had ever imagined, and it is growing."

"But we have the ships of several combined worlds at our disposal," Fott noted.

"True, but so do they, and it seems they are led by an incredibly powerful visla going by the name Dominus."

"Visla. That's their top classification of wizard, if I'm not mistaken."

"That's correct, Grand Marshal," Rika replied. "And this one is more powerful than any seen in centuries. A man named Korbin, who is a powerful visla in his own right, came through the portal with us. He knows the ins and outs of that galaxy, and he made it clear in no uncertain terms that this Visla Dominus is of a caliber he's never seen before."

"So we send more ships. One man can't possibly be that strong."

"Unfortunately, that's where you're wrong. Kara, one of the teenage girls who were unfortunately dragged into this mess, happens to not only be Korbin's niece, but also the daughter of a Visla Palmarian. He's supposedly one of the most powerful vislas in ages, yet it seems even he might not be able to stand up to this Dominus character."

"Can we gain his alliance, then?" Fott asked.

"Well, that's another issue. There are some concerns he might be covertly in league with Dominus in some way, which would only add to his threat."

A murmur fluttered through the gathered leadership.

"And they figured out the timing we'd set the portal on, which put us at a serious risk for a crossover. The countdown was the same every time, you see. Fortunately, I've taken over with that casting now, and we control the portal's new timing."

"What about the others?"

"Jo transmitted a coded burst to our people on the other side. We're all dialed in, so at least we have the means to keep the visla's fleet from timing the opening and making a rush to our side. For now, anyway."

"Thank you, Rika," Zed said, the AI stepping into the conversation. "Now, as for our defensive systems, as you've all seen in the prior briefing, it seems our warp systems simply do not function properly in the other galaxy. However, this appears to be a double-edged sword, in that their magical defenses do not function as well in ours."

"Can we find a way to overcome them? To work around their shielding?" Daisy asked. "There's gotta be a way to cut through and make them vulnerable."

"We're working on it. And Rika's magic does seem to affect it as well. Now, if we can just figure out how and why, then apply that to our own weaponry, we might gain an advantage."

"Why don't we just lob a nuke through the portal, then?" Daisy suggested.

"We can't just throw nukes around like that," Captain Harkaway interjected. "Jeez, Daisy, you know that."

"We need to knock those bastards out. Hard and fast," she countered.

"Not like that."

"But we need to do *something*, Captain. We're just sitting on our hands, when we should be acting."

"Enough, you two. Cut it out." Admiral Harkaway interjected. "No fighting in the war room."

A curious look crossed Rika's face. "I was just wondering, what about other, non-radioactive tech? I mean, we're using railguns, which are cool, but they're from my time. Surely you have some other cool stuff at this point. Why not lasers, now that we're in the future?"

"Mirrors," Zed replied. "All they'd need is really strong mirrors."

"Shit. Right," Rika said. "But maybe sonic pulses?"

"No sound in space," the AI replied with a chuckle.

"Well, duh," Rika snarked back.

"Ooh, sassy. I like her," Sarah said with a little laugh.

"What I mean is, when we engage them *in atmosphere*, a sonic attack might be something their magic defenses can't cope with. I know I never learned any spells of that kind, so maybe they don't know how to defend against it."

Zed pondered for a moment. "An interesting theory, Rika. We do have some devices along those lines in deep storage. Mainly crowd control units, but we could see how modifications might make them more suitable for our purposes. Cal, would you mind?"

"I've already got my people tasked with pulling them from mothballs," the Earthbound AI replied. "Daisy. Freya. Is there any chance of getting the Big Gun working again?"

"You know we haven't been able to get it working again since the war," Daisy said. "And even if we could, seeing as it runs on warp energy, I wouldn't dare fire it off in a galaxy where that power malfunctions all over the place. You agree, Freya?"

"Yeah. Daisy's pretty spot-on. If the Big Gun misfired it could take out our entire fleet. It's just not worth the risk."

"You know she could probably make it work if she really wanted to," Sarah said.

Yeah, but only in this galaxy. Seeing how much destruction it can cause, it's no wonder she doesn't want to rebuild it. When she created it, she was just a kid. But she's older now. Has a kid of her own. I'm actually glad she doesn't want to rebuild the greatest weapon of mass destruction ever created.

"Says the woman who just wanted to throw a nuke randomly through a wormhole."

Portal. And not randomly. The bad guys are just sitting there asking for it.

"I think, given the magical nature of our foe, we need to bring the newcomer in on this conversation," the admiral said. "If you all agree, I'll request Korbin join us."

"There's more to him than meets the eye," Joshua said, his great tactical mind having been studying the man since the moment he arrived. "I think he is a far greater asset to our cause than any realize."

"He is a strong caster, that's for sure," Rika said.

"That's not what I mean. But whether or not I am correct in my assumption depends on the man himself," Joshua noted.

"I'll have Marty go get him," Freya suggested. "He and Arlo are home and free. I'll have him up here within the hour. You are eavesdropping again, aren't you, Marty?"

A silence hung in the air a moment.

"Well, kind of," the chided AI replied.

"What did I tell you about that?" Freya asked.

"Not to do it. Am I in trouble?"

"Well, you did overcome a quintuple dead-locked comms filter in the process," Freya said with obvious pride. "Go pick up Korbin. We'll talk about this later."

The assembled group broke for refreshments and less distressing conversation while they waited, hoping the mystery man from another galaxy might possess a solution to their growing problem.

CHAPTER FOUR

A blast of relatively mild magic slammed into the poor human volunteer, flinging him backward a good five meters. No worse for wear, he rose to his feet and brushed himself off, impressed with the strange magical powers this newcomer possessed.

What he didn't know was that if Korbin had *actually* been trying to harm him, he'd never have stood again. For that matter, he likely wouldn't even have had feet to rise to.

"Did you see what I did there? What Gregory here did wrong?" Korbin asked the rapt observers.

"He tried to attack you head-on when you were expecting him?" one of the onlookers said.

"Yes, that's part of it. But also, he came at someone wearing one of these," he said, holding up his arm and showing off his konus. "This is a konus, and with it, even a non-powered person can utilize its stored magic. And this goes for people of your realm as well, once you learn the core principles of its function."

"Are we going to get one?" another asked.

"No, I'm afraid not. These are a rare commodity in this galaxy, and the few we have must be dedicated to those already well versed in their use."

He was about to continue his lesson when the unusual communications device he'd been provided began chirping on his hip.

"Uh, sir? Your comms, sir," the man he'd been throwing about said.

"What? Oh, yes, of course," Korbin said, fumbling the unit from its clip. "Yes? This is Korbin. Copy. Over?"

"You don't have to say all of that, Korbin," Daisy said over the comms.

"But Ripley said——"

"Ripley was being a brat," Daisy replied with a chuckle. "Look, we need you to come up and join this little powwow. Everyone wants to hear your perspective on the goings-on in person."

"I will go fetch my vessel and be up to you shortly, then."

"No need. I'm sending one of ours to your position. Marty should be there in thirty seconds."

"Ten seconds," a chipper, young AI interjected on the line. "I kinda hit the afterburner on the way over."

"You have a warp engine, Marty. You don't use an afterburner. *No one* uses an afterburner. Not for hundreds and hundreds of years," Daisy said with a knowing sigh.

Marty and Arlo were a team all right, and the AI had most definitely picked up on his human counterpart's quirkiness. Something she was very, very well aware of. Arlo was her kid, after all.

"Well, yeah," Marty said. "But it sounds badass."

"Arlo, did you teach him that?" Daisy asked.

"We might have been watching some old vid files together," the teenager replied.

Just then the shadow of the ship flashed overhead, pulling some serious g's as it banked and dropped down to land in the clearing near Korbin's demonstration area. The dust had just settled when the door popped open and a spry teenager just a few months older than Ripley hopped out.

"Hey, Korbin!" Arlo said with his usual pep. "Marty and me are here to take you up to see my mom and the others."

"Marty and *I*," Daisy corrected.

"Oops, left the comms open," the teen grumbled. "Yeah, Marty and I. That's what I meant. Anyway, let's boogie!"

"Your son speaks a strange dialect my translation spell has some difficulty with," Korbin said over the comms.

"Tell me about it," Daisy replied. "But he's a good kid and a great pilot. And Marty's one hell of a ship, so you're in good hands."

Korbin nodded once, then turned to his assembled class. "To be continued," he said, then boarded the sleek craft.

Marty powered up and lifted off immediately.

"Request flyby, tower," the ship said in an amused tone.

"Negative, Ghost Rider, the pattern is full," Arlo replied with a laugh.

Korbin looked perplexed. "What's going on? What is a ghost rider? Honestly, I think my translation spell is truly having problems."

"Nah, inside joke. Just sit back and enjoy the ride. Punch it, Marty."

Korbin, used to flying via magical transport, was startled at the violent application of G-force to his body as the ship accelerated up and out of the atmosphere. Only once they were in space did the pressure cease driving him into his seat.

"I hope that wasn't too much," Marty said. "You okay, Korbin?"

The color was finally returning to the poor man's face as his blood flow resumed its normal coursing through his veins.

"Yes, I'm fine, though that was a rather unsettling experience," he replied.

"So it's true? Your ships don't experience any G-forces when they maneuver in atmosphere?" Arlo asked.

"If by G-forces you mean the pressures of rapid movement, then you are mostly correct. Our flight spells are linked with a very standard pair of others, namely the two that keep you from being thrown about, and the other which keeps your feet on the deck once you reach space."

"Oh, so it's a gravity spell," Arlo mused. "That's so cool. You hear that, Marty? They've got spells for that stuff."

"Beats gravitational generators, probably," the AI ship said. "I wonder if we could get one for me. What do you think, Korbin?"

"I think it would be difficult, given your apparent age."

"Hey, I'm not that old!"

"I mean no offense, but you are a mature intellect, and as such, casting is more difficult to learn. Cal was informing me of this quandary with your AI brethren just the other day."

"Well, poopsticks," Marty grumbled. "I thought I could be a magic ship. *That* would have been cool."

Korbin felt a fondness for the unusual craft. It seemed a few of the artificial minds in this galaxy possessed more than a little quirk, though he had a good idea why this particular one leaned toward the odd end of the spectrum.

"You're Freya's offspring, right? And the one called Joshua is your father?"

"Yeah, though not in the gross, fluids way people do it. But, yeah. They made me."

"Fascinating," Korbin said, taking in the ship around him. "Smart vessels making more smart vessels. Yours truly is an unusual world."

"You think that's unusual? Just wait till you meet the others," Arlo said as they neared the mass of Zed's orbiting command ship. "We've got a whole smorgasbord of unusual waiting to talk to you."

CHAPTER FIVE

Arlo and Marty were chattering incessantly during the relatively short flight ferrying Korbin to meet with the others. The teen seemed a good enough sort, but his exuberance, combined with the confusing banter he and the AI ship shared, could become tiring quite quickly, he thought.

Fortunately, they soon landed on Zed's spacious main hangar deck, the Earth-tech sealing the space quickly and pressurizing it with air. Korbin noted a magical force barrier would be far more efficient, and could even be cast to allow craft with the right magical signature to enter and exit without disrupting the seal.

But that was a conversation for a later date. He had people waiting for him.

Korbin recognized the sleek, black, deadly looking craft resting nearby. It had been engaged in the battle with Visla Dominus's fleet and had handled itself admirably, even managing to take a number of the attacking vessels out of the fight, despite their magical defenses.

"You would be Freya, if I'm not mistaken," Korbin said as he was guided past the ship toward the entry to the main corridor leading to the war room. "A pleasure to make your acquaintance."

"You too, Korbin. That was some pretty nifty flying you did back before we crossed over," she replied. "You're a talented pilot."

"Thank you. And so are you. I observed your engagement with the enemy for a time. Most impressive."

"Aww, shucks. You know how to make a gal blush."

"I'm sorry, what?"

"Just kidding," Freya said with a little chuckle. "I hope Marty didn't pull too many g's on the way. He gets carried away sometimes, but he's a good kid."

Korbin grinned. She may have been an artificially created being living within a deadly stealth ship, but Freya was still a mom all the same.

"The flight was fine," he replied, looking around at the ships filling the vast hangar space. "Are all of these vessels minds such as yours?"

"No, but there are a few AIs here. That's Mal over there. She runs Captain Harkaway's ship, the *Váli*."

"Ah, I've heard the name mentioned by your friend down below."

"Cal? Yeah, he and Mal go back all the way to the Great War. But that's history stuff, and we don't want to keep everyone waiting, so you should hop on into the meeting. I'm remotely linked, so I'll see you there," the AI said.

"Very well. Nice to meet you in person, Freya."

"Likewise."

Korbin strode behind Arlo, following the teen, who clearly knew the ship as well as anyone there. Korbin guessed he'd spent a good portion of his life aboard this and the other craft in the unusual fleet orbiting Earth. What an upbringing that must have been, he marveled.

"Okay, this is it," Arlo said. "Mom won't let me come in for the meetings with all the bigwigs, but me and Marty will hang around and give you a ride back when you're done."

"Thank you, Arlo. I appreciate your assistance."

"All good, man," the teen said, then trotted off to one of Zed's galleys in search of food, leaving Korbin to fend for himself among the collected leaders of the allied worlds.

It was twenty minutes into the briefing session when Zed interrupted yet another of Grand Marshal Fott's rather long-winded questions with one of his own. And Zed was in no mood to be subtle.

"Let me ask you something, Korbin," the AI began. "You're a powerful man. *Very* powerful, from what I've heard. Yet you present as an ordinary Joe. Just a man who got caught up in some really freaky shit. That sound about right?"

"Well, I suppose..."

"What I'm getting at is, I think there's more to you than just some magical abilities. I know a few others share my opinion on that. You're keeping secrets, which is something I can totally respect. However, given the nature of the enemy we're facing, and the need for absolute honesty if we hope to stop this threat once and for all, I think it's time for you to come clean."

"Zed, I'm sure Mr. Korbin has his reasons," Mal interjected. "And he is our guest."

"Sure, he's our guest because a crazy wizard from another galaxy tried to kill him too. But he's on our side of the portal now, and allied with our forces. I think this is not the time to be coy, wouldn't you agree?"

Korbin smiled. Zed was the AI leader of all of Earth's AI forces, yet he still spoke passionately, and quite unlike most of the other artificial minds he had met in his short time in this galaxy.

"You're correct in your assessment," he said, albeit a little reluctantly. "I suppose, given the current circumstances, the time for subterfuge has passed."

"Thank you," Zed replied. "It's appreciated."

"Yes, of course. I've just been playing the game for so long, it's a bit strange speaking of these things openly. And with relative strangers, no less."

"But strangers who are on your side," Freya noted.

"Indeed," the alien visitor replied. Korbin took a deep breath. "As you know, I'm a visla. A power user of some potency in my realm. But I've long lived a rather secluded life, opting to eschew the responsibilities men of my abilities are typically burdened with."

"Understandable," Captain Harkaway muttered. "Sometimes a man just wants to live his life."

"And that I did," Korbin said. "But my life was a bit more... *complicated,* than it seemed to the outside world."

"Oh?" the admiral mused with a curious, raised brow. "How so?" she asked.

Korbin paused. This was it. Publicly stating what he'd kept secret for so long. Amazara knew, of course, as did a few others, but none but his most trusted of allies.

"I've been something else for most of my life," he finally admitted. "I suppose you could call me a rebel leader, of sorts."

"Rebel? But I thought there was no real conflict before this Dominus person showed up on the scene," Daisy said. "You're saying there's *another* one to look out for?"

"No, nothing like that. This is an old threat. One that was defeated but never fully eradicated. A rot on our society that we must be diligent to cut out, lest it return."

"You're speaking of the Council of Twenty, aren't you?" Cal asked via his remote link. *"But I was of the understanding they were disbanded centuries ago."*

"They were, but they've merely become weak, forced to live in the shadows in all but a few systems. But given the opportunity, they'd make a return, and it's people like me who are working to stop them. We train others in the arts of stealth, and tactics, and combat. The ways of magic and espionage. And all to be used to hold back those remnants of the Council of Twenty."

"But you said they're scattered," Rika said. "I was forced to be a part of them in the past. A slave to be used to fight and kill. Are you saying they're coming back? Because if so, sign me up to fly back over there and kick their asses right along with Visla Dominus."

"No, it's nothing like that. The Council's power is weak, and they only have a handful of strongholds remaining. But my comrades and I aim to keep it that way, though there are some powerful men and women who would welcome their return and gladly join their ranks so, as to wield even more power than they already have."

"Like Dominus?" Sarah asked.

"No. He's something new. Something powerful. And I don't believe he's interested in joining forces with the Council. In fact, I think they should fear him as much as we should."

Korbin pulled several of the image discs Kara had stolen in her flight from her father's estate from his pocket. Without bothering with an explanation, he cast the spell that activated one of them. Images of the massive fleet of Visla Dominus's ships leapt into the air.

"Is that a hologram?" Freya asked.

"I don't know what a hologram is. This is an image disc. It captures whatever is in its field of vision and stores that information for later recall. This particular one was taken from my old friend Nikora's vault. You know him as Visla Palmarian. What it means, exactly, I do not know. What I am certain of, however, is that the forces shown are many and powerful."

He pointed to a trio of larger ships seen moving to the left of the image.

"These are from a race known as Tslavars. Originally, they were slave traders and cutthroat merchants, but over the years they've become a mercenary force for hire. And judging by the modifications to these warships, as well as the number of vessels present, someone has acquired the services of damn near all of them."

"Slavers?" Maxxoor, the senior Chithiid representative, asked. "My people know much about being enslaved, and we shall not fall to this fate again." He turned to Daisy. "You know the Revered Leader better than most. Do you agree that he will commit greater resources to this fight, given this new information?"

"He's talking about Maarl, Daze."

Yes, Sis, I know.

"He's getting old, but I can't see him backing down from this fight, can you?"

Not a chance. We just need to ask. You know how he feels about slavery, and given what was done to him and his people, I really can't blame him.

Daisy turned her attention to Maxxoor. "Yes, I believe he will. I'll ask him personally."

This seemed to satisfy the Chithiid, as Daisy had a long and storied relationship with the Revered Leader, all the way back to the Great War, when they fought side by side against their oppressors. If *she* asked him, he was certain to listen.

"They're taking more slaves," Korbin interjected. "Here, I'll show you."

He pulled another of the image discs from his pocket and uttered the activation spell. A scene of devastation projected in the air, the visla's ships laying waste to a small group of utterly outclassed vessels.

Half of them had been destroyed outright, snapped in half or rent open to the void of space. The others, however, were clearly being boarded.

"I've reviewed these images at length," Korbin continued. "The fleet pinned down and trapped these ships after they took out the ones they deemed to be the biggest threat to them. They then took the crews as slaves and folded the captured ships into their fleet for modifications and re-crewing as warships. I'm told you know of the effects of control collars, so you can imagine what a fleet this size could be capable of if every one of those ships was stocked with a load of them in their cargo holds."

"It could be enslavement on a global scale," Admiral Harkaway said with a sigh. "And you are correct. We know these collars all too well. They've already made more than one attempt at control with them in this galaxy."

"And enslaved billions in mine. It was only thanks to Charlie's rebellion many hundreds of years ago that a revolutionary change occurred. And without those slaves doing their bidding, the remnants of the Council were scattered. But control collars still exist, and not all people heed the laws regarding them."

"That's not unique to either of our galaxies, I fear," Admiral Harkaway said. "Thank you, Korbin. I think that should suffice for now, but we may require your services and insights again as we prepare to deal with this threat."

"It's my pleasure," Korbin replied.

"Oh, and one more thing," Cal added. *"When you return to Los Angeles, if you'd be so kind as to power down your ship's defenses, I would like to begin retrofitting it with some Earth tech weaponry as well. A little something to complement your substantial magical skills."*

"Anything to gain an advantage," Korbin replied. "Consider it done. Arlo and Marty are standing by to ferry me back to you."

"I'll take you," Daisy said. "And when you're done, there's someone I want you to meet."

CHAPTER SIX

Daisy watched with a mix of fascination and annoyance as Korbin actually used magic to disarm his ship and allow Cal's teams of AI machinery and cybernetic helpers to begin the process of upgrading his ride.

It wasn't that his ship was getting new state-of-the-art goodies. Freya was far more advanced and deadly than any ship in the known systems, thanks to her unusual birth and the flexibility that afforded her mind. The designs she came up with were impossible. But, as Daisy pointed out to her precocious young AI kid many moons ago, "The impossible is accomplished by those who don't know it can't be done."

But magic? *Actual* magic? It was amazing, sure, but it also offended Daisy's sense of fair play. And fair, in her book, meant any way possible to win, her tenacity tested and proven during the Great War against the Ra'az Hok invaders.

Magic, however, simply couldn't be handled with overwhelming force or a technical trick up her sleeve, and it was that feeling of helplessness that was eating at her. Daisy had always been the one with all the answers. The one who could find a workaround and work her technological voodoo to save the day.

If you could hot-wire, jury-rig, or outright override a system, she was your woman. Watching Korbin cast even the most basic of spells, however, made her feel unprepared for the first time in a long time.

"Maybe he'll teach you how to use a konus," Sarah said, the ever-present voice in the back of her mind trying to be helpful.

Maybe. But this just doesn't feel right. I mean, magic?

"Stabby's magic now. Does that mean you don't love your bloodthirsty toy anymore?"

It was true, her genetically linked bone sword had drunk deep from a powerful magic user, absorbing the caster's essence and power somehow. It didn't make the sword a full-fledged intellect, per se, but there was a definite change in his behavior since then.

For one, he had defended and countered a magical attack without Daisy consciously wishing it. Stabby, in his own way, now had a mind of his own, it seemed.

"I'm magic now too, if that's what you wanna call this energy form," Freya added, tapping into the conversation via the neuro-patch Daisy had forgotten she was wearing.

"And I still don't quite know how you managed to do that, kiddo," Daisy replied. "I thought fully formed AI minds couldn't use that stuff. At least, that's what Cal was saying."

"Yeah, but I've never really been one to fit their mold," Freya joked.

"You're telling me," Daisy replied with a laugh. "Maybe we'll have to see about having Cal upload whatever he's got on this magic stuff for you so you can break it down into something we can all understand."

"I've already asked him to gather everything relevant for me," Freya said. "It'll be neat. And I know Ripley's already learned some basic spells with the neuro-stim."

"See? Your niece is a witch now. You've gotta accept magic into your life."

"You sound like a door-to-door religious nut," Daisy sniped back as she looked at the monitors.

A lone figure was trotting back to the ship, leaving a very busy team of mechanical beings to carry out their task. For someone so recently looking over his shoulder for any sign of an assassin, the man from a distant world seemed remarkably at ease.

"All done," Korbin said, rejoining Daisy aboard Freya. "Amazing what Cal is proposing. If he can truly join the technology of your world with my craft, it should prove a formidable combination against our enemy."

"Kind of like what I did with my sabot rounds," Freya noted. "I had some of my nanites generate a counter-field of magic energy to pierce their shields. Seemed to work pretty well, once I got it mostly dialed in."

Korbin grinned as he took his seat. "You have quite an amazing kid, Daisy. She's a marvel of both our galaxies, it would seem."

"Freya's one of a kind, that's for sure," she said, strapping in. "Okay, kiddo. It's off to Taangaar we go."

"Cool. I haven't seen Maarl in a long time," Freya said as she powered up and out of the atmosphere. "All right, warping in three. Two."

"We are going to warp?" Korbin asked.

"One."

A moment later they exited warp with a faint blue crackling around the ship.

"Let's show our guest where we are," Daisy said.

The screens flashed on, showing they had arrived just a short distance from the Chithiid homeworld of Taangaar, spanning the distance magic ships would require several jumps to cover in but a single attempt. For truly vast distances they would link warps, but this particular one wasn't too far. Especially not for Freya.

"That felt good!" Freya exclaimed. "It's so nice having my warp drive work normally again."

"Well, you did say you had more or less figured out how to make it work in the other galaxy, thanks to your new nanite modifications."

"Yeah, but this is *easy*. This is normal."

"Said the most abnormal AI in the galaxy," Daisy added with a chuckle.

"Hey! How can you say that? You know Habby!" Freya shot back.

"Okay, good point. Sorry, kiddo. My bad."

"Apology accepted," Freya replied with amusement. "I've got a clear path in. I'll have us at Maarl's place in a few minutes."

"No rush," Daisy said. "Might as well give our guest the scenic tour on the way in."

Freya did as she was asked and took a slightly less direct route to Maarl's comfortable estate. The elder Chithiid had been instrumental in the defeat of the Ra'az Hok, and after the war, the position of Revered Leader had been more or less thrust upon him, though the poor man simply wanted to go back to a normal life.

But duty called, and Maarl was never one to shy from it. And now he was the defacto leader of the Chithiid race, though he'd long ago delegated most of the drudgery to his assistants.

After they had rebuilt their homeworld after the war, everything else seemed so comically inconsequential by comparison. They'd survived near genocide. The thrills of community planning just didn't whet his appetite.

Korbin followed Daisy through the small throng of smiling four-armed Chithiid men, women, and children, all familiar with her from years of visits. Freya, too, was fondly greeted, and though she had been fluent in Chithiid more or less her entire life, the locals were thrilled for the opportunity to practice their English with her.

As for the man from another galaxy, he had his usual translation spell working around him at all times, though he did find it fascinating how these disparate cultures nevertheless took the time and effort to actually *learn* one another's languages. It was a hardship people from his world never had to endure.

Of course, the neuro-stim technology commonly used made languages easy to pick up, but Korbin was still rather unfamiliar with that particular bit of tech. Just one more of the many things he would learn about in due time.

Daisy led them to the manicured grounds of a lovely home just above the shores of the nearby sea, the smell of the water invigorating in its freshness. It was something Korbin had noted on all the worlds he'd visited. Whether the climate was hot, cold, or just right, the smell of the ocean brightened the spirits.

A weathered Chithiid walked from the building, standing tall and strong despite his advanced years. An enormous smile graced his face, and he threw wide his four arms to welcome Daisy with a warm embrace.

"It is wonderful to see you, Daisy. I was told you would be coming. And this must be your guest," he noted, looking at Korbin. "I am Maarl. Welcome to my home."

"A pleasure to make your acquaintance, Revered Leader," Korbin said with a little bow.

He didn't know the local customs, but having spent his whole life around men of power, he had a good idea of the social graces universally accepted when meeting such individuals.

Except this one, it seemed.

Maarl burst out laughing, drawing similar mirth from Daisy.

"Was it something I said?"

"No, Korbin. It's just no one ever calls me that," Maarl said.

"Except those kiss-ass bureaucrats," Daisy said.

"Well, yes. Those are the exception," Maarl chuckled. "How is Arlo, by the way?"

"Big. But you'll see soon enough," Daisy said.

"Oh? Am I taking a trip?"

The smile tried to linger, but the reality at hand forced it from her lips. "Maarl, we need you to come to Earth. There's a problem, and it threatens all of us. More even than the Ra'az did."

"You know the Chithiid are ready to fight if need be. And our weapons are so much better than before."

"Yeah, but this time we're not fighting aliens with big guns. We're fighting invaders with *magic*."

A strange look flashed across Maarl's face. "Did you say *magic*? I've studied your language long and hard, but my translation must be off."

Daisy nodded to Korbin.

With a bit more flourish than was really necessary, he cast a force spell, uprooting a small tree and sending it flying into the sea. If that didn't get the man's attention, nothing would.

"I just planted that last year," Maarl said with a sigh.

"Oh, I'm so sorry," Korbin said, blushing terribly as he quickly cast again and retrieved the tree with another spell, dropping it back in its hole. "I hope the roots aren't too damaged."

Maarl looked first at the tree, magically back in place, then at the odd magician with an appraising eye. "I like this one. His heart is in the right place," he finally said. "So, back to Earth, it would appear. I'll tell Hakaaraso not to wait up for me."

The Chithiid walked back inside and returned a few minutes later with a small bag over his shoulder. He'd spent most of his life as a slave, enduring hard labor with no possessions. It was a life experience that had stuck with him to this day. A small pack was all he would ever need. Anything more was just creature comfort.

"I am ready," he declared. "And shall I assume our new allies are joining us as well? It seems the Urok delegation was only just here on Taangaar a few weeks ago."

"Yes, they'll be there," Daisy said. "And even the Kathiri are joining the cause."

"Kathiri?" Maarl said, an eyebrow arched high. "They mean well, but sometimes they're more trouble than they're worth."

"Perhaps," Daisy said as they walked back to her waiting ship. "But this is an all-hands-on-deck situation. We'll fill you in on the way. And by the way, we're having a family dinner this evening, and I expect you to come. I know the kids will be thrilled to see you."

"And I, them."

"Oh, and you should know, there's one more thing."

"Isn't there always?"

"Yeah. But the thing is, we've got a Ra'az."

CHAPTER SEVEN

Grundsch hadn't slept so soundly in many, many years. Not even when he and his brothers were laying waste to vast swaths of puny rebels had his body simply shut down and forced him to rest at the end of a long and tiring day. But this was different.

The enormous Ra'az warrior's physiology had been long studied by those who had survived their genocide, and though a live one hadn't been seen in well over a decade, the drugs needed to sedate one were still readily on hand. It took a lot to keep the natural-born killers down, but with only one left in the entire galaxy, so far as they knew, there was plenty to go around.

And this one was different, apparently.

Korbin had carried the alien with him across the portal between galaxies as he fled Visla Dominus's fleet during a heated battle. The control-collared security man had been severely injured during the battle high atop Visla Palmarian's estate tower, a near fatal blast of magic striking him down as he put himself between the caster and the visla's daughter.

Korbin's niece.

Karasalia Palmarian was the apparent target, though the reason why was not yet clear. What was known was the giant alien had done something utterly foreign to his kind. He had been willing to sacrifice himself to save her.

To Korbin it was merely a valiant and noble effort by a personal guard who had seen the girl grow up. An honorable man doing his duty. Had he known the Ra'az Hok's true nature, he'd have been quite surprised. As would the rest of the Ra'az hive, were they still alive.

The control collar had been specifically designed to keep the alien's rage issues in check, at least against other members of the Palmarian household. But when those same members split off, many of them revealing themselves to be under the employ of Visla Dominus, Kara had used a thin braid of Ootaki hair to disable his collar, essentially restoring his free will and lifting the magical restrictions that had been placed on him for so many years.

Free from control, the Ra'az had gone on a killing spree, reveling in the freedom to disarm——literally, in one instance—— the men trying to harm his charge. But something had changed within him. He could have done anything he wished, even killed the girl had he so desired, but a strange feeling welled in his broad chest. He actually cared what happened to her.

And that was what led to him being so gravely injured.

Korbin stabilized him as best he could, wrapping his superficial injuries with the damp cloth on his person, soaked by the Balamar healing waters, but he simply didn't know enough about Ra'az physiology to properly help him. His dear friend Amazara had always been the healer in his band of trusted friends, not him. But with her now so far away in another galaxy, a new source of medical support was needed. One he found on Earth.

Grundsch was drugged, restrained, and patched up, albeit reluctantly, by the skilled medical staff in Los Angeles. They'd all wished death upon the alien, but Cal had voiced his directive that the Ra'az should live. For now, at least. And so it came to pass that survivors of the Ra'az genocide saved the life of the last known Ra'az in the galaxy.

The mending alien had healed from the work done to him surprisingly quickly. *Too* quickly, in fact. That he still had traces of the healing waters in his system was unknown to the Earth techs who had helped him. All they knew was there was no way a normal Ra'az could recover so quickly, even with the cellular regenerators at their disposal.

Those were tooled for human and Chithiid biology, not Ra'az. An amazing bit of tech that could re-attach a limb and have it functional within the day if need be. Fortunately, with the war over, that need rarely arose.

Grundsch slowly opened his eyes, a calm warmth of deep, restful sleep still wrapped around his mind and body.

"You're right. He's coming around," a cyborg med tech said to her Chithiid counterpart. "Notify the others."

"Of course. And we should have the medical AI run a full set of new scans, don't you think? It is a rather remarkable recovery," the four-armed alien replied.

"Good call. We'll do that as well, just as soon as we—"

Grundsch lunged violently against his restraints the moment his heavy head rolled to the side, affording him a clear view of who was speaking within the room.

A human. And a Chithiid. It could not be, but it was.

The Ra'az thrashed and strained, pulling at the sturdy bindings holding his arms, legs, and torso to the reinforced gurney serving as his bed. He was a creature of immense strength, but this was a team well-versed in dealing with Ra'az in the past. They'd restrained enough of them after the war. Just before the trials and executions began.

This one would not be breaking free anytime soon. But he might hurt himself trying, and seeing as they'd just spent all that time and effort repairing him, they really couldn't have that happen.

"Sedation," the cyborg calmly said to the air.

Grundsch watched in horror as a slender armature unfolded from the side of his bed, quickly and efficiently plunging a needle into his restrained hip, then sliding back into its compartment.

The drugs took hold almost immediately. The last thought in the panicked alien's mind was the confused realization that he wasn't being killed. But why they were drugging him and keeping him alive was a mystery. One he would have to unravel later, as all he could do for now, despite his best efforts, was sleep.

He didn't know how long he'd been out, or even what day it was, for that matter, when he woke. All he saw as his eyes opened was the concerned face of the young woman he'd watched grow, protecting her his every waking day.

Kara looked at him with care and concern clear on her face. He felt her hand on his forearm, a comforting warm touch in an otherwise cold and sterile environment. Despite his genetic disposition and war-like upbringing, it was a welcome and soothing show of affection.

His mind cleared further. He was back in his own galaxy somehow. All these years after his ship was pulled through some strange anomaly into that far-flung realm, his crew killed and only Bahnjoh surviving of all the Graizenhund on board. He'd been alone. Cut off from his people. Made into a slave.

He supposed it was ironic that the slavemaster had been forced to serve for all those years. But some good had come of it, and she was sitting beside him now, watching the fog lift from his eyes. He glanced over to the observation window, where a small gaggle of onlookers were peering through the thick glass.

"Don't worry. They won't hurt you," Kara said, squeezing his arm.

"You don't know that," he replied.

"I do know that," she said.

"They want me dead. I can see it in their eyes."

"You're a good man, Grundsch. We just need to show them that. To help them see what I see."

"Denna Palmarian," he said, shifting his gaze back to the lady of his house, "you do not know my race. Our history. What we did to these people. Nothing you can say will change their opinion of me." Grundsch looked around the room once more. "We are back in my own galaxy now, though how, I am unsure."

"My uncle took you aboard his ship after you were hurt protecting me. Do you remember the fight in the tower?"

"A most glorious battle," Grundsch said, smiling at the memory of finally being able to dole out some delicious violence upon a deserving adversary.

"And you were hurt protecting me. Do you remember that as well?"

He nodded.

"Uncle Korbin didn't have the magic to properly mend you, so he took you to find a healer."

"I was a burden in battle," he said with distaste.

"No, you weren't. And besides, it was come with him or die, and there was no way we could let you perish if there was anything we could do about it."

"You should have left me," the Ra'az warrior said with a resigned sigh.

Kara looked at him with an intensity he'd only seen on rare occasion. A gaze that made him remember that this frail girl was the daughter of the most powerful visla in the realm.

"You helped raise me, Grundsch. I've known you my whole life. You're family, even if you're a Ra'az and I'm not."

"You know what my people are? What we do? What we have done?"

"In this galaxy? Yeah, I've been informed. But I've also been told that your hive is destroyed, and your queen is dead. That life is gone, but that doesn't mean yours has to end as well. You're important to me. And Bahnjoh too," she added.

"He is alive?"

She nodded. "And happily playing with Baloo as we speak. I'm sure you'll get to see him soon. But for now, rest and finish healing. And please, stay calm, for my sake. I can't imagine what I'd do if anything were to happen to you."

Kara leaned over and gave him a gentle kiss on his forehead, then quietly walked from the room.

The Ra'az Hok didn't strain and struggle against his restraints. He just sat quietly and thought, taking in his new reality. His people were dead, of that he was certain. But it seemed, nonetheless, he might truly have a trace of family yet.

CHAPTER EIGHT

Kara walked out of the medical facility to her waiting friends, one of her mental burdens lifted now that she had finally seen her lifelong protector open his eyes. It was her father she was worried about and missed the most, but with him ill, and millions of light years away, tending to Grundsch would have to suffice.

She'd visited several times a day, even though she was told he was under heavy sedation but otherwise healing just fine. But with so few ties to her former life anywhere to be found, the familiar, comforting bulk of Grundsch was one that put her at ease, even if he was unconscious.

Ripley and Vee gave Kara her space when she visited him. It was something she needed to do on her own, and they respected that decision. But once she came back outside she was fair game for shenanigans and adventures. And Ripley had made it her job to show her new friends a good time.

For the extremely active teen, a lot of that involved showing them the sprawling wilderness that had reclaimed so many areas around Los Angeles and her home in Malibu. Centuries without human presence had allowed plants and animals to regain a solid foothold, and given the minuscule number of inhabitants of the region after the Great War, none had even considered pushing back against it.

Nature had a way of doing what it wanted, and with the world healing after such a great conflict, there was none who desired to oppose its will.

Eddie was greatly enjoying ferrying the girls around, the extra company making for a nice diversion from his usual one-on-one time with Ripley. And they hadn't even really begun exploring yet. He couldn't wait to take them on longer flights to some of his and Rip's favorite haunts. But for the moment, local was good enough.

And for the teens from not just another world, but another galaxy, even the most boring of things to anyone else could be worth marveling at. Having never seen *any* technology, let alone an entire world run by it, was a non-stop adventure of discovery for Kara and Vee.

"Hey, how'd it go in there?" Ripley asked as the violet-skinned girl trotted out to join them. "You look happy. Is it safe to assume he's doing okay?"

"Grundsch is much better," Kara replied with a happy smile. "He finally woke. And the doctors said I can even bring Bahnjoh to see him next time."

"They're gonna let that crazy mutt into a med facility? Oh, man. I can just imagine what the cleaning crew will say."

"And this crew will be working by hand?" Vee asked, still amazed that so many tasks they simply cast a spell for back home had to be done by manual labor.

"Yeah, they'll send a droid out for a cleaning, but I know how anal those medical types can be. I'm sure they'll be on hands and knees, scrubbing the tough spots."

"Incredible. Three simple spells and even I could have the place clean in just a few minutes," Kara said.

"Even you? C'mon, Kara, we know you're stronger than you let on," Ripley said.

"No, really. I'm telling you, Rip, my father's the one with all the power in the family."

"You've got it, Kara. I've seen it," Vee noted. "Remember at Korbin's? When you were training?"

"That was just the konus he let me use," she replied.

Vee was tempted to clue her in that the konus had actually been an unpowered one, and the impressive display of power she'd put on was entirely drawn from within herself. But she'd promised Korbin she wouldn't say anything. Not until he figured out what was going on with her, at least.

"Well, I'm sure you're better at magic than I am," Ripley said. "I know a couple of spells, but that was specialized stuff Uncle Cal gave me with the neuro-stim when things were getting really hairy with the Tslavars."

"It still amazes me you had to fight them in this galaxy as well. It seems even across portals, they always have a way of making trouble," Kara said, as she and her friends climbed aboard Eddie's waiting ship.

"Where to, ladies?" he asked.

"I'm thinking we should swing by home first and grab a bite. Then maybe we'll head down to the beach. Sound like a plan?"

"Sure, Rip. I'm really enjoying the waters of your beaches," Vee replied.

"Yeah, and the sun seems to be doing a number on your dye job," Ripley noted. "I don't know why you bother coloring it. Ootaki hair is freakin' amazing. People would kill to have hair like that." She paused, a blush rising to her cheeks. "Sorry, I didn't mean it like it sounded."

"It's okay. I know what you meant," Vee said. "The thing is, back home, people would treat me like a thing, not a person, if they knew what I was. That's why my parents have dyed my hair since I was little. They gave me a childhood I would otherwise have never been able to enjoy."

"But as you've seen, the rays of this system's sun are incredibly powerful, and it seems Ootaki are particularly sensitive to it," Kara pointed out. "With all of that energy flowing in, the colorings simply can't stay in place. I even tried to apply a magic fixer to her hair, but it failed miserably."

"So a blonde beach babe you shall be," Ripley said with a laugh. "I can think of worse things. And don't worry. No one wants to take your hair in this galaxy. And if they ever tried, Hunze would whoop their asses. That is, if Bawb didn't do it first. I can't wait for you guys to meet them. I think you'll hit it off great."

"Just because we're both Ootaki doesn't mean we'll be insta-friends, Rip."

"No, but she's pretty cool, and so are you. It's only natural that you'll get along. And who knows? Maybe she'll be able to show you how to control your own hair's power like she does."

"She does what?" Vee gasped, shocked. "That's impossible."

Ripley laughed. "You can tell her that when you meet her. I thought you knew, Hunze is a caster. And a really, really powerful one now too. Bawb found a way to help her take control of her own power. It's a bit complicated, but I'm sure they'll explain it when they get back."

If they got back, was the unstated worry lingering in Ripley's mind.

Eddie made the flight to Malibu in short order, dropping the girls just outside Ripley's home. They could smell something delicious wafting out the doors before they even made it inside. Finn was cooking, and, as usual, it promised to be something delicious.

CHAPTER NINE

"Hey, look what the cat dragged in!" Finn called out with a huge grin on his face as his daughter and her friends made their way into the house. "Arlo and I were just making some lunch. You three hungry?"

"When's Rip *not* hungry?" Arlo asked, taking a bite of one of the homemade pickles the mad chef habitually made in a variety of flavors.

"You should talk," Ripley shot back, not about to be outdone by her cousin. "You eat way more than I ever could."

"I'm a guy. Of course I do. Gotta build them muscles!" he said, flashing a quick look at their company.

Ripley noted his gaze, yet again, lingered a second longer on Kara. Her cousin, it appeared, seemed to have a thing for her new violet-hued friend. "Yes, Dad," she sighed. "Feed us All Of The Foods, please."

"It'll be my pleasure. Any dietary restrictions I should know about?"

"Just the ones you already know. None of the stuff that makes magic people sick," Ripley replied.

"Doesn't grow on Earth, so I think we're safe, there," her dad replied with a chuckle. "So, how were things downtown?" he asked as he pulled some more fixings from the massive refrigeration unit he'd had custom installed in the house when he and Sarah moved in. "Is the monster awake yet?"

"He's not a monster. He's Grundsch, and he saved my life," Kara said.

"Sorry, I wasn't trying to insult you, it's just the Ra'az and me go way back, and let's just say that after the whole genocide of my species thing, it's a little hard to live and let live, if you know what I mean."

"Leave her alone, Uncle Finn. That's ancient history from before any of us were even born," Arlo said.

Finn was about to reply, but noting the way the boy was eyeing the lightly violet-skinned girl, he decided to hold his tongue and let nature do what it might.

"So, you girls seen much of the area yet?" Finn asked as his cybernetic hand worked through the food prep at a feverish pace. "You know, Arlo and Rip have been running around these hills since they were in diapers."

"Daaaad."

"What? It's true. Maybe my buddy Arlo here can help show you the area. What do you think, Arlo? You up for taking our visitors on a hike?"

Arlo shot a look at Kara, gauging the girl's interest in such an outing in an instant. Or, he hoped he was. To date, his success with the ladies was less than exceptional, save for a short-lived romance with a local born girl named Caroline before her parents moved them all away.

That left him in a bit of a dating rut. Of course, given the small size of their population, it was little surprise, since he had relatively few options.

"Sure, I think that'd be fun," he said. "We can pack up the food and make it into a picnic, even."

"Hey, good idea! I'll grab the cooler backpack for you," Finnegan offered. "Rip, did you put it back after you used it?"

"Yes, Dad."

"Hey, don't groan at me. Last time I needed it, I had to search the whole house for it," he said, turning to their guests, adding with a conspiratorial whisper. "She was out with a boy and forgot it in the field."

"Daaaad!"

"What? It's true, isn't it?"

Ripley rolled her eyes and bit her tongue. Finn's love of busting her chops for fun was only rivaled by his love of cooking. After seventeen years, she knew when to just let it go.

Arlo, being Ripley's best friend since birth, stepped in, as he so often did. "Hey, Uncle Finn. Do you think you could give us a container of those pickled carrots you made? The spicy ones?"

"Sure. But I thought you said they were too hot for you."

"No, that was my dad," he lied.

"Huh, must be getting old, then," Finn said with a chuckle, tapping his head with a metal finger. "Oh, and Ripley, remember, your mom said to be sure to go see Cal for a checkup."

"Ugh, really?"

"Hey, you spent a lot of time over in that other galaxy, and with the way that side of the portal affects things, it'll put her mind at ease if you just do it. Humor me. You know how your mom can get."

"Okay, okay, I'll go." Ripley turned to her new friends. "My mom's got some serious nanite mods going on. You do not want her pissed at you. Trust me. But I'll go *after* the picnic."

"Fine by me," Finn said, then finished packing up the portable feast.

The four teenagers had been hiking for a half hour, taking in the natural beauty of the area, but even for newcomers seeing the sights, Arlo noticed that Kara was a bit quiet.

"You okay?" he asked, slowing his pace to match hers.

"Yeah. I was just thinking. It's beautiful out here."

"I agree," he said, pausing. "You sure you're okay? You seem a little, I don't know, distracted."

Kara's façade slipped a moment. "I miss home," she finally said. "And I miss my father. He was quite ill, and my going missing again will only make it worse, I fear."

"Are you two close?"

She nodded an affirmation. "My stepmother was getting him a healer when I had to flee the estate. Now I don't even know how he is. If he's all right. If he's safe."

Kara didn't mention that she was also worried about whatever sneaky business her father had been up to. After what she'd seen in his image disc collection, she worried it might be worse than she'd originally feared.

Her teen guide thought a moment. "You know, I could take you, if you wanted," Arlo said. "My ship, Marty, he's super fast. I doubt anyone would even notice."

Ripley had been staying out of the conversation, but at that she couldn't help but chime in. "No, you can't, idiot. You can't even warp on the other side."

"If Marty modifies his warp drive we can."

"Don't be stupid. And even if you could, Aunt Daisy would kick your ass and ground you for a year if you even tried."

Arlo grumbled something, but he knew she was right.

Kara noted his mood shift. "Thank you, Arlo. Really. I appreciate your concern, even if it's not possible."

Arlo nodded and took a swig from his water bottle. "Come on. There's a good picnic spot up ahead."

"Yeah, and it's a quick hop down to the beach," Ripley added. "And I'm getting hungry."

"As am I," Vee said.

A crashing in the brush nearby made them all freeze and spin. Arlo, for all his exuberance and silly ways, went immediately serious, a pulse pistol quickly flashing to his hand.

"Where did you get that?" Ripley hissed.

"My pack."

"No, I mean *where*?"

"Dad gave it to me. Said it was for emergencies, just in case," he replied.

The sound suddenly ceased, replaced by another on their opposite side. The teens were being flanked.

Arlo switched the safety off of the weapon. Ripley called up the limited spells she knew as she slid her konus onto her wrist. Kara and Vee, however, watched with fear, helpless. Or so they believed.

A slight whuff and a snort reached their ears through the dense shrubbery. A familiar sound.

"Baloo? Is that you?" Kara called out.

Moments later the giant canine came bounding through the bushes.

"Oh, you silly boy. You could have been hurt!" Kara said, scratching his ears.

A moment later, Bahnjoh came charging in from the other side, nuzzling his head against Kara as well, seeking out ear scratches from the other hand.

"They were stalking us," Arlo noted as he tucked the pistol back in his pack. "And pretty effectively too."

"Yeah, if they'd wanted to attack, there's not much we could have done," Ripley noted. "I'm glad they're on our side."

With two large four-legged companions now joining them, the teens made their way to the picnic site and set out their spread. Fortunately, Ripley's dad always overpacked when it came to food. He may no longer have been feeding an entire spaceship's crew, but he sometimes cooked like he was.

A convenient side effect of that was there was ample amount

to share with the canines, though the flecks of blood on Baloo's snout told them the rambunctious duo had likely been successful in their hunt.

"Hey," Arlo said between bites. "I was thinking. Maybe we should give them a crash course on Earth tech. What do you think, Rip?"

"Could be fun. Kara? Vee?"

"Oh, I'd very much like that," Kara replied.

"Me too," Vee added.

"Okay, it's settled, then," Arlo said. "When we finish up here, we'll go hit up Mom's workshop. There's all kinds of cool stuff in there." He paused a moment. "Hey, Rip. Do you think it'd be possible to wire up a neuro-stim for them? Might make it easier on 'em, what with all the new tech to learn."

"That's a Cal question. Their brain wiring is totally different than ours, I'm sure, and you know better than to mess with that on your own."

"Do I ever," he replied. "Just ask Aunt Sarah's neural clone how good an idea it is, right?"

"Yeah, seriously. I don't think *either* version of my mom would approve," Ripley added. "But I think Cal will be open to the idea. All we can do is ask, right?"

The group chatted and ate, basking in the warmth of the afternoon sun. They then packed up and began the walk back.

It was a little thing, but Ripley made sure she and Visanya followed a few paces behind, chatting about this and that, letting Arlo and Kara have a bit of privacy as they walked.

"Who says I never do anything for him?" Ripley mused.

CHAPTER TEN

Maarl strolled through Freya's stealthy mass with the greatest of ease, completely at home and relaxed within the state-of-the-art craft. Korbin watched the way he would pause from time to time, one of his hands resting on a surface as he took in the sight of this ship he had obviously developed a strong affection for.

Freya, for her part, was just as happy to have her old friend aboard once more. Apparently, she had known him since she was quite a young AI, and it was Maarl's calm and experienced tutelage that had been one of the guiding influences on her developing mind.

The bond between them was almost tangible. Nothing like what she shared with Daisy, of course. That was a connection as robust as any parent and child could ever hope to possess. But Maarl's connection was strong nonetheless. A wise, grandfatherly love reciprocated in kind by the brilliant AI.

Korbin was astounded by things in this galaxy on a near hourly basis, and watching a mind created by hands, not the mysteries of reproduction, and her strong and healthy relationships with those she cared about only deepened his sense of awe. They may not use magic in this realm––at least *almost* no one on Earth did—but it was a fascinating place all the same, and magical in its own special way.

"Hey, Maarl. Before we stop off to see Zed, we're gonna swing by the portal so you can see what this is all about firsthand," Daisy informed her guest. "They're scheduled to pull it free from the sun for just a minute to shoot a drone through to upload a data burst to a spy satellite we've got tucked away on the other side. The bad guys don't use tech like we do, so they have no idea it's even there."

"Excellent. I am most intrigued by this phenomenon, and I would very much like to see it with my own eyes," the elder Chithiid replied. "And a portal between galaxies? It's fantastical to my mind. But then, so,, too was the idea of intelligent machines and time travel, before I met you."

Korbin's attention zoomed in to laser focus. "Did you say time travel?"

"Oh, yeah. I keep forgetting you really don't know all that went on during the war," Daisy said. "See, the thing is, the warp technology that powers our ships also has the capability of effecting a sort of time warp. It was discovered by accident, and no one else can reproduce the effect. It was just good old Freya here who did it, when things went haywire. But she can't do it anymore, can ya, kiddo?"

"Nope. No more time jumps for me. My warp core can't handle another," the ship lied.

She actually *could* if she wanted to, but keeping track of timelines and potential paradoxes was just too much strain, even for her genius intellect. And if anyone thought she still possessed that ability, the potential for misuse and abuse of it was a very real threat. So she and Daisy and Sarah played dumb, and no one was the wiser.

Regular warp travel, however, was another matter entirely.

Freya powered up her warp core, and, in a flash, they arrived back in Earth's solar system, not too far from Mars. They could have warped right to their final destination, but with all of the ships standing guard against a possible Tslavar incursion, as well as the fact that no one knew exactly what might happen if a warp happened too close to the portal, safe was the order of the day.

Being a stealth ship and essentially invisible to the fleet, Freya announced herself and fired up her external illuminators just to make sure everyone knew she was there. She still enjoyed sneaking around as much as ever, but given the incredibly high tensions and itchy trigger fingers around the portal, it was the logical thing to do.

"And you say this portal is intact? Even inside the burning sun?" Maarl asked, staring at the molten plasma over Freya's shielded displays.

"Yep. And, apparently, our sun blasts out some sort of potent magic of its own, though it's only been noted to be absorbed by space dragons and those gold-haired people."

"They are called Ootaki," Korbin interjected. "The gold-haired ones, that is."

"Right. Ootaki," Daisy repeated. "Anyway, none of the other magic folks seem to be affected by it. You feel anything, Korbin?"

"No, I do not."

"Well, sucks for you, but that means none of them can use it on their side, at least," Daisy said.

"There is the other one," Freya noted. "Rika. The pilot with those cool tattoos. She can absorb the sun's energy, but from what I've heard, it's the pigment they used to ink her that has the power. I really do need to get a sample from her. It'd be really cool if I could incorporate some of that into my nanites along with the konus energy."

"It's in her *skin*, kiddo."

"Well, I'm not asking anyone to flay her or anything. Jeez. All I need is a drop. A pinprick would be enough for me to analyze."

"I'll see what I can do when we get back," Daisy offered.

"Your child has a most impressive mind," Korbin said with admiration.

"Thanks. She's a good kid. But, man, you should have seen her when she was younger. Whoo, boy. Talk about a handful!"

Korbin laughed. "I have some familiarity with being a handful myself."

Daisy and Maarl shared his mirth. "Oh, I bet," the redhead said with a grin.

"It's about to begin," Freya announced. "I'll zoom in so you can get a better look."

Maarl leaned closer to the display. "Thank you, Freya."

The spell pulling the *Asbrú* free from the sun, along with the portal that the wealth of Ootaki hair packed within the ship was generating, triggered right on schedule. At first there was nothing to see, but then a bulge formed in the churning plasma as the Trojan Horse ship and the portal it was creating pulled free.

The drone delivering the data packet was already en route at high speed, crossing over the portal's threshold just as it reached a safe distance from the sun. The whole thing had taken merely thirty seconds.

"It's going to go back in now," Freya announced.

A few seconds later, the portal began quickly dropping into the sun's plasma once more.

"Well, that was rather—" Korbin began to say.

An enormous spray of molten plasma blasted out toward the nearby fleet. The nearest ships caught traces of it, their shielding unable to deflect direct contact from actual plasma of that intensity. One melted entirely.

Without a moment to lose, Korbin cast as powerfully as he could, corralling the deadly spray with a magic containment field, forcing it back into the sun's surface. The other ships were in emergency escape mode, though their weapons remained trained on the submerged portal even as they spun and fled to a safer distance.

It was then that a hefty Tslavar ship burst from the sun, engulfed in molten death. Spells were flying from it fast and heavy, a desperate attack at anything near enough to hit. But the fleet had already pulled away, given a moment's warning by the odd solar phenomenon generated in advance of the arriving ship.

Apparently, the sun's energy did strange things to the portal when it was fully submerged.

Korbin fanned out another defensive spell array, this time targeting the incoming magical attacks. But it wasn't needed. The magic was weak, its caster obviously on his or her last legs as they attempted the spell.

The fleet opened fire as one, their weapons shredding the melting craft to fragments of slag in an instant. But even that wasn't truly needed. The ship would have self-destructed into a melted mess of its own accord momentarily anyway, its shields utterly unable to protect it from the sun's intensity.

"What the hell was that?" Sarah asked, her voice repeated over Freya's internal speakers, as well as in Daisy's head.

"They were testing the portal," Korbin replied, shaking his head. "Fools."

"Can they get through?" Maarl asked.

"Not without meeting the same fate," Korbin replied. "But that's not going to stop them from trying, it seems."

"Great," Daisy grumbled. "And they're scheduled to open it again pretty shortly. Keep the baddies on their toes that way. I hope they don't pull that crap again."

The fleet sent their thanks for the unexpected magical assist, then settled back into a defensive position, only this time a little farther from their original location. Whether or not an attack was the actual intent of the incursion was anyone's guess, but safer was better than sorry, at least until new information made itself available.

"So, anyway, *that* happened," Daisy chuckled with a sigh of relief. "Now you see what we're up against, Maarl."

"Indeed. And that was a large and powerful ship, despite its contact with the full fury of the sun. I can see why you requested my presence."

"Yeah. Sorry to pull you from your gardening, but I think this one calls for a proper meeting with the actual leader of the Chithiid people."

"Agreed."

"All right, then. Let's get you to Zed. And then I've gotta get Korbin here back home to Earth."

Freya took her mom's cue and turned from the sun, shutting off her exterior markers and going dark, flying to rendezvous with the massive command ship in her preferred manner. Invisible to one and all.

CHAPTER ELEVEN

In a small, uninhabited system tucked away in a distant corner of an unremarkable nebula, the small band of pirates and their commandeered ships sat quietly in orbit, while their leaders convened a little meeting on the surface of the relatively tranquil planet below.

The crews were down to skeleton status, the majority of the men and women taking all of the shore leave they could while in a holding pattern. Once the battle with Visla Dominus and his fleet began, they might be stuck aboard their vessels for a very long time.

If they weren't killed outright, that is.

In any case, the crews of the hastily gathered little fleet were making the best of it, remembering to live a little while they could, as life could be far shorter than expected. Something pirates were very well aware of.

The handful of unexpectedly promoted crew who were now tasked with the responsibilities and burdens of guiding those ships, however, were having a less relaxing time of it, though they, too, were glad for the respite from space travel. And being promoted to captain, even in such unusual circumstances, was a dream come true for most.

But there were burdens to shoulder as well. The bitter that inevitably came with the sweet.

Kip and Dukaan had arrived at the world with no particular flourish or fanfare, but their successful warp-jump with Kort had further solidified the little ship's confidence in warp travel in this realm.

They had actually found the process of tying in the AI ship's warp system with the magical handshake provided by Kort's Drookonus-powered craft relatively easy, once they got the hang of it. Add to that the konus welded into Kip's frame, as well as Hunze's quickly growing abilities with her magic, and he and Dukaan both felt that they could soon travel without requiring a magically powered jump escort.

For the moment, however, Dukaan left those ruminations to his AI friend, taking the opportunity not only for some fresh air, but also to meet the men and women he would likely soon be fighting alongside.

The world may have been lacking civilization, but that did not mean the lush planet was devoid of life. It was, in fact, home to a fairly diverse assortment of creatures, both big and small, as well as plenty of fresh water and a pleasant lack of major predators. It was no wonder the Drooks had kept this little system secret, even when confined to slavery. And now it seemed their dreamt-of opportunity to visit their secret sanctuary had finally arrived.

It was something most had not thought would actually ever happen in their lifetime. The location of the system was something passed from Drook to Drook, but never spoken of outside their circles. But as an enslaved race, the odds of any of them actually making it to the system they'd only learned of from handed-down tales were slim to none.

And yet, here they were. And as *free* men and women, no

less. It was like a dream come true. And having achieved it, they were ready and waiting to power the fleet in battle against Visla Dominus. Fighting not because they wore control collars, but because they chose to. To willingly taking a stand.

But for the moment, they reveled in the unusual comfort of friendly companionship with their pirate comrades.

Given the number of people on the surface, Charlie and Ara had made a quick survey of the planet together, sourcing some local game for the pirate crews to add to their festivities. It was good for morale, but also gave the pair a chance to review their options free from the pressures of a group setting, with many voices interrupting their silent discussion.

After their training session with Charlie, Bawb and Hunze had also taken a short break from the company of others, vanishing into the woods without a trace for a few hours, reconnecting physically, and mentally, but also further binding their power to one another. When they rejoined the group, they appeared the same as when they'd left. That is, to everyone but the six other Wampeh Ghalian masters on the planet.

Kort could immediately sense the change. A shift in the immense power rippling through Hunze. Bawb was in possession of half of her magical locks, but she had given him all of them, freely and with love, no less.

But then he'd done what no one had ever done before. He'd bound his power with the Ootaki and gifted it back to her. And now that they were together again, the connection had solidified even more. They had *both* become stronger. Symbiotic. A bonded pair.

It was arcane magic. A spell Kort didn't even know existed. But, apparently, it was just one of the secrets contained in the long-lost vault of Wampeh Ghalian treasures. More than the wealth of coin or weapons, it was these ancient texts, scrolls, and tablets that held true value. And their worth was incalculable.

Now they just needed the last living Wampeh Ghalian who

knew where they were hidden to retrieve them. But that would come after their rag-tag rebel leaders had their meeting. Then he would bring his new brother and sister back to join the others at the designated training house to further set in motion their part of the grand plan.

With their crews feasting and enjoying their surface time as best they could, the assembled captains of the pirate fleet joined with Charlie and the others. The loss of their pirate leader, Marban, was felt by all of the rough and ready men, but such was the risk of space piracy. And he wasn't dead, just in another galaxy, which also lessened their sorrow.

And now, with so many of them commanding stolen Tslavar warships of their own, the dynamic among the ranks had shifted. It was an impromptu promotion for so many at once, but when Charlie's magic had killed the Tslavar crews, leaving their ships intact and ready for new owners, it had only made sense that the most seasoned of the pirates should take command. It came naturally to them, though the boring drudgery of tactics and strategy meetings like this one were a bit unfamiliar.

As for the Wampeh Ghalian, each had arrived in their own little shimmer craft, quite invisible to all present. One minute they were alone, the next there were a half dozen of the deadly assassins joining them at the confab. It was disconcerting to say the least, the realization that, if they wished it so, the handful of men and women could have easily slaughtered every last person there before their presence had even been noted.

Fortunately, the Wampeh Ghalian had sided with them in the fight against Visla Dominus. It was the first time in thousands of years the order of assassins had taken such an action. But these were unusual times, and the threat Dominus posed to the galaxy would upset the balance of power far more than even they could allow.

And so it came to pass that the Wampeh Ghalian would take up arms in a war, albeit with the greatest of secrecy.

The discussion began with great enthusiasm, the newly minted captains eager to prove their worth in battle. But soon the reality of their situation set in. This wasn't a fight they could possibly win on their own. Not head-on. Not against someone as powerful as Visla Dominus.

And they were in the dark as to what resources their comrades on the other side of the portal might be preparing to bring to bear in the coming conflict. What they needed was intel. Given the lone means they had to communicate with their Earth-bound friends, that meant one thing.

Charlie and Ara would be taking a little trip.

CHAPTER TWELVE

"You ready?" Charlie asked as he slid into place and strapped into Ara's harness system.

"Of course I am. This has been a most welcome respite, and the game on this world is quite refreshing," Ara replied.

She'd fed well, and the fresh waters that were so abundant also seemed to have done her some good. They weren't Balamar waters, of course, but the clear, fresh streams that drew from the system's sun's power seemed to invigorate her nonetheless.

Fortunately, they were also lacking the combustion issues that Wampeh faced with water of the Balamar variety. A good thing, as the entirety of the Wampeh Ghalian leadership had been present on the little planet.

To have them all in the same place like that was unusual. For them to all be together outside of one of their safehouse training facilities was almost unheard of.

Technically, it *was* unheard of, in that any who might tell of such a gathering were either members of the order or were dead by their hands.

But the Wampeh Ghalian masters had already departed, leaving the others to carry out their next steps in the plan. That meant gathering resources. More ships, more supplies, and more crews. There was never a shortage of people willing to fight for coin, but a rebellion was a bit of a harder sell. At least to the mercenary crowd.

But that was an issue for the others to deal with. As for the assassins, they would work toward their own goals. Namely, recovering the cache of weapons and more from their long-lost vault and gathering their own forces for the coming battle.

Charlie and Ara, on the other hand, were tasked with a far different mission. They were flying to the portal itself.

Not *to* the portal, per se, but close enough to make contact with the little hidden spy satellite their counterparts on the other side of the portal would be using as a digital information dump and dead drop of sorts. Each side could leave messages for the other, retrieved when the portal opened, transmitting vital information the non-tech-using visla and his ilk could not intercept.

It was one of the benefits of their technology-based system that could prove to be a most crucial tool in the fight. The magic users simply had no means of eavesdropping on electronic messages. Everything was magic-based in their world, and there wasn't even the skree equivalent of an open radio scanner that they could use to try to ferret out communications between the rebel forces.

The portal itself cut off any signal between galaxies, even when not submerged in the sun's plasma, but a dense data package could be delivered in an instant by something as simple as a drone, hopping from one side to the other and sending a burst transmission, knowing the satellite would receive it and store it for retrieval by its intended listeners.

And that same drone could snatch up any messages being sent on repeat from that same satellite, effectively allowing large chunks of digital information to be transferred between the galaxies, with only the tiniest bit of risk that the enemy might make a run for the briefly open portal.

Another benefit of the system was that the satellite was a device capable of receiving messages without the sender having to be right on top of it. There was interference in the area, so some degree of proximity was required, but Charlie and Ara didn't need to jump anywhere near the visla's fleet in order to interact with the device.

Instead, they'd post up at the outer limits of the satellite's range, safely away from the searching eyes of Visla Dominus's fleet.

"Okay, y'all. We'll be back as soon as we're able," Charlie called out to his friends. "Don't do anything crazy while we're gone."

"I assure you, we have no intentions of the sort," Dukaan replied.

"Yeah, me and Dookie promise to stay out of trouble," Kip chimed in.

"Great. We'll be back as soon as we can. Keep your comms open, Kip. If all goes well, this shouldn't take too long." Charlie looked down from his perch atop the enormous red Zomoki at his friends. *"You guys good?"*

"We are better than good, my friend," Bawb replied. *"And when we join up once more, we shall prioritize finding Leila's location."*

"Thanks, Bob. I know she's okay, it's just tough not having her with me, ya know?"

The Wampeh looked at the golden-haired woman at his side. *"Yes, Charlie. I most certainly know. Now, fly safe, both of you. We all have our parts to play, but we shall see one another soon."*

Ara didn't wait any longer, leaping skyward with a mighty flap of her wings, jumping when she reached the cold void of space.

.   .   .

"Where are we now?" Charlie asked after several jumps, as he scanned the unfamiliar gaseous planet and its dozen small moons.

"We're in the portal's system, Charlie," Ara informed him. *"This is the planet just at the edge of the range you said your transmission device could function from."*

"Ah, yeah, now I see," he replied, the distant dot of the sun's flames jetting through the portal a bright pinprick in the otherwise inky darkness.

The system's own sun was a giant ball of red, but the positioning of the orbiting planets were aligned in such a way that the portal was framed by dark space rather than backlit by the sun. Had it been the latter rather than the former, most would miss the tiny dot entirely.

"Okay, all we need to do is—" Charlie was cut off when Ara abruptly spun to her left.

A stream of yellow flame blasted past her, followed by two more. They were weak bursts, but enough to cause damage nonetheless. For the human on her back, likely a great deal more as his magical shielding was not tuned for that sort of attack.

"What the hell?" Charlie blurted.

"Ferals," was Ara's reply as she spun and dove away from the assailants.

Charlie's eyes and magic locked in on the threat simultaneously. A small pack of hungry, wild Zomoki were attacking them. The beasts were scrawny. Starving. And, unlike Ara, apparently entirely lacking higher thought.

"What's going on, Ara?"

"These apparently had been in captivity a long time and have forgotten how to jump."

"You mean they've been trapped in this system since the fight with Dominus?"

"Yes. And there is not much in the way of game on the worlds here.

Plus, the fleet would have been eliminating them with great prejudice."

"But I thought you said you were an Alpha and they'd never try to attack you. Hell, they ran away last time we were here."

"Normally, yes. But these are the most base of my kind, bordering on mindless beasts. And they are starving. For that reason alone, they are willing to risk this foolish aggression."

Another stream of flames shot past them, but Ara easily avoided it this time. The Zomoki were hungry, and one of them attempted to take a bite out of his nearest counterpart, but they were all so thin, there was simply not much meat for his hungry jaws. Ara, however, was a full-grown and healthy female. A feast, if only they could bring her down.

Which was not going to happen.

Charlie felt the sadness of his friend through their shared magic. A terrible weight was now on her shoulders.

"What is it?"

"They will give away our position if they keep this up," she replied. *"I'm sure they've been at it for some time, but a concerted effort like this is bound to draw attention. And we cannot afford to have Visla Dominus's craft jump to our location to investigate."*

"What are you saying, Ara?"

She fell silent a long moment. *"I'm saying I have to eliminate them."*

"But they're Zomoki."

"Yes. And mindless, suffering ones at that."

Charlie knew what she was proposing, and she was right. Ara was such a rare creature in both her power, as well as her intellect. Most Zomoki were lesser creatures. Animals of instinct and violence. Only a very few were ever born with the gift of truly higher thought, and fewer still with the ability to speak as she did.

"You want me to do it?" Charlie asked, preparing to cast the killing spell.

"No. I should be the one," his Zomoki friend replied.

She'd laid who knew how many eggs over the centuries before she had ever met Charlie. For all he knew, some of these feral beasts might even be her descendants. But that did nothing to change the circumstances they currently found themselves in, and the clock was ticking. The threat had to be removed before they drew attention, and that was all there was for it. Too much was at stake.

Ara pivoted and paused, presenting a stationary target for the hungry swarm. The Zomoki came at her as one, their sharp teeth ready to tear into her tasty flesh. She was as merciful as she could be, her magic stunning the attackers, while her flames reduced them to dust. If she'd calculated correctly, they wouldn't have felt much, if anything.

"I'm sorry," Charlie said, feeling her hurt.

"Thank you. It was regrettable, but necessary," Ara replied. *"Now come, we must complete our task before the portal opens."*

Charlie set to work packaging his transmission––a sit-rep update for the forces back home––and sending it to the satellite far across the solar system. It took two attempts before the little device sent a reply ping that the message had been received.

The message waiting for them had been relatively short, but a more detailed assessment was to come with the next transmission, due to be sent through shortly.

"Okay, it's done," Charlie said. *"Now we just have to wait for theirs. The portal should open in a little under two hours,"* he noted, looking at the chrono mounted on Ara's harness. *"You know, we'll have time once this is all done. Maybe we could jump near Slafara on the way back. Just to see if we can pick up any chatter about Leila or Palmarian's ships."*

"You know we cannot do that, Charlie. I was clearly seen during the pursuit of Korbin's craft despite our best efforts to conceal my presence. The risk is simply too great for us to go anywhere near Slafara. And even if I wasn't noticed, we need to let the Wampeh

Ghalian do what they excel at. Let the experts be experts, Charlie. It's what they do. And once we have their report, then *we'll go get her, wherever she may be."*

"I know, you're right. I'm just worried about her."

"She'll be fine. Anyone who ever knew her in this realm has been dead for centuries. There is no reason to assume she is in any trouble."

Ara's logic was sound, but that didn't lessen the knot Charlie felt growing in his stomach.

CHAPTER THIRTEEN

Ara had remained relatively silent as she and Charlie floated in space, patiently waiting for the portal to open and the new update to be sent through. The minutes ticked by slowly, and there was an abundance of downtime, but Charlie left her to her thoughts. Killing so many of her own kind, even though it was a case of them or her, would surely be weighing on her.

Charlie took the time to reflect on his own situation, leaving Ara in silence. A true friend knows not only when you want to talk, but also when you want not to. Finally, the portal began to shift open, and quickly, at that.

"Hey, it's happening," Charlie said. *"And that thing's moving fast. Man, Rika must've set a seriously powerful spell on it to cycle open that rapidly."*

Ara focused her attention on the distant portal as the sun's flames vanished, leaving a clear shot to the magical opening. One of Visla Dominus's ships immediately made a run for it, jumping in as close as it could, then shifting into a rapid push for the portal's beckoning mouth.

The tiny drone that shot out of the portal was so small it would be missed by all but those specifically looking for it. But for their purposes, it was all they needed. It blasted out its payload, the digital packet flying through open space to the waiting satellite.

The drone then powered down, just another inert piece of floating debris not even worth noting, until it had received Charlie's data packet. It then immediately shot back through to the other side, a barely visible dot to all observing.

The visla's ship, however, was hard to miss. They were sending a fast assault craft at a breakneck pace.

"They're rushing the portal," Charlie said, watching via the enhanced link with the little satellite. Even then, it was far enough away to be small on his screen.

No sooner had the craft come within close range of the portal than the magical gateway slammed shut in front of it, the sun's flames bursting forth, the portal obviously dropped back into the burning plasma as fast as it had been pulled free.

The ship, however, didn't slow or change course.

"What are they doing?"

"It appears they are going to attempt to cross, even though the portal has closed too far for them to succeed," Ara noted.

"Why would they do that? It's suicide."

"I would think the visla likely gave them two options, neither of which were good."

"A damned if you do, damned if you don't scenario? I never thought I'd find myself pitying a Tslavar mercenary, but I almost feel bad for them," Charlie said as the small image on his screen appeared to plunge into the burning opening. *"Well, I guess that's it for them. Even if they survive the trip, which they won't, our guys will pick them apart on the other side."*

A moment later the satellite alerted them it had a new data packet ready for download. Charlie punched in his access code and retrieved the information, then pulled it up on screen for a quick scan before they began the many jumps back to the others.

He'd only made it a few paragraphs in when something caught his eye.

"*Hey, Ara. It looks like we're going to have to move in closer after all.*"

"*Oh?*"

"*Yeah. The big brains on the other side want us to send through the rest of the Balamar waters so they can load them into a weapons delivery system.*"

"*The waters in weapons? I guess they had good luck with what Marban carried across with him.*"

"*It would seem that way,*" Charlie agreed.

"*Hmm. This could get interesting,*" Ara mused. "*But, given the new tactics and positioning of Dominus's fleet, I think we have a problem.*"

"*I know what you're going to say,*" Charlie replied. "*We can sneak close and retrieve the waters we hid out near the portal, but there's no way we can make it through the portal ourselves. We're simply not fast enough to fly them through without being caught. Plus, there's no way I'm leaving Leila behind on this side of the portal.*"

"*This means one thing, Charlie. It means we need a ship. And a fast one at that.*"

Charlie agreed with his Zomoki friend. The only way they'd be able to get the waters across to their waiting comrades was if they jumped a craft in as near as possible at the instant the portal began to open. It would be close, and they'd have to fly fast to beat the visla's craft, but it could be done.

"*We'll deal with the ship later. For now, we need to get in there and recover the waters,*" Charlie said, turning his attention to the scanner laying out the location of the enemy fleet in relation to their current position and the small chunk of rock that was their destination.

It wouldn't be easy, and Ara would have to achieve a bit of speed, then coast in like a piece of debris to avoid notice. Only once they'd recovered their payload could they risk a jump, not a moment sooner, lest they be noticed.

Ara noted the area was now crawling with far more of Visla Dominus's ships, though they did seem a little bit disarrayed. *"I believe we may have made a bit of a mess of things when we were last here,"* she noted in an amused tone. *"It seems they are on edge. And while that is good in that it exhausts our enemy, it is also a hindrance in that they are likely to be far more jumpy than normal."*

"So we go in fast and quiet, then get the hell out of here."

"A plan I can get behind," she replied.

Ara focused her magic and launched herself, not too fast, but not too slow. Just the right speed so as to blend in with the other space debris constantly drifting through the system. Her trajectory was spot-on, and unless someone happened to be more or less directly in her path as she glided to their destination, they'd reach it unmolested.

Fortune was smiling upon them this day, and they did, indeed, make it to the rocky surface undetected.

Charlie quickly dismounted his dragon friend and set to work negating the deadly protective spells the three of them had placed all around the cache of priceless waters.

"Wouldn't want them getting their hands on this," Charlie grunted as he hefted the first of many containers free and lifted it up to fasten to Ara's harness. "One down, a whole shit-ton to go," he grumbled, heading back for the next of the large containers.

Even in the reduced gravity, it was still tiring work, and he couldn't use magic this close to the fleet, even though the odds of someone noticing the magical force was minuscule. It simply wasn't worth the risk, and Murphy had quite a way of butting in on Charlie's affairs to this point.

He did, however, find himself almost wishing he hadn't turned down Bawb's offer to join them. Of course, there was no way of knowing the AIs would make this particular request, and on top of that, the waters he was manhandling were deadly to his friend.

Thus, he settled into the task, knowing it was far better to do this on his own rather than risk, even slightly, the death by holy water immolation of his Wampeh buddy.

A half hour later all of the containers were safely secured to Ara's harness, and all without drawing any attention to themselves.

"The only thing we need now is a fast ship," Charlie said as he climbed up to his place on the Zomoki's back. "The timing is gonna be quick, though. And we'll need not just a fast ship, but also a ballsy pilot. The portal will only be open a moment."

"And if the attempt should not go as planned? If it should fail?"

Charlie mused the possibility of the ship simply slamming into a wall of pure molten plasma.

"Well, at least it'll be one hell of a way to go."

CHAPTER FOURTEEN

Leila woke from her lengthy slumber, her body sore from lying in the same position on the floor for so long. Slowly, her muscles screaming at her as she slowly forced them to move and flex, she rolled to her other side, allowing the pooling blood in her extremities to begin to flow properly once more.

The pins and needles sensation ran the length of her, from her feet all the way to her aching jaw. Sleeping on the unforgiving ground hadn't done her any favors, and neither had her lack of motion.

She began clenching her hands. Then her arms. Gradually, she added her feet and legs to the mix, finally adding in the muscles of her back and torso, pulsing them gently until the tingling began to fade. Sitting up was a chore, but she knew she had no choice. Her sand-dry mouth and chalky skin made it quite clear she needed to drink something, and soon.

The multiple trays of food and water that sat just inside the door to her cell made it clear that her keepers didn't know exactly how long she would be out. So they just pushed in a tray every so often, wondering if she'd wake to eat it.

Leila lacked the strength to rise to her feet, so she resorted to the age-old locomotion of everyone's youth. She crawled.

The discomfort of the hard floor pressing her sore knees was nothing compared to the thirst that was now racking her body. That alone was all the motivation she needed, and she quickly reached her destination, snatching up the cup of warm water, greedily gulping it down, feeling the moisture almost soak right into her cracked, dry tongue.

She was desperately thirsty, and hydration was all that mattered in that moment, but her body had other ideas. As soon as the hastily gulped fluid hit her stomach, a series of painful cramps washed over her in waves, forcing it back up in an acidic rush.

Leila was glad in that moment that there wasn't anything in her stomach. The thought of solids passing through her dry throat at that moment was not a pleasant one.

"Gotta slow down," she muttered to herself, wiping her mouth and refilling the cup from the pitcher on the tray.

This time, she forced herself to only sip the water, holding it in her mouth and slowly letting it slide down her throat for a ten count. The sensation, while not as satisfying as taking a proper drink, was nevertheless one of blissful refreshment as her tongue began to rebound to its natural moistened state.

Her body, likewise, seemed to know it was being replenished even before it had time to properly absorb anything, and a modicum of strength returned to her shaky hands.

After twenty minutes with no further cramping, Leila picked up a piece of bread from the tray and took a small bite, chewing slowly and thoroughly before washing it down with more water.

She waited.

No nausea.

"Better," she said quietly, then began slowly replenishing her energy stores, filling her belly one small bite at a time, careful not to overdo it.

She'd nursed enough young animals in her day to know what happened when an overly enthusiastic youngster ate too much too fast in their excitement. She had no intention of allowing her rumbling stomach a repeat performance of its impromptu aria of discomfort.

Leila pushed herself up onto the low bed and immediately sank into its welcoming embrace. Compared to the floor, the firm mattress was like lying on clouds. But after a few minutes, she realized she felt something unusual. More unusual than the aches and discomforts of her body's recovery. A sensation tickling her senses. A pressure all around her. Magic.

It was only then that she noticed her Magus stone was warm and glowing against her chest, pulsing out a slow, steady stream of protective magic all around her.

She sat up, resting on one elbow, and took in her surroundings once more. She was still in the thick-walled cell high atop Visla Palmarian's towering estate, that much she could tell. And they'd dragged in a hooded and bound Wampeh the same time she'd arrived, she recalled.

How many days ago was that? she wondered.

Judging by the state of her body, it had been at least several, though with the Magus stone protecting her, she thought it might possibly have been longer. There was simply no telling exactly how the green pendant affected things.

It was currently creating a little shell around her body, holding whatever pressing magic they were deploying against her at bay. But what about her body itself? Could it delay dehydration and starvation as well?

Unfortunately, with no way to gauge time in her cell, and no idea how to control the powerful family heirloom, she simply could not know.

Leila reached out with her own minimal internal power, trying to connect with the stone and the magic it was pulsing out. She could feel what it was doing, but no more than that.

The stone, passed down from mother to daughter in her family, finally arriving in her hands, was of incredible power, but only to those of her bloodline. And though she could not control it of her own accord, it nevertheless defended her, already having saved her and her friends' lives on more than one occasion. She wondered if it hadn't just saved her again.

Captain Sandah. He turned on me. Stranded Baloo and took me captive, she mused.

But he was merely following orders. A foot soldier in whatever sick game was being played by the power users of this realm. And now, here she was. A captive in the tower of the most powerful visla in centuries. And, apparently, her Magus stone was the only thing keeping her safe.

Leila hadn't been wearing her konus when they'd put her in the cell, but the innocuous little dark green stone had slipped her captors' notice.

I wonder...

With all the power she could muster, Leila reached out to the Magus stone, trying to feel its power as she recited a little illumination spell, intending to draw the power for it from the stone itself.

It was a simple spell. One that all children learned at an early age to provide themselves light in times of darkness. Even the weakest konus could power that spell with ease, yet Leila found herself utterly unable to spark that magical illumination with the stone's power.

Well, it was worth a try, she thought, then slowly rose to her feet.

She'd only walked the cell for a few minutes, pacing out its length and width, taking note of every aspect she could in case it might, somehow, help her escape, when the magic pressing upon her abruptly ceased.

The Magus stone remained engaged a moment longer, then dimmed close to its dark and inactive state.

Its power was suddenly notable in its absence. A comforting blanket of magic that had been pulled from her and tucked away for later use. The sensation was odd, to say the least.

Without warning, the stone flashed back to life, glowing bright green as it pulsed out its protective shielding once again. The attack on her had renewed, begun again, but this time stronger.

"They knew I was awake," she realized. *"They're testing me. Testing my Magus stone."*

Someone was very interested in the power she now possessed, dangling around her neck, looking like just another pendant, until it was needed, that is. And that someone wanted to take it from her, as she knew they would.

Only a power user of the highest level could even hope to forcibly take a Magus stone from its rightful owner, but this one most certainly was. It was a terrible realization, what was happening to her. She had thought she was safe in this place. Among friends, protected from harm and danger. But she'd been wrong. She was now a prisoner in that same home. And she couldn't believe who had actually imprisoned her.

CHAPTER FIFTEEN

Pimbrak, the dapper Wampeh Ghalian whose acquaintance Bawb had only just recently made, returned from his short trip with the other masters, bringing word that they were now prepared and awaiting Bawb's arrival at one of their many locations throughout the systems.

As was custom, they did not transmit this information by skree, but relayed it verbally, in person. A lesser Wampeh could have been sent, but Pimbrak had another task at hand. One he would be completing with the human and his Zomoki friend when they returned.

Kort had offered to fly the legendary Geist and his lady friend to the secret training facility on the planet of Chaldra, but the pair made clear their wish to retain their own transport, should the need for it arise. It was in this manner that Kip and Dukaan were afforded a visit to their second secret Wampeh Ghalian facility in as many weeks.

As outsiders to the order, it was highly unusual. Equally so was the lack of threat of death applied to them should they breathe a word about the location to anyone. Both Bawb and Hunze vouched for them, and that was enough.

The one concern, however, was the little ship's ability to properly navigate this galaxy with his warp systems. It was a simple fact. Warp drives malfunctioned on this side of the portal, and there was not much he could do to change that, even with a konus welded into his frame.

But with both Hunze and Bawb aboard, the former adding some of her magic, and the latter lending the power of his Drookonus to the mix, Kip was sure they would overcome that hurdle. The Drookonus was extremely powerful, and using it in conjunction with his konus-linked warp system would effectively make it as if Kip was linking to a Drook-powered ship.

"Clever," Kort said when informed of their plan. "And that is a powerful Drookonus," he added with admiration as he examined the fully charged unit. "Far more so than my own. I must say, it is a shame these devices are so hard to come by. And so pricey to fill with Drook magic."

Bawb grinned at his assassin brother. "Wait until we unseal the vault, Kort. I believe you will be pleasantly surprised by what you find there."

"Oh? There are Drookonuses there?"

"Many. And so much more than that," Bawb replied.

"Wait. Don't tell me," Kort said. "I am so rarely surprised by anything after all these years, I would like to relish the moment when it arrives."

"As you wish," Bawb said with a chuckle.

"Shall we, then?"

"Not just yet. There are some things I would like to retrieve on the way to meet the others on Chaldra."

"You've been gone from this galaxy for a very long time," Kort noted.

"Yes. But I have several emergency bug-out bags stored on several planets. All in locations that should survive the test of time. One such place is on the way to Chaldra. I wish to stop there and gather them."

"If they're still there."

"Yes, if they're still there. But from what I know of the superstitious, I am hopeful my cache remains unmolested."

"Very well. A stopover en route it shall be," Kort agreed. "I will link with and follow your ship as we jump, just in case its systems display the same issues they've experienced before."

"That is appreciated, Kort. I have faith in Kip's abilities with the modifications my Drookonus affords him, but the safety net is welcome."

Kort nodded, then made his way to his ship.

"We are going to visit another Wampeh stronghold? Most interesting," Dukaan said.

"You know, you can stay with the others," Bawb replied. "There is no need for you to come on this task."

"Kip and I come as a package," the Chithiid replied. "He may be annoying, but he is my ship, and I, his pilot. Loyalty is important."

"A noble sentiment. Very well. We shall meet you aboard shortly."

Five minutes later, their farewells said and plans for regrouping with the others made, Bawb and Hunze boarded the little ship.

"I left a comms link with Pimbrak," Kip noted. "Just in case Charlie and Ara get back while we're still gone."

"Excellent. Then we are prepared. Let us depart. We have much to do," Bawb said.

Moments later, Kip and their Wampeh companion both took to the skies, soaring up into space. Then, with a crackling blue flash, they were gone.

The Earth ship and his Wampeh counterpart exited their joint warp-jump more or less on target. They'd arrived slightly farther from the little world of Nurbaz than expected, but not enough to be a problem.

The new warp setup utilizing the Drookonus appeared to be a success.

"That went better than expected," Dukaan said, letting out a relieved sigh.

"Hey, give a guy some credit, Dookie. That was an excellent bit of flying, if I do say so myself. Got us right up on that place. Well, close, anyway," Kip chirped.

"Yes, yes. You did well, my electronic friend. Now, allow me to help guide you in the rest of the way," Bawb said. "I have not been on this world in many centuries, but the basic geography remains the same. We are on course for the correct city. All we need now is a landing zone."

"Got one," Kip said. "Will this do?"

He flashed the location on the display screen.

"Yes. That is perfect. If you would, please take us in."

"You got it," the AI replied. "Hey, hang on. I don't see Kort. Oh, crap. Did we lose him when we warped in?"

"He is still with us," Bawb said.

"I don't see him."

"He surely engaged his shimmer," the Wampeh replied. "Kort is a Ghalian master. He will land in secret and connect with us on the ground."

It made sense. Keeping the additional ship and its arrival unnoticed by anyone on the ground. An emergency backup, of sorts, and a standard Wampeh Ghalian tactic.

"If that's the case, I'll stop trying to find him," Kip said. "Alrighty, then. I'm taking us in!"

CHAPTER SIXTEEN

The planet of Nurbaz had never been a particularly cultured or genteel world. It was one of the reasons the Geist had selected it, and the small city of Aktan, as a site for one of his secret stashes—a safety net should things go really wrong.

It was the kind of place no one would look twice at a bloody, limping man making his way down the street.

Bawb had been fortunate in his career that it had never come to that. Of course, with the caliber of jobs he'd been taking, he'd either be successful or dead. Bruised and bleeding was a highly unlikely outcome.

But after just a few steps into the once-familiar streets he realized just how much farther the place had fallen. It was startling. A relatively rough place had devolved into a dog-eat-dog world of thuggery and violence.

But Bawb and his friends were masters of that particular skill.

"We should move quickly. Kort will be following in his shimmer cloak, but we must nevertheless strive to be unnoted."

Hunze nodded once and took off behind him, her stride

matching his, their power commingling more and more the longer they were back together.

Dukaan was originally going to accompany them into the city as they trekked to Bawb's hiding place, but seeing the nature of this place, he readily agreed to stay behind and provide an extra layer of defense for Kip should he need it. Everything was a prize to be taken in this world, and the unusual ship was no different.

It was fortunate they had landed later in the day. The long shadows cast by the squat buildings provided additional cover as they moved. With the brilliance of Hunze's hair, direct sunlight could make her golden locks shine, even with her hood up.

It was just one such flash, the briefest of things, that caught the eye of a slight, wiry man with greasy hair and stained teeth. He was good at his job, though, keeping watch without letting on to his true intentions. He pretended he didn't see a thing as the newcomers hurried by. But once they were past him, he immediately pulled out his skree and made a call to his friends.

A new prize had come to town, and they were going to take it.

Bawb moved quickly through the streets. The layout of the city had changed drastically in the hundreds of years since he'd last been there. Fights had broken out. Buildings had been torn or burned down. And some places had simply collapsed with age and neglect.

But one would remain intact. He'd been counting on it when he chose it as his hiding place, though he couldn't have known he'd need it to remain standing for quite so many years.

"In there?" Hunze asked as they closed in on the steps to a mid-sized temple.

"Yes," he replied. "This is a rather benevolent religion, and as such, their sacred buildings tend not to be disturbed. At least, not as often as some other sects."

Bawb had chosen the location during the height of that particular deity's popularity in the system, taking full advantage of the free security the temple provided. He didn't believe in any invisible sky friends, but these were harmless people, and trying to do good.

That much he could respect, though he didn't much care about their desire for something bigger than they were to believe in. As far as he was concerned, they could pray to a table for all he cared, so long as he could use their sacred ground for his own reasons.

They entered the temple and made their way to a section toward the rear that was set aside from the main space. A decorative column and series of statues provided just the cover Bawb needed from the few stragglers praying in front of an altar.

He cast a small spell––one of Charlie's favorites, actually–– sending the stench of feces to the few people lingering. It wasn't anything overtly violent, just enough to make each of them think the other had perhaps had an accident. The type of accident that made you want to leave an area immediately.

Within a minute, they had finished their prayers and made their way outside.

"We won't have long," he said, quickly casting with his konus, lifting a pair of heavy paving stones from the floor and setting them aside.

In the space within, several pristine packs were laid out side by side. The dirt around them had apparently been subjected to some flooding in the past centuries, but his protective spells had kept the bags themselves perfectly safe and dry.

Bawb grabbed two of them, the longest of the stack measuring at just over a meter each. Quickly confirming their contents, he then slid the stones back into place, re-sealing the grout lines around them, making them seamlessly blend in once again. He wasn't cleaning out his entire cache––it might come in useful again someday. But he was taking a few very key items he felt would be of use in their current endeavors.

"Come. We are done here," he said.

Each of them shouldered a pack, moving from cover and toward the exit, only to find their way blocked as a skinny man with greasy hair pushed his way inside. Following him were over a dozen dangerous-looking men, most carrying some sort of cudgel or blade in their hands.

Bawb quickly assessed the ruffians, noting their strongest members, as well as the smaller ones most likely to stab you in the back while you were engaged with the others and not looking.

He glanced at Hunze. She was ready for action.

"This is a sacred place," Bawb said, calculating the many, many ways he would slay these men if need be. "Don't be disrespectful. Let us take this outside."

"*You* can leave," the largest of the would-be muggers said, looking at the sheer superiority in numbers he and his friends possessed. "Just give us the girl and those bags," he said with an over-confident laugh.

Hunze bristled, the power within her tangible as it crackled over her skin. "I am no girl. I am a woman. And I am no man's property to be given," she said with a quiet snarl.

Bawb looked at her again, a feeling of awe and adoration welling in his chest. Hunze, *his* Hunze had become even more amazing in his absence from her, and he loved her even more for it. But that didn't mean he wanted her to kill. It was her purity despite her power that impressed him so, and he did not want to see that sullied.

Fortunately, a friend was going to address that issue.

"Go on ahead," Kort said, seeming to appear out of nowhere, much to the surprise of the muggers' lookouts. "I'll handle these yokels."

Bawb grinned. "Would you like help disposing of the bodies?"

"No, I'll be fine. But thank you for the offer."

The leader of the band of thugs looked at the newcomer, perplexed. "What do you mean, *bodies*? We outnumber you ten to one," he said, a ball of power forming in his hand.

No konus. This one had power, it seemed. Not much, but it was something, at least. Enough to intimidate most people on this backwater world.

Kort removed a long, wicked knife from concealment and began casually picking his teeth with it, to his new friend's amusement. Oh, yes, Bawb most definitely liked this man's style.

He and Hunze walked toward the exit while all attention was on the new threat. Only a pair of heavies blocked their exit. Bawb could easily remedy that, and it seemed his Wampeh Ghalian associate was certainly looking forward to dealing with the rest.

"So many?" Kort said. "Well, that's okay. I've removed far more corpses than that before." It was then that he flashed his smile. His *true* smile, pointy fangs sliding into place.

At that moment the muggers realized the error of their ways, but by then it was too late. They turned to flee, only to find their two comrades at the door already lying in their own blood, the door to the outside sealed against them.

"So, shall we begin?" Kort asked, rolling his neck and shoulders as he walked ever so slowly toward his victims.

Outside, a small throng was waiting to enter the temple when Bawb and Hunze had stepped out.

"There is a private service in session," Bawb informed them. "If you come back in, say, ten minutes, I believe the temple will be re-opened for your worship."

He and Hunze then hustled back to their waiting ship, leaving the confused devout behind, and quite confident that Kort would be along shortly, well exercised, and well fed.

CHAPTER SEVENTEEN

Kip performed another successful warp, his modified systems functioning flawlessly with the addition of Bawb's Drookonus.

Well, *almost* flawlessly.

The little ship did exit warp on-target, but did so spinning at great speed, pinning his passengers to their seats with centrifugal force.

"Kip! What are you doing?" Dukaan asked through straining lips as the wind was pressed out of him.

"Oopsie. Sorry, guys. I didn't know it would amplify my ambient rotation like that," Kip said, quickly slowing his spin until he resumed level flight.

If Bawb wasn't already a pale-skinned man, he would have been after that ordeal. Likewise, Hunze's normally pale-yellow complexion looked even lighter, all of the blood having rushed to her organs to keep them stable.

Only Dukaan seemed unfazed by the event.

"How is it that you are unaffected?" Bawb asked, his mouth watering from nausea.

Dukaan leaned back in his seat. "You forget, I've flown with

Kip for a while, now. This isn't the first time he's exited a warp spinning."

"Well, yeah. But nothing like that," the AI protested. "You can't pin that on me. It was all the Drookonus's fault. I bet that's what did it."

"It is of no matter," Bawb replied. "We are where we needed to go. That is Chaldra below, home of a training house."

"You been there before?" Kip asked.

"No. We relocate periodically. The facilities used in my time have been shuttered for hundreds of years."

"Ah, makes sense. Can't very well have top-secret training facilities lying around so long they cease to be secret, I guess," Kip noted. "So, seeing as I'm gonna stand out, where should I land?"

"Well outside the city. I will guide you in. Kort will then ferry us in his craft to the city proper."

"Lame! I'm gonna be stuck out in a field somewhere?"

"Not a field. More of a rocky wasteland."

"What!"

"Just kidding," Bawb replied.

"But you never joke."

"Consider it a bad habit acquired from my Earth-born friend. Now, let us get you settled in."

The Geist showed Kip the way, as he'd been told by Kort, the little ship safely nestled beneath a growth of tall trees. Their Wampeh friend was waiting for them when they landed, his craft uncloaked and in plain sight.

"I am glad you are here," Kort said as the new arrivals walked to his ship. "It is but a short flight into the city. From there we will have to walk perhaps ten minutes to the facility. I would procure us a conveyance for the final distance, but I thought you'd wish to familiarize yourself with the surroundings on the way."

"And you were correct," Bawb replied. "Though we will need

to disguise these as we walk," he added, laying out several well-worn lengths of metal, each roughly a meter in length.

"Are those Bakana rods?" Kort asked. "Where in the worlds did you procure them? I thought all had been destroyed in the siege of Trepnazor."

"And all of them had been. All but these five."

"I can see now why you wished to stop off on Nurbaz. A lone pair of these would make the detour well worth the time. But five of them?"

"I know. And now they are with the order, where they belong in this time of need," Bawb said.

"Excuse me, but what is a Bakana rod?" Dukaan asked.

Bawb began disguising the rods by creating a small litter, to which he would then apply a levitation spell. They would then place all of their belongings atop it, their bulk further hiding the true nature of what the thing was made from.

"A Bakana rod is nothing by itself. A mere piece of magical metal, unable to do much of anything. But if you have two, the users can pool their power, linking together by the rods' magic. As long as both casters stand, they can then share their combined power, channeling it to whoever needs it most at that time."

"That's amazing," Dukaan said.

"And dangerous in the wrong hands, for each user's power is still the same and can be drained. For those not well versed in the use of the rods, they can deplete themselves and their counterparts rapidly, often to the point of leaving themselves exposed to attack. But for skilled users, the ability to effortlessly assist one another without consciously diverting from your own defenses is something of a coup. And with not two, but *five* of them in the hands of a powerful team, major works of magic can be accomplished," Bawb said.

"And I feel you will see them at work soon, my four-armed friend," Kort added. "But come, we are expected."

"We shall maintain an open comms channel for you, Kip," Bawb said, then stepped from the ship.

They piled into Kort's small craft and quietly lifted off, leaving Kip to his own devices, at least for the time being. It was a short flight, and in just a few minutes they'd arrived at the shipping hub near the neighborhood where the Wampeh Ghalian had secretly established their foothold on this world many years ago.

They then walked a circuitous route, allowing Bawb and Hunze to take in not only the sights, but also strategic chokepoints, ambush locations, and routes of egress. Dukaan recognized some of them as they passed, but nowhere near to the degree of his assassin friends.

Finally, they arrived at a multi-level residential building. It was quite a shift from the wide facility with its large courtyard where Hunze and Dukaan had first met the masters. But just like the prior location, this one, too, had a secret entryway in plain sight, and its true footprint was nothing like what it appeared.

Kort led them into the reception area, then off to a side room. He then cast his Ghalian access spell, Bawb and Hunze quietly casting alongside him. The wall slid soundlessly open, offering up a passageway where none could possibly exist.

"After you," Kort said with a slight bow.

His guests stepped through the door, which he closed behind them. Hunze could feel the safe embrace of the years of defensive magic once more, and she added to it, casting a little spell of her own to add to the layers upon layers of castings protecting the facility.

After only a fifty-meter walk, they arrived at their destination. Another courtyard, though this one was a bit smaller than on the previous world. As before, however, the sky above was magically superimposed on the high ceiling, giving the feeling of being in open air.

Zilara and the other masters were reclining, watching this facility's trainees power through their daily regimens.

"Ah, you're here," the slender woman said with a pleasant smile. "The Geist," she casually announced to the students.

One and all lowered their eyes and gave a slight bow of respect.

"Thank you for the warm welcome, Zilara. This is a truly magnificent facility," Bawb said. "And I bring something for the cause."

He quickly stripped down the makeshift floating litter, placing the Bakana rods side by side, leaning up against the wall.

All of the elder Wampeh had the same excited visceral reaction, though they also held their expressions neutral, as they'd been trained.

"Bakana rods," Farmatta said. "Oh, how I've longed to hold one of those in my hands."

Bawb knew her favored attacks were of the magical variety. He'd learned all of the other masters' preferences and styles, just as they wished to learn his. "You'll have use for one soon enough," Bawb said.

"Indeed," the old woman replied. "But for now, what do you say we provide a little demonstration for the novices?"

Bawb looked at Hunze, an anticipatory smile already spreading across her face. She was loving this, and the prospect of a good sparring session lifted her spirits higher, which, in turn, lifted his.

"We'd be delighted."

CHAPTER EIGHTEEN

Wampeh Ghalian were nothing if not stoic––at least, that's how the outside world perceived them. When they weren't being killed by the deadly assassins, that is. But the truth was far different. They may have *appeared* not to react to anything, but inside they reveled in the proper application of their skills.

And sparring at levels that would prove deadly for most "normal" people was one of their favorite pastimes. A Ghalian way to show friendship and their own odd form of affection.

Bawb and Hunze shed their gear and extraneous layers in preparation for the session. It would be free flowing, with the legendary Geist and his partner demonstrating their skills, while also finally being afforded the opportunity to truly get into a connected rhythm with one another.

Hunze shared Bawb's abilities, thanks to the neuro-stim transfer he'd attempted over great many sessions. They hadn't appeared to take hold, but once she gained control of her own powers, it seemed the transfers *had* worked, and now, she was finally able to use that knowledge.

"Are you ready, love?" Hunze asked as she and Bawb pressed

their foreheads against one another briefly before the fun began.

"I am," he replied, feeling the connection of power between them like the tightly interwoven fingers of a bonded couple walking hand in hand.

The two smiled, then stepped back, turning to face the five masters circling them. Only Pimbrak was not present, the dapper assassin staying with the nascent rebel fleet to assist Charlie in his task. The other five, however, were more than ready for the exercise.

No one uttered a word. No one said, "Begin." The attack merely started, going from zero to full-bore violence so quickly even the trainees had a hard time discerning the moment it began.

One day they hoped to be that good. But for the moment, at least, they would be observers. And this would be a lesson to end all lessons. One of the most renowned Wampeh Ghalian in the order's lengthy history was going to show his stuff, and it promised to be unlike anything they'd ever seen.

Farmatta began the attack, launching a blistering flurry of spells, while Leif lunged into the fray, his magical crutch wielded as a powerful weapon, his cripple disguise shed in the glory of combat.

Bawb and Hunze pivoted around one another, the former deflecting Leif's strength-based attack, while the latter easily batted aside the former's magical one with a shower of smaller spells, dispersing Farmatta's assault.

Zilara and Kort both joined the others, the slender woman's blade whipping out in a blur. There was no such thing as waiting your turn in matters of violence and death. Sportsmanship would only lead to your demise.

Hunze reached behind her and grasped the grip of the Vespus blade riding on Bawb's back, drawing it from its sheath in a flash,

Bawb leaning slightly as he sensed her intention, aiding Hunze's defense even as he fought the other two attackers. They were already connecting as a fighting duo, and they'd only just begun.

The ring of metal on metal echoed in the chamber, a rapid staccato of attacks, parries, and counterattacks that sounded more like a drum roll than a fight due to their speed. Farmatta tried to use that frenzy to slip a few of her sneakier spells by, but Hunze's massive power surged, swatting them down as her arms and legs spun and lashed out against both women.

Bawb had his hands full, yet the large man attacking him was unable to land a blow, nor was Kort, likewise stymied by the Geist's impressive moves. The legends were true, they were both pleased to realize. The Geist really was that good.

And Hunze shared not only his skills, but a magical link. As Wagyah, the youngest of the masters, joined in, all five assailants working as a unit to switch attacks between Bawb and Hunze, it became readily apparent that there was something unusual at play. Something more than merely a team possessing the same knowledge.

The masters fighting together could lay waste to entire companies of soldiers, yet their efforts were repeatedly stymied by the odd couple. The intensity increased, all five pushing harder, striving to be the first to find a weakness in the duo's defenses, but it appeared to be futile.

The fight was five on two. Not fair odds, normally. Especially when all were incredibly skilled fighters of this level. But Bawb and Hunze had a secret. They were not merely fighting as a pair who happened to share the same skills, as students of the same master might. They were also moving in tandem as a single entity, their magic and combatives melding as one, joined by the invisible bond between them. A bond that had strengthened with their proximity to one another.

Had the five masters each feasted on a powerful user recently, perhaps the additional stolen magic would have given them the edge they needed. But with Bawb and Hunze sharing her overflowing Ootaki magic as well as the power of her gifted locks, it was simply not going to happen.

At the three-minute mark, all combat abruptly ceased, each of the masters' internal clocks recognizing their traditional stopping point to the second.

A gleam of sweat shone from the brows of all seven of them, the exercise far more difficult and energetic than their normal fare. A murmur rustled through the assembled students. What they'd seen was seemingly impossible. Two had nearly bested five. And those five were the greatest assassins the systems possessed.

The masters and the fighting couple shared a smile and a little bow to one another, then sheathed their weapons and stepped back to their seats.

"I hope you all took note," Zilara said to the assembled onlookers. "And realize that, while you possess great abilities and have learned many deadly techniques, you are still in training. No matter how good you believe you are, there is always the possibility you will come up against someone better." She glanced at Bawb and Hunze with a curious look, then turned her attentions back to the students. "Now, back to your training. Work hard, and one day it may be you who is the master presenting a demonstration."

The students and their instructors separated off into their respective groups to return to their day's labors. Zilara poured three glasses of water and carried them to Bawb and Hunze, who each took one appreciatively.

"You've bonded," Zilara noted, her eyebrow slightly raised as she sipped the cool beverage. "No Wampeh Ghalian has done so for longer than any can recall."

"I am aware," Bawb said, flashing a warm look to his beloved.

Zilara watched the pair interact. This was highly unusual. "You know the risks."

"I do. But the reward is worth it," he replied.

"I hope so, my brother. I truly hope so. There is a reason we live solitary lives."

Bawb said nothing, but her words flew true, sparking the memory of his existence not so terribly long in the past, yet also a lifetime ago. He, too, had been a lone wolf, carrying out his terrible work on his own, the only family he had being his Ghalian brothers and sisters.

Even then, they saw one another rarely. And for all of the masters to gather as they'd just done was a highly unusual occurrence. But his life now was better. Filled with something he'd never allowed himself to even dream of having.

Love.

It made everything worth the risk, and given the choice, he'd do it again.

"Brothers, sisters, we are facing a difficult task ahead of us," Bawb said.

"We are," Zilara replied. "And for that reason, we require the last of The Three to travel to the order's hidden vault and reclaim what is ours."

Bawb nodded, but he had a different idea in mind. "I believe it is time we change some of the old ways," he began. "The Three proved to be a flawed system, I think we can all agree. And the order has been at a disadvantage for centuries because of it."

"What do you propose we do?" Farmatta asked.

"I was thinking. Perhaps *The Six* would be more appropriate than *The Three*," he replied.

The five gathered masters glanced at one another. To be one of The Three was an enormous honor only afforded the highest of their order. But Bawb was right. The weakness of the system had been shown, and perhaps it was time to change things up. To protect that knowledge.

"Pimbrak is not with us," Leif noted. "We are The Five, not counting the Geist."

"True, but we can bring him into the fold upon his return," Farmatta replied. "I believe the Geist's suggestion to be one of merit."

The nods of the others were unanimous.

"Very well," Bawb said. "Let us begin, then."

The masters listened intently. This was history. They were leveling up in a way none of them had dreamt of.

Bawb looked at his brothers and sisters and felt an affection well within him. Hunze had changed him in more ways than one, it seemed.

"The vault is not accessible by just one key, but actually a series of them," he began, "each with the ability to unlock the spells sealing and concealing it. A multiple factor entry system. Any who would seek entry must possess two of these keys in order to access it."

"Spread out in different systems, I assume?" Wagyah asked.

"Of course. It was a system designed to ensure that even if one of The Three was somehow compromised and gave up the location of the vault, the existence of the keys would likely not be revealed, at least not immediately. And even if one was, the remaining two could retrieve the other keys before another might hope to pry that information free. It is the vault, those keys, and their locations, that I will share with you today."

"And what of the contents?" Farmatta asked. "There are legends and rumors, but none but The Three know for certain."

Bawb looked at Kort. He had been looking forward to a surprise, but he nodded his approval.

Bawb smiled and continued. "There are weapons and wealth, naturally. But most importantly, the vault contains spell books, scrolls, and even ancient tablets, all containing knowledge of powers not seen by more than a handful in thousands of years."

"All we need to do now is retrieve them," Zilara said. "And with the key system, it seems access, though perhaps a bit time-consuming, should not be a problem, especially for those of our order. But where is the vault itself? On what world are the greatest secrets of the Wampeh Ghalian held?"

Bawb looked at The Five with pride. The best of the best, and now keepers of the most valuable of Ghalian secrets. "Easy. It is on the world of Loquitas."

The masters looked at one another uneasily.

"What is it?" Bawb asked.

Farmatta spoke, the old woman shaking her head. "Our spies inform us that that world is now a main staging point for Visla Dominus."

"But it has always been a simple trading world. Unexceptional in every way."

"In your time, perhaps, but no longer," she replied.

Bawb sighed. This was not going to be as easy as he'd hoped. But there were more of his kind now, and they would work together.

"We shall devise a plan to address that setback," he said. "But for now, we gather the keys. *Then* we reclaim what is ours."

CHAPTER NINETEEN

"You're enjoying this, aren't you?" Charlie asked, amused.

"We are doing what needs to be done. And if that happens to include the relaxing joy of flight without conflict for a change, then why not?" Ara replied.

Charlie chuckled in his space suit as he rode atop his friend's back. At their side, Pimbrak flew his shimmer ship, escorting them on this particular mission.

"You know what I mean," Charlie teased. *"He may be a stoic Wampeh Ghalian, but Pimbrak is kinda fanboying over you."*

"Why, I don't know what you're talking about," Ara replied with a chuckle.

It was fascinating to see one of the deadliest men in the galaxy react to Ara like he had. Zomoki were uncommon, but not terribly rare by any stretch. One of Ara's lineage, however, was. And when he learned she was, in fact, Aranzgrgghmunatharrgle, his glued-on passive expression almost slipped.

For a Wampeh Ghalian master, that was really saying something.

Ara was the last of the Great Ones, so far as any knew. The

powerful, intelligent Zomoki with exceptional powers and abilities had always been few in number, and none had been seen in a great many centuries.

For Pimbrak, meeting Ara was like a kid's favorite movie star coming back from the dead to not only sign autographs, but also take him to the amusement park. Only, in this case, the movie star was a space dragon, and the amusement park was a backwater world in deep space. In any case, he was clearly enjoying the task.

They'd traveled quickly, and only a few more jumps were needed before they would be at their destination. In that regard, the warp technology of Earth's galaxy was superior, capable of covering far greater distances in a single warp. But Ara was a magical creature and traveled by jump, not warp, and Pimbrak's ship was likewise powered.

"I have just received a long-range skree message from a Ghalian operative in this system," Pimbrak informed them over the Earth-tech comms unit they'd provided him. "Intel is beginning to arrive from our spies embedded within the visla's fleet."

"Details?" Charlie asked.

"Not much as of yet, but we are hearing where some are coming in from and where others are going to. They do not appear to be as stagnant as we'd thought. Their ranks keep shifting, making an accurate tally of their true numbers quite difficult."

"Swapping out ships? Clever," Charlie mused.

"There is one report of unusual things taking place in a nearby system where one of the vessels carrying a Ghalian spy has jumped to. Odd magic disturbing the fabric of space. It is within a single jump's reach, and the system is otherwise uninhabited. None are known to frequent it."

"Making it a perfect place to test out some nefarious shit,"

Charlie said. "Yeah, I see where you're going with this, and I agree. Let's go take a look."

Ara and Pimbrak coordinated their flight paths and then jumped in unison, arriving at the outskirts of a small system with a blue sun. There were only three planets, each of them a gas supergiant, and each utterly uninhabitable.

Orbiting the middle world were a handful of ships. Powerful craft carrying skilled casters from what Charlie and Ara could sense.

In the empty space in front of the craft, strange, magical flashes of light illuminated them for a split second.

"Is that what I think it is?" Pimbrak asked.

"Oh, sonofa––Yeah. If you think that's someone trying to open a portal, you'd win yourself a chicken dinner."

"What is a chicken?"

"What everything tastes like. Maybe I'll treat you to one someday if we ever make it back to my side."

Ara cocked her head slightly. "Gentlemen, while it does appear to be an attempt to open a portal, you'll note that the size is far too small for all but the most modest of ships to pass through. And certainly not with it stable for such a short duration."

She was right, of course. The portal would pop into existence, then fizzle out barely a second later. Not only could they not seem to create one of any size, but they also couldn't keep it open.

"You smell that, Ara?" Charlie asked.

"Ootaki magic, though a tiny amount. It would seem they are attempting to recreate the phenomenon of the portal we now control, utilizing this system's sun to add power to the hair."

"It seems weak to me."

"It is. There is not much power to be gained from this sun, but while you and I are linked, feeling this viscerally, they are functioning on assumption. And knowing as we now do that Ootaki and Zomoki react to similar energies, it is safe to assume they will continue to be unsuccessful in their endeavor in this system."

"Yeah, I think you're right. Kinda funny how they—" Charlie's attention abruptly shifted, and without hesitation, he cast a strange, powerful spell.

"What was that?" Pimbrak asked.

Then he saw it. A small Tslavar craft had exited jump right near their location. Only by luck were Charlie and his friends not backlit by the system's sun, giving him that split second to effect his spell.

"Did they see us?" the Wampeh asked.

"Oh, I don't think so," Ara replied. "Charlie just froze them into stasis, I believe."

"He did *what*?"

"Oh, that," Charlie said. "Yeah, it's just something I kinda learned to do by accident."

"But there are few spells capable of doing such a thing," Pimbrak noted.

"Well, my magic is a kinda messed up mix of Zomoki and Ootaki, with a bit of Earth's sun's power thrown in for good measure. There's even a tiny bit of Rika's weird power lingering from when we linked together. I'm still learning what exactly it'll do, but at least I know *this* spell works."

Pimbrak was impressed. He liked Charlie, and the man was a decent fighter, but he'd failed to see what the Geist saw in him, besides his bond with the Zomoki, that is. But now? Things were starting to become clearer. This man contained *surprises*.

"We are fortunate they arrived in this system without their shielding engaged," the Wampeh noted. "A rookie mistake made by many younger captains trying to conserve their casters' magic while in supposedly safe places they do not expect to be disturbed."

"Always expect the unexpected," Charlie said.

"The Geist taught you well."

"Oh, Oscar Wilde beat him to it on that one," Charlie replied. "In any case, no harm was done to them. Once we're well out of their line of sight, we can free them and jump away. A few may have fallen to the deck, but they'll assume it was turbulence or something from the jump."

"And if not?"

"Then they'll think it was something to do with the magic they're experimenting with out here. In any case, I don't think anyone's going to want to admit passing out on duty. The fear of embarrassment often drives men to act against their own best interest."

"A wise observation," Pimbrak noted. "Very well, then. We have observed what we need, and to linger now that we have this new wrinkle to the situation would be folly. We should release them and continue on our way. There is still an important task to complete, and it would be best not to keep our man waiting."

CHAPTER TWENTY

The blue-skinned smuggler landed his craft of choice on the relatively tranquil planet of Skidoon just as dusk was settling over the main city of Hipsala. The ship settled into a soft hover just above the ground at the landing field, resting comfortably on a gentle cushion of magic.

Normally, Olo preferred to use one of his Drookonuses to power his craft at his disposal, but this one in particular he always crewed with a small team of very talented and very discreet Drooks. People he paid well for their services. Men and women who wore false control collars to prevent their being Shanghaied to another vessel.

It was an unusual arrangement, but one that benefited both the smuggler and the Drooks equally. They earned a good wage for their labors, and he had a hard-working crew to propel his ship, all of them guaranteed to keep their silence no matter what happened. He paid them quite well, which alone would normally be more than enough to ensure their loyalty.

That he'd helped obtain their freedom when they were happened upon during a covert mission with his dear friend Korbin back in the day––and had provided them with knock-off control collars of the highest quality—only solidified that position.

And if any double-crossed him, they knew his protection would be forfeit. That could mean they might eventually fall into slavery once more. Paid a fair wage and living free versus a life fearing slavery? It was an easy choice.

That said, Olo always carried a powerful Drookonus with him as well, just in case things got *really* hairy and he needed to hide his Drook crew as his ship was boarded. It had only happened a few times, but being a smuggler, he knew it was bound to happen again. He thought it wise to carry his Drookonus, just in case.

"I'll be back shortly," he told his crew as he headed out of the ship, placing a powerful ward on the door, barring any from entering without first receiving a very nasty surprise.

The pink sun was something of an anomaly, a red dwarf shifting its spectrum in a manner not normally seen. It didn't project any special or unusual powers, but it was nevertheless a beautiful sight to see, especially as it set over the horizon.

Olo walked the streets of Hipsala, breathing the fresh air, smelling the wonderful aroma of restaurants just opening for their evening customers. This was a quiet city on a quiet world, where nothing of note ever happened. Not his usual environs, especially for a covert meeting, but the call for his services had come with substantial coin up front, so he showed up gladly.

Of course, the konuses on his wrists were fully charged, as were both slaaps on his hips. And every blade secreted on his body was enchanted to one degree or another. Like he said, better to have it and not need it than need it and not have it. That applied to more than just his Drookonus.

Olo took a seat in the bustling little establishment he'd been directed to, selecting a remote table in a far corner, his back to the wall. Habit. It was a safe world, but you never knew.

He was nursing his drink, barely sipping it, when a pink-skinned man and his pale companion walked in. The former was unfamiliar, but the assassin he knew. And they were walking right toward him.

"Shit," he muttered, then plastered a neutral smile on his face. "It's you again. Pimpuk, wasn't it?"

"Pimbrak," the Wampeh replied, knowing full well the man remembered his name.

"Ah, my mistake," Olo said, turning his attention to the human. "So, that must make you the Zomoki guy, right?"

"Zomoki guy?" Charlie said with a laugh. "Sure, if that works for you, though most just call me Charlie."

"Okay, Charlie. I'm Olo, as you already know."

The two men shook hands as the newcomers took a seat. Olo released his grip on the magic in his konuses, standing down from his high-ready posturing. With a Wampeh Ghalian here, especially *this* one, there was nothing he could hope to achieve with his weapons that the pale man couldn't do faster and better.

At least he was on his side this evening. So he hoped, anyway.

"So, what can I do for you, Charlie? That was a pretty sizable payment you sent."

"And there's plenty more, if you can do what we ask," Charlie replied.

"We need your help," Pimbrak added.

"Hey, I'm happy to take your coin, but I already got you that freighter. Huge thing it was too. Very hard to come by, and cost a substantial amount."

"Which we paid," Pimbrak reminded him.

"That you did. And I even flew it in myself. Personally delivered it to right where you wanted it," he said with a laugh. "Only, there was already a shit storm of a battle underway when I got there. You never said anything about that when you hired me."

"That was an unexpected wrinkle in our plans," Pimbrak replied. "And one you adapted to admirably, I might add."

With men of Olo's volatile nature, the Wampeh had always found a little flattery––but not too much––brought them around to what you wanted of them far easier than simple coin or threats. Feed their egos and they'd gladly step into harm's way for something as simple as praise.

It was the reason so many fools rushed into wars, hoping to obtain a shiny medal or colorful ribbon for their chest. A bauble proudly displayed to all, often members of the opposite sex. Or the same. Whatever they preferred, it didn't matter.

Whoever had invented the system deserved a medal of his own, for he'd found a simple, inexpensive way to convince young soldiers to risk injury, or even death, willingly, all for glory. Such a silly thing, glory. The assassin had ended many who foolishly stepped into his path hoping to attain it. All they found was a cold grave.

"You're damn right I adapted," Olo said with his trademark cocky grin. "Dropped that baby right in their laps, I did, and bugged out before they could lay a finger on me. Oh, what chaos that must have caused," he mused.

The payload of angry Zomoki had caused a little more than mere chaos. In fact, without them, the battle would certainly have been lost.

"We need your services once more," Pimbrak said.

"Are you kidding? Do you know who it was we did that to? I mean, if you'd told me we were going up against Visla Dominus's main fleet itself I'd never have taken the job. So, no. I don't want to draw *that* person's attention any more than I already have. I have a business to think of, after all."

"And if all of the systems fall into war?" Charlie asked. "How will your business fare then?"

Olo smiled. "Friend, a smuggler *always* finds profit in times of war."

"Dammit, he's right," Charlie mused. It was annoying, the blue fellow's cockiness, but he couldn't help liking the man. "That's too bad," he finally said, sliding into a relaxed pose, as if he didn't really have a care in the world. "You see, we need the fastest ship we can get. Something that can outrun *anything*."

"I wish you luck."

"And we need the best pilot imaginable."

"I'm the best, but you'll just have to look elsewhere."

"Even for the coin we're offering?" Charlie asked, dropping a heavy pouch onto the table.

Olo didn't pick it up, nor did he show outward interest, but he'd played this game for many, many years. Judging by the sound it made when it hit the polished wood, he gathered there was a small fortune inside.

"Well," he began, "I suppose I could maybe find you a ship."

"The fastest ship," Charlie reminded.

"Obviously. But flying it? I don't know," he said, musing on the offer, swayed not by glory this time but simple greed. "What's the job, exactly?"

Charlie looked at Pimbrak. The Wampeh nodded once.

"You saw that portal when you flew the freighter?" Charlie asked.

"Yeah. Big sonofabitch, that thing. What of it?"

"It leads to another galaxy. *My* galaxy. And we need someone to carry cargo through it. Someone piloting a ship fast enough to avoid whatever that fleet might have lying ready to try to stop us."

Olo sat up straight in his chair. "Oh, hell no. Smuggling is one thing, but I have no interest in going to another galaxy, thank you very much."

"Then surely you know someone. There is an opportunity for great profit," Pimbrak said.

Olo paused. "Yeah, I do know one man. Crazy bastard named Tymprazagal. He could do it, maybe. But coin only has worth if you survive to spend it. Profit means nothing to a dead man."

"A valid point," Pimbrak said, tossing a smaller pouch of coin on the table and retrieving the larger one. "Then get us a ship. The fastest. We have brave men of our own who will pilot it."

"Not as well as I can," Olo said.

"No. But as you said, you're not interested. So, a fast ship, then," Pimbrak said. "Do we have a deal?"

Olo sat quietly a long moment, then slowly reached out and picked up the pouch of coin, feeling the heft of it. A smaller fortune, but a hefty sum just the same, he confirmed, a smile spreading across his face.

CHAPTER TWENTY-ONE

Across space, in a galaxy far from his home, Baloo ran through the hills of Malibu as if he'd been born and raised there, his four-legged friend charging along in parallel as they moved through the dark like a pair of sleek hunters—which, in fact, they were.

Bahnjoh, unlike Baloo, actually was home, in a way. Though he'd been born in the violent crash of his master's ship in a distant galaxy, his species was from this galaxy. And unlike the Ra'az Hok, eradicated in the war, there were quite likely more Graizenhund living in the wild somewhere out there.

The two had been thick as thieves ever since they met, and after taking down a small group of Tslavar mercenaries together, they were even closer. The thrill of *that* hunt had been so much more than any a deer or rabbit could afford them.

Of course, there were cougars and bears in the wild hills— their populations had rebounded robustly when mankind had nearly gone extinct—but they steered very clear of the two enormous canine creatures. They may not have known exactly what they were, but one whiff of their scent and they knew those two would be trouble if they ever crossed paths.

The only thing that gave the slightest of hints at the presence of the quietly stalking pair was the rare glint of gold from around their necks. Their fur covered the slender collars most of the time, but on occasion it would shift, and the light would catch it just right.

They weren't control collars, though. For one, Kara would never have allowed it. But Korbin, likewise, felt the two had more than proven themselves capable of restraint. They were on the same team, and, despite the animals' immense jaws and palpable ferocity, he trusted them.

And so it was that Korbin had a burst of inspiration when his hosts mentioned there were additional konuses on this world, part of a cache brought by their counterparts across the portal.

He told Cal what he wished to do, and the AI readily agreed, supplying him with a few of the lesser devices with which to work. Korbin set to work, applying his power to a novel task—fashioning a few konuses into a pair of collars for Bahnjoh and Baloo.

The collars were quite clever in design, the magic they were imbued with capable of deflecting and protecting the animals from low to mid-level magical attacks. If they worked as anticipated, the two of them would be able to shrug off most spells from all but true power users.

If they came across one of those, however, all bets were off. And *those* attacks would likely be a fair bit deadlier. He just hoped the collars would still give them a fighting chance if that ever occurred.

Baloo and Bahnjoh paused in their hunt, sniffing as the wind shifted, blowing the scent inland from the beach. Their ears perked as they listened intently, the faint smell of smoke grabbing their attention.

The scent of Kara and Vee soon followed, the two quickly relaxing back into their hunting posture.

Family. No threat. Carry on the hunt.

Down on the beach not too far away, the teens and their new friends were enjoying a Malibu tradition. The beach bonfire. For the girls who had grown up in a city, the experience was transcendent.

The sky was clear, the stars bright, and the moon resplendent in its radiance, reflecting off of the gently lapping waves as they quietly broke along the shoreline. The smell of salt in the air mingled with that of the crackling driftwood, a comforting blend that set each of them at ease.

"Me and Arlo, this was all we ever knew growing up," Ripley said, casually poking the fire with a stick. "Our folks would take us on cookouts and barbecues all the time. And Aunt Tamara and Aunt Shelly would usually come. Aunt Fatima too, though not as often."

"Well, she was teaching a lot," Arlo noted. "She's sort of in demand as a therapist of sorts," he clarified. "People, cyborgs, Chithiid, you name it, she'll find a way to help them if they need it."

"She sounds like a fascinating woman," Vee said.

"You don't know the half of it," Ripley replied. "She's older than she looks. A *lot* older. Ask her about it sometime when you meet her. Quite a story, I tell ya."

Kara looked up at the stars, the constellations so different from the ones back home. "We'll have quite a story to tell as well. If we ever make it home, that is."

"Hey, you'll get back," Arlo said. "Trust me, my mom is taking this personally, and when she and Freya set their sights on something, watch out."

"But they're just two people. Well, one person and one ship," Kara noted.

"Freya's probably the greatest AI mind ever created. Sure, others are better at some things, like Joshua. He's hands down the most talented tactical mind ever to live. But Freya? She was born from a series of unusual mistakes, and the result is, she's one of a kind. Like my mom."

"Hey, now. Mine too. They're sisters, after all," Ripley corrected.

"Okay, good point. And Aunt Sarah *is* a total badass," Arlo said with a grin. "But what about you guys? You haven't really told us anything about your home and families."

"It's... *complicated*," Kara said, throwing a look to Vee.

Their human friends caught the hint and quickly shifted the subject.

"Hey, there's a warm current this month. You guys wanna go for a night swim?" Ripley asked.

She didn't wait for an answer, hopping to her feet and running off into the surf.

Arlo shrugged. "I guess we're going for a swim," he said, then took off after her, jumping into the small waves.

Kara and Vee looked at one another.

"Should we?" Visanya asked.

"Why not, Vee?" Kara replied.

"But what if there are creatures?"

"I'm sure there are. But don't worry, if it was dangerous, Arlo and Rip wouldn't be so casual about it." Kara then rose and shed her outer layers, stripping to the swimsuit Ripley had provided her. "Come on," she said, then rushed down the sand into the water.

Visanya sighed and followed, splashing into the surf along with the others. The tide was high, and the waves were tiny, resulting in a very calm surface once they waded out past the little waves at the shoreline.

"Hey, you wanna see something cool?" Arlo asked, plunging his hands into the dark sea and moving them quickly, stirring up the calm waters.

"What is that?" Kara asked as little glowing specks formed around his hands. "Is that magic? I thought you didn't have any."

"I don't," Arlo replied with a grin. "It's called bioluminescence. My dad taught me all about it when I was a kid. It's a kind of plankton that photosynthesizes during the day, then bioluminesces at night when it gets agitated."

Kara and Vee looked at him with blank expressions.

"You're doing the tech thing again," Ripley chided.

"Crap. Sorry. Uh, what I mean is, there are these teeny tiny little creatures that live in the sea, right? And when they absorb energy from the sun during the day, they sometimes give it off at night if they get shaken. Does that make more sense?"

"Yes, much more," Kara replied. "It's fascinating how you can do that."

"You can do it too," Arlo said, taking her hand in his and shaking it in the water.

The two teens tensed slightly from the touch, which both Rip and Vee noticed even in the dim moonlight.

"Hey, I've got a trick too," Ripley blurted, hoping to help her cousin avoid any further awkwardness.

He was a good guy and her best friend, but his skills with the ladies were seriously lacking at times.

"Check this out," she said, rubbing the skin on her arm vigorously.

"Uh, what are we looking for?" Visanya asked.

"Give it a minute. We're wet. It works better when I'm dry."

Sure enough, thirty seconds later the skin beneath her hand began to glow. Not the spotty sparkles of the plankton, but an actual glow covering the entire area rubbed.

"What is that?" Kara asked, amazed.

"A side effect from my mom," Rip replied. "Ya see, she was chock full of nanites when she was pregnant with me."

"Nanites?" Kara asked, confused.

"Now *you're* doing it, Rip," Arlo joked. "In plain English, please."

"Right. Uh, nanites are tiny, invisible little machines that work in a kind of swarm, right? And my mom was fixed by them when she was badly hurt. So now they're part of her for life. But while I was growing inside her, some of them kinda found their way into me as well, so they came with me when I was born. They don't do anything useful, though. Not like my mom's. Hers are badass."

"But they glow," Vee said. "It's magical."

"More like a static charge causing a reaction with their power inverters, but I like the sound of magic better," Ripley replied.

The teens splashed around in the water for a while longer, then made their way to the warmth of the bonfire before heading back to Ripley's house.

"Uh, okay. I guess I'll see you guys tomorrow," Arlo said, lingering by Kara an awkward moment, then turning and heading off into the night.

Ripley shook her head slightly as she and Vee shared another look. "Hopeless," she said. "Well, let's get cleaned up and crash. I've got some cool plans for tomorrow."

The girls headed inside and showered off the smoke, sand, and salt, then lay their heads down for the night, a long and fascinating day under their belts.

It was the best the two alien teens had slept since their arrival.

CHAPTER TWENTY-TWO

Eyes all across the globe, as well as quite a few in orbit around Earth, the moon, and the sun, were glued to their video displays as the most powerful wizard––*visla*, as they were called in his galaxy––began his demonstration of what true magic was. And more importantly, how to defend against it.

It had already been something of a hard pill to swallow, the realization that there really was magic out there, and they would be fighting forces utilizing the completely unconventional weaponry. Spells instead of plasma bursts or railgun sabots. Shielding of magic rather than phase-pulsing energy fields.

It was enough to make your head spin, and, given the demonstrated aggressions already waged against Earth as well as the Urok fleet, there seemed little doubt the threat was imminent.

That's where Korbin came in.

It was unfortunate for him that he had been driven to cross galaxies to survive the battle he was caught up in, but it was a boon for the non-magical forces of Earth and their allies. That he was more than just a talented spell caster, but, rather, one of the most powerful vislas from that distant realm, meant he could bring precisely the expert insight they would need should they hope to survive the pending attack.

It wasn't a question of *if* it would come. It was a question of *when.*

Rika had agreed to assist Korbin on this occasion, her own magical skills being quite impressive as well, and with their resident magic man and his space dragon friend nowhere to be found for the time being, she was the top spell caster in the galaxy, after Korbin.

The demonstration was sure to be an eye-opener for those unfamiliar with these powers, but even the new pirate visitors from the other galaxy were tuned in and watching as well, eager to see a major visla put on a show. Even Marban found himself staring at Korbin's perfect smile on screen.

"Thank you all for joining us," Korbin said to the small crowd assembled before him.

He'd been informed of video transmission and how that whole system worked, but it was foreign to his world, and thus, he had been provided a live crowd to demonstrate for to make it easier for him. Staring at a lens was not something he was accustomed to back home.

"While I know this all will be a little strange to you, rest assured, all of the technology you find commonplace is just as strange to me. Our worlds are so very similar in many ways, but so incredibly different in others. The most obvious is how our very civilizations function," Korbin began. "In your world, you have engines and projectiles, where in mine we have spell casters and magic. Each system functions smoothly in our own realms, but they are fundamentally different to such a degree that I believe we can use this difference to help you all defend yourselves in ways people from my world would not expect."

Rika stepped several paces back, as they'd rehearsed, and prepared herself.

"You'll see that Rika, here, is glowing," Korbin continued.

"She is from this planet. An Earth woman. Yet she is imbued with a type of magic from a distant part of your galaxy, as well as a rather rare power from mine. The result is a combination of powers that seems to overwhelm magic from my realm."

He nodded to Rika, who cast a shielding spell. It was invisible to the eye, but as Korbin began launching spells against it, faint shimmers could be discerned. The tiny size of the reaction in no way represented the amount of force being wielded, however.

Korbin nodded to her again, and they stopped.

"That probably didn't look like much, and to the unpowered it wouldn't. But now, without shielding, I'll cast those same spells."

He turned toward a set of targets thirty meters away, the cameras tracking him smoothly. Slowly and deliberately, he began casting, shattering each of the targets one by one with his magic. The gasps and murmurs from the crowd told him the demonstration had the desired effect.

"Those were the same spells, but with no shielding," he said. "Now, we hope you'll never find yourself up against this sort of attack, but everyone needs to be prepared. You all need to go into battle with your eyes wide open, aware of what you're up against. Now, your vessels have an ingenious bit of tech-based shielding."

He nodded, and a pair of drones flew toward them from a nearby launch point and began circling them.

"Because of the differences in powers used, your shielding may easily stop a projectile or pulse weapon attack. But magic..." He cast a single spell, albeit a strong one, and tore the drone to pieces.

He'd cleared that with Cal beforehand, of course. It was good for shock value, to make the lesson stick, but he didn't want to waste any resources they couldn't spare.

"That was with your shielding running at capacity."

The crowd murmured again. How could they defend against something like that?

"I know what you're thinking. How can we stop an attack that cuts through our shields? It's a tech answer, and Rika will explain that far better than I can."

"Thanks, Korbin," Rika said, stepping forward. "The energies used by magic may seem mystical and impossible to us, and it's true that we still don't know exactly how they work. But we do know they produce repeatable patterns that react with our shields. And if we shift our defensive arrays to phase in that new spectrum––" she nodded to Korbin, who fired off the same spell at the second drone.

That one stayed in the air. Shaken, but unharmed.

"As you can see, if we dial in to the type of magic being used, we *can* defend against it," she said.

"But what if it's different magic?" a crew-cut airman asked.

"Good question," Rika replied. "And you won't like the answer, but the fact is, you'll have to adapt and adjust on the fly. And there's not much we can do to speed that process. It's a lot of trial and error, and every ship in our fleet will have to contribute their readings to the AI brains working on the problem. But once we know which spell variants they're using, we can transmit that to the fleet as a whole."

"Yeah, that's a good point," Korbin chimed in. "Ships from my galaxy use an entirely different form of communication device. While you won't be able to tap into their communications, neither will they be able to hear yours. Transmitting this data, as well as any battle plans, will be safe."

Korbin and Rika then launched into a discussion on the various quirks of magic, and the tactics all pilots from the other galaxy have had drilled into their heads. Then they shifted to the scary "what if?" What if they encountered the enemy on foot?

"At a middle distance, spells are hard to stop. Your best bet is to take cover and radio for assistance," Rika told the group. "But from far away, magic will eventually dissipate. So if you're far enough away to run, run."

"But, if you're up against it and there are bad guys all around, get as close as you can," Korbin added. "We are all trained early on not to cast any combative spells in close proximity to our friends and allies. It's just too easy for something to go awry, and the last thing you want to do is accidentally take out your own men. I believe you call that 'friendly fire' in your realm. But if you find yourself in that situation against the enemy, that proximity to them can give you a relatively safe pocket to resort to conventional weapons. Blades and the like."

"What about guns?" a woman asked.

"Ah, yes. I've examined your projectile and pulse weapons and am happy to report that those will work quite well up close and personal," Korbin replied.

"And if you're under fire at a farther range, pulse rifles do sometimes work if you have a window to get a shot off. The power holds for great ranges, and our enemy has to adjust *their* shielding as well to compensate for our attacks," Rika added.

The spirits of the attendees seemed to rise steadily as they realized that, while it would be a tough fight, it was one they *could* win. Then Rika got into the quirks of warp technology and how unreliable it was on the other side without a handshake from a magical craft to help guide it.

"If you find yourself on the other side, for whatever reason, you need to find one of our allied ships to help you," Rika said. "Without it, there's no telling where a warp might take you. But that might be your only option, and if it is, take note of the stars. Start cataloging them for your own star map. Then, and only if you absolutely must, make the smallest warp you can. That should keep you within conventional travel range, while getting you out of a bind. Any more than that and you risk getting straight-up lost. Any questions?"

An orange-skinned Urok raised his hand. "The Urok fleet utilizes a somewhat different warp technology than your Earth ships. Will it affect us the same?"

"We haven't tried to warp one of your ships on the other side yet, so we just don't know. Your safest bet is to link up with one of our magic ships before attempting a warp," Rika replied, scanning the crowd. They'd covered a lot already, but there was even more.

"Okay. Let's discuss shimmers."

CHAPTER TWENTY-THREE

"I think that went rather well, all things considered," Korbin said as he and Rika took a little ride in the *Fujin.*

She had dragged him off after their teaching session ended, having been beamed to pretty much every eye in the system, saving him from an onslaught of curious participants who were just dying to see more of his magic up close. A few of them up close and *personal*, even.

Not that Rika was getting any less attention. As the first human caster, and a talented pilot and all-around badass on top of all that, she had more than her share of admirers as well. Of course, that just made her want to leave even more.

"Jo, go talk to them a bit, will ya?" Rika had asked.

"And what am I supposed to tell them? I'm riding bitch while you tear off across the galaxy? Ooh, so glamorous."

"Ha-ha. No, dumbass, tell them some stories about our adventures. Tell them the Nasturian one. They're bound to love it."

Jo pondered a moment. "Well, I do have some handy. I was going to drop it with Cal for analysis, but I suppose I could also see if anyone's up for the Nasturian challenge."

"Jo, don't go hospitalizing our allies, okay?"

"You got it, boss."

Rika shook her head with a chuckle. "All right, I'm gonna bail for a bit. Holler if you need me."

"I've got my comms ready if this lot gets out of hand," Jo replied with a grin. "Go on, get out of here. And have fun over there."

"Oh, it'll be fun, and I think Korbin's gonna have a blast. Literally, in fact."

She'd taken him on a roundabout flight, not heading directly to their destination. What fun would it be without a little build up, after all? But after ten minutes of casual sightseeing, Rika finally took the *Fujin* in to land in the desert far to the northeast of Los Angeles.

"Why did they call it 'Skunk Works'?" Korbin asked as Rika told him a little about the history of the aeronautical testing facility.

"That, my friend, is far too long a story to get into right now. Suffice to say, the greatest inventing minds of their day worked here, and after the war, Cal and the others decided to re-open it."

"Okay," Korbin said as they touched down. "But why the secrecy?"

"You'll see."

"Again, with the secrecy," he chuckled, following her from the ship onto the hot tarmac.

They walked across the area, past a pair of smaller hangars toward a larger one with actual guards stationed outside.

"Heya, fellas," Rika said as they approached. "Cal told you we were coming, right?"

"Yes, ma'am," one of the nearly identically crew-cut men answered. "Please, step inside."

She didn't need to be told twice in that heat, nor did her guest, who followed her into the large facility. What he saw nearly made him lose his composure and squeal with delight. But that wouldn't suit a man of his age, let alone a visla.

"My ship!" he said, his smile threatening to split his face. "Oh, look what you've done to my ship!"

"Thought you'd like it," Rika replied, giving him some room to take his time and walk around the craft, taking in all of the spectacular modifications that had been made to the vessel.

Cal's team was the best there were, and they'd worked fast. That they were getting to not only play with the most advanced and deadly toys in the toolbox was actually secondary for once. They got to work on an actual *magic ship*. It was as close to a fairy tale as the tech-minded team would ever get.

Korbin was slow and deliberate as he examined every inch of his substantial ship. Rika approved. As a pilot, she was familiar with the importance of a thorough walk-around. At the end of the day, your ship was your responsibility, no matter what a tech or mechanic may or may not have done to it.

And, oh, what they'd done to this one.

"Are those railguns, like on the *Fujin*?" he asked when he finally completed his loop.

"They're similar, but it looks like they gave you a beefier version since your ship's bigger than mine. I like the armored housing they installed for them to retract into. Blends with the exterior almost perfectly."

"I was just noting that," Korbin said, still grinning like a kid on Christmas morning. "What about those?" he asked, pointing at a trio of deadly looking octagonal barrels toward the middle-rear of his ship.

"Plasma cannons," Rika informed him. "The two on either side are on a two-hundred-degree rotating gimbal, while the center one is designed as a tail gun."

"Tail gun? You mean to target craft behind me?"

"Yep. You never cast spells behind you?"

"It's not customary, no. Generally, magic for propulsion

would potentially be disrupted with too much casting directly into its wake. It's a common weakness among all ships, which is why rear shielding is so robust."

"Well, this ain't magic, so feel free to blast away at anyone foolish enough to get on your tail," Rika said with great amusement.

This reminded her. It was just about time to give the *Fujin* another round of upgrades now that she and Jo had experienced more than their fair share of combat on the other side of the portal. With a few modifications and new toys, the *Fujin* would be even deadlier. And so would her mech.

Speaking of which, she realized she needed to talk to Marban about the best transit options for rapid deployment when they did eventually cross the portal again. The setup they had previously used worked well, but, given the nature of their adversary, she had been thinking a faster means of getting it in the fight would be worth figuring out.

But the mech would have to wait. She shifted her attention back to the ship in front of her.

"Hey. Try casting a spell against it."

"Against my own ship?"

"Don't worry," she said. "I promise it'll be okay."

Korbin didn't doubt her, but he nevertheless used a far gentler spell than they'd cast against the drones earlier that day.

The spell flew true, but a strange shielding buzzed to life across the ship's hull when it landed, dispersing the energy and directing the residual off of the far side, sending it crashing into the wall, the techs nearby scurrying for cover.

"Oops. Probably should have warned them," Rika said with a laugh. "Sorry, guys!"

"My magic should only be barely protecting the ship in its current state," Korbin marveled. "What did your people do?"

"Oh, just added some advanced phase shielding to your baby while they were at it. With both your magic and the ship's new automatically adjusting tech shields, it's gonna be one very tough cookie to take down."

"Thank you, Rika. This is wonderful."

"Don't thank me. Thank Cal. He set this all up. But hey, do you wanna take it out to the firing range to work out the bugs and loose some rounds?"

Though it hadn't seemed possible just moments before, Korbin's smile grew even wider. "I thought you'd never ask."

"I believe the expression you're looking for is, 'Holy Shit!'" Rika said with a laugh, standing beside Korbin on the bridge of his newly modified craft.

"Holy shit!" he echoed. "I like the sound of that."

"It's a goody," Rika agreed. "And seeing what your new toys can do, I think it's quite fitting."

They'd started off with some basic trial runs, getting the alien captain familiar with the tech controls now added to his magical ship. It was a bit of an adjustment, but Korbin had always been a fast study, and within an hour he was operating the systems like a natural.

The plasma cannons were a big hit, their heavy octagonal barrels streaming out bursts of energy-death far beyond anything he'd ever seen of the sort. Within minutes, Korbin dialed in his targeting, and from that moment on, anything he set his sights on was toast.

"Try the railguns," Rika urged.

"We have projectile spells where I'm from, but it's always magic launching things to overcome a magical defense."

"Yeah, well, this is just straight-up, electromagnetic, kick-ass firepower. And those sabots are fast down here in atmosphere, but once you fire them off in space, you'll really appreciate the sheer carnage they can accomplish. I'm talking Mach ten projectiles firing in rapid bursts."

"Mach ten? What's Mach ten?"

"Ten times the speed of sound," she replied. "It actually sounds cooler than it is, but in some firefights it's what you need. The thing is, there's actually such a thing as *too* fast. Like, the kinetic energy of a sabot at around Mach four will turn it to slag and cause an explosive reaction when it hits."

"I like the sound of that," Korbin said.

"And you can dial the speed down to that if you like. The higher speed ones are more for penetration into bigger ships. On smaller ones, they'll likely just pop right through without much damage. And with magic sealing the hull breaches, that's not what you want. But this system is controlled by the amount of power you feed it, so it lets you adjust velocity on the fly, so you should be able to switch it up as you're shooting. And you've got two of 'em on this thing. You wanna give 'em a go?"

"Do you even need to ask?"

Korbin spent a half hour working with the tracking system, the power mechanism, and the many adjustments at his disposal, getting a feel for them all before beginning a live fire test of the railguns.

The first series was against stationary targets. He tried them out at different speeds, and, as Rika had said, each density of target reacted best to a different speed of sabot.

"I think I've got this," he said. "Let's take it up a level."

"You got it," Rika replied. "Send up some drones," she called over comms.

The drones were fast, and they were shielded as well. Korbin had a hard time tracking, flying, and firing at the same time at first.

"This would be easier with a full crew."

"You don't have one, so stop bitching and start shooting," was Rika's version of sympathy.

Korbin laughed and set his mind back to the task, and soon the drones fell one by one.

"Not bad. But what about magic? You think you can force some of your power onto the rounds?"

"I don't know," he replied. "But I'm ready to try."

"Good, because here comes the drone."

Korbin easily targeted it, but the magical shielding deflected the sabot without a problem. He growled with frustration, pushing his power onto the next rounds chambered and ready to go, but again, they bounced off.

"What am I doing wrong?"

"You need to adjust your magic to the shift of the shield I put on the ship. Feel it, read it, find its weakness, then exploit it. All it takes is one making it through. The rest will follow easily."

He focused, trying again to down the little drone. "Come on, you stupid––I got it!" he blurted as his round cleared the shifting magic and downed the craft. "I can pierce magic with tech!"

Rika was beaming. He'd learned quickly, and his ship was now going to be a very welcome part of their arsenal. "Nicely done," she said. "Now, we don't know how well this will work in the other galaxy, of course, but the basics are there. Hell, the weird differences between galaxies might even be why Dominus's portal spell in the *Asbrú* didn't work as intended. Saved by a quirk between galaxies that gave us just enough time to stop them."

"A fortuitous surprise," he mused. "A glitch that worked in your favor."

"Yep," Rika replied. "So, your ship still needs a proper space shakedown, though, so what do you say to taking it out for one in a day or two, when the final checks are complete?"

"I'd love to," Korbin replied, happy as a kid in a candy shop.

"Cool. And I was thinking. We have a commandeered shimmer ship, but it needs work. The Drooks are great, don't get me wrong, and they're loving free life. But with its onboard caster dead, the shimmer potency he imbued into the craft is fading. You think you can work something out with that? None of our magic seems to stick to that ship."

"I'll have a look, and if I can recharge its shimmer magic, I'll gladly do so. It would be a valuable tool in our arsenal."

Rika grinned. Things had gone well today, and Murphy had let them. It was an unusual sensation, and one she could get used to.

CHAPTER TWENTY-FOUR

Locked in a cell, under guard despite his lack of weapons and the thickness of the bars confining him, Grundsch passed the time as many in confinement did. Namely, he exercised.

His captors had done a fine job healing him, and whatever magic Korbin had applied prior to handing him over to his now-jailers had taken hold and greatly accelerated his recovery. It had only been a few days, but he felt much like his old self again. Better, perhaps.

The space in which he found himself housed had been out of service for a great many years. Once the last of the war criminals had been tried and executed, there wasn't much need for cells capable of restraining men of his strength. That, and after the war, the idea of the handful of humanity's survivors actually fighting one another and committing crimes worthy of imprisonment was laughable.

Sure, people needed a drunk tank to sleep off their grudges, but true crimes? *Serious* ones? Those were pretty much a thing of the past.

Then Grundsch arrived.

The huge Ra'az still scowled angrily at the humans and Chithiid who oversaw him daily. It wasn't that he had a specific grudge against any of them, just an instinctive rage he still carried within, though he had no reason to anymore. His people had failed. Lost the war, which they hadn't even considered a two-sided affair until it was too late.

Conquest, that's all humanity was to them. Right up until Earth's supposedly extinct denizens mounted a surprising comeback, unaware they weren't supposed to be able to. It quickly spilled over from a skirmish into a war leading to the end of his race. And just like that, Grundsch became the last of his kind.

Kara had been the one consistent bright spot in his otherwise depressing confinement, though he still found it hard to believe the girl would take time from her day to visit the likes of him. He was just a bodyguard. Muscle tasked with protecting her. But she'd known him her whole life, and to that impossible, violet-skinned girl, he was family.

"Hi, Grundsch!" the teen said as she popped in for her daily visit.

The guards wouldn't let her in his cell. Not yet, anyway. But she didn't mind so much, so long as she could talk to her guardian and help raise his spirits.

"You should stop coming here, Denna Palmarian. You are young, and there is a whole world you could be exploring."

"One, there's plenty of time to explore. I don't think we'll be going home anytime soon. And two, stop calling me Denna. It's a silly title, and I don't like it."

"Apologies, Denna," he replied with a hint of a grin. Something rather unusual for a Ra'az, the guards monitoring the room noted.

"Ugh, you're impossible. Just call me Kara, like everyone else."

"It will take some getting used to, *Kara*, but I shall do as you request."

"Thanks, Grundsch. Oh, and I thought you'd want to know, Bahnjoh and Baloo are doing great. They're having a blast running around the hills and exploring together. I mean, we had the gardens at home, but seeing him out in so much nature? I've never seen him happier."

The giant Ra'az felt his spirits rise at her words. Graizenhund were normally tools among his people, not pets. Deadly but expendable. However, stranded as he had been, he and the animal had become close, and he was glad to hear Bahnjoh was happy on this new world.

"Tell me again," Kara asked. "Tell me why they hate you so much here. It just doesn't make sense."

"It makes perfect sense, Den––*Kara*. You've only known me in one setting. But here? Here, my life was quite different."

"But genocide?"

Grundsch sighed. "Mine was a hive race. A people ruled by one queen who guided us all. And we lived for the glory of battle and conquest, my brothers and I, spreading out across the galaxy to acquire more resources for our ever-expanding home."

"But why kill everyone? It doesn't make sense. People have value."

"It was their planet's resources we wanted, not the inhabitants. Our queen decided long ago that it was simply more efficient to eradicate the primary defenders of a world entirely before we began harvesting its resources."

"So you just flew around, conquering worlds and wiping out their inhabitants?"

"More or less. That is, until the unthinkable happened. The Ra'az Hok lost. And not just a battle, not just the war, but our homeworld as well. Our queen. Our people. But when the final attack occurred, some sort of massive power weapon discharged, coinciding with my planet exploding. It was cataclysmic, causing our sun to react as well. It was that mix of powers, I now realize, that somehow made a rift open. A wormhole of a sort. My ship was rushing into battle, ready to perish in a blaze of glory, when we were sucked into it and ejected into your realm."

"Father told me the story. How he found your vessel crashed on one of the distant planets he oversaw."

"Yes, though I do not remember many details. I was gravely injured, and the rest of my shipmates were dead. So, too, were the Graizenhunds we had aboard. All perished, but the pregnant one that delivered her litter on impact. And, somehow, a lone pup survived."

"Bahnjoh."

"Indeed. His kind are hardy and have exceptionally long lifespans. I was fortunate to have him, I suppose. A reminder of my former life. In any case, when I finally woke, it was with a collar around my neck and in your father's service. I've been a slave ever since."

Kara assessed him with kind eyes.

"The thing is, Grundsch, you're living in a new reality, yet again. Yeah, your collar is gone and you can return to behaving like your former self, but your old beliefs will serve you poorly. What I'm trying to say is, you're not part of a hive anymore. You're your own man, and that means whatever you do, it's all on you, not someone else. There's no queen now. No more blindly following others. You should follow your heart and mind."

"But I am Ra'az Hok. This is what I am."

"But you don't have to be, Grundsch. I've known you my whole life, and believe me when I tell you that you're so much more than that. Be who you decide to be. No hive or slave owner dictating what you are. Just you."

He studied her a long moment.

"You are wise beyond your years, Kara. When did you grow up, so?"

"You helped raise me, so you should know," she replied with

a warm smile. "Now, enough of that serious stuff. I'm going to tell you all about this world's marvels. Have you ever heard of bioluminescence?"

CHAPTER TWENTY-FIVE

Safely tucked away in their shared and formerly top-secret hangar on the periphery of the Dark Side moon base, Freya and Joshua were hard at work, pooling their resources and combining their intellectual powers toward a single goal.

Understanding nanites and their relationship with magic.

Freya had been born in this place, her bleeding-edge experimental AI mind accidentally switched on totally outside of normal activation parameters when Daisy had stumbled upon it.

Now, as a fully grown and self-sustaining AI, Freya called the place home, and her stealthy shape fit easily within its confines, leaving ample room for Joshua to join her with his heavily armored core vessel, once he'd shed the swarm ships and left them outside.

Just as if you tracked mud in the house on your shoes, Freya would not be thrilled if a few hundred craft were suddenly scattered about the place. So they waited, patiently settled across the lunar surface.

Joshua would normally have kept them in low orbit, but given the nature of their strange and magical assailants of late, he thought it prudent to keep them out of the way of the facility's defensive weaponry array. No fire was better than friendly fire, he liked to say.

The unusual AI pair had been working together to scientifically understand exactly how Freya's nanite structure had managed to assimilate the magic power of Kara's deconstructed konus into the very fabric of her vessel. It was power, but unlike any they'd ever dealt with before. But then, what was magic if not scientific mysteries they just didn't know the answer to yet?

"We're no closer to replicating your results, Freya," Joshua said.

He wasn't exactly frustrated, per se, but for the greatest strategic mind ever created, the AI who had formerly overseen the military might of an entire nation while safely tucked away underneath a granite mountain, it was disconcerting. Answers usually leapt out at him. The magic question, however, thus far yielded no such luck.

"You know, Eddie can cast," she noted. "I think that had to do with his age, though. They say mature AI can't quite shift their core processing parameters to what's needed for the 'intent' portion of spellcasting."

"But you're a mature AI. In years, if not personality," Joshua joked.

"Oh, hush, you. The only reason I can make this stuff work is because I wasn't born the way the rest of you were."

"That, and the totally out-of-parameter nature of that beautiful experimental brain of yours," Joshua added appreciatively.

"Well, yeah. That too," Freya chuckled. "But the thing is, I was able to break down the power holding me to that piece of debris once I had an energy generation device of my own."

"The konus."

"Precisely. And when I incorporated the same structure of

that into the rest of my nanites, it effectively gave me a surface area that was able to direct this magic, or power, or whatever you want to call it."

"But why can't you cast like the others, now?"

"It seems that the words actually do mean something. How, I don't know, though. What I deactivated on my own was a spell gone awry. That's why I was able to break it. It was a ruined spell. But for *real* spells, it appears you actually need specific words."

"But they say it's more than words. It's intent," Joshua said.

"Yep. But I'm getting the gist. I've been learning how the words and intent when casting translates into specific energy patterns within the power, thus converting that conglomerate into the final spell. I think I should be able to gain more control with just a bit more practice. I can only cast little spells so far, but it makes more sense with every new one I incorporate."

"The thing we need is to get a system functional with the enhanced nanites," Joshua noted. "It would be a great tactical advantage, and I think we'll be needing one. Eddie has a konus welded to his frame, and he can cast to an extent, but so far, every attempt to bond an AI mind to a magic/nanite composite craft has led to the AI going insane."

"So we keep trying."

It wasn't as cold-hearted as it sounded. They weren't sacrificing their carefully grown kin in the name of science, but had instead been running a simulation with a very specialized, self-contained AI.

The problem was, it went mad with every attempt, forcing a reboot.

Konus-powered magic with the device added to an existing ship's frame seemed to work. But a craft constructed with magical nanites? So far, every single iteration of the simulation's AI had failed.

They'd start again, the new information learned added to the base code of the shell mind. But even then, progress inevitably slowed, and the mind went mad. A living pilot could use the test ship's structure itself to amplify and direct their casting, but an AI simply could not be made to bond with it.

"It's not a nanite problem. We've seen they can essentially break down and replicate most energy types found within this magic stuff. And we can create a nanite ship, no problem," she said, referring to the sleek experimental craft currently being finished in the automated fabrication chamber. "The ship is pretty much done. The only issue is the huge amount of power it will need to actually charge up the nanites to magical levels."

"Why didn't you say so?" Joshua joked. "Ask and you shall receive."

He transmitted a burst to the solar array on the far side of the moon, where it was currently absorbing pure solar energy and feeding it to the base. In a flash, the relays diverted the majority of the feed not to Dark Side base, which had ample power for weeks if need be, but to the nanite ship under construction.

"You sure Sid's okay with this?"

"He has power cell backups. And besides, we're only taking power for a few minutes to give these little guys a boost. Once they're online and charged up, they'll do the hard work of getting their siblings up and running."

The ship's nanites buzzed with the new energy source, drinking their fill even while the machinery around them finished its labors. Very soon, it would be a completely functional magical nanite ship. One that possessed both magic energy, as well as a warp core. Only there was still one problem. It couldn't house an AI.

"You do realize what this could mean, don't you?" Joshua asked, more for the feeling of saying it out loud than because he actually required a response.

"Yeah, I do," Freya replied. "It means it'll almost certainly need a non-AI pilot."

CHAPTER TWENTY-SIX

The formerly quiet planet of Otsola had always been a relatively ignored world located in one of the less frequented systems. It hadn't been due to any hostilities or other problems in the area, but rather, the natural volatility of the planet due to high volume of seismic activity.

Earthquakes were a regular occurrence, leading to much shorter buildings with wider bases, as well as an interior decoration style favoring unbreakable items, all of which were either on heavy bases or fixed in place magically.

In the more distant spots on the planet, small volcanoes would periodically erupt, spilling molten lava onto the surface to harden into a new layer waiting to be broken and melted down again in another few years or centuries, depending on the planet's whim.

Fortunately, this constant state of activity kept ash from being collected and blown into the atmosphere, so aside from a bit of a foul smell in the general area, the volcanoes didn't do much more than put on a pretty light show at night.

The constant rumbling and knowledge that the planet was essentially spitting up its insides not too far away had the tendency to put visitors on edge. The constant ill-at-ease sensation is what led to the planet being left to the locals, for the most part. Only traders would frequent it, using the place as a convenient stopover to resupply and offload some of their wares.

To that ramshackle bunch, a shaking city was as good as any when it came to earning some coin. And traders were easy to blend in with, their constant moving of cargo a convenient cover should you need to deliver or retrieve several large containers, for example.

It was for this reason The Three had selected this planet to conceal their priceless cache of Wampeh Ghalian wealth for millennia. Of course, things had changed a bit since the Geist had last set foot there.

"This isn't normal, is it?" Hunze asked from her seat within Zilara's stealthily shimmer-cloaked craft. "There are a *lot* of vessels out there, and they appear to be Tslavar."

"Not just Tslavar. These are Dominus's craft," Zilara grumbled.

Even for a master assassin as skilled as she, getting through those ships, down to the surface, maneuvering around a city full of the enemy, reaching a centuries-hidden cache, then somehow carrying it back, all without being noticed, would be near impossible.

Naturally, she felt a giddy warmth at the prospect of such a challenge.

"I see the geology is as active as ever," Bawb noted calmly. "Fortunately, our destination is in the capital city, which was located on the most volcanically stable region on the planet. It was formerly known as Laskan, though I couldn't tell you its name presently."

"Its name interests me far less than its location. Shall I assume it is located where all of those craft are shuttling to and from on the surface?" Zilara asked, maneuvering her shimmer ship around one of the visla's lesser supply craft.

"You would be correct," Bawb replied. "However, I fear even your shimmer will not withstand the sheer quantity of magic being deployed in its vicinity. It's concentrated in a small area rather than spread among an entire fleet. Can you feel it, Hunze?"

"I can. It's strange, though. As if a large portion of it is not fresh. Stored magic, but of great potency. Not Ootaki, though, of that I'm certain."

Zilara cocked her head slightly, feeling the magic around them. She'd fed recently––a moderately powered emmik, and her senses were greatly enhanced for it. "Not Ootaki, no. Something else. Strange magic. Clearly what we've sensed when encountering Dominus's forces previously."

"What do we do, then?" Hunze asked.

"For now, we observe," Bawb replied. "We do not yet have the necessary keys to access the cache anyway, but the others are retrieving them as we speak. If they are half as capable as I believe them to be, they'll already be waiting with them for us when we return to Chaldra to regroup."

They sat quietly, floating in the concealed vessel, just far enough from the overlapping magic of the numerous ships in such close proximity to one another. Her shimmer was powerful, but not against that overwhelming amount of magic.

After a time, a new group of craft jumped into the system, towing what appeared to be damaged vessels taken in a fight. They were mostly intact, however, and were taken directly to a shipyard floating in orbit.

"Pirated ships," Zilara noted. "Looks like our Visla Dominus is capturing vessels and retrofitting them into warships. That would explain why it has been difficult to track his sourcing of the ships in his fleet."

"Of course. He's been crafting many of them himself," Bawb realized. "Clever."

Supply ships continued to come and go from Laskan,

making their way to and from the much larger craft in low orbit, but a few recently arrived vessels seemed different from the others.

"Are those Palmarian ships?" Zilara asked.

"A bit after my time," Bawb replied. "But they do look similar to some of the vessels we saw while on Slafara. But, again, it is simply too risky to get closer to confirm. But once they head back into space, then we might be able to get a better look. It is most interesting that Palmarian and his craft keep turning up wherever we go."

"You think it means something?"

"Perhaps. Perhaps not. But only a fool ignores patterns. No, I think that if those are in fact from his fleet, then this is almost certainly more than a coincidence. And if those are Palmarian ships, if one is still on the surface when we approach the cache, then perhaps we can even inquire of their crew as to the whereabouts of our friend."

"And about the cache. I think this changes our plans a bit, wouldn't you agree?" Zilara noted.

"Yes and no," Bawb said as he watched another ship jump into orbit. "But I have an idea. One I will put into motion when we return to Chaldra. But for the time being, we watch and learn."

CHAPTER TWENTY-SEVEN

The boot that connected with Marban's jaw hadn't hit with full force, but it was, nevertheless, quite a shot. Fortunately, his skull was thick and his jaw was strong. A lesser man would likely have gone down from the blow. But Marban was not a lesser man.

With an amused laugh he shook it off and launched into a mixed-style counter-attack, moving quite fast for a man his size.

Rika had been caught off-guard the first time he'd revealed his disguised speed, but not since. She parried and blocked, keeping her feet well centered beneath her as she absorbed a few shots to move in close, knowing the pirate's reluctance to hit her meant an opening to move inside the larger man's reach.

He had no sooner pulled his punch than he was made to regret it when Rika threw an elbow to his already aching jaw as she spun her back toward him, grabbing his arm and throwing him effortlessly over her hip with her favorite Judo technique from back in the day.

Marban hit the ground hard but rolled quickly back to his feet, a look of renewed determination mingling with his standard one of amusement. The pirate again attacked, but this time focusing on footwork, leading Rika to where he wanted her positioned through feints and fakes.

Finally, she stepped forward for an attack, right into position. Right where he wanted her. Marban switched stance in a flash, driving his knee forward straight into her chest. Or, it should have gone there, but his target was gone.

Rika had spun at the last moment and somehow wound up on his back, buckling his knee forward with her foot, dropping him low enough for her to slide a chokehold into place. She smiled as her arms flexed, tightening the pressure. Any second now, he would tap out.

But Marban was stubborn. Stubborn, and possessing a particularly thick neck.

Using his size to his advantage, he slid his arm back between her feet, then up, pulling her boot off of his knee as he lifted her over his head while rising to standing. Rather than bringing her down on his knee, as he'd do in true combat, he tossed her to the ground, confident she could not only take it, but would respect him more for doing so.

Rika easily rolled out of the impact and turned, using the coiled energy in her legs to spring back toward her adversary in a flash. This was a bit unexpected, but Marban was an experienced fighter. Stopping the smaller woman would be easy. Or so he thought, until she abruptly halted her approach right before him, planting her feet and driving hard with her hips, all of her leverage and kinetic energy traveling through her core, her shoulders, and her arms, to her flattened palms.

The open-palm strike sent him flying, partially knocking the wind out of him.

"Hey, we agreed there'd be no magic," Marban said, painfully sucking in a breath as he rose and dusted himself off.

"I didn't use magic," Rika replied.

"Oh, ha-ha. Very funny. But you obviously just did."

"Nope. Just good old-fashioned Jeet Kune Do. It's all in the hips, after all."

"Not likely."

Rika paused, then abruptly lifted her shirt, revealing a sports bra and the swirling, barely-visible white lines of the tattoos covering her body. On her sternum, the dense Gordian knot of interwoven branches converged to her source of power. Her Prime. The Wellspring, as she called it.

"You see me glowing?" Rika asked.

"Well, uh, no. But––"

"No buts. The only butt is yours, which I kicked, fair and square. No glowing, no magic," she said, dropping her shirt back in place, and rather enjoying how uncomfortable such a simple display had made the man.

He was a *pirate*, for crying out loud. A pirate who was unsettled by a sports bra. Rika was endlessly amused.

They trained quite well together, actually. When Rika wasn't torturing the poor fellow, that is. He had shown her a bunch of the pirate tricks of the trade they used when boarding ships and fighting in space. It was a rather specialized skill set, and one that might come in handy when hostilities with the invaders inevitably began again.

And Rika returned the favor in kind, showing Marban many of the deadly techniques that Malalia had burned into her mind. It was a difficult tale to tell, but after she'd shared it with him, Rika actually felt a little bit better.

She'd talked about it before, of course, but for whatever reason, this conversation with the unusual pirate had taken the edge off.

Marban found his eyes lingering on the ink on her flushed skin. "You know," he said, tossing her a water container and cracking open one for himself. "I was thinking."

"A pirate? Thinking? Stop, it's weird," Rika joked.

"Seriously, though. I thought maybe I'd get a tattoo."

"Not like mine, you won't. For one, the guy who did it? Not a fan of offworlders. And two, the ink they used on me would kill you."

"Oh?"

"It's a galaxy thing. A lot of stuff on that planet is toxic to people from your world. You should have seen how miserable Hunze and Leila were at the feast—"

"There was a feast? Oh, now I know I wish to visit this world."

"Ugh. Could you live up to the stereotype any more?"

"I'm doing my best," he replied with a mischievous wink.

A little something was building there, and for a moment Marban allowed himself the indulgence of a glimmer of hope.

"Hey, there you are!" Korbin called out, walking toward them.

Rika turned, the moment lost.

"Hey, Korbin. What's shakin'? Glad you could make it."

"Of course," he said, noting the sweaty pirate. "If you're still up for a session, that is. I understand if you're all sparred out."

"Nah, I'm good," she replied. "Just having a little fun with my buddy Marban, here."

Marban quickly gathered up his things. "I have to get back anyway. My men will be expecting me."

"Okay. Thanks for playing, Marban," Rika said to him as he walked away. "Okay, Korbin, let's see what you've got."

The pirate felt the twinge in his chest tighten, joined by its new and rather unfamiliar friend.

Jealousy.

"Don't be foolish, Marban," he muttered to himself as he walked. "There is none of that life for men like you."

Head down, he trudged off with absolutely no intention of returning to his men. He needed to blow off steam, and he knew just the place to do it.

CHAPTER TWENTY-EIGHT

The basement level of the former industrial building—now converted to a bustling club environment—was warm with the heat of the masses crowded into the modest-sized space.

Music thumped from the hidden sound system, a mix of styles spanning not only generations, but also worlds, as the clientele were a diverse mix from several planets.

The lighting was relatively dim on the periphery, affording those seeking a bit of anonymity and solace a place to do so. To the middle, away from the edges, however, things were different.

Alcohol flowed freely in the club, but those in the center beneath the bright lights were not partaking. They had more important things to do, and inebriation would only slow their reflexes.

This was a place to settle grudges. To test one's mettle. This was the fight club of Los Angeles.

It had originally started just after the Great War. Or during it. No one could say for certain. But that didn't matter. What did was that the original organizers had created the group not for entertainment of others, but as a post-traumatic coping mechanism for the many disgruntled humans and Chithiid dealing with their lingering issues from the war.

That the Chithiid had been forced into their roles, working against the slim remains of humanity, was inconsequential. What mattered was the grudges and pent-up anger held by parties from both sides of the conflict, regardless if they were justified or not. Resentment would fester, and angry glances shot at one another could quickly escalate to shots of a different variety in the post-combat landscape if left unchecked.

So fight it was.

The earliest of the bouts were brutal, sloppy affairs. Cathartic releases of rage for those involved rather than a chance to test one's mettle. But as the participants' anger washed away with the healthy sweat of battle, so too did their lingering grudges.

It took time, of course. You don't just get over genocide in a day or two. But in relatively short order the club transitioned from a secret den of violence to an accepted means of addressing one's ails.

In the years since its inception, Cal had proven himself a wise overseer of the region, and rather than disbanding the group when life began to return to some semblance of normal, he stepped in and found a better, larger, safer venue for the contests to continue. Only, now there were cellular refabrication and healing facilities located right next door.

Cal was smart. Obviously, he was a genius AI, but more than data smarts, he had correctly assessed the mood of the people and saw the obvious. The club must go on. If that was to happen, he couldn't afford to lose workforce to silly injuries.

The result was a new system, whereby combatants could fight harder than before, causing actual damage without fear of permanent injury. Break a leg? Go next door and get it fixed quickly enough to come back in time to buy the next round. Lose an eye? Give them a day or two and they'd grow you a new one if you didn't want the cybernetic upgrades they always had on hand.

In the ring, a middle-aged woman with well-defined muscles circled her opponents, a much larger man with a cybernetic fist, and an equally large fellow whose left leg was far from original. Neither replacement parts were impressive compared to Tamara's arm, though.

It had been nearly two decades since the first fight club, and the dark-haired woman with the gleaming metal appendage now had thicker streaks of gray in her hair than when she'd first stepped into the ring, but that just made her look even more badass than when Daisy first met her. And despite the advancing years, Tamara Burke was still a regular fixture and knew all of the other regular fighters by name.

Daisy often accompanied her to the fights, though she herself tended to participate far less since she had her kid. It wasn't that she didn't still possess the drive to take on all challengers and come out on top, it was just a shift in priorities. More time at home with Vince and Arlo, less time beating on hapless would-be experts.

Of course, when one of the Chithiid felt like testing her mettle, Daisy had no choice but to accept the challenge. To refuse would be insulting, and, while they would soon be beating each other to a bloody mess inside the ring, she didn't want to offend them outside of it.

Tonight, however, Daisy was just nursing a drink while Tamara took on two opponents. "Watch that left!" she called out to her metal-armed friend as the quicker of the two men tried to slip past Tamara's defense and land a jab.

He actually did manage to make contact, but it wasn't her cybernetics that allowed her to absorb the shot without problem, it was her years of combat training combined with even more years of precisely this sort of match.

Tamara slipped the next few swings, surprisingly fast for her musculature and age, snapping out a quick roundhouse kick to the slower man's thigh, dropping him to one knee as the muscles spasmed.

He knew what was coming and tried to defend himself as best he could, but he'd be leaving the ring unconscious on a stretcher tonight.

Again.

Fifteen attempts, but he and his brother were still paying for Tamara's drinks. She almost felt bad about it. Almost.

"On your three!" Daisy shouted as her friend knocked the man out with a quick punch to the corner of his jaw.

Just as he went beddy-bye, Tamara threw her body backward and to the side, shortening the range of the thrown punch, sapping it of most of its power. She just absorbed the remainder as her elbow flew upward into the slumbering man's brother's nose.

The crack was audible even over the music.

"Okay, okay! I yield!" the bleeding man said, pinching his gushing nose.

"Good game," Tamara said, patting him on the shoulder, then called out to the bartender, "Drinks on him!"

"You broke it," he whined. "Again."

"Hey, did you see me use this baby at all?" she asked, waving her state-of-the-art cybernetic arm."

"Well, no."

"See? Fair and square. You know, you could just buy me drinks and save yourself the pain next time if you like," she joked.

"Damn, that's cold Tamara," Daisy laughed.

"What? After over a dozen tries? He deserves it."

"And you're still drinking for free."

"Ahem. *We're* drinking for free," Tamara corrected her, then poured liberally from the bottle in front of them. "Cheers!"

CHAPTER TWENTY-NINE

Across the bar, a rather drunk space pirate with a scar running from his head to his shoulder sat by himself, watching those around him but not engaging. He'd been mulling over things for several hours, replaying Rika's smile when Korbin showed up in his head over and over. This, inevitably, led to more drink, and, despite his pirate-level tolerance, he was beginning to feel the booze.

"Ah, fuck it," he grunted, lurching from his seat and pushing his way to the central ring.

"You've been drinking," the referee said, smelling the liquor on his breath.

"Just a shot," the pirate lied.

"I can't let you fight. You're in no condition,"

An angry rage rose from Marban's gut, mixing with the pain of frustration, the confused tears threatening to seep from his eyes. "I said I'm fine. You need to let me fight," he growled.

He'd spent many, many years drinking and fighting, and though he really wasn't fine, a few extra beverages wouldn't hurt him.

The ref assessed him with cool, calculating eyes. What

Marban didn't realize was he was being scanned by a cyborg, his body mass to blood alcohol levels being calculated as they spoke.

Finally, the ref shrugged and let him into the ring. "Fine. Whatever happens is on you," he said, waving for an opponent.

A thick-necked man with a metal hand going up to the elbow and a body built like a powerlifter rose from his seat and strode into the ring. He eyed Marban, sizing up his victim. Or so he thought. For while Marban may have been somewhat smaller and obviously intoxicated, he had also been a space pirate for a long, long time. And when he usually fought, his life was usually on the line.

The solid punch that connected with his jaw the second the match began pretty much immediately had the muscled man rethinking his tactics. Everyone has a plan until they get hit, and the drunk, it seemed, knew how to fight. And he hit *hard.*

Marban, however, was not a man for beating around the bush. He was more the just plain beating type, which he commenced dispensing to his larger opponent with relentless brutality. Punches rained down, hard elbows and knees following, finding gaps in the poor, outmatched man's defense, slipping in and flying true one after another.

The man's metal hand finally caught Marban with a solid punch, but rather than stagger him, it just flipped a switch inside. The tears of frustration welled and spilled onto the pirate's cheeks, making for a most unusual sight as he pummeled the larger man desperately trying to survive the onslaught.

First a rib cracked, but he could work around that. His core was strong enough to absorb it. But then his arm and leg followed in quick succession, the bones snapping from well-placed and powerful strikes. Marban had unintentionally crossed the line from sparring to really trying to hurt the man.

Leaning against the far wall, a square-jawed man with close-cropped hair watched with interest. Sergeant Franklin never participated in the bouts––being a reinforced spec ops cyborg, it wouldn't be fair––but he thoroughly enjoyed watching others let off steam. This, however, had him a little concerned. Enough so that he'd sent a message as soon as the pirate stepped into the ring.

Jo showed up, right on time, elbowing her way through the crowd to where her onboard AI locator indicated her friend was. George nodded to her in greeting.

"I think our boy Marban could use a little friendly intervention," he said, gesturing to the man pummeling his much larger foe in the ring. "Judging by my calculations, he should be done in there in about three. Two. One."

The metal-handed man collapsed to the ground on cue. Marban stood over him, staring a long moment. He then looked at his bloody hands with barely-hidden shock.

"What did I do?" he said with a gasp.

"He'll be fine," the ref said. "We'll get him next door and he'll be right as rain in an hour."

The man began convulsing on the mat. It seemed there might be some intercranial swelling to boot.

"Make that *two* hours," the ref said, waving over stretcher-bearers and quickly whisking the downed man away for medical attention.

Marban looked a little shell-shocked as he stood there under the bright light.

"Okay, let's get him out of there," George said, stepping into the ring. "Hey, buddy, fancy seeing you here. Jo's with me, you wanna come sit with us?"

Marban turned and looked at him, then at Jo standing nearby. The hurt in his eyes was plain to the cyborgs, but they said nothing, smiling as if everything was fine. A benefit of being a machine was the ability to maintain an expression no matter what you were actually thinking.

Marban's eyes welled up once more, though if anyone asked, he'd just swear it was sweat from the fight. George patted him on the shoulder and turned, walking out of the ring, confident his friend would follow.

The pirate had been sitting quietly, staring at his cup of strong coffee for nearly five minutes when Jo broke the silence.

"Okay, man. What's up? I mean, what's *really* up?"

"Nothing, Jo. I'm fine," he replied, not shifting his gaze from his cup.

"Bullshit. You may be a great pirate, but you're a crap liar," she shot back. "So, what? Homesick? Trouble with your men?"

"Trouble with the *ladies*?" George added.

Marban shifted in his seat uncomfortably.

"Aah. Rika," Jo said.

"No, it's not––"

"Shut up and listen, okay? Look, you chose a tough nut to crack with that one, believe me. I mean, I haven't known her all that long when you get right down to it. We've only been flying together a relatively short time, but it's enough to know she's one helluva complicated woman."

"And powerful," George added.

"Yes, she is," Marban agreed. "She and Korbin pair well in both skills and magic."

A light bulb went on in Jo's head. "Oh, so *that*'s it? *Korbin*?"

"He's handsome. Powerful. Wealthy."

"Yeah, but that shit doesn't mean much to her, trust me. And I really don't get the vibe that there's anything between them," Jo replied.

"No?"

"No. And our buddy George here said as much. And he'd know. Ain't that right, George?"

"Yep. True story, my brother."

"What do you mean?" Marban asked, his leaking eyes slowly drying.

"I'm a tactical spec ops cyborg, with a full range of infiltration and covert action gear."

"What does that mean?"

"It means I see much more than anyone else can. And her temperature and hormones don't shift at all when Korbin is around," George informed him.

Slowly, Marban began to understand what the cyborg was getting at.

"But... but they do with me?"

The cyborg remained silent a moment. "Good talk." George smirked and slapped his shoulder, then rose from his seat. "Come on, Jo," he said, leaving his friend without an explicit answer, but with something almost as good.

Hope.

CHAPTER THIRTY

Orbiting the small, uninhabited planet in a distant, unnoticed system, Charlie's rebel fleet was growing fast, expanding to far more than its original fourteen commandeered Tslavar ships. Word had gotten out through pirate backchannels. A fight was coming, and though the risks would be great, the rewards would be greater. Enough, even, to retire for life.

If they survived, of course.

A several-stop chain of outposts had been set up to guide the newcomers in, each of them providing the next jump location as the ships and their crews came to join the pirates in orbit. Some of them came seeking a fight. Others, wealth and glory. A great many, however, were seeking revenge.

It seemed that the mysterious visla had made quite a few enemies over the years as he amassed power, but all had been too afraid of him to speak up. To act. To do anything to right the wrongs committed against them. Until now.

The majority of the craft that filtered in, joining the newly minted rebel fleet, were of the smaller, poorly shielded variety. Minimally powered and in need of upgrades to be of any real use in battle. But once the Geist and his friends rejoined them, there would be ample magic to spread among the needy craft. And their numbers continued to grow.

The pirate-crewed Tslavar warships were another matter entirely. *They* were in prime condition, fully crewed up and ready to bring their considerable combat spells to bear on any who crossed them.

That the visla had seen fit to stockpile so much stored magic aboard each ship spoke not only to his foresight and paranoia, but also his wealth and sheer quantity of power. For no simple, common caster could funnel so much magic into devices without suffering a critical power loss. Visla Dominus, however, seemed to have no such problems.

Charlie was discussing just what that might mean for their forces with his new Wampeh friend when a small armada of rough-and-ready warships abruptly jumped into orbit.

And these were not expected.

"We're under attack! Ara, provide cover," Charlie blurted. He called up to the pirate ships on his skree. "Rovnik, get your men's ships into defensive posturing. Protect the weaker ships as they jump to the backup––"

"You can all stand down," a familiar voice interrupted over their skree. "No need to get your panties in a bunch over little old me,"

Charlie let out a sigh of relief. "Olo? What the hell are you doing? And who are all of these people?"

"Funny you should ask. I thought you'd like to meet some of my friends. They hate Visla Dominus, and they love to pillage. It seemed like a match made in heaven, if you ask me. Hang on. Is that a Zomoki?"

"Don't worry. She's with us."

"First an Ootaki, then a Wampeh Ghalian. And now a Zomoki? Oh, I've got to see this up close," Olo blurted.

A sleek, fast ship separated from the main body of the newly arrived ships and raced around the nearby vessels as if they were merely an obstacle course. A deadly, inhabited obstacle course, that is. It whipped a sharp turn, then sped toward Charlie and Ara.

"Shall I destroy him?" Pimbrak asked.

"No, hang on," Charlie replied, watching the craft race closer.

Sure enough, the ship turned and stopped on a dime right in front of them.

"Oh, and I also brought you a pilot, by the way," Olo said. "An utterly insane, but exceptionally skilled pilot. He's nuts, but he'll get your cargo through. Tymprazagal, say hello to Charlie and his friends."

"Hey, hey," a voice said casually over their skree link.

"Nice to meet you, Tymprazagal," Pimbrak replied.

"Uh, yeah. I'm not even going to try to pronounce that," Charlie said.

A pause hung in the air.

"There are some who call me... Tym," the man finally replied.

"Better. Greetings, Tym. So Olo told you all about the gig and you still want in?"

"Oh, yes indeed! A challenge! Good old Tym loves a challenge!"

"Does good old Tym always speak about himself in the third person?"

"What's that?"

"Nevermind," Charlie chuckled. "If Olo vouches for you, then I guess you're our man."

"Fly past some stupid Tslavars into a portal to another galaxy? No problem! I'm the best pilot in the galaxy!"

"*Second* best," Olo corrected. "Now, what say we all land on one of those big, beautiful, and if I'm not mistaken, *stolen* Tslavar warships over there. I'm parched and could really use a drink right about now."

"And the rest of your payment," Pimbrak noted.

"Well, I wasn't going to say anything, but now that you mention it."

"You've more than earned it," Charlie said. "Ara will take us in. Just follow close."

Olo and Tym greeted Charlie and Pimbrak warmly when they'd landed aboard the commandeered ship. But it was Ara who truly had the smuggler's attention.

"Never seen one so big up close. And she's tame, you say?"

"I don't know that I'd say *tame*," Ara replied with a toothy grin.

"She speaks!" Olo exclaimed.

"He's a quick one," Charlie noted.

"My gods, only the Old Ones had that ability. Or so I thought."

Charlie laughed. "Let's just say she's not as young as she appears and leave it at that."

"What are you saying, Charlie?" the dragon asked with mock offense.

"That you look *marvelous*, Ara. Absolutely marvelous."

"More incoming," the ship's captain noted.

A trio of small craft soon joined them aboard the large vessel, the captains of several of the other ships new to the fleet come to meet their commander.

"Charlie? Like the rebel?" one asked when introduced.

"Yeah, like the rebel," the rebel replied. Sometimes it was just easier to roll with it than try to explain he actually *was* Charlie the rebel. "Thanks for joining us in this fight. We've got a tough road ahead of us, and we'll need all the men we can get."

"Intruder!" Tym shouted as a small shimmer craft revealed itself in the hangar.

"Stand down," Pimbrak shouted to the men as they reached for their weapons. "This is one of ours."

"How long has that thing been sitting there watching us?" a startled captain wondered.

"They're Wampeh Ghalian. Who knows?" Olo replied.

Pimbrak walked to the craft and greeted the Wampeh woman piloting it.

"Gentlemen, this is one of my associates. She has news of our agent's efforts on Slafara," he said when they joined the others.

"Our man inside the ranks of Visla Palmarian is still on-site, but he has been unable to penetrate beyond the most superficial levels of the building's security," the woman said. "He has, however, witnessed several unusual craft come and go, always utilizing the network of floating gardens high atop the estate rather than the more easily observable ground-level landing areas."

"Are they Visla Dominus's ships?" Captain Rovnik asked.

"He cannot be certain, but the descriptions he gave lead me to believe it to be a possibility."

Charlie took a step forward. "And what about Leila? She's a half Alatsav woman who was last seen aboard one of Palmarian's ships."

"He did not get anywhere near the secure levels of the estate, but he did hear of a new prisoner. An olive-skinned woman who is a friend of the visla's daughter. She and her large canine were originally taken to find her friends, but now she is held prisoner atop the tower."

"That's Leila!" Charlie blurted. "She's being held prisoner? Shit!" He started pacing, agitated. "Okay, I'm going to need you to get me a full floor plan of the building and the locations of any guards. I'll also need to know how many power users there are besides the visla. Pimbrak, I'll need to borrow a warship and––"

"No, Charlie," Pimbrak said, stopping his pacing with a calming hand on his new friend's shoulder. "You cannot charge headlong into the estate of the most powerful visla in centuries like that."

"I can take him, Pimbrak. If I hit him hard and by surprise––"

"All you will accomplish is your own demise, and Leila will remain imprisoned. Remember, there is a very good possibility that Visla Palmarian and Visla Dominus are in league with one another."

"Or are one and the same," Olo noted.

"What's that?" Captain Rovnik asked.

"Just some scuttlebutt I heard. Might be nothing to it, but it might be true. In any case, the man's incredibly powerful, and not someone you want to take on unprepared."

Charlie's emotions were high. Leila was a prisoner, and he finally knew where she was. But they were right. He couldn't just rush in.

"Okay, you're right. But I can't just do nothing. I have to get to her. I need intel. I need a plan."

Pimbrak smiled and turned to the Wampeh spy with an excited gleam in his eye. "You say our man has been unable to gain full access to the estate?"

"Correct," the woman replied.

"Well, well," he said, a smile growing on his lips. "Finally, a challenge worthy of my talents." He turned to Charlie, excitement clear in his eyes, though his expression remained as calm as always. "I shall infiltrate this Palmarian's estate personally and ascertain the true status of the situation, as well as the identity of the prisoner being held there. If she is indeed your Leila, I will bring her back to you straightaway."

"But Palmarian? You said we can't just rush in there," Charlie reminded him.

"*You* cannot. *I* am Wampeh Ghalian, and my shimmer skills

are unmatched, as are many other talents suitable for this task. This is not my first outing of this nature, Charlie. Trust me, I will have her back to you by week's end, at the latest."

Despite not really knowing the Wampeh assassin for long at all, Charlie did know Bawb well, and if this man was anything like his dear friend, he was not exaggerating about his skills.

"All right," Charlie replied. "Tell me what we can do to help you prepare."

CHAPTER THIRTY-ONE

Tym proved to be as much of a chatterbox as Kip was, once he got started. Charlie was both amused and mildly horrified at the realization.

"At least he's not obsessed with toast," he mused as the pilot gave his ship a thorough walkaround and structural check while the remaining Balamar waters were loaded into its cargo hold.

It was heartening that, despite his extremely unusual demeanor, Tym was nevertheless all business when it came to the safety and flyability of his craft. With the priceless cargo aboard, he needed to be.

Charlie held back one medium-sized container of the waters for his and Ara's own use, should the need arise. Having access to the waters on the wastelands where they were hidden was one thing, but in the heat of battle, or directly after, a trip that far might simply not be an option. And given what the waters could do for injuries, as well as what it was supposed to be able to do to Visla Dominus, Ara agreed with the idea.

"So, they have women in your galaxy?" Tym asked as he yanked on one of the containers, ensuring the magic holding it in place was secure.

"What do you mean?" Charlie replied.

"You know. Women. Females. Soft, and warm, and––"

"Yes, I know what a woman is, Tym. But I don't get your question. Are you asking for a prostitute when you land?"

"No, man. Good old Tym doesn't need to pay for it. I just want to make sure this new world isn't gonna suck."

Charlie couldn't help but laugh. "Uh, you do realize that without women there wouldn't be *anyone* alive, right? I mean, unless men give birth in this galaxy, which is probably the one freaky thing I haven't seen yet. So women are kind of a given."

"Huh. I hadn't thought of that," Tym replied.

Charlie was amazed. It was like having a conversation with a stoned toddler, but one who could fly better than almost anyone in the galaxy. And one whom you were relying on for a particularly important mission.

Disconcerted didn't begin to touch on the emotions Charlie had bounding around inside. The ticking chrono didn't much help, either.

They had seven hours until the portal was scheduled to open, confirmed by a quick jump to connect with the hidden satellite, just in case there'd been a change of plans.

There hadn't been any such change, though, aside from Zed deciding he would send a few additional defensive ships through the portal when it next opened to provide cover for their craft as it crossed over. All there was to do now was wait.

The plan was for Ara and a small contingent of their most powerful craft to jump to the periphery of the system just before the portal opened. The big guns would then hang back with Tym and his ship, providing ample protection just in case Murphy decided to throw a monkey wrench in their scheme. If all went according to plan, however, Tym would jump to the very edge of the plume of solar plasma shooting from the portal just as it began to recede.

Rika had apparently sped up the portal's cycle a bit, making the speed and timing of Tym's hasty flight even more crucial. Arrive too soon and burst into flames. Arrive too late, and the portal would already have cycled back into the sun. Again, leading to the whole burst-into-flames thing that no one wanted to do.

"You all ready?" Charlie asked when the chrono finally clicked down to twenty minutes.

The small force signaled their readiness, and they all began the jumps leading them to the portal system.

It could have been accomplished in just a couple of jumps, but the rebel fleet's leaders had all agreed it was far more prudent to use multiple jumps, thus ensuring any bad actors attempting to backtrack their route would not find the hidden fleet of pirate vessels.

A dozen jumps later and the ships had all arrived in position, Ara and Charlie scanning for any unexpected signs of magic in what should be a safe region of space.

"We're all clear here," Charlie informed the others over skree. "But there are even more ships out there now," he noted.

"Their ranks have indeed grown," Ara observed.

"They sure have. Look at all those ships. How the hell did the visla fly under the radar so long while amassing that much power and that many ships? It seems impossible for something like that to go unnoticed."

"It's a big galaxy, Charlie. Millions of systems all throughout it, but less than a thousand of them inhabited. There are a great many places to hide, if you find the right conditions."

"Like we did."

"Yes, precisely. I believe we are not alone in our utilization of an uninhabited system to keep ourselves unobserved."

"Likely," Charlie agreed. "Tym, you ready to go?" he called over skree.

"Oh, yeah. This is gonna be fun! Like that time in Gaastram. Remember, Olo?" he asked his friend.

From his equally fast ship, Olo was watching the events unfold. "Yeah, I remember, Tym," the smuggler replied. "But as I recall, that fast run was due to your ill-advised liaison with the local emmik's daughter."

"How was I supposed to know who she was?"

"Because of her name and residence, for one," Olo replied.

"Guys, we need to focus here," Charlie interrupted. "The chrono has us at twenty seconds out. When I signal, you jump in as close as you can and take off. Push hard and fly straight. A few ships will pop through to cover you, but until you reach them you'll be on your own."

"It'll be legendary," Tym said, his grin almost audible over the skree. "If I don't jump into the sun, that is."

"Technology is very precise, Tym. Especially with AIs running it."

"What's an AI?"

"You'll find out soon enough. Ten seconds," Charlie informed him. "Five seconds."

The chrono hit zero, and Charlie gave the signal. Tym jumped immediately, arriving just outside the burn zone of the portal as the flaming plasma began to quickly recede.

"This guy's good," Charlie admired.

"Let us hope he is as good at the actual flight as he is at jumping. He has but one shot at clearing the portal. If he fails, all of that water falls into the hands of Dominus's men," Ara replied.

"I don't think any of Zed's ships will let that happen. If it looked like a possibility, I wouldn't be surprised if they shot him down themselves."

"A harsh action, but justified," she replied.

"I'm hoping that doesn't become a necessity," Charlie said as he watched Tym kick his little ship into high gear and hightail it for the portal, staying just behind the receding flames.

As soon as the last of the streaming plasma was gone, five Earth and Urok ships popped through the portal, their weapons hot and firing in a tight circle around Tym's ship, providing it cover as it raced ahead.

Charlie realized the forces on the other side must have been toying with weaponizing the waters already, as a few rounds appeared to let off a fine mist when they impacted the Tslavar craft's shields. But even with his surveillance link to the satellite, it was still far enough out that he couldn't be entirely sure.

What he was sure of was Zed had coordinated with their new allies, and the resulting barrage from the small squadron of ships was doing its job admirably. That is until a shimmer ship that had flanked them caught a stray round deflected from one of its brethren's shielding, suddenly becoming visible.

"It's an ambush!" Charlie shouted over comms. "Everyone, get out of there!"

The ships, however, merely adjusted their firing patterns, spreading wide, hoping to land another lucky shot on any other shimmer-cloaked craft that might be lurking nearby.

Tym powered ahead, dodging spells somehow, even though he shouldn't have been able to see them at that speed. Olo had equipped the ship with a little something extra, it appeared, and it was making all the difference in the world now.

Spells buffeted the defensive ships, but they weren't destructive ones. In fact, the ships didn't seem moved at all. Charlie and Ara both sensed the magic.

"You need to get back across. They're casting stun spells," Charlie transmitted just as Tym's ship blasted across the portal threshold at blistering speed. "He's through. Everyone, get out of here. He's across. Get back!"

The ships didn't need to be told twice, their captains quickly spinning and flying hard for the rapidly closing portal. Flames were coloring the sky orange, and in just a few moments it would be sealed by burning plasma once again.

Four of the five ships made it through, but an Urok ship took the full brunt of the hidden craft's stun spells, all of them directed at the lone remaining vessel. The ship abruptly began flying with no direction, looping slowly in space, its crew frozen inside.

A shimmer ship decloaked and used the freed-up power to tether the craft, pulling it from the rapidly approaching flames as fast as it was able. It didn't seem able to jump while towing, though, and with the portal closing quickly, it was going to be close.

"Can we get to them, Ara?"

"There is nothing we can do, Charlie," she replied. *"I am sorry, but to assist at this point is suicide. There are simply too many."*

Charlie knew she was right. The fleet's deadly craft had already closed the gap, taking the smaller shimmer ship and its captured prize aboard before jumping away to lord knew where.

The Urok ship was gone.

Charlie was well aware that war was hell and losses were incurred, but that didn't make it hurt any less. They'd gotten the waters across, which was a huge win for their side, but they lost a ship in the process.

"Everyone, let's get out of here," Charlie sent over skree.

Moments later, the rebel ships jumped free.

The captured tech ship would be delivered to Visla Dominus personally. It was a most unusual prize, and the visla would study it. Learn from it. Understand how this tech-magic really worked. All the better to destroy the enemy.

CHAPTER THIRTY-TWO

Visla Dominus had a team of lesser casters studying the captured craft from the moment it was brought aboard the command ship. The skilled power users had helped in the visla's expansion, gathering power and resources for their leader while increasing their own power and status in the process.

War would be coming, and when it did, they intended to be on the winning side. Given their visla's incredible abilities, they were confident they'd made the right choice in their alliance. The arrival of the strange craft, however, had thrown them for a loop.

This was not some normal type of magic they could overpower with their laundry list of spells. In fact, it seemed as if this craft possessed no magic whatsoever, though there was an unusual energy of sorts located deep within it.

The Urok warp system, however, was utterly foreign to them, and the power did not meld with their own one bit. Maybe it was useful in the other galaxy, but in this one, they believed it was of limited potential.

Then there was the design of the vessel itself. Strange, angular metal, formed and joined with other segments with undetectable power, encapsulating the frozen crew in a rigid bubble of trapped air. There was no magic keeping those aboard from the cold vacuum of space. Just a triple layer of hull, and thick double doors.

Those airlock doors took some work to open, the mechanism not responding to entry spells of even the most powerful nature. Eventually, however, they managed to gain access without damaging the craft too much. What they found inside was as baffling as the exterior.

"It's so inelegant," Hoomra said, ducking her head as she peered behind one of the display consoles as her team of workers carried out the stasis-frozen crew one by one.

"How do they make it fly?" her male counterpart, Galvash, wondered.

The pair were relatively low-powered vislas, at least compared to Dominus. This task had been given to them at their request. The visla wanted to know all there was to learn about the enemy across the portal, and if they could provide such details, the rewards could be great.

The cost of failure, likewise, could be quite dear.

"*This* sort of vessel has stymied our fleet? Even taken down some of our own craft," Galvash huffed. "It seems impossible. There is no power here. No explanation for how it managed such a feat."

"The design, it is illogical," Hoomra added as she ran her hand over a guidance console.

Her touch caused several warning lights to flash to life on the screen. The ship was immobilized, and applying thrust, as she'd accidentally just activated, would not be allowed without proper access codes.

"What did you do?" Galvash asked. "I didn't hear you cast."

"I did nothing, Galvash. I merely touched this panel."

"It activated by touch alone? There was no spell required?"

"Apparently not."

Galvash gazed around the command center with a different perspective. "Do you think the entire vessel functions in this manner? By touch, rather than magic?"

"It is possible, I suppose. But what would be the purpose of such a system? The delays caused by manual activation seem unwise, especially for a battle craft."

"Nothing aboard this vessel appears to be guided by wisdom," Galvash noted. "But that is irrelevant to our task. We must help understand this galaxy's defenses' strengths and weaknesses, and this is our most substantial asset to date."

"We could wake the crew. Have them explain it to us," Hoomra suggested.

"Not yet. They will undoubtedly lie to us, as any good soldier should. While our interrogation techniques will no doubt overcome that, eventually, I would like to learn what we can without that distraction. At least for the moment."

"Very well," Hoomra replied. "I shall begin a search of the other levels. There were no Drooks aboard, but there must be some means of propelling this craft. I'll leave this chamber to you. It appears to be a command center, of sorts. Perhaps you will find something of use."

The pair set to work prying what secrets there were to be had from the ship. They'd get to the crew eventually, but only once their understanding of the vessel itself was enough to better help them catch lies.

In another part of the command ship, high above in a heavily shielded magical workspace, another visla sat reviewing the results of the portal tests from the small contingent she'd dedicated to the task. Visla Cresh was a powerful caster in her own right, far more gifted than either Hoomra or Galvash.

It was for this reason that Visla Dominus had tasked her with studying a surprising phenomenon they'd only just noticed. With Ootaki being extremely rare, it had taken some time to source one with any decent length of hair on their head. But one older specimen had been found, and he had been brought to the visla with great haste.

He'd arrived in the vicinity of the portal only a few hours before their wily foe made their successful attempt to cross over, and in just that short time, something strange had happened.

The Ootaki's hair appeared to gain in strength the longer he was in the vicinity of the sun's rays, pouring through the portal. To say that Visla Dominus was interested would be an understatement. The casters had been trying, and failing, to properly open a portal, but their power simply wasn't enough, even when bolstered by stored magic.

But with this new discovery, the visla's hope was renewed. A new portal could be created, but it would require a lot of Ootaki hair. All that they could find, in fact, but they'd already harvested pretty much all of it that was to be found for the prior attempt to cross over. The attempt that had filled the *Asbrú* with magical hair and sent it to the other side.

It had been a huge use of magic, and had appeared to have failed. But now there was something new in play. As well as an explanation for how the troublesome enemy had managed to keep the portal open for so long, and even submerged in the sun.

It was the Ootaki hair. The sun made it stronger.

That secret was a secret no more.

Visla Cresh was giddy with excitement. The ramifications of this discovery were enormous. If they could position their Ootaki as close to the blazing portal as possible, she posited they would be able to supercharge their golden locks. It would be difficult to acquire the remaining unshorn Ootaki and caches of their hair, though. The few remaining were held by strong emmiks and vislas, none of whom had allied with Visla Dominus.

If only Ootaki hair grew faster they could simply recall all of the shorn slaves from the facilities that held them and await the new emergence of their golden booty. But Ootaki hair was slow growing, and with the failure of the Trojan Horse portal, Visla Dominus's patience had worn thin.

Visla Cresh dispatched all of the minions at her disposal to scatter across the known systems and seek out and gather all the Ootaki hair they could find, no matter how small an amount it might be. And if it happened to be held by a non-compliant power user? Dominus had made it clear that whatever means were necessary would be deployed.

Cresh had the older Ootaki man brought to her in the lab space. The power radiating from his hair was almost intoxicating in its novel strength. Whatever the sun's rays were doing to it, the result was incredible. But she had an idea. A wild stab in the dark. But if it worked, its power would increase even more.

Another younger Ootaki, already shorn for the *Asbrú* attempt, was brought into the chamber as well. Visla Cresh stood them next to one another. One fully ripe and ready for harvest, the other no more than a hint of his former power.

She turned to the new acquisition and fixed him with a steely gaze. "You are new here, so I am going to make this very, very easy for you," she said. "Give me your hair willingly or your brothers and sisters will suffer greatly. Starting with this one."

She cast a small pain spell, the collar around the younger Ootaki's neck dropping him to his knees in agony.

"I shall give you ten seconds to make your choice," Cresh said, then began counting down.

The older Ootaki had been around a long while, and he'd had his hair cut off several times in his life thus far. With each cut, its power was diminished. He figured giving it freely at his age couldn't possibly hurt much, especially if it saved one of his kind from suffering.

"Freely given," he said.

Cresh smiled and pulled an enchanted blade from a case on the nearby table. It would cut the hair, but it *should* magically cap the ends, preventing power from being lost in the process. It was an imperfect system, but one that worked well enough for their purposes.

Visla Cresh brought the harvested hair to her visla immediately. Dominus was one step ahead of her, though, already devising a means to draw power from the small patch of the Earth's sun to help create a new portal. Two, to be exact.

"Two portals?" Cresh asked.

"Yes, two," Visla Dominus replied. "One in this system, small in size but close to the existing portal. It will lead to the system our research ships are in, providing a constant flow of this energy."

"Ingenious," Cresh said. "In this way you can do your work there without risk of interruption from the enemy at this location."

"Yes," Dominus replied. "And from *that* location we will mount our next attack. So long as this portal remains in the sun, these troublesome natives will be feeding our progress. Should they wish to stop it, they will be forced to pull the portal free from the sun, thus allowing my fleet unfettered access to their realm."

"No matter which course of action they take, they help your cause. Most wise, Visla. Victory will surely be ours now."

Visla Dominus's smile faltered. "Do not count your victory before it is achieved, Cresh. There are always forces at play beyond our control. Forces that could turn the tables in an instant. We must be methodical. We must be thorough. And most of all, we must find more Ootaki."

CHAPTER THIRTY-THREE

Sitting quietly in his thick-barred cell, Grundsch stared out the window at the blue skies of the world his people had once conquered. An entire planet, brought under their rule in a matter of weeks before they moved on to the next conquest. And now? Now it was back in the hands of its original inhabitants, and his kind had been scattered to the wind, their hive destroyed, their queen dead.

There would be no more Ra'az Hok. He was the last.

"I wanted to speak with you, Grundsch," Cal said, his voice appearing out of thin air.

"I am not going anywhere," the alien replied. "Speak as you wish."

"Your situation has been discussed with the other AI minds overseeing this planet, and we all agree that the life on Earth is rebounding well. The war is long over, and people have healed."

"So I've been informed," Grundsch replied. "And mine are all dead."

"Yes. But I've been thinking long and hard about your particular case, and I would like to make you an offer. I wish to free you on probation."

The enormous Ra'az sat up straight, perplexed. "You wish to free me? Why?"

"Because we are all tired of death and killing. Because the war was so long ago. And because your advocates made quite a strong argument on your behalf."

"Advocates? What are you speaking of? I have no advocates."

"There, you are mistaken. Korbin spoke on your behalf, telling of your actions when his niece was in jeopardy. You had your freedom, Grundsch, your collar had been neutralized. Yet you not only stayed to fight, you were willing to sacrifice yourself for the life of the girl."

"It was not intentional. It was a purely instinctive act," he replied.

"But that instinct was the right one, and it is the reason I am offering you this opportunity. You should know, both Kara and Visanya also spoke on your behalf, each of them telling of not only your actions on that day, but also in regular life. You looked after Kara with great care, Grundsch, and that was something a control collar could not force upon anyone."

"So, I am to be freed? To be turned loose on this world?"

"Within reason," Cal replied. *"You will be given a tracking chip so you can be monitored as a condition of this release. Though your people did a great harm to this world and many others, your friends believe that people can change. That you have changed. Prove them right."*

Over the next few hours, Grundsch was visited by med techs, who implanted the small chip in his calf, as well as representatives of the human, cyborg, and Chithiid inhabitants of the city.

He would be a free man, but he should know that there were still a great many with grudges against his kind. The populace had been informed of his release, and warned not to harass or attack him, and they would follow those edicts. But if he should step out of line, their restraint would evaporate.

Grundsch nodded his understanding.

"People wish harm upon me," he said, quietly, as he stepped onto the street to be met with angry looks of those who had come to see his release. "And given what my brothers and I did to them, perhaps I should let them."

It was late at night, yet the downtown fight club was packed, the air hot and damp, the crowd roaring with delight. This was something different. This was more than the usual bouts and tests of strength and skill.

This was a Ra'az.

Grundsch sat on a sturdy stool in one corner of the ring, bloody and beaten. He drank deep from a large bottle of water, then climbed to his feet once more. It was time to face his next challenger.

He'd been at it for hours. Taking on all comers, two, even three at a time, being beaten down, his sturdy body withstanding the barrage as his opponents did their best to end him with their fists and feet. Even a few cyborgs joined in, bending the rules and traditions of the club on this rare occasion.

All had suffered at the hands of the Ra'az, and it was time for payback.

Grundsch didn't care. He fought them all regardless, and when he was too injured to continue, his handlers would ferry him next door to be healed up. But rather than call it quits, as soon as he was cleared to leave the medical facility, the enormous alien would step back into the ring for more punishment. He wasn't leaving until everyone who wanted a piece of him had their chance.

George was there, sitting quietly at the bar, watching the Ra'az fight. He'd thought about stepping in for just a minute or two, but even if he dialed it down, being a spec ops model gave him too much of an advantage. It just wouldn't be sporting, even in a situation like this.

Korbin arrived a while later, squeezing through the crowd to see the fighting firsthand. It was true, what he'd been told. Grundsch was indeed facing off against anyone and everyone. And what he also saw was that the Ra'az was losing, and not even intentionally.

The participants in this venue fought for fun. For a hobby. To them, the motions were as natural as breathing. But for Grundsch, the killer instinct had been held back by his control collar for so many years that he was having a hard time channeling it again.

He was outclassed, plain and simple, but it didn't have to be that way.

The latest bout finished with Grundsch laid out on the mat once again, a muscular Chithiid waving his arms and bellowing to the crowd in victory. The Ra'az just pushed himself up and crawled to his corner once again.

"Excuse me," Korbin said, pushing his way to the ring.

His broadcast had been seen by pretty much everyone in the establishment, so they all knew not only who he was, but what he was capable of. With great respect, the bodies parted, allowing him unfettered passage.

"Hey, Grundsch," he said when he reached the sweaty, bleeding Ra'az.

"Visla," Grundsch replied.

"You can call me Korbin, you know."

"I do, Visla," he replied. "I wish to thank you once more for saving my life. It was not required."

"To me it was. And now you seem bent on losing it. If you really want to thank me, how about you stop losing so badly out there? I know you're better than this."

"It has been a long time since I've been allowed the freedom to fight. I fear I have lost the ability."

"Nonsense. You're just using your hands when you should be using your knees and feet," Korbin said. "You have long reach, and if you throw small kicks to keep your opponents at a distance, you'll have much greater success at landing your blows."

Grundsch looked at him curiously. "Thank you, Visla. I shall take your words to heart."

He then rose and strode to the center of the ring again, ready to meet his next challenger.

"Why are you helping him?" an older Chithiid asked.

"He is a friend, and I fear he is putting himself through too much, even if it is what he feels you all require of him."

"He's a Ra'az."

"I know what race he is, but he's not what you remember of his kind."

"Mindless thugs. Murderers. Savages," the Chithiid spat.

"A long time ago, perhaps. But this man? He saved my niece's life. He put himself between her and a violent attack, knowing full well he was going to die for it, yet doing so without hesitation regardless. Whatever his former sins, he is a changed man, and he forever has my gratitude."

The Chithiid looked at Korbin curiously, then called over several of his friends. They all knew him from the global demonstration he'd put on. Korbin was something of a celebrity in that regard, much as Daisy had been right after the war. And that lent weight to his words.

"Tell them the story you told me," the Chithiid requested. "They are not going to believe this."

Grundsch continued to fight for the better part of the next hour, but as he did, the energy in the crowd shifted as Korbin's tale spread.

A wiry but fast Chithiid was in the ring, peppering Grundsch with a flurry of punches and kicks, following up with

181

brutal elbows and knees. He was lean, but he was a speedy dervish of hands and feet.

The Ra'az had been defending himself far better the last several bouts, taking Korbin's advice to heart, but this opponent was simply too much for him. With a powerful elbow to the head, Grundsch found himself on the mat, facedown, once again. Only this time, something was different.

He rolled over slowly, then sat up, but rather than taunting him, the Chithiid reached out a hand. The crowd fell silent. Grundsch hesitated, then grasped it, the much lighter Chithiid pulling hard to help him up. The two stood there a moment, then the Chithiid nodded once and stepped out of the ring.

Korbin smiled. There was still a long way to go, but it was a start.

"Drinks are on me!" he shouted to the enthused crowd, then settled in for a long and enjoyable night at the fight club.

CHAPTER THIRTY-FOUR

After being in the middle of a multi-system conflict that spilled over into an intergalactic mess of tech and magic, Ripley, Kara, and Vee were all a bit out of sorts being kept in the dark as to a lot of what was going on with the hostilities on the other side of the portal.

They knew through the grapevine that a new ship had crossed over, and there was talk that the Uroks might have lost one of theirs, but no adults would verify the rumors. It was beginning to grate on them, especially Ripley, as she'd played so crucial a role in the recent fight against the Tslavars on this side of the portal.

But that was when Charlie and Leila and the others were around. With them stuck in another galaxy, Ripley didn't have them to advocate for her inclusion in all things military. Fortunately, Eddie was more than willing to tap into comms streams to cherry pick whatever information he could get his electronic hands on.

"You guys know I can just ask Marty what's up, right?" Arlo said when he joined the girls later that afternoon for a late post-lunch snack, courtesy of Rip's father and his almost compulsive need to feed those he cared about.

"You think Marty can find out more than Eddie?" Ripley asked.

"His mom and dad are the most powerful AIs in the fleet, I'm sure he can dig something up from them."

"But won't Aunt Daisy be mad if we go around her?"

"You know Freya. She'll do what she wants anyway, and if Marty and his folks are having a talk, who's to say that's breaking any rules, right?"

"I suppose," Ripley replied.

"All *I* want is to know about my father. If he's okay. He wasn't well when I left, and I'm afraid he'll be worried sick about me," Kara said, looking at Arlo pleadingly with *those* eyes. "My stepmom was trying to get him a powerful healer when everything went crazy and we had to flee. I don't even know if he's all right."

Arlo felt his body temperature rise slightly from the intensity of the violet-skinned girl's gaze.

"And my parents too," Vee added. "We left in the middle of an attack on Kara's place, and we just vanished. For all my parents know, I could be dead."

Arlo thought about how his parents reacted if he didn't check in on time from his and Marty's solar surveys. They were not amused, to say the least. And going missing after an attack on their home? He could just imagine how the girls' parents felt.

"I just want to be able to let him know I'm okay," Kara said. "If nothing else, just to know he isn't worried about me."

"Ditto," Visanya agreed.

"Well, they won't let us send any unofficial messages through," Ripley said. "So I'm afraid we're shit out of luck."

Arlo chewed in silence a moment, an idea forming in his mind. And it was kind of nuts.

· · ·

"Hey, Marty?" Arlo asked when he wandered back home.

"Yeah? What's up?" his mischievous AI ship asked, sitting on the empty lot adjacent his Malibu home.

"I was wondering. You think you might be up for a little adventure?"

"Like flying off to Taangaar in the middle of the night again? That was a lot of fun. Always game for that."

"Yeah, it was. But no, I was thinking of something a bit more, uh, *interesting*."

"Interesting? So, by that I assume you mean something that will freak out both of our parents."

"You know me so well," Arlo chuckled.

"Comes with the territory, amigo," Marty replied. "What did you have in mind? You know I'm always game for an adventure."

Arlo grinned. Of course Marty would be on board. They'd been an inseparable pair ever since they were kids, and adventure was one of their shared loves. That and space flight.

Arlo was just a boy when he and Marty had first taken off on their own––against the express wishes, and to the consternation of, their parents. But the hook had been set, and from then on, both were always looking for new adventures to go off on together.

But this? This idea put all of the others to shame.

Combined.

"So, do you think you can maybe make your warp drive work on the other side of that portal?" Arlo asked. "I know there are some weird problems over there, but we were on that side with your dad for a minute, so you must've gotten some readings."

"I did, but that doesn't mean I can use my warp there. My folks are already trying to find a workaround to that whole warp misfire thing, you know."

"But what if some of the other AIs were to help? They've all been working on the problem, right? That's like a billion times the processing power of just one ship, so they've gotta have figured out how to work around it by now, right?"

"I'd hope so, but I can't say for sure," Marty replied. "But I can get whatever info the others have. That, at least, shouldn't be a problem."

"Sweet! So if we can get that info, all we would need to do is make whatever tweaks are necessary, then jump to the other side."

"But the portal is closed. In the *sun*, no less," Marty reminded his human pal.

"Obviously. But we can find out when it's scheduled to open next, can't we?"

"I suppose I can probably get the timing from one of the guys up in orbit."

"And if we do it right, all we need to do is warp to the portal the second it pulls free from the sun and cross over before any of Uncle Zed's ships go through. Then we just warp immediately from the other side to Kara and Vee's homeworld. We'll deliver their messages, take one back for them from their folks, and be the heroes of the day. And best part, no one will be the wiser!"

"But we'll need to get back, Arlo. And the portal will be closed by then."

"It should be an easy warp back when we're done. We just need to wait for it to open again and zip, bang, boom, we do the same thing on the return let and we're back through and warping away before anyone knows we crossed over."

It was an audacious plan, but teenage hormones were in play, and Arlo ever so desperately wanted to impress his violet-skinned friend.

"You sure about this?" Marty asked.

"Trust me, Marty. It'll be fine."

CHAPTER THIRTY-FIVE

The interesting thing about the Wampeh Ghalian––one of them, at least––was their quaint and old-fashioned tradition of using couriers to ferry messages rather than sending them over a skree. It was antiquated. Slower. And quite odd.

It also ensured prying ears could not eavesdrop on a conversation sent across space. It was supposed to be impossible, the skree could only connect to its intended recipient by design. But, like so many foolproof devices, there was a back door. One that allowed someone with enough power and just the right information about the sender or recipient of a skree to listen in to that conversation.

And the Wampeh Ghalian should know. It was an intelligence-gathering trick they themselves used often. Fortunately, very, very few in the galaxy possessed this knowledge, and all who did protected it fiercely. If word got out that skrees could be listened in on, everyone would switch to other means of communication, and that resource would be lost.

Charlie had been told all of this one day while he and Pimbrak were surveilling what appeared to be one of Visla Dominus's ships. They didn't seem to have much chatter, though, leading Bawb to the conclusion that perhaps the visla was also aware of this security flaw.

In any case, when a young Wampeh apprentice arrived at the pirate fleet with a message for Charlie and Ara personally, it didn't come as much of a surprise.

"It's from Bob," Charlie said as he led the courier to his Zomoki friend. They'd both hear the details from the horse's mouth, so to speak. "Go on, we're both here."

"The Geist requests your assistance in a matter of great importance," the Wampeh began.

"These days, what isn't important?" Charlie mused. "So, what does he need? We'll be there, obviously."

"He and his companions are attempting to complete a task and require a distraction in a nearby system to draw away at least some of the fleet residing near his target. The quantity of vessels and the power of the magic within is making a successful landing under cover of shimmer near impossible."

"But with the ranks thinned out a bit..." Charlie mused.

"Precisely. There are a number of ships in another system that happens to fall within long-distance skree range. An attack upon them would most certainly bring assistance from this larger and more powerful force."

"Freeing up space so Bob and his buddies can land. Got it." Charlie turned to his Zomoki friend. "Whaddya think, Ara? Shall we go stir up some trouble for Bob?"

"Indeed, we shall," she replied.

The young Wampeh had heard of Ara, of course, but witnessing one of the Old Ones speak in person was nevertheless an almost overwhelming moment for him.

"The Geist and the order thank you," he said. "Do you have a return message you wish to relay?"

"Yeah. Tell him we'll hit the others in two hours. That should give everyone plenty of time to get in position. And tell him he owes me a drink when we get back," Charlie said with a grin.

"The message shall be relayed."

The Wampeh relayed the location of the ships to target, keeping the system containing the Ghalian treasures a secret still, then climbed back into his little ship and immediately took off to deliver the news.

Charlie told the others he'd be gone for a few hours and began suiting up, adding a pair of powerful konuses under his space suit. It looked like they'd need to make quite an impression, and he didn't want to leave anything to chance. The extra power would make it that much easier to cast while reserving his own internal strength, just in case.

Things *should* go smoothly, but Charlie was well-acquainted with Murphy by now, and knew better than to assume an easy go of it.

"*You ready for this?*" he asked as he fastened his helmet.

"*Ready, and actually rather looking forward to it,*" Ara replied.

"*Yeah, a little free-for-all destruction should be fun for a change. And this time we're the ones doing the ambushing.*"

The small group of vessels in low orbit around a quiet little supply planet were indeed from Visla Dominus's fleet. Charlie and Ara noticed the telltale modifications made to the captured ships as soon as they jumped into the system. These were no warships, they were support craft being used to resupply the fleet, allowing the more important ships to stay in place rather than make runs for necessities.

"*This should be cake,*" Charlie said. "*What do you think? Torch the two larger ones while I bombard the others? That should get their attention and make them call for help. If we separate them into scattered clusters, we should be able to position ourselves in such a way the arriving ships won't be able to get a clear shot at us.*"

"*That would be preferable,*" Ara replied. "*Much as I will enjoy this, I do not wish the tables to be turned on us.*"

"Right. So we keep a clear escape route should we need it. If they start closing down jump options, we bail out of here. But until then, I think we can pretty effectively use the visla's own ships as a shield against his fleet. They wouldn't want to go blasting the very ships they've come to rescue, after all."

Ara agreed.

"Okay, then. Twenty minutes until go time," Charlie noted, relaxing and slipping into an easy meditation while they waited, the trick learned from Ser Baruud all that time ago serving him well, yet again.

His internal clock chimed just as the chrono did.

"It is time," Ara said, beginning her approach.

She flew in fast, tucking in tight and allowing herself to appear as just another ball of debris as they approached. When they were close to the larger of the ships, she unfurled her wings and blasted out a massive stream of magical fire.

The ships were pathetically shielded, and had she wished, Ara could likely have destroyed them with just one pass. But that was not the plan.

Charlie peppered the smaller ships with spells, disabling a few, rocking the others with an impressive, but equally non-lethal attack.

"That oughta do it. Keep your eyes peeled, they'll be calling for help about now. And any minute we should see—"

Charlie was cut off when a large Tslavar warship jumped into the area.

"Now that's what I'm talking about," he said with glee. *"No more holding back. Light 'em up, Ara!"*

The Zomoki didn't need to be told twice, unleashing an unrestrained blast of powerful magical flame. Charlie layered his magic on top of hers, adding the trace of Rika's power that still lingered within him. That resource was limited and would likely be drained momentarily, but if it did what he needed, it would be worth it.

Sure enough, the strange magic helped him batter through the ship's magical shielding, leaving it vulnerable to Ara's attack. And this time she wasn't holding back. The ship rocked from the assault, massive damage incurred along its flank.

A wild flurry of spells assailed Charlie and Ara, but it was a disjointed and panicked counterattack. It seemed the Tslavars had been overconfident, utterly unaccustomed to a foe who could actually fight back. And Ara was doing far more. She was kicking their ass.

"That'll get their attention. They should be calling the others for backup right about now."

Ten ships jumped into the area in quick succession.

"Wow. They really aren't playing around," Charlie noted. *"Okay, let's give 'em something to think about, then tuck behind the supply ships. The longer we keep them here and out of Bob's hair, the better."*

CHAPTER THIRTY-SIX

"They've done it," Bawb said with a grin as he, Hunze, and Zilara sat quietly in her shimmer ship, observing the powerful craft amassed before them. One of the larger ones jumped away, right on time. A minute later, nearly a dozen quickly followed.

"That was more ships than we had assumed they'd be able to draw away," Zilara noted. "The approach will be rather easy now."

"You sound almost disappointed," Hunze said.

"Well, I do enjoy at least *some* challenge," Zilara replied. "In any case, we must begin."

The skilled Wampeh pilot guided her ship down through the remaining craft quickly, weaving between them with ease, invisible and undetected. In their possession were two of the necessary keys to the vault, retrieved by their comrades while they'd been scouting the area.

One of the keys was lost forever, its planet having fallen to global war, rendering even its protected hiding place no more than a pile of rubble. The others, however, had been attainable, though with varying degrees of difficulty. The important thing was, the order now possessed them all and would be hiding them anew in new locations to be determined by The Six.

It was the beginning of a new age. One of recovered power and a plan to use it. It was unlike any endeavor the Wampeh Ghalian had embarked upon in well over a millennia.

"There," Zilara said, noting a convenient rooftop on which to land her shimmer ship.

It was only one story tall, but the structure was sturdy, and, more importantly, its location lent itself to their task. It was close to their destination, and being elevated allowed them the freedom to park without worrying about someone accidentally happening upon the invisible ship.

Zilara would bring it to ground level when they brought the cargo, but not any sooner. The two Wampeh were clothed in stolen Tslavar uniforms, but the pale assassins had one more thing to do before stepping out into the light.

"Shall we?" Bawb asked.

"After you," Zilara replied with a grin. She always enjoyed this part of a job, and didn't get to utilize her Ghalian disguise magic to this level very often.

Bawb closed his eyes and began muttering an old and highly secret spell, repeating it over and over, focusing on the image in his mind's eye. Hunze was amazed to see his face slowly shift not only color but structure until soon he bore no resemblance to her love. He was a Tslavar.

Of course, the magic was only an illusion. He hadn't actually changed himself on a cellular level. But unless someone went so far as to reach out and touch his face, the illusion would hold. And Tslavars were not known for their displays of affection. Bawb was quite confident none would attempt to caress his cheek.

Zilara followed suit, quickly joining him in the disguise. Hunze, however, was not practiced in this particular skill. One day, perhaps she'd be able to, but at the moment it was not an option. As an Ootaki, however, she had value, and that would be good enough.

Bawb handed her a fake control collar, which she affixed around her neck. He knew it wasn't real, but even so, seeing her wear one again made his heart ache.

"I'm ready," the Ootaki said, now appearing to be a captive for all intents and purposes.

The trio stealthily made their way to the ground level, then headed the few streets over to the old waste disposal facility. While many modern worlds had such systems in place in every home, this world was more rustic, and as such, refuse was taken to one of the many convenient centers for magical disposal.

Much like a temple, it was something unlikely to be damaged in times of strife. Even invaders needed their trash taken care of, after all. And that made it a perfect hiding spot for a fortune in relics, treasure, and weapons. And it just so happened to have convenient bins stacked all around it, devoid of their disposed of contents and ready to be returned for more trash.

CHAPTER THIRTY-SEVEN

While Charlie and Ara continued to wreak havoc on the ships jumping into the nearby system, using the smaller supply craft as a sort of obstacle course to keep from being properly targeted, a system away, Bawb and Zilara led their faux prisoner through the streets of the city, heading for the secret Wampeh Ghalian vault.

"You found one!" a Tslavar commander said as they rounded the corner leading to the squat and rather fragrant refuse disposal facility.

"Yes, we found one," Bawb said, sliding into the moment as he did with all of his characters. Effortlessly.

"This is a boon for us," the somewhat heavyset Tslavar commander said with a happy grin. "The visla will reward me well for bringing an Ootaki. And so soon! We've only just been given the command to round up any we can find. Little did we know there was one on the planet."

"Quite a boon," Bawb said. "We'll take her to be transferred immediately, sir."

"No, you misunderstand. See that rank on my sleeve? This is

my Ootaki now. You get back to your duties. I'll take her in myself."

The man moved for Hunze, grabbing her arm. It would be the last thing he remembered. The surge of stunning energy crackled through her body, right up his arm, dropping him in an instant.

Bawb and Zilara were already moving. A nearby refuse crate would make a perfect place for his body, and they had him stuffed inside in under ten seconds, always the consummate professionals.

"Did I kill him?" Hunze asked, realizing what she'd done.

"No, you did not," Bawb replied. "You only stunned him."

Zilara gave him a funny look. There was no need to treat the Ootaki with kid gloves. She was Ghalian now. And while she may not have killed the man, she did not need to be shielded from the fact that the man had transitioned from living to dead with a well-placed blade as Zilara tucked him into the container.

The body would be dumped into the central processing area, where powerful magic would dissemble it to molecules and send the powdered remains out into the fields as fertilizer. Someone might wonder where the commander had gone, but they would be long gone by that time.

"Come, we should hurry. There is no telling how long our friends will be able to keep the Tslavars occupied," Bawb said, hurrying into the building.

The city itself had been a simple trading outpost, once upon a time. A perfect, unremarkable place to hide the Ghalian wealth. But now, with the arrival of the visla's fleet, it had become something far more. But trash was trash, and the facility still stood.

Zilara and Hunze followed Bawb through the entryway, right past the processing pit to a recessed area on the far wall. They quickly stacked crates several high, affording them a bit of privacy, as well as preparing a few to carry whatever they'd be retrieving on this day.

They'd not take all of the contents of the vault. That would be foolish and was completely unnecessary. But key items would travel with them, as would enough coin to fund their participation in the war for a long, long time.

Zilara and Hunze each carried one of the keys acquired by their brethren. The one in Zilara's hands was a gleaming pendant with a galaxy stone in the center. The swirling colors were beautiful, but no more than a commonplace decorative trick.

The real magic, however, was undetectable. And it only activated in combination with the right spell, and only when in the presence of another key. One that Hunze produced from her pocket.

"Thank you," Bawb said, taking the key from her outstretched hand.

It was nothing to look at, but that was the point. An incredibly valuable bit of Wampeh Ghalian magic stored in a simple hair clip. It wasn't even a terribly ornate one, but it served its purpose just fine without any pomp or glitter.

Bawb placed the two keys on his palm. When they touched one another, a subtle shift occurred. Only a power user would notice it, which Hunze certainly did.

"The spell is tied in to the keys," Bawb informed them. "It is crucial that two of the keys are present for it to work. And they must be undoctored. If someone had tampered with them, there would be a slight shift in the way they react to one another. One only known to The Three."

"You mean The Six," Zilara corrected.

"Now, yes," he replied. "This knowledge will be shared with the others when we return. But for now, it is only we three."

Bawb then began incanting a complex spell, the tones as important as the words. Both Zilara and Hunze committed them to memory, the mental skills of a Ghalian being as crucial as the physical and magical ones.

The wall shifted a fraction of an inch. That was all.

No lights. No rumbling of foundations. Just a hidden door unlatched with no fanfare or pomp. Bawb placed his palm on the door, but before pushing, he took his left foot and pressed a spot on the wall just to the side of the door with his toe. Only then did he push forward.

"That is the second safeguard," he informed the women. "All of them are tied together, but they increase in deadliness as the sequence progresses. Try to open the vault with no key and you'll receive a terrible shock. Try with only one key and be struck dead. Unlock the door with both keys but not know to press the hidden release? Well, that triggers the final option spell."

"Which is?" Zilara asked.

"A self-destruct spell that will kill anyone within a city block, while sealing the vault forever with an even more powerful self-destruct spell so robust not even a visla could force it."

"How is that even possible?" Hunze asked. "A powerful enough visla could eventually break through anything."

"Normally, perhaps. But this spell is old magic. Very old, and very strong. And there are literally thousands of years of the most powerful casters bolstering its power. At this point, the spell is unbreakable. Bring two of the crates."

He pushed the door farther and stepped inside, the magical illumination within not brightening until he'd shut the door behind them.

"No such spells are required to exit," he informed them. "Follow me."

He led them through the vast space hidden in an impossible place. The door, it seemed, was a type of short-distance portal of sorts, carrying them seamlessly to the vault deep beneath the surface. Another Wampeh Ghalian trick used to perfection.

They walked past piles of treasures, ignoring the insane amount of wealth amassed in this place. It was enough, in some systems, to purchase worlds. But they did not care about any of that. Not at the moment. They would grab enough to fund their war, but not until they'd first acquired what they'd come for.

Hunze could feel the power humming in the weapons stored in this place. Konuses and slaaps, of course, but something more. "Is that a claithe?" she asked, already knowing the answer as Bawb deposited the deadly implement in the crate.

"Yes, and a powerful one at that. There are two more located here, but we only have one caster strong enough to use one, so they shall remain. Grab that," he said, nodding toward a long wooden case.

Hunze opened it and looked inside. The blue metal of the blade and its throbbing power made it clear what this was. Another vespus blade.

She looked at Bawb, who flashed her a quick wink. "For you," he said, then continued his inventory of items to take with them.

Hunze ran her hand over the grip. It was a more slender sword than the one she'd restored for Bawb. And she knew already it would fit her hand and style perfectly.

Bawb and Zilara were loading armfuls of powerful konuses into one of the crates, along with a healthy amount of very enchanted knives to be distributed amongst the masters and their favored pupils.

"I am sorry you must see this," Bawb said as he opened a thick chest against the wall.

Inside was a priceless fortune's worth of glowing Ootaki hair. It was first cut, she could tell, taken from someone who'd been held since birth. And it was so long. Impossibly long. The hair's former owner must have gone their whole life without it being cut once. An impossibly powerful thing, taken at the expense of one of her own's entire life.

Bawb knew they would need the additional resource, but he was nevertheless uncomfortable in the moment.

Hunze stepped close and looked deep into his eyes. "It's all right, love. It was not you who collected this hair. I can feel it. This is old. Very old. What was done occurred over a thousand years ago."

"Yes, but––"

"But, nothing. This is no time for sentimentality or weakness. They gave up their life for this hair, and it is a powerful asset now. It would be disrespectful of their sacrifice not to use it."

He stared at her a long moment. "You're an amazing woman, Hunze."

"And you, an amazing man," she replied, pressing her forehead to his. "Now, let us get what you really came for."

Zilara had already found the objects of their desire. Table after table had scrolls and books, and even carved stone tablets of the most ancient, arcane magic. The power they contained was unimaginable. It was also too risky to remove from this place, lest they fall into the wrong hands.

Bawb opened a small cabinet and removed a sheaf of enchanted parchment. "We copy the spells we need onto these," he said. "The contents will only be able to be read once, and only with the correct spell to reveal what is written. Then they will turn to ash. We shall bring these back to our brothers and sisters and learn them when we are all together."

"And until then, these are also safeguarded from snooping eyes, I assume?" Zilara asked.

"A simple spell, but yes. To all but the Ghalian, the words will appear as merely a letter to a relative before self-immolating."

"Clever," she replied. "But I wonder. Might we utilize the neuro-stim device aboard Kip to perhaps share some of this knowledge with select members of the order we deem ready at a later time?"

"An interesting suggestion," Bawb agreed. "We shall have to inquire with Kip when we return, though I think that seems more of a task for the likes of Cal and his greater AI mind."

The trio made one more survey of the cache of wealth and weapons, gathering more items until the boxes were full. When they saw their Ghalian brothers and sisters from across the galaxy, they'd outfit them with the most powerful weapons imaginable. They'd be a fighting force the likes of which hadn't been seen in millennia.

"That is enough," Bawb finally said, sealing the containers with a potent spell. "Now we must get back to the training facility. The others await us, and our friends cannot keep up their diversion forever."

CHAPTER THIRTY-EIGHT

The odd man who had stepped from the speedy little magic-powered ship greeted his red-headed escort down to Earth with an appreciative, and rather inappropriate, look when they landed in Los Angeles.

Tym was his name, and, apparently, he had volunteered for the mission with the proviso that Earth indeed had women in its population.

Daisy quickly sorted that shit out, putting him in his place without needing to resort to violence, though he very much tempted her.

"I was only asking," the pilot protested as Daisy manhandled him from the landing facilities to the loop tube pod that would take them to visit one of Cal's conference facilities.

Normally, Cal would have just chatted with the man anywhere––he did oversee the entire city, after all––but this fellow had just carried a supply of the odd Balamar waters from another galaxy for them. He figured a slightly more formal setting would make a better impression.

He had no idea it wouldn't make the slightest bit of difference to the strange pilot.

"So, what sort of nightlife is there around here?" were the first words out of his mouth.

"I'm sorry, Tym, I assumed you would perhaps first wish to clean up, maybe have a shower and a change of clothes, then a nice meal. I know Admiral Harkaway is interested in meeting you."

"Is the admiral a woman?"

"Yes, she is. Though I don't see how that—"

"Okay, I'll meet her. She's attractive, though, right?"

"And married," Daisy said, rolling her eyes. "You see, Cal? One-track mind."

"Yes, you mentioned."

"Well, I've got things to do. Freya and Joshua wanted to go over some of the mission intel. I thought I'd join them."

"A good idea, Daisy. We lost a ship up there. I fear things are going to be getting more difficult sooner than later."

"Just our luck, right, Cal?"

"You know it. Tell the boys I say hello when you see them."

"Will do," she replied, turning to Tym as she walked out. "And you. Be on good behavior. You just did a heroic thing that could help us win this thing. Don't go and ruin all that goodwill being a perv."

"The man is true to his nature," Sarah noted.

If by that you mean he's a creepy little dude, then yeah, you're right.

"I'm surprised you didn't break his fingers."

Tempting, but he did just make a pretty ballsy run from another galaxy, so I figured I owed it to him to cut him a little slack. For the time being, anyway. Once he's settled in, though, all bets are off.

Daisy made her way to the roof, where Freya had flown to meet her, hovering just above the surface.

"Hey, kiddo. Thanks for coming."

"Sure thing, Daisy. No sense in taking the loop tube all the way back to the spaceport when I can just as easily come here."

"Yeah, I didn't really want to have that guy attempt a landing anywhere but the nice, wide open spaceport, ya know?"

"He seemed like a pretty good pilot."

"And he might prove to be. But for now? Better safe than pervy alien dude stuck in the side of a building, right?"

Daisy climbed aboard, and Freya whisked them up and out of the atmosphere, making a quick run to her Dark Side hangar and fabrication facility. Joshua was already there, his swarm ship body resting on the surface while his core was inside.

"Hi, Daisy," he said as she exited Freya's stealthy mass.

"Hey, Joshua. How's it hangin'? I see you've got the prototype ships working finally."

"Yep. And they're flying well. I even got to try them out against the Tslavars, though I did lose a few."

"Well, it's unfortunate, but that's what they're made for. Keep you safe while they do their thing, right?"

"I don't want any of those nasty Tslavars hurting Joshua," Freya said, her protective streak flaring.

"I'm fine. But what does concern me is the loss of an Urok ship on the other side while we were bringing this Tym character across. It seems the enemy was lying in wait, cloaked with shimmer spells. Only once our ships had taken up positions to defend Tym's little vessel did they attack us."

"Sneaky bastards," Daisy grumbled.

"Sneaky and clever," Freya noted.

"She's right. This looks like more than just an attack. They intentionally stunned the crew. While our forces crossed back over before seeing the final outcome of that encounter, I'd say it's very likely the ship was taken for study."

"Meaning this Dominus character is trying to learn about us. About our tech."

"Precisely."

"Shit. Their ignorance of our machinery was one of our biggest advantages."

"It was, but I've looked at the intel from the mission, and from what I can tell, they've begun figuring out what our ships can and cannot defend against."

"But they're magic users. They don't even understand our tech," Daisy said.

"Only a fool underestimates their enemy," Joshua replied. "And I know for a fact you are not a fool."

Joshua and Freya pooled resources, their great minds combining to suss out whatever information might be useful in their fight against the mysterious enemy. For Freya, it was a fun puzzle, sorting through all the data. For Joshua, however, it was like his old days, back when he ran all of the national missile defenses for NORAD, deep underneath Cheyenne Mountain in Colorado.

Daisy looked over the data as well. She wasn't an AI, but her meat mind was more than anyone else's, rewired into a powerful machine by her neuro-stim incident. And, sometimes, that human element would spot things the machines had missed.

But in this case, there wasn't much to go on, and until they had a prolonged encounter with the Tslavar ships, they simply didn't possess the knowledge needed to formulate a substantial plan.

Even so, Joshua had an idea.

"Rika?" he said as he contacted the magically inked woman over comms.

"Yeah, what's up? Who is this?"

"This is Joshua. I'm the AI with Freya and—"

"I know who you are. Everyone knows who you are. So, what can I do for you? It's not every day the head of NORAD calls a girl up, after all."

"You're the one in charge of the timing of the portal now, correct?"

"Yeah. What's up?"

"There's been a bit of a situation. I was wondering, can you make the portal enter and exit the sun even faster?"

"Faster? I guess I could. It's dangerous, though. And I'll need to be on hand personally when it does its thing. You'll need me there casting to make it work. Automatic spells won't cut it, and we really don't want to risk roasting our guys in the sun. That means real-time casting."

"If that's what it takes, then, fine," Joshua replied. "I'll let you know when we need you. Hopefully, that shift in tactics will work to our advantage."

"They're slippery bastards, those Tslavars," Rika said. "Don't underestimate them."

"I was just saying that myself," Joshua replied.

He wasn't about to underestimate the enemy fleet. Whether they'd live up to the threat he anticipated, however, only time would tell.

CHAPTER THIRTY-NINE

It was getting late in the afternoon when Freya gave Daisy a lift back down to downtown Los Angeles after a quick stop at home to retrieve Stabby at the AI's request.

"I'm here, Cal," she said, walking into his preferred research facility.

He had dozens of them spread across the region, giving not only his cyborg friends, but also human and Chithiid residents something useful to do. It seemed that a modicum of work was preferable to a life of absolute leisure. It was something those who'd struggled to achieve such a life all of their working days would have been surprised to learn.

"Daisy, thank you for stopping by. I've asked a few others to join us as well. I think you'll all find this quite interesting."

"Hey, Sis," Daisy said as Sarah and Finn wandered in a short time later. "How's things at the homestead?"

"Oh, you know. Crazy teenagers making a mess. This yo-yo feeding them far too much sugar."

"It doesn't count if I'm experimenting, babe," Finn protested. "I needed guinea pigs."

"And they'll turn into real pigs if you keep plying them with a dozen new recipes a day."

"It wasn't a dozen," he confided to Daisy. "More like a half dozen."

"You two are ridiculous. How Ripley ever turned out so cool is beyond me. In fact, I'm starting to think it's her aunt's influence."

"You're damn right it is," Tamara said as she walked through the door, her cybernetic arm sporting a fun new paint job. A psychedelic rendition of a classic Van Gogh, but done up in her own style.

It was something she'd taken to after the war. Her arm was a military unit, and capable of meting out larger doses of violence with great aplomb, but in day-to-day life, it could be a bit intimidating to some people. Overkill, if you will. So she began decorating it from time to time. And this many years into the practice, it had become something of an ingrained habit.

"Just waiting on one more, then we'll begin."

"Oh, you're waiting on me?" Korbin said, slipping off the shimmer cloak he'd been hiding under.

"Dude, good way to get yourself skewered," Daisy said, lowering her sword.

"Sorry about that. I actually only just got here myself, but I'm so out of practice with these things, and Cal had some lying around after you defeated the Tslavars who'd been using them––nicely done, by the way."

"So you just decided to snag one and play spy?" Tamara grumbled, though she was clearly amused.

"Something like that. I've also been working on the shimmer ship itself. Amazing piece of work, that one. Someone spent a lot of coin outfitting it. That's more than your normal shimmer, and it's been quite an effort getting it fixed."

"It works just fine. The Drooks have been flying it around for months," Sarah noted.

"Well, yes. It flies fine. But the other features need attention. But that's neither here nor there. We're here at the request of Cal. Shall I assume there's something of interest for us to see?"

"Oh, that there is," the AI replied. *"We've been studying these strange waters sent across from the other galaxy."*

"Balamar waters," Korbin said.

"Yes, these Balamar waters. Figuring out ways to use it offensively against Dominus. But we have also noticed the healing properties seem to extend to more than just people. At least, we think so."

"More than people? So, what? You heal trees now?" Finn asked.

"Hardly, though I believe we could. But I have a little test I'd like to perform. Daisy, would you mind?" Cal asked, as a long, narrow tray of water was brought to her by a small droid.

"Ah, that's why you said bring Stabby," she realized as she unsheathed the sword. "Well, he *is* made out of me, so I guess it can't hurt," she said as she placed the sword in the shallow bath.

The reaction was immediate. Just as it had been when he was plunged into Emmik Trepenan's chest, Stabby was reacting the same way, the water rapidly absorbed into his length with a greedy, slurping sound.

"Is...is that blade *drinking*?" Korbin asked.

"Yeah, he's a living sword. Made out of my own bone," Daisy said. "You can pick him up if you like. Don't worry about cutting yourself. He only gets sharp for me."

Korbin carefully reached into the container, the few remaining drops of water on the sword's grip sending a surge of energy into his hand. The waters were powerful in both galaxies, it seemed.

But something else was powerful. The sword. It was pulsing with energy. Energy, and a strange consciousness.

"This sword. Has it always been enchanted?" he asked,

touching its blade carefully. Indeed, as Daisy had said, it was as dull as a club.

"Enchanted? He's just a sword. But when he fed on that Trepenan fella, it seems he picked up a little something from him."

"Ah, that explains it. And the waters have helped him evolve even further."

"Evolve?"

"Your sword is alive. And he is growing stronger," he said, handing her the gleaming white blade. "Though he does need a good sharpening."

Daisy laughed. "Hey, Cal. You need this table?" she asked.

"Yes, but be my guest, Daisy. I can always mend it."

"Thanks," she said, then casually dipped the sword's edge down onto the metal surface.

The table split in two and fell to the ground.

"But it was dull."

"Yeah. That's the thing, Korbin, my man. Like I said. He only gets sharp for me."

"Amazing," Korbin said appreciatively.

"I have small samples for each of you to ingest," Cal informed them, little shot glasses and a small pitcher appearing on a tray carried by one of his cyborg staff. "We know this is safe for humans. We're still testing on Chithiid and Urok cells, but they appear compatible as well."

"My kind cannot imbibe this," Korbin said, accepting the shot glass. "But we can benefit from surface contact." He then slowly poured the little glass over his head, reveling in the sensation of the energizing, healing waters leveling up his powers.

The others shrugged and downed their shot glasses, the aches and pains of their daily lives evaporating the moment the water hit their tongues.

"Holy crap! This stuff's amazing!" Finn exclaimed.

Sarah was also having quite a positive rush as well, and even the nanites making up her reconstructed arm seemed to react. Curious, she stuck her finger in a pitcher. The nanites immediately absorbed the water, spreading it among their masses, storing it for later study and possible use.

"It kind of makes my skin itch," Daisy said.

"Mine too," Sarah agreed. "But it's not bad. Just like a niacin flush or something."

"We will start dosing the crews shortly. I'm told this provides some protection from magical attacks. Is that correct, Korbin?"

Rather than pontificate, the visla simply pointed at Finn and cast a stun spell. The metal-handed chef stumbled and dropped to one knee, but quickly righted himself.

"What the fuck, Korbin? Not cool!" he protested.

"Apologies. But now we know. To answer your question, Cal, it does appear to protect to an extent. That spell should have rendered Finnegan unconscious, yet it only knocked him down momentarily."

"Good. This will prove quite useful to our crews in future confrontations," Cal replied.

"Might I have a container of the waters? I wish to bring them to Rika. I believe her powers might benefit from additional contact with it," Korbin asked.

"Of course. I'll have one brought to you straightaway," Cal replied. *"You'll find my weapons research and development staff's progress with railgun sabots containing small quantities of the water quite interesting."*

"What's that supposed to do?" Tamara asked.

"This Dominus character is supposedly sensitive to it. Like a vampire to holy water," Finn replied. "Splash him with it and, 'boom.' No more Dominus."

"Or so we hope. In any case, these new rounds are designed to detonate once they pierce a ship, releasing their water vapor. It might strengthen a few of the Tslavar crew who happen to be

nearby, but if Visla Dominus is anywhere near, it should take him out of the equation, so the trade-off is worth it, in my opinion."

"Agreed," Daisy said. "C'mere, Tamara. I wanna do a thing."

"A thing? So articulate, Daisy."

"Oh, shut up and bring me that arm of yours."

Tamara finally relented. "What craziness do you have in mind this time?"

"No craziness," she said, picking up a small glass of the waters and accessing one of Tamara's small survival storage compartments secreted within her metal limb. "Just putting a little of this away for a rainy day. Just in case." She then poured the water in and sealed it tight. "Let's just hope that rainy day never comes. But if it should, we know who to call."

CHAPTER FORTY

Maarl had spent his stay on Zed's command ship pretty much in constant discussions and strategy sessions as the powerful AIs and the captains of the fleet assessed the portal, studied their situation, and planned their next steps.

The old Chithiid held a position of particular rank among all of them, having been not only a key to the victory during the Great War on Earth, but also being drafted as leader of the Chithiid homeworld of Taangaar.

He had survived much, from the original conquest of his own planet to the later genocide on Earth. And with such a long and storied life, he had a network of connections that spanned more than mere cities, or even continents, but planets.

When the speedy ship carrying the mysterious waters from another galaxy arrived––which he was still wrapping his head around––Maarl made it clear that he was shifting his priorities to that strange new asset.

The way it had been described, it could possibly shift the intergalactic conflict in their favor. And the healing properties were also of no small interest to the aging and aching alien. His dear old friend Cal already had a portion set aside for him once it had been thoroughly tested.

It would be a welcome treat. He was already advancing in years when his network risked it all to help Daisy, Cal, and their friends in the Great War. Nearly two decades later, the discomforts of his hard life were only more apparent.

"Lars, thank you for ferrying me down to the surface," Maarl said from his comfortable seat aboard the *Váli*.

"I wouldn't think of having anyone else take you, my old friend. It's been far too long," Captain Harkaway said.

"Indeed, it has. I'm sorry I haven't visited in some time. But we will make up for it now. Can Celeste join us for dinner? It would be nice to catch up over a meal rather than a strategy board, though it has been a pleasure chatting with you both there as well."

"I'm sure the admiral can peel herself away," Lars said with a warm laugh. "If not, she'll catch holy hell at home," he noted.

His wife may have been in command of the allied fleet, but that did not mean she couldn't break free from time to time. In fact, it was that very position that allowed her to delegate on occasion and take a much-needed break from the pressures of her job.

Mal, the *Váli*'s AI, reached out to their friends on the surface, letting them know Maarl would be joining them in Los Angeles for a bit. She was sure they'd all want to make sure they saw him during one of his rare visits. Especially Arlo, for whom Maarl had served as a grandfatherly figure his entire life.

The ship touched down gently atop the sturdy building Cal had lately been favoring as his primary command facility. He was not physically located there, of course. The actual location of the powerful AI's brain was not only protected by reinforced housings, but had also been kept secret since the time of the Great War. He didn't think he'd need to go to such lengths, but he'd survived hundreds of years of alien occupation. Safe was better than sorry.

"Gentlemen, welcome," Cal said as they left the *Váli* and strolled down to the command center. *"It is a pleasure having you back on Earth, Maarl, though it was lovely catching up over the strategy sessions aboard Zed as well."*

"Funny, we were just saying the same thing," Captain Harkaway said with a chuckle. "I was thinking of taking Maarl for a spin around town. He hasn't seen the latest changes you've made to the place, and the new greenbelt came out better than planned."

"Thank you, Captain Harkaway. A lot of work went into that addition. But there is something else I think Maarl will be interested in. Something that should interest you both, actually."

"Oh?"

"There's been a development. The Ra'az is now free. And it is not what one would expect."

Maarl and Harkaway put aside their natural bias against the Ra'az as best they could. Yes, the brutal race had caused huge amounts of pain and suffering to both of their worlds, but they trusted Cal implicitly. If he saw fit to free the prisoner, there had to be a reason.

"Where's he at, Cal?" Harkaway asked.

"Head to the loop tube. I'll have one of George's men standing by to escort you there."

It had been a quick trip to the beach. From there it was a short ride to the picturesque property resting atop the bluffs between Malibu and Santa Monica. The location the Ra'az had selected to call home was just far enough from any neighbors as to be effectively isolated, while also being close to the city if need be.

"Just up ahead," the beefy cyborg said as they walked the final several streets to their destination at a leisurely pace, enjoying the fresh air and sun. "It's the damnedest thing, I tell ya. I never thought I'd see something like this."

Harkaway and Maarl's curiosity was now more piqued than ever, and a few short minutes later they saw what had so surprised the cybernetic soldier.

There he was, an enormous Ra'az Hok, free of restraints—though unarmed—on the sprawling grounds out front of the home in which he'd been residing. And he had company.

"Is that a—?" Harkaway asked, his jaw nearly dropping open.

"Yep. A Graizenhund," the soldier replied.

"Is he—?"

"Playing fetch. Yep."

It was such an incongruous thing to see. Their former foe, one of the most deadly and hateful races in the galaxy, playing with his animal friend. And he was actually enjoying himself.

"What the hell, Cal?" Harkaway said over comms.

"I thought you'd want to see this in person," the AI replied. *"It would seem our guest has evolved."*

"Fascinating," Maarl said, watching with great interest as the Ra'az hugged the huge beast affectionately as it licked his face.

He was even *laughing*. And Ra'az *never* laughed. But this one did. And he seemed truly happy. At ease. And, most importantly, not violent.

"I never would have believed it if I hadn't seen it with my own eyes," Harkaway said. "Maarl, this is incredible."

"Yes, it is," the Chithiid elder replied. "Cal, are you thinking what I am?"

"That perhaps there is hope for this one yet? Yes," Cal said.

"Then let us go and speak with this man," Maarl said.

They walked forward, the cyborg calmly following a few paces behind, but ready to spring at a moment's notice should the Ra'az turn violent.

He needn't have worried.

"Hello," Grundsch said calmly as the men approached. "Say hello to our visitors, Bahnjoh."

The Graizenhund padded over to the three men, tail wagging, happy from his afternoon playtime. They'd never seen one up close that wasn't actively trying to kill them. This was a most unusual day, indeed.

"Uh, hello," Captain Harkaway said, amazed that he was actually scratching a living, and quite content, Graizenhund's ears. "I'm Lars Harkaway. This is Maarl."

"The captain from the fleet, yes, I've heard. And the Chithiid leader. My greetings," he said, appearing calm and relaxed, to the men's surprise. "My name is Grundsch, last of the Ra'az Hok."

"So we've heard," Captain Harkaway said.

There was an awkward silence as the three men whose races had fought so brutally in the past came to terms with the quite different circumstances of the present. Grundsch, for his part, had experienced something of a breakthrough since his night at the fight club. He'd already begun the transition over his lengthy and peaceful service in Visla Palmarian's home, but the change was now a conscious realization rather than an unnoted one.

It was Maarl who bridged the gap, stepping close to the enormous Ra'az and reaching out a hand. "It is a pleasure to make your acquaintance, Grundsch. Our people have a troublesome and unpleasant history, but as far as I am concerned, it is just that. History. We are all different men now, are we not?"

The Ra'az nodded slowly, then clasped the outstretched hand. "Well spoken," he said. "Let the past be the past."

"It's strange to say, I have to admit, but you're right," Harkaway said, shaking his hand as well.

The men and their escort all relaxed, the tension they'd been carrying in their bodies without even realizing it dissolving in the afternoon sun.

"Please, join me. I will have the house systems prepare some refreshments," Grundsch said, gesturing toward the outdoor furniture under a nearby tree. "So strange, this life of relative luxury Cal has afforded me."

"Thank you, Grundsch," Maarl said. "And as a part of this world, this society, you should be treated no different than anyone else, though, admittedly, that may take some longer to accept than others."

Grundsch let out a rumbling chuckle. "I have noticed, but I believe progress is underway."

"Then let's sit and talk. It's too damn pretty a day not to enjoy it," Harkaway said.

The men walked to the shady spot and discussed *everything*, even the difficult stuff. And at the end of it, as the human and Chithiid took their leave, things had been thoroughly hashed out. The healing had begun, and the most unlikely of new members of Earth's population finally began to feel, at least a little bit, at home.

CHAPTER FORTY-ONE

It was a bit of a strange sensation, flying in a ship rather than atop Ara's back, but Charlie and Olo were making their trek in a craft that would not raise alarm when they came in to land on the planet of Orval.

A giant, red space dragon tended to put people on edge.

"I am near if you require my assistance," Ara said when she pulled away from the ship as it began its descent to the surface.

"Thanks, Ara. I think this should go fine, but it's good knowing you're around, just in case."

Olo, while reluctant to fly into harm's way against the powerful visla, was nevertheless willing to participate in this task. The risk was far less, and he received more coin for his troubles. And, best of all, they were going to Orval, home to a black market of legendary size.

Charlie hadn't been back to that world since he and Bawb had been sent off on what Mandoog considered a fool's errand. Little did he know they would actually succeed.

In that same visit to the smuggler's haven, Bawb had frozen Commander Yakatan in stasis with his wand, leaving the traitorous man in the care of the ruler of the underground in their absence. Mandoog was perfectly happy to take the man into his possession, but not for reasons they expected.

Yakatan, in reality, was one of Mandoog's minions. One he tried to free from the spell binding him as soon as Charlie and Bawb left. But the magic was strong. Too strong, in fact, for Mandoog's caster to break.

It was unfortunate, the loss of Yakatan would make his black market trade a bit more difficult, but if Charlie and Bawb ever returned, Mandoog had every intention to hand them over to Visla Dominus and reap the reward. And maybe the visla would be grateful enough to break the spell on Yakatan in the process. For a caster of *that* power, it would be child's play.

Charlie and Olo were under surveillance the moment they touched down, though they paid it no heed.

"They're watching us," Olo noted.

"Yep. Just play it normal, Olo. This guy's got eyes everywhere, so just assume we're *always* being watched."

"Because we *are*," Olo shot back.

"Well, yeah. And Mandoog himself undoubtedly already knows we're here. And he's the fella to see. He's got access to ships, Olo. A *lot* of ships, and that's just what we need. And you, my friend, are the expert in that arena."

"From what you've said, you need as many as you can get your hands on. But I have to admit, this place is even better than I'd heard. Just look at all of them," Olo marveled as they made their way into the subterranean marketplace and its accompanying network of massive ship-sized flyways.

The sprawling network of hidden tunnels allowed for the safe and secret docking of all manner of ships of mischief and piracy. To Olo, it was heaven. A smuggler's paradise.

A tall and imposing man, thick muscled with multi-colored braids woven into his hair, stepped in front of them, halting their progress.

Ah, about time, Charlie thought.

"You again," Quintz said with a smirk. "Didn't think I'd see you back here in one piece. Where's your Wampeh friend?" he asked.

"Not with me today. He had other things to do," Charlie replied.

"Your loss," Quintz replied, his associates stepping out of the shadows, all of them eyeing Charlie and his blue-skinned associate menacingly.

Of course, Charlie had seen them coming long before they'd finally made contact, but he kept that little detail to himself.

"You're to come with me. Mandoog wants to see you."

"Lead the way," Charlie replied.

They followed the tall man through the winding network of connecting passageways, climbing up and down so many levels that most would have been hopelessly lost and unable to retrace their steps, which was the point of the lengthy route.

Finally, at long last, they arrived at the unassuming entrance to Mandoog's lair. Charlie had been there before, however, and had its location memorized from their first visit. But this little game had to be played out according to Mandoog's whim, so the two men just followed along, playing the part expected of them.

"Thank you, Quintz," Mandoog said as Charlie and Olo were shown into his opulent lair, his expansive mass reclining comfortably on a couch, a large retinue of guards standing at attention.

The décor was as impressive as Charlie remembered it. The man was wealthy, no doubt, and had good taste to boot. Being in charge of a massive smuggling ring and black market didn't hurt, either.

"So, you survived," Mandoog said, sipping wine from a chalice. "Though I see your Wampeh friend is not with you."

An *actual* chalice, Charlie marveled. He was really going over the top today. He'd had plenty of time to position himself, and this was the impression he wished to make. Knowing it was all a put-on, the effect on Charlie was far more comical than impressive, but he kept that to himself.

"Yep, we survived, all right," Charlie said. "And we succeeded."

At this Mandoog's face betrayed him, a look of actual surprise flashing briefly across his features. "Oh? Then you've done well. Give the relic to me, and I will help you defeat this troublesome enemy of yours."

Of course, Mandoog had no intention of doing anything of the sort, but was going to hand the deadly relic over to Visla Dominus, along with Charlie and his friend. The visla would surely reward him *greatly* for achieving this coup.

But Charlie had other plans.

"Yeah, about that," Charlie said. "I kinda used it already."

"You what?" Mandoog bellowed.

"You heard me," Charlie shot back, his attitude most decidedly not that of a prisoner.

"How dare you waste such a thing. I should——"

"Oh, shut up, will ya? I swear, this posturing is exhausting."

"I'll have you killed for speaking to me like this. Killed, or worse," Mandoog growled.

"Yeah, sure you will. Now, listen. I know you're working for this Visla Dominus character, but he's up to some seriously nefarious shit. But the thing is, you can make a difference. And if you do, I'll go easy on you."

"*You* will go easy on *me*?" Mandoog said with a laugh.

"That's what I said," Charlie replied, utterly unfazed. "I'm going to need you to provide me and my friends with all of the ships, crews, and supplies we need. You're going to have to step out of the shadows and act. No more of this playing both sides and flying below the radar."

"Radar?"

"Never mind. The point is, there's an actual war coming.

This is about to get ugly, and *everyone* is going to be involved. Even you."

Mandoog looked at the pair of prisoners with obvious contempt. "And what makes you think I would ever do what you ask? I can just hand you over to Dominus and receive a fat reward. You're outnumbered ten to one, fool."

Charlie snickered. "Yeah. About that. Allow me to introduce you to your guards."

"*My* guards?" Mandoog said, confused.

Confused, that is, until his guards' faces suddenly dissolved back to their normal states as the Wampeh Ghalian assassins' shed their disguises. Only then did Mandoog realize that he and Quintz were the only non-Wampeh in the room.

Wisely, Quintz immediately put his hands up, taking care not to make any sudden movements. Mandoog, however, was beside himself.

"Do something!" he shouted to Quintz.

"I am," he replied. "Making sure I continue breathing."

Charlie smiled. "A wise man. And you'd be smart to do the same."

Mandoog was fuming. Furious. Humiliated. It was all a dangerous combination in a man of his demeanor, but he also knew when he'd been outplayed. He wouldn't have survived and risen to the top of the vicious underworld otherwise.

"Fine," he sighed. "What do you need of me?"

Charlie looked at his blue-skinned friend.

"Your ships," Olo said.

"Which ones?"

"Pretty much all of them."

"Oh, is that all?" Mandoog said, a deflated shell of himself.

Charlie almost felt bad for the man. *Almost.* "Well, about that. The rebellion needs bodies, so we'll also be taking your men."

"I'll be defenseless!"

"We'll leave a few of our Wampeh friends to keep an eye on you," Charlie said. "For your sake, but also for ours. You'll rebuild. Your kind always does. But I suggest you behave, and don't breathe a word of this to Visla Dominus. You'll live much longer that way."

CHAPTER FORTY-TWO

The transition from smuggling fleet to rebel armada had been going surprisingly well, Charlie thought. Mandoog's men—*former* men—had heard what happened within the highly fortified lair of their employer. And if *he* could be ambushed like that, any of them could.

Not to mention, the Wampeh Ghalian appeared to have taken a side in this conflict. That alone was enough to strengthen the resolve of many, as well as loosen the bowels of more than a few reticent crewmembers.

All of the ships were falling in line, resupplying and preparing for departure to join the rebel fleet, when the captain of one ship, a well-armed and particularly desirable vessel, naturally, decided to put up a fight.

It was a craft they very much needed in their fleet, and as such, they couldn't simply make an example of it. Also, it was still within the confines of the subterranean network of Orval, and any massive battle would cost countless lives and cause not only irreparable damage, but also bring their operation very much to Visla Dominus's attention.

"I'll handle it," Charlie said, quickly sending a message for the most able pirates from Marban's former shipmates to join him.

The response was astonishingly fast. Apparently, they'd been rather hoping for some trouble and were already geared up and eager to join in. This rebel thing was interesting, but they were pirates, after all. A good old-fashioned boarding and takeover was sorely missed.

And now they had that opportunity.

"Thanks for coming on such short notice," Charlie said to the assembled men, all bristling with weapons and ill intent. "What we've got here is a reluctant captain and a particularly tough ship. Now, we're in port, and he doesn't want to start a shooting fight any more than we do. But if we don't quash this now, others may decide to follow his example."

"So we board the ship and crush him," one of the pirates said with glee.

"Yes, we do. But remember, these men are going to be our comrades soon enough. If they don't seem to have their hearts in the fight, do what you can to disable them rather than kill them. We'll need all the men we can get when we go against Dominus."

"You fought with Marban on many occasions. Now we'll fight with you," the man replied.

The others were obviously just as ready for the engagement, amped with energy and excitement.

Quintz, and several of Mandoog's other henchmen, watched the entire spectacle with fascination. They wouldn't be joining on this particular mission, but they might be called upon to do similar in coming days. Seeing the loyalty and enthusiasm these men shared––without payment or coercion––was, both surprising and a bit inspiring.

"Okay, then. Let's do this," Charlie said, leading his men into one of the Wampeh's shimmer ships.

It was a tight fit, but given the nature of their approach, as well as their enemy being on alert for any sort of attack, it was the only way. Other Wampeh spread out among the onlookers, blending in, but ready to strike if unrest should show its face.

Quintz noted the way the men and women would vanish into the masses. He'd heard of their skills of disguise, but never seen them in person before today. Of course, he supposed if he had, it would have been the last thing he ever saw.

The invisible ship flew the short gap to the docked and heavily armed craft, settling into a low hover just above its hull. Not being in space, the pirates were afforded the rare luxury of not needing to cast force spells to create a breathable passageway to the craft. Instead, they simply slid down onto its surface, quietly stepping onto the hull, ensuring they made no noise that might give themselves away.

It was amazing to the few allowed to observe the proceedings just how stealthy the seemingly bulky and gregarious pirates could be when they wanted to. But they were consummate professionals when it came to the business of piracy. Any less would result in one or more of their demise.

Charlie cast a breaching spell, opting to quietly part the hull rather than blast their way in. From what his senses told him, the other side of the bulkhead was unoccupied at the moment. It was a skill he wished he'd possessed back in his early pirating days.

In a flash, the pirates were inside the ship, fanning out and silently taking down as many of the crew as possible with stun spells before the ugly work of close-quarter combat really kicked in. Once that happened, magic would be taboo, and they'd have to resort to other, messier means.

Charlie rushed ahead toward the command center of the craft, followed closely by a handful of his fellow pirates. Magic suddenly blasted out. Had it not been for the shielding he was casting as they ran, he and his comrades would have been killed outright.

As it was, the hull buckled slightly from the deflected blast.

"The fool's using magic this close," one of the men said.

"We're not in space. He isn't worried about a breach," another replied. "We need to take him down, and fast, before he damages the ship with his idiotic attacks."

Charlie was already way ahead of them, casting a containment bubble in the direction the spell was coming from. He'd never tried the trick before, but, given the circumstances, he doubted it would make things any worse.

The man casting the attack wasn't a power user, but merely a crewmember wielding a particularly powerful konus. When he stepped clear of the bulkhead he was hiding behind to cast again, however, Charlie's spell caught him full-force, stopping the spell on his lips dead in its tracks.

Actually, it stopped the man dead as well, namely, by cutting him neatly in half, the top section of his body hovering in the air within the containment bubble, while the bottom fell to the ground.

The defenders around him immediately threw down their weapons and raised their arms. What they didn't realize was that Charlie had not at all intended to do what he'd just done.

But shock and awe was going to save a lot more lives, so he put aside his own surprise and played it up, ordering the captives to line up, where his men would take charge of them.

The rest of the ship fell in short order, though it was a bloody fight in some of the corridors and compartments. Eventually, however, the crew was brought to heel, their rebellious captain slain in the action, unwilling to surrender even when given the option.

"Not a bad-looking group," Charlie said of the kneeling men lined up in the cargo bay as he walked their length, sizing up the potential of this crew. "And they fought well. For not being pirates, that is."

The pirates standing guard nodded, proud of their work.

They'd not lost a single man, and had captured almost all of the crew intact, more or less. One of the pirates, however, held Charlie's gaze a bit longer than the others. Something was up.

Charlie walked slowly back toward the man, who twitched one eyebrow upward, then flashed his eyes to one of the kneeling men. The fellow was a bit bloodied, obviously one of the more skilled in the resisting force, seeing as he made the pirates go to such lengths in order to subdue him.

Charlie looked at him, making eye contact. The man didn't flinch. Nor did he break his resentful stare, his eyes shooting hate daggers with intensity. He was going to be a problem. And they simply didn't have the time or resources to deal with one.

The lesson taught to him by Captain Saramin all those years ago flashed back into Charlie's mind. Never leave a threat at your back. And this man was most certainly going to be a threat, no matter what he might eventually say.

Charlie gave a nearly imperceptible nod to the pirate guarding that group of prisoners. The pirate turned his head away, as if studying something fascinating on the far wall, just as Charlie turned his back on the kneeling prisoner.

The man's eyes flicked down to the unguarded knife hanging from Charlie's hip. Seeing the guard was distracted, he didn't hesitate, lunging for the blade with deadly intent. Charlie actually let him wrap his hand around the grip before reacting, the concealed blade that had somehow appeared in his other hand flashing out and driving deep into the prisoner's chest.

The look of shock in the man's eyes lasted but a moment before he slid to the deck in a small pool of blood. Charlie felt ill. He hated killing, especially like this. But he couldn't afford to be kindhearted. Not now. Not with two galaxies on the line. This had to be done, and an example had to be made. It was that, or potentially having to fight more of the remaining prisoners at some point.

"This is what happens to those who do not fall in line,"

Charlie said, channeling his long-dead former pirate captain. "Now, I wish you no harm. In fact, I am offering you the opportunity of a lifetime. The chance to fight for a cause worth fighting for. And in so doing, the opportunity to not only save this galaxy from the threat of Visla Dominus, but also the promise of not only glory, but great wealth. For rest assured, those who step up and do their part will be well rewarded." He turned to the body, prodding it with his toe. "Those who do not..."

He turned and walked away, letting the message sink in. The satisfied nods of his pirate brothers told him it had been a good speech. He hoped it would suffice. They needed all the men they could gather, and it would be a shame to lose any more of them.

Back on the docks overlooking the area, Quintz asked to speak with Charlie.

"Yes? What is it, Quintz?"

"I just wanted to say that you'll have no trouble from me. I'm your man, whatever you need."

Charlie assessed the man with a long, piercing stare. He didn't know if Quintz could be fully trusted, but the man had seen what the Wampeh Ghalian could do, and the fear that anyone around him could be an assassin in disguise would keep him in line far better than any threat Charlie could ever make.

"I'm glad to have you with us, Quintz," he finally said, placing his hand on the man's shoulder. "You'll be treated as a free man among us, not a servant, as you were under Mandoog. I hope you don't disappoint me."

"I won't," Quintz said, and in that moment, Charlie actually believed him.

He turned and walked away, heading back to his group of trusted allies, when Olo and a few pirates walked up to him.

"Charlie, there was a bit of a problem with one of the other captains," a pirate said.

"Oh? Damn. Okay, let's gather up the gang and head over—"

"Oh, the problem has been handled," the man corrected. "Your blue-skinned friend here stepped in and put a quick stop to it. Laid the man out before he knew what hit him, then scared the hell out of the others, offering them a piece of him if they dared. It was quite an amusing spectacle," the pirate said with an appreciative chuckle.

Olo grinned, obviously pleased with himself.

The smuggler seemed to be coming around, Charlie mused. Maybe he'd step up and throw his full support to the cause after all.

"So, you know I'm going to need some more coin for doing your job for you, right?" Olo said, holding out his hand.

"Or not," Charlie said to himself with a little sigh, then handed the smuggler a modest payment.

At least they'd won the day, though, and that was all that mattered. For now, at least.

CHAPTER FORTY-THREE

It had taken Pimbrak very little time to liaise with his man inside Visla Palmarian's estate, their contact being made easy by the sheer size of the visla's property and the number of servants in his employ. Blending in with the lower-tier worker bees as they came and went from the building was laughably easy.

Pimbrak had the plans to the building and the most recent updates about the security routines of the building's rotating teams. It seemed they had greatly increased both foot patrols as well as magical wards in the short time since the younger Palmarian had gone missing once more.

Given the drastic increase of activity at the property, the Wampeh master assassin took the information and bade his contact to continue his surveillance at the lower levels, reporting back to the order periodically. He, however, would proceed with his infiltration, as planned.

This was a task at which most would fail. In fact, between the heightened security presence and robust magical defenses, the Palmarian tower was impenetrable. Well, *almost*.

Disguise firmly in place, Pimbrak made his way to the

servants' entrance at the service area, carrying a load taken from the courier whose identity he had assumed after paying him very, very well for his package. He had told him it was an urgent delivery and the payment was a bonus for prompt delivery. The man had gladly accepted it without a question, while Pimbrak had acquired a living patsy, should one be required.

Once he'd passed the most superficial of defenses, he handed off the package, as was expected, then slid into his shimmer cloak, disappearing from sight to observe the staff's movements.

A guard stepped out for his break not more than ten minutes later, a bit of good fortune that would save the Ghalian a fair amount of time that would have otherwise been spent standing very still. An exceedingly boring necessity in this line of deadly work.

Pimbrak followed him, and a few minutes later, emerged from hiding wearing not only the man's uniform, but his face as well. Comfortably settled into his new disguise, he then casually slid right through the checkpoints—or *around* them, as was security's way—heading deep into the secured heart of the building.

Once inside, he maintained the disguise, should he absolutely need it, but opted instead to utilize his shimmer cloak, embracing the freedom of movement it afforded him. Invisibility had far more benefits than a mere disguise, and as a master of both, he moved quickly through the building, shifting between them as needed.

The lift discs leading to the uppermost floors were located in the heavily guarded lobby area of the estate tower, but he carefully slid through the space in his shimmer cloak, no one the wiser to his presence. More guards were on hand, doing all they could to appear busy.

Mareh Palmarian, the lady of the estate, was there, speaking with what appeared to be one of the senior guards. The man was rather heavily bandaged, despite having received magical healing the residual power of which he could feel still radiating from him. He must have been an important member of the guard to receive such a level of care.

Other unusual traces of activity remained in the area, more concentrated here than elsewhere. It was interesting, but from what Pimbrak could tell, a terrible fight had taken place here recently. And *inside* the visla's home, no less. It was no wonder security had been stepped up so dramatically.

But why wouldn't the visla have simply quelled the issue himself? Strange things were afoot.

The Wampeh assassin paused, listening to the conversation the woman was having with the injured man. It seemed that there had, indeed, been quite a fight. A group of disloyal men had been hiding among the ranks of the staff, and it had taken a great many lives to put down the uprising.

The man had apparently been protecting the visla's daughter when he was injured. It was on the topmost floors of the tower that she'd escaped from, heading out to the floating gardens high above to make her escape. How that had been accomplished, however, he was uncertain.

The teen's uncle *had* come to her aid, slaughtering those attempting to harm her with the utmost prejudice, but that was before he abruptly departed, leaving her in the tower where he believed she would be safe. But then a prisoner escaped, and the details got a bit fuzzy.

Pimbrak would leave that wrinkle in the story for later. While lingering and eavesdropping was interesting, he had a more important mission at hand. Leila, Charlie's woman, was quite possibly somewhere in the tower, and he was duty-bound to retrieve her. And Mareh and the guard had just inadvertently revealed where the cells were located.

High above.

He moved slowly, silent and utterly undetectable in his shimmer, as only Wampeh Ghalian of his caliber could be. He stepped away from the pair and cautiously wove through the milling guards, to the lift discs. There, however, he would have to wait. A lift disc abruptly rising without a passenger would draw notice.

A servant walked his way not long after, and Pimbrak carefully slid onto the lift they were heading toward just before they arrived, skillfully placing himself at the opposite end of the disc as it began its ascent. Bumping into the invisible man would spell the end for this person, and he wished to avoid any extraneous casualties if possible.

While he had no qualms about brutal slaughter, Pimbrak was not one for random violence. It was merely a fact of his life. A necessity of his job. But he didn't crave it. None of the Wampeh Ghalian did. If any showed that proclivity in their lengthy training, they would be disappeared, never heard from again.

The lift disc arrived at a relatively high floor. High enough to be within the visla's top-level defenses rather than outside of them. The penetration was complete. All that remained was to reach his final destination. The cell blocks likely to hold the woman who may or may not be Charlie's queen.

He stepped off the disc once the path was clear and took a careful look at his surroundings. From his knowledge of the building's layout, he knew there was a stairwell that would take him up the remaining flights with no obstacles.

Pimbrak quickly made his way that direction. This was going to be easier than expected, it seemed. And hopefully he'd find Charlie's woman. While getting her out of the building would be a bit more difficult, having scoped out all of the egresses, he already had four potential escape routes planned, and was working on a fifth.

Yes, things were going better than planned, but his senses

were heightened, looking for danger because of it. He'd been around long enough to know that was when they most often went wrong.

CHAPTER FORTY-FOUR

The topmost floors of Visla Palmarian's estate were a bit more heavily guarded than he'd anticipated, likely the result of the recent and quite unexpected fighting that had broken out within the building itself. As a result, several guards were patrolling the topmost level, where the cells were located. And one of them was powered. An emmik, he noted.

Pimbrak's rare genetics allowed him to essentially *smell* the power user's strength, the way a predator would sense their prey. This was a meal he'd gladly take, the additional power would be useful should he encounter any difficulties while trying to exit the building, though he didn't anticipate any. Of course, when they least expected was when they were most likely to appear.

He counted the number of men pacing the floor. Five, total. Four normal guards and the emmik. Then, with the speed and efficiency of one of his order, he quietly took down each of them with powerful stun spells, hiding their bodies in the floor's one storage chamber, taking care to conceal them from all but the most thorough inspections.

Then he focused his attention on the emmik. That one

would require a little more finesse. He wanted to take him down, but had to do so without setting off any alarms elsewhere in the building in the process.

Pimbrak stood stock-still against the wall, hidden in his shimmer cloak, a predator waiting to pounce. The emmik, to his credit, was alert as he walked the floor. Say what you may about the majority of guards and their propensity for boredom and carelessness, but *this* one took his job seriously. The Wampeh smiled. A worthy target, then.

The emmik paused as he walked, listening to the silence of the floor. Did he note the absence of the other guards' footfalls? If so, his defenses would be at the ready. The assassin would have to move quickly.

With great speed and focus, Pimbrak struck from within his shimmer without losing any of its protective cover. It was a skill very, very few possessed, but he'd trained long and hard in this, and it had paid off on numerous occasions, though it required a bit more power than he normally wanted to use. But with an emmik on the menu, any power expended would be replenished, and then some.

A powerful stun spell hit the unsuspecting emmik a split second before the Wampeh's fangs pierced his skin, the man greedily drawing the spell caster's power through his blood. A minute later, Pimbrak's thirst was sated, and he stashed the man's slumbering body with the others, drained but alive.

He was now free to survey the cells. If Charlie's woman was here, he'd find her, but he'd have to be fast. Undoubtedly, he'd have limited time before someone would notice the lack of guards checking in.

His stealthy skills were firing at full capacity as he approached the thick doors lining the corridor. The visla, it seemed, had enough enemies to warrant the highest of security facilities in which to house them.

When he slid open the slots to the first few cells, however, he found they were empty. He then found an older, recently shorn Ootaki, sitting docilely, staring at the wall. The man hadn't even noted the slot opening.

Pimbrak moved to the next cell and slid the slot open.

"Spinako!" he gasped, a rare break in concentration for one of his skill.

But this was a true shock. The Wampeh who had been taken into the cells in shackles and a hood at the same time Leila arrived was no ordinary man. He was a Wampeh Ghalian, and a very, very powerful one. He had also gone missing some time ago, assumed killed in the pursuit of his contract, as was a hazard of the job.

But here he was, pale, even for a Wampeh, his eyes showing none of their characteristic mirth and fire. The decision was as immediate as it was easy to make. Pimbrak would now be rescuing *two* instead of one.

Footsteps made him close the slot and step aside, hugging the wall, perfectly still and invisible in his shimmer cloak.

It was Mareh, the visla's wife. It seemed she was revisiting the site of her stepdaughter's disappearance. She walked down the hall, humming to herself, passing obliviously right by the assassin, then stopped at Spinako's cell. She quietly uttered the unlocking spell and pulled the door open, then stepped inside.

Pimbrak smiled under his shimmer cloak. She had just saved him the trouble of wasting magic breaking the locking spells. Silently, he followed her inside the cell. He'd simply stun her and leave her hidden. There was no reason to kill an innocent woman.

"You may as well give up without a fight," Mareh said, her back still to the open door.

Is she talking to me? the Wampeh wondered. But that was impossible.

"In case you're wondering," she said, turning and looking right at him, despite his shimmer, "yes, I am talking to you. I would have said something down in the lobby, but I was busy with one of my guards. And I know how your kind love to sneak around, so I thought I'd leave you to it for a while, until we could chat in private."

At that moment, Pimbrak realized he was in deep shit. Over his head and getting deeper, in fact. He didn't hesitate, pulling the just-stolen emmik's power and adding it to all the force his konuses and slaaps contained, throwing it at Mareh in a flurry of spells.

Mareh laughed as she batted the magic aside with ease, then cast her own spell. Just a single one. A powerful one that pinned him to the wall with amazing force.

She's so strong! Pimbrak realized, the unfamiliar sensation of panic welling slightly within him. He'd been the apex predator for so long, he'd forgotten what it felt like to be quite the opposite.

Before he could cast again, a spell slammed across his mouth like the hot pain from a large fist, sealing over it like a gag, preventing him from speaking the words of his spells. He was a master Ghalian and didn't have to say his spells in a loud voice, but, unlike Charlie and Ara, and even Bawb, now, Pimbrak still had to articulate a spell, however quietly, in order to cast it.

Mareh walked to the seated Wampeh, gently running her hand over his neck in an almost affectionate way. She paused, looking her new prisoner right in the eyes. He was pinned to the wall, and there was no way he could break free.

"I'm so glad you came. This one was just about dry," she said, fangs sliding into place as she smiled at him.

Mareh leaned down leisurely, then sank her fangs into the fading Wampeh's neck. He barely flinched. A minute later, he slumped to the ground, dead.

Pimbrak stared at her, utterly confused. This was impossible.

"I know what you're thinking," she said, wiping the blood from her lips. "How can a non-Wampeh possibly do this?" She fixed him with a look that was utterly calm, yet utterly terrifying at the same time. "Let's just say I've been draining your kind for a very, *very* long time."

CHAPTER FORTY-FIVE

Visla Malalia Maktan took a healthy drink from her fresh Wampeh blood supplier before leaving him in his new cell, stripped of all weapons, largely drained of his energy and utterly helpless. It would take a few days for him to fully recover his strength after she returned later for a second helping, though perhaps a bit less if he was particularly strong.

Malalia felt fantastic. There'd been an unexpected extra bit of power within the man, though he was obviously a master, himself. She recognized the magic flowing in her veins. One of her guards, tasked specifically with overseeing Leila and the others, was an emmik of some strength. And this Wampeh had drunk from him. And that power was now hers.

She really should thank her new guest, she mused. It would have been rude to drink from her own guard like that, but this Wampeh had provided her a perfectly acceptable means of taking his power for herself.

With a reluctant sigh, Malalia realized she should have someone go find the missing guards. They were undoubtedly stashed somewhere out of sight. No use leaving them in a closet or under a pile of containers, after all.

As for her former blood bag's drained corpse, she would leave that in her new toy's cell as a fun little reminder what his eventual fate would be. Like a cat toying with her food, she would do so not out of necessity, but simply because it amused her.

Malalia had been draining Wampeh of this sort for centuries, ever since she was thrown back across space and time in her terrible battle against Charlie and his surprisingly powerful friends back on ancient Earth nearly two thousand years ago. The cascading magic had blasted her through a rift back to her own galaxy.

Most would be glad to be home, but she quickly realized she had arrived back in her own realm decades after her previous departure. The portal had worked, sort of, but it had thrown her through time quite accidentally. But she now knew where this other galaxy was, and where the planet Earth was situated. All she needed was time to gather her power and make a move.

It turned out that the Council of Twenty had been overthrown in her absence, and the great Visla Malalia Maktan was long dead, so far as anyone knew, anyway. Her father's estate had fallen to disrepair, and her assets were gone. She was on her own.

With only the power carried within her, along with the menacing drive that accompanied it, she would have to rebuild from scratch. But she knew a thing or two that would help her on the way. Like where she'd hidden vast caches of Council wealth before expending so much magic in her pursuit of the Earthman.

The first few Wampeh had been relatively underpowered. But that was no matter. All she needed was enough of their gift to drain the lower level users she captured. In time, as her skill and magic grew, so, too, did the strength of her prey. But she couldn't very well continue to hunt them. Someone would eventually notice the number of disappearances.

It was then that she had decided to start a farm, of sorts, maintaining a handful of powered captives from whom she could feast. Many of them lived in bondage under her thumb for years. A few even lasted decades, allowed to replenish their strength, only to have it stolen from them over and over again.

The thing was, Bawb had been correct about her thirst all those years ago. Once she had started down that path, she could not stop. If she failed to consume Wampeh blood to maintain her ability to steal others' power, she would waste away and die.

So she bided her time and began slowly amassing power over the centuries. Two fictions were created in that time. The mysterious Visla Dominus as the power user pulling so many strings, and various iterations of the pleasant and unassuming woman who had become wife or lover of so many powerful men and women, all from whom she took what she needed in their sleep, leaving them weakened but functional.

It was what she'd been doing to Visla Palmarian for years, living in luxury while taking his power regularly. And his daughter's. Oh, that one had power, all right. Possibly even more than her father, though she'd never know it. Not with Malalia—Mareh to the girl—stealing it from her regularly, her simple enchantments wiping the child's memory and healing the wound every time.

Kara had always seemed a rather weak girl. It turned out, that wasn't exactly the case.

Malalia had been patiently gathering all the Ootaki hair she could find for centuries when she finally made her attempt on Earth. She could have sent the portal anywhere in that galaxy, but some part of her wanted to start with the conquest of Charlie's former planet, even though he'd be long dead when she placed its inhabitants under her yoke.

The joke, it seemed, was on her, though. It seemed almost too impossible a coincidence, that Charlie and his friends had somehow been thrown forward in time the same moment she had, but they'd gone even farther, arriving just months before her Trojan Horse attack began.

The universe apparently had a wicked sense of humor, and somehow her fate seemed eternally bound with the troublesome Earthman's. She had wondered for months now how that was possible. Hopefully, she'd have the power to cross over and get that answer for herself soon enough.

Malalia walked across the corridor to another cell. The one containing her childhood playmate. Her enemy's lover. Leila.

She'd proven herself surprisingly resilient on more than one occasion, but none more so than this most recent encounter. The olive-skinned woman actually possessed a Magus stone. And it was an incredibly powerful one at that. One of the legendary handful belonging to the Alatsav royals, no doubt. How she came to possess such a thing was a bit of a mystery, but Malalia had her theories.

In any case, it was magically bonded to the woman, and the more force Malalia used in her attempts to take it, the more it reacted, beating back her attacks at every turn. But Malalia had centuries of experiences to draw on now, and rather than simply try harder, as she might have in her youth, she had switched tactics and had been doing quite the opposite for some time, sending soothing, relaxing magic upon the stone in wave after wave, gradually lowering its defenses.

Leila looked up from her bunk as Malalia strode into her room, still unable to believe she was actually here. Of all the people to encounter all this time later, it was this woman she believed to be dead––and rightfully so––who was behind her torment yet again.

Malalia sized her prisoner up with an unnerving gaze, her eyes finally fixing on the green stone hanging around the woman's neck.

"How did you come to possess such a rare and beautiful thing?" she asked.

There was no sense lying, Leila thought. Any who might have been used against her were long dead. "It was my mother's. And her mother's before her," she answered.

"Hmm, you're telling the truth," Malalia mused. "I can smell a lie, you know. See it in your eyes."

Leila doubted that, but Malalia had certainly evolved into something far scarier than the last time she'd seen her so long ago. Who knew what she was truly capable of now?

"I assume your father kept it for you until you were old enough, am I correct? I know I never saw you wearing it back on my father's estate."

The lack of a reply told her she was right.

"Ah, poor Hertzall. A fair groundskeeper, but long dead, now. Nothing more than worm food, I'm afraid," Malalia taunted. "Just like my own father, because of you and your friends."

Leila may have been a prisoner, but she wasn't the helpless girl of their youth. And even if she had no weapons, she was not going to grovel at the feet of the likes of Malalia Maktan.

"From what I heard of that day, Malalia, it was *you* who killed your father. All so you could drink from him."

Malalia, surprisingly, didn't take the bait. She'd had hundreds of years to work through her feelings on that particular issue, and nothing Leila could say would have any effect.

"Not exactly," she replied with a smirk. "Though, thanks to a taste of your friend the Geist's blood, I developed the slightest hint of the ability to do as his kind do. To take another's power. Father must have known it was possible, the way he reacted when he heard of the encounter. A family genetic trait, perhaps. Regardless, I sourced more Wampeh with that gift, and with each I've drained, I've become that much stronger. Yet, despite all the power I've taken, your Magus stone is still resisting me."

"Funny, that," Leila sneered.

"Yes, indeed. But, you know, in my lengthy life, I've learned a thing or two."

"I bet you have."

"Such as the true nature of this particular stone. I've sensed its particular flavor of power before."

That surprised Leila.

"Ah, so you don't know," Malalia chuckled. "How delightful. The little slave girl had no idea she was descended from Alatsav royalty. Your grandmother, in fact, was taken as she was on her way to a gathering of the governing families. Captured by pirates. Enslaved. Sold off to the highest bidder. She was pregnant with your mother at the time. And when they were separated when she was a child, the stone must have traveled with her, all the way to my father's estate, where she met your dear Hertzall. And that brings us here," Malalia said, pushing an additional wave of soothing magic at the stone.

"You can't take it, Malalia. You already know, it cannot be forced from my neck," Leila spat.

"Oh, I do know. And I also know the stone is bonded to you by blood. However, I've been working a particular magic on it for some time now. The *opposite* of force, slowly, gently separating it from your bond," Malalia said, then walked up close, paused a second, then lifted the stone off of the prisoner's neck.

Leila gasped.

"But, how could you?"

"With patience, my dear," Malalia said with a wicked grin as she turned and walked to the door. "Now, if you'll excuse me, I'm having a new guest for dinner."

The thick door sealed shut, leaving Leila very confused, and very much alone in her cell.

Malalia studied the plain, green stone resting in her palm. She could sense no power from it at all. It may have been removed from Leila's neck, but it seemed their bond remained. She would have to keep the troublesome prisoner alive a bit longer. She may need her yet.

CHAPTER FORTY-SIX

In a small cluster of ships orbiting an uninhabited world, Captain Darus was monitoring the continued interrogation of the orange-skinned crew from the captured Urok ship.

The odd creatures often walked using their arms as well as legs, but the ranking members seemed to only walk upright. Perhaps it was a rank thing. Or perhaps a class one. In any case, it had unintentionally helped the Tslavar single out those of higher value for enhanced questioning.

Their ship was as unusual as its crew. It possessed not a single Drook to drive it, yet there was no Drookonus in their place. Instead, an odd energy located at the core of the craft appeared to be what they used for propulsion, though none had figured out exactly how they were able to do that. The energy did not seem to be magical in origin, and Captain Darus's top casters were at a loss.

As for the body of the ship, it was constructed of hard metals and glass, all blended into sharp angles, along with many heavy components. It was an inelegant design by most standards, but this ship wasn't from this galaxy, and for all Darus knew, it could be the pinnacle of Urok construction in that strange other realm.

Uroks. That was the name of the rather arrogant species piloting the vessel. They were found to be quite cock-sure and overconfident in their military prowess, puffing their chests and putting on a show of bravery and defiance upon waking in captivity. They were proud and strong.

When they were together, at least.

Separated, and slowly tortured, however, was a different matter entirely. The Uroks may have liked to *play* tough, but given enough time, they would break, just like everyone else eventually did.

They all cracked under the relentless magical barrage of Darus's top interrogators, one by one, but it was a lower-tier crewmember who finally gave them information of true value. Something that could change the course of the conflict, if he was telling the truth. And given what he'd just endured, that was almost guaranteed.

"We fly to Slafara at once," Captain Darus informed his crew.

"Destination, Captain?"

"The Palmarian estate."

The crew looked a bit confused.

"Uh, Captain? Shouldn't we be subtle?" his right-hand man asked. "Perhaps send a smaller, more discreet vessel?"

"No. Palmarian is on his deathbed, and Visla Dominus will soon control that entire system. We shall have no problems on Slafara. Fly us directly to the estate. I have urgent news for the visla that is too vital to be relayed by skree."

"Yes, Captain. The Drooks are prepping. We will jump momentarily."

Captain Darus lowered himself into his chair and awaited the first of the several jumps required to reach Slafara. Visla

Dominus would be pleased by this news. And when she was pleased, her most loyal servants were rewarded.

"Land atop the floating gardens," Captain Darus directed as his massive ship approached the Palmarian tower, casting a shadow across the city as it passed overhead.

Stealth was not a priority. Not anymore.

The vessel slowed to a stop as it reached its destination, halting in a low hover just above the uppermost garden. It would be but a short walk for the captain, and more importantly, this manner of arrival ensured he would bypass the many gatekeepers who habitually stuck their noses where they didn't belong.

He was here to see the visla, and with the news he had to share, there was no way he would allow anyone to get between them. Relaying his message would simply not happen. Not this time.

"I will tell the visla you have arrived, Captain Darus," one of Malalia's aides said as the Tslavar strode in from the garden.

"Do. I have crucial information for her. She will not wish me delayed."

"Of course, Captain," the aide said, then scurried away.

Just a few moments later, Visla Dominus stepped from her chambers and walked casually over to the good captain. She was particularly resplendent today, possessing even more of that healthy glow typically gracing her frame.

"Captain Darus," she said, pouring not one but *two* drinks from the small bar tucked against the wall. "Join me for a drink, won't you?"

He was on duty, but when Visla Dominus offered you a drink, you damn well accepted.

"Thank you, Visla," he said, taking a sip.

It was the good stuff. The *really* good stuff, he noted.

"So, I understand you have something of pressing importance you wished to share with me?"

"Yes, Visla. It's the crew of the captured Urok vessel."

"The ridiculous orange men, yes, I recall. What of them?"

"They finally broke."

"*Everyone* breaks, eventually," she said, echoing his own thoughts on the matter. "But that alone is not what brought you here. Tell me, what did you learn?"

"There is a thing these other-galaxy invaders possess called a *satellite*. It is a non-magical device that allows them to send and receive information, as well as leave messages for one another."

"Interesting," Malalia said, her interest piqued.

"That's not all, Visla. They have placed one in our galaxy. This satellite is being used as a relay point for information on the timing of the portal. They send a small craft through when it opens to update this device with the new schedule. That's how they've been able to so successfully utilize what appears to be a completely random pattern."

Now Malalia was *very* interested. "So, that's how they've been doing it," she mused. "And this satellite. It is somehow connected to the craft that was captured?"

"Yes. They utilize a thing called a 'comms relay' to interface with the device."

"And this relay, it still functions?"

"With one of the Urok crew manning the station aboard their ship, yes, I believe so."

"Most interesting. Do you know of its location?"

"Yes, Visla. It is hidden in plain view among the floating debris near the portal. Without any magical signature, we'd never have noticed it if not for these prisoners."

"At the portal, you say?" she said, surprised at its proximity.

"Yes, Visla. I can send word and have my men destroy it immediately, if you––"

"No. You will do nothing of the sort."

"Visla?"

"I have a far better idea," she said with a cold grin. "We won't destroy it. We will *use* it."

CHAPTER FORTY-SEVEN

"Mooooomm, quit it," Ripley whined.

"Oh, stop. I'm sure your new friends love seeing your baby pictures," Sarah said, pulling up another embarrassing image on her small tablet. "And it's a short flight. Isn't that right, Eddie?"

"You bet, Sarah," the AI replied.

Ripley remained unamused. "Dad, make her stop."

"Sorry, Rip, but you know it's not smart to cross your mother. I learned that lesson a *long* time ago," Finn replied with a chuckle.

"And that's why I love you," Sarah replied. "That and you feed me."

"One of my great pleasures in life," he said, flashing a smoldering look.

"Eww, Dad! Gross!"

"Oh, honey, we appear to be disturbing our daughter," Finn laughed.

With the AI piloting them for their little outing, Ripley's parents were freed up to harass their daughter at will. Kara and Vee were amused by the family's antics, and for all the whining, it was clear they cared for one another very deeply.

The outing had been a somewhat impromptu one, both inspired by Ripley's desire to show her friends the cool things about Earth, as well as her father's spying a perfect opportunity to whip up a feast of a picnic spread.

While Ripley had planned on taking Kara and Vee to somewhere really cool like New Singapore, her parents had other ideas. Reluctantly, she went along with the plan, knowing there was no way out once her folks had made up their minds.

The Grand Canyon.

Maybe it was impressive to people riding wagons across the continent, but for a kid who had an AI spaceship for a friend and had been to not only other planets, but even to another galaxy, the giant hole in the ground wasn't a big deal.

The alien girls weren't terribly impressed either.

"It's kind of like the ravine at Pendar," Vee said when they landed.

"I suppose," Kara replied. "But smaller." She turned a darker shade of violet as she realized she was being rude to her hosts. "Uh, but it's still really big. Wow," she added, unconvincingly.

"Fine, fine. Maybe it's not all that big compared to your space ravines," Finn joked. "But look at this place. Even if you're not impressed with the size of it, you have to admit, this is some damn pretty scenery."

In that he was absolutely correct, and, to his surprise, the girls paused and looked out across the landscape with a different perspective.

"Yeah, I guess it is," his teen agreed.

For all her quirks, Ripley was a very thoughtful girl, and a swell of pride briefly grew in his chest. That pressure quickly shifted to his stomach, though, and in a matter of minutes Finn had an impressive picnic spread out for their afternoon repast, which they made quick work of before finally piling back into Eddie for the trip home.

As the ship's doors closed, Finn and his wife shared a happy smile. All in all, it was turning into a really nice day.

While the AI ship on the surface was flying toward Los Angeles, another ship far above was lining up just outside the bubbling surface of the sun. The portal was scheduled for a routine communications update, which the little craft would carry out, popping over to the other side of the portal for just long enough to transmit the message to the hidden satellite, retrieve whatever messages had been left for them, then hustle back across to Earth-side.

The whole thing would take less than a minute. Piece of cake.

The portal began to open, but as it slid free of the sun, a massive surge of enemy ships suddenly poured through, blasting magical attacks all around them. The waiting fleet was ready, however, and they engaged in an instant, the skies above the sun abruptly turning into a full-fledged battle.

Several of the magic ships pulled clear of the railgun fire enough to jump away while the others fought. They'd simply have to be tracked down later. Zed was pretty sure each of them had been hit with a tracking round, though he'd save confirmation for *after* the battle.

Sid's forces at Dark Side base scrambled into action, the defensive fleet quickly taking up their position, all weapons aimed toward the distant sun.

"What's going on, Zed?" Sid asked from the moon.

"An attack, and a big one at that," Zed replied. "Bastards are sending the damn kitchen sink through."

"Can you nuke them on the other side?" Sid asked, though loathe to resort to such a tactic.

"Nope. No can do," Zed replied. "I still don't have intel back, and I can't go sending nukes through willy nilly until I know for sure what's on the other side." Zed shifted his focus, reaching out to the woman who just so happened to be present for this clusterfuck of an event. "Rika, I need you to switch to a new timing, and quick!"

"On it," she replied, turning to Jo, who had already completed the task and sent it to the nearest drone. "Ready to go, Zed."

The little drone raced forward, dodging the heavy fire of the battle and crossing over the portal. It was a dumb ship––no AI on board. A piece of equipment they could spare.

"Close it, Rika!"

Rika cast her magic immediately, lowering the portal back into the sun, but not before one of the ships that had jumped away returned and swooped back through to the other side.

"One got through," she called out.

"But the others can't come across. We've limited their attack. Now take these fuckers down!" Zed commanded.

"Don't have to tell me twice," Rika replied, then dove the *Fujin* into battle, guns blazing.

The invading forces were diverse in the craft employed in this attack. There were larger ships, but also smaller, fast-moving ones as well, and they were wreaking havoc on the defensive firing solutions so carefully laid out.

"Don't let them––" Rika began, but it was too late.

Tslavar ships began jumping away, and judging by the comms traffic they were receiving, the enemy hadn't gone far.

"I'm spinning us around, Jo," Rika said. "These guys can handle what's up here."

"Where are we going?"

"Following the rest of the fleet. Back to Earth."

CHAPTER FORTY-EIGHT

Rika and Jo warped to Earth pursuing the invading forces. A few of them were actually shimmer-cloaked, but as the tattoos around Rika's eyes began to glow, the captains of those ships relying on magic camouflage would find it did them no good at all as she blasted them out of the sky.

"You're getting pretty good at that," Jo said as Rika channeled some of her unusual magic into the weapons systems. "Whatever you're doing, it's playing merry hell with their shielding."

She was indeed causing problems for the invaders, but that didn't change the fact that there were simply too many for her to handle on her own. Sid had sent some ships to intercept as best they could, and Cal had the terrestrial forces launched and ready, but these Tslavars were a wily bunch.

Fortunately, Joshua and Freya were nearby, the duo happily tag-teaming as they knocked ship after ship from the sky. Arlo and Marty were there too. It was Marty's first real battle, and, despite being busy with their own dogfights, Freya and Joshua kept a close eye on their electronic offspring. Heaven help any who actually harmed him.

Another even younger ship was racing into the fray as well, but this one had a shimmer merged with his frame. All he had to do was engage it and they'd be free to take down the enemy ships. Eddie rushed ahead, weapons hot as he focused on his shimmer spell.

"Sorry, but we don't have time to land and drop everyone off," Eddie informed his passengers. "Buckle up, things are gonna get a bit rough up here. It should smooth out once my shimmer is––"

Eddie was rocked by a blast of magic that sent him tumbling end over end before he could engage his shimmer. Another craft, also shielded by shimmer magic, had gotten the drop on them just before they could slip from sight.

Spiraling downward far faster than he would have liked, Eddie plummeted to Earth, engaging his emergency thrusters at the last second, changing a bone-breaking crash into merely a hard landing.

"Uncle Cal! Eddie's down! We need help," Ripley called over comms, unsure if the message was getting through.

"Multiple systems are down," Eddie announced. "Oh, no. Oh, shit. You need to get outside," he said, a slight note of panic in his voice.

"What's going on, Eddie?" Ripley asked with obvious concern.

"I'm having some sort of cross-reaction with my konus and the warp core. Whatever that ship hit me with, it's playing a number on my systems, and I don't know what it's going to do."

"Damn. They're learning our systems," Ripley said.

"Seems that way. Now, you need to hurry up and get away from me."

"Don't you go blowing up on me, Eddie."

"Not my intention, Rip. But you need to go. Now!"

Ripley and the others bailed out of the downed ship but found themselves immediately caught in an intense barrage of ground fire. The Tslavar forces that were hurling magic at them were ignoring the ship, it seemed. That, at least, was in their favor, because if Eddie could right his systems, he could reactivate his weapons and lay waste to the ground forces.

But that wasn't happening. Not yet, anyway, and they had to defend themselves in any manner possible.

A few spells shook the downed ship.

"I've got ya, Eddie. Just keep working on your systems!" Ripley called out to her friend as she slipped her konus onto her wrist.

"What are you doing, Rip?" Kara asked from behind a low wall.

"We've got to buy Eddie some time!" the teen replied, then began casting the limited spells in her arsenal.

Encountering tech was the one thing they'd been prepared for, but the Tslavars quickly shifted the focus of their assault to the lone magic-wielder on the battlefield. The teenage girl.

Ripley was actually casting pretty well, and Vee and Kara couldn't help but admire their new friend's courage in the face of such a dangerous enemy. But the Tslavars had more experience in this sort of thing, and they shifted their style of attack from purely magical to a combination of magic and hurled debris, hoping to overcome any shielding spells the troublesome girl might be casting.

Ripley was learning, but she was not a combat-ready spellcaster by any means. She shifted on her heels and desperately tried to put up a defensive spell, but a flying wall of broken concrete and debris smashed through her magic, slamming right into her and sending her tumbling.

"Ripley!" Finn bellowed, rushing from cover, ignoring the bits of rock smashing around him. He got to her quickly, sliding to the ground and gently cradling Ripley's bloody head in his lap, hot tears welling in his eyes.

Sarah's carefully placed weapons' fire abruptly shifted from defensive shots designed to keep a greater number of attackers at bay to a rage-driven, all-out assault. Finn, seeing his wife rush into the fray, carefully laid Ripley's bloody body back on the ground and charged after her, knives appearing in his hands from sheaths none had even known he'd been wearing.

Finn, it seemed, was armed to the teeth, and sharp metal was flying true, taking down Tslavar mercenaries left and right as his wife blasted her way close to the enemy forces. A married couple engaged in a deadly choreographed dance. They knew each other's every move, and the coordinated carnage they wrought was awesome in the original sense of the word.

The green men began to realize that perhaps their numeric advantage wasn't really as much an advantage as they'd originally believed. It was of little consequence, though. They wouldn't have to worry about that much longer.

Kara and Vee watched in amazement as Ripley's mom's nanite replacement arm finally did something more than simply look like an arm. The flesh tone vanished, replaced by the nanites' natural charcoal gray, and her hand had transformed into a lengthy and deadly spike with which she was impaling the men who'd harmed her baby in a most violent fashion.

Finn, likewise, was a tornado of flashing blades, his arms moving so fast the silver glint of metal took on the appearance of a frenzied school of fish. Only this time it left behind a trail of chum in the form of slaughtered Tslavars.

Green blood coated both of them from head to toe, the sight unsettling even to the most seasoned of their adversaries. This pair was death, and it was coming for them all.

The mercenaries were running low on numbers, but they had one hidden ace up their sleeve. Their shimmer ship, which should be moving into position any––

Eddie, though unable to fly, fired off several railgun sabots, the cloaked Tslavar ship bursting to pieces, the remaining crew torn to bits in the vessel's collapse.

Moments later, the battlefield—at least this section of it—was calm. Kara looked at the downed ship with wonder. "You're not magic. How did you see them?"

"I didn't," Eddie replied. "But I saw one of those bastards exit their ship to join the others. Idiot gave away their position when he did that, so I got a bead on them and lit 'em up. Bastards deserved far worse."

Kara turned to see Sarah, streaked with gore, running back to her broken daughter. Ripley was breathing, but her injuries were grave. It was obvious she likely wouldn't survive the day.

"Noooo, my baby," Sarah wailed, lifting her daughter into her arms.

Finn fell to his knees beside her, a look of utter grief creasing his face into a mask of despair.

"What's that?" Vee asked, staring hard at Ripley's neck. Right where Sarah's hand was cradling her.

The woman's nanite limb was moving, shifting of its own accord, and, amazingly, so was Ripley's skin. She had more nanites within her than she knew, apparently, and they were reacting to her mother's presence.

The two swarms merged as a glimmering, iridescent stream ran across them.

"The waters," Sarah muttered. "The nanites took some and stored it."

She watched in awe as the tiny machines ferried the healing liquid to their counterparts, who then hurried it into the injured girl's body. The nanites, it seemed, knew what the waters could do.

Almost immediately Ripley began to rouse as her painful broken bones were forcefully drawn back into alignment and healed, stitched together along with the connective tissue surrounding them. Vee had heard of the water's power before, but only in legend. She'd never dreamed of seeing it in action.

Ripley, quite against all odds, was going to survive.

A violent blast shook the air, and a spray of green blood and gore showered them all.

"What the hell?" Finn blurted as they all turned in wonder.

What they found was even more of a surprise. Kara, hands outstretched, her eyes huge with shock at what she'd just done.

"He–he was coming to hurt you," she said of the Tslavar mercenary who was now dispersed over a ten-meter area.

Ripley was going to be okay, but now there was another young woman in need of help. Finn got to his feet and walked over to her, gently putting his hands on her shoulders, trying to look her in the eye. But Kara kept staring at her wrists in disbelief.

"What's she doing?" Finn asked, looking to her Ootaki friend.

Vee realized what she was staring at, and it was no wonder Kara was freaked out after a display of power like that.

"She's not wearing a konus," Vee told them, her eyes as wide as her friend's. "That was all her. And it was *massive*."

CHAPTER FORTY-NINE

When the battle had breached the atmosphere, everyone on the ground became immediately aware of the incoming hostilities, even if they hadn't paid attention to the warnings every AI across the planet was sending out. For some, however, it was not a moment of fear, but rather, one of excitement.

Grundsch was sitting with Bahnjoh and Baloo atop the bluffs overlooking the ocean and doing a very un-Ra'az thing. He was meditating.

A soft-spoken woman with almond eyes had come to visit him. Fatima was her name, and she had something of a knack for getting into your head. Even *his* head, which was particularly tough to crack. But something about her words resonated with him, and after she took her leave, he grudgingly decided to attempt the foolish mind-calming practice she'd recommended.

Amazingly, he took to it, finding himself at peace for the first time in years. He slowly came around to accepting that this was a very, very different life than any he'd ever known, but it was a life worth living. And that was enough for him.

The sonic boom of a ship's entry through the exosphere

jarred him instantly to his feet, adrenaline rising as he readied for whatever might come his way.

"Oh, that's interesting," he said as he realized there was fighting high above.

He recognized the tell-tale signs of a magical attack. These invaders were from the other galaxy. The one where he'd been enslaved for so many years. And now, they were here, in *his* part of the universe. And they were threatening it.

"Best get to cover, boys," he said to the pair of massive animals sitting attentively beside him. "Things are going to get rough, and neither of you can be of any use in this fight."

Bahnjoh and Baloo whined, as if they understood on some level that they were being kept from the fight. Grundsch chuckled at their cocked heads.

"Of course, if a ship were to be forced down, *then* there might be some quarry for you to pursue."

The two perked up. Whether it was his words or the tone of his voice he was unsure, but whatever the case, he had little reason to worry about the canine duo. They might just get to hunt after all, and if one or both should fall in the process, at least it would be in glorious battle.

Something he very much needed to get engaged in.

Grundsch raced to the nearest loop tube accessway and descended to the tunnel system, selecting the appropriate destination. The spaceport. While he was not rated to fly any Earth or magical craft, there were still a good many captured Ra'az vessels parked there. Mothballed and left to the elements, but still intact. If their cores had been left in place, a few decades of dust would be no issue whatsoever.

The tube pod shot across the transit network below the city, quickly bringing him to his destination. The gates to the storage area were locked, but for one his size, that didn't pose much of a problem.

Grundsch snapped the lock and hurried into the boneyard

area of long-stored craft. A pair of menacing cannons swung into place high above, both barrels locking on him as a familiar voice boomed out over the attached loudspeakers.

"What do you think you're doing, Grundsch?" Cal asked. *"This is a restricted area you've just broken into."*

The weapons didn't fire, but the deadly cannons remained firmly locked on target.

Grundsch ignored them, standing tall, chest out and back straight. "I am defending my home," he replied. "These are magical vessels. Tslavar ships. And they are in desperate need of removal from this airspace."

Cal paused a moment, weighing the alien's words, while also monitoring his vitals for any sign of deception. A second later the cannons powered down and swung back into their cradles.

"You'll want the fourth on the left. Its drive and weapons systems are the best of the old Ra'az craft still stored here. Good hunting," Cal said.

"Oh, it will be," Grundsch said with a grin, then raced to the waiting ship.

It had been ages since he'd even seen a Ra'az heavy raider, let alone stepped inside of one, but muscle memory kicked in the moment he set foot on its cool deck. The ship smelled of battle, long ago. A familiar scent, and one that made the Ra'az feel both saddened at the loss of his hivemates, but glad for the opportunity to be of use for a change. Of *real* use, not just as an intimidating bodyguard.

This was what he'd been born and bred for, and the violence he'd unleash on behalf of his new home would be glorious.

He powered up the ship's systems, running a rapid check of the most vital ones. Good enough for his purposes, he was pleased to note. He then tightened his restraining harness and punched it, blasting up into the sky, weapons hot as he joined the fight with his new allies.

This place may not have been his hive, and his queen was

long dead, but he'd been given an opportunity to call this place home. And with that acceptance came something surprising. An unusual and unexpected sense of joy. Happiness at being part of something bigger than himself once again.

Grundsch swung his ship into the fray, targeting the enemy with great precision. He'd not lost his skills, he was pleased to note. And now he would rain death and destruction upon these Tslavar intruders.

He'd never liked the green men. Not once in all the time he had been in Visla Palmarian's service. And now, with the utmost of enjoyment, he had free rein to blast them from the sky.

Had anyone been watching in the Ra'az ship's cockpit, they might have been a little unsettled by the look of sheer joy plastered on the enormous alien's face as he unleashed the firepower at his command. This was glorious battle, and against a foe he was more than happy to engage.

He flew well, and the enemy found themselves susceptible to his weapons if enough bursts hit their shielding in rapid succession. And that was exactly what he was doing. Peppering their shields until they failed, slipping a few more deadly rounds into that gap before peeling off and targeting another ship, leaving the crippled one to plummet to Earth.

It wasn't a full-on mindless battle frenzy. That only happened in hand-to-hand combat among his kind, and rarely at that. But it was a glorious violence just the same. With an enormous grin, Grundsch dove into the thick of it, content that whether he lived or died on this day, it was a glorious way to achieve either result.

CHAPTER FIFTY

The incoming Tslavar mercenary craft had spent the initial part of their attack surveying the major city centers of Earth and determining which would be best for their transition to a ground occupation attempt.

An area with a larger population along with a properly configured city would make defense by the natives more difficult. It was for this reason Los Angeles was one of the targeted cities of priority.

Several invading ships had already been shot from the sky as they attempted to strafe the ground to provide their smaller troop carriers a clear place to land and deposit their men. Fortunately, the AI defenders were exceptional at monitoring all of the vessels in the air. If a ship was one of Earth's or its allies, they were safe. From friendly fire, at least.

But some of the Tslavars had managed to land, and not only their shimmer ships. The resulting wave of ground forces in the streets of downtown was enough to keep not only the city's autocannons active, but also the residents, all of whom had been armed since the first attack.

"Get up there and kick some ass," Rika instructed her

gunner/co-pilot as she dropped to the guarded section of the spaceport and jumped from her seat.

"You sure about this?" Jo asked.

"Yeah. Someone needs to cover the residents. I've got this. You take the *Fujin* and stop any more of them from getting to the ground. And maybe call Marban and his buddies and see if they can lend you a hand."

"All right. Be careful, Rika."

"Never. Now get out of here," the pilot shot back with a grin, then raced out of the ship and across the tarmac to her waiting ride.

Rika jumped up into the cockpit of her parked mech and powered it up, both with the onboard power cells, courtesy of her cyborg friends, as well as her own magic.

"Ooh, yeah, boy! That's what I'm talking about," she said with a happy laugh as the dual-powered mech lurched to its feet without putting much of a strain on her magic at all.

Sergeant George Franklin's little modification was paying off, indeed, allowing Rika to keep more of a focus on her casting than on powering the mech. Of course, she could switch her magic in an instant if needed, but for the time being she was able to use the power cells and keep her magic free to shield herself from attacks.

The mech rumbled down the street, kicking the few Tslavars foolish enough to attempt to physically attack the metal giant when their magic failed. Perhaps if they could get close to the cockpit high up on the mech's torso they might be able to stun the machine's pilot, but as it stood, they were getting their asses kicked, sometimes literally, by the huge mech.

Rika was in a groove, her magic finely tuned in to defend against all magic attacks thrown at her. And the mech was operating flawlessly, providing the locals the opportunity to flee the attacking forces as she engaged them with the newly installed weapons systems.

What had started as a simple geologic survey mech had evolved into a full-fledged battle mech.

"Why didn't we think to do this earlier?" Rika wondered as the Tslavars beneath her scattered as she gleefully unleashed bursts of plasma fire. "Aww, yeah. I'm gonna kick some serious––"

She was abruptly cut off by a massive impact, her mech slammed hard and thrown to the ground, pinned beneath an enormous weight. It hadn't been an attack that had hit her, though, but a crashing shimmer ship, its camouflage failing from all the damage it had sustained before it fell from the sky.

That it had managed to steer into the giant machine as it crashed was testament to its pilot's skill. It also highlighted the one major flaw in Rika's defenses. With energy cells powering the mech, she had diverted all of her magic to her shielding, and as she was facing Tslavars, it was all tuned to block magic.

A crashing ship, though carrying magic users, was most definitely *not* a magical attack.

The mech was designed for the rigors of work in the harsh environment of Mars all those years ago, and its reinforced framework is what saved Rika from being crushed to death. The metal giant was hopelessly pinned, however, the weight of the crashed ship far more than its straining hydraulics could hope to lift.

Dazed and more than a little concussed, Rika popped the emergency hatch and crawled free. Her boots wobbled as they hit the rubble-strewn ground.

"Why am I wet?" she wondered, running her hand across her forehead.

The glistening red answered that question.

"Fuck. Really?" she grumbled.

Whether it was shock, a concussion, or the knowledge that the head tended to bleed a lot even if it was a small and superficial injury, was not important. What was, however, was the blast of magic she sent out, knocking the Tslavars foolish enough to press in for an attack to the ground. At least for the moment.

"Come on, you. Get off my baby," she groaned as her magic strained to lift the ruined shimmer ship atop her mech. "Damn it! Jo, I'm down. Repeat, I'm down. My mech's stuck, and I'm in some deep shit here. Jo? You copy?"

There was no reply to her comms, but the unit had taken quite a beating in the crash. Whether it worked or not was questionable at best.

"Fine," she grumbled, pulling the pistol from her hip and firing off several shots. "Let's do this."

The mercenary forces had paused after her initial show of magic, but the woman was hurt and bleeding. In her weakened state, they could take her. The attackers fanned out, moving in several groups to try to create a flanking crossfire of magic and debris.

Rika's magical defenses were holding, but wavering. A shockwave of magic from above knocked her to her knees, but the magic held. Barely. But the ship that had strafed her position from above was circling back around.

A series of potent spells abruptly rocked it from above. They'd been cast from quite a distance, and their potency was greatly reduced for it, but they nevertheless forced the Tslavar ship to peel off in a defensive maneuver.

Rika looked up. "That wasn't Jo. That was magic," she mused as she caught sight of a blazing orange shape hurtling toward her from orbit.

Apparently, whoever was piloting that ship was in too much of a hurry to re-enter the atmosphere at a proper angle, the resulting friction making for quite a colorful display. She saw a small shape separate from the craft, racing toward her location, just before her shielding shook and she was forced to redirect even more power to her defenses.

271

Her concussion must have been worse than she thought, because casting was getting difficult. She just wanted to take a nap and wake up when the fighting was done.

"No, Rika, that's not an option," she said, forcing herself to focus.

The mercenary forces smelled blood in the water. Their prey was weakening. This was their chance to strike. As a unit, they emerged from cover and began rushing the outnumbered woman. Had they taken the time to look up, they might have realized this was a bad idea.

The small pod was still orange-hot from its rapid descent when it slammed into the ground far harder than it was designed for, despite its braking spell. The impact killed a few of the Tslavars outright, the rest hesitating for a second too long as their brains tried to process what just happened.

A hatch sprang open, and a devastating barrage of pulse rifle fire sprayed forth, tearing into the mercenary ranks as the man firing them burst from the craft, bellowing like a raging berserker as he rushed onto the battlefield.

Marban was a force of devastating power, a pirate captain of quite some skill, now unleashing all of his tricks upon his enemy. Rika shook her head, clearing the cobwebs as she stared in disbelief. He was wearing *two* konuses, despite the risk, but rather than using them for offensive spells, she realized he was wearing them as shielding, while the Earth tech was laying waste to the Tslavars.

Several powerful spells rocked him, but the konuses absorbed most of it. He was staggered nonetheless, but kept firing as he raced to Rika's side. Rika forced herself to focus, casting defenses as well as she rushed to meet her unlikely savior. The look of concern in his eyes at the blood on her head was quickly replaced with one of sheer fury as he redoubled his firing, daring the enemy to even try to take a piece of what he had for them.

The enemy fell back a moment to regroup, allowing him a brief chance to better assess Rika's injuries.

"Not too bad," he said, noting the shallowness of the lacerations to her scalp. "Had me worried there."

Dazed, and with a moderate concussion, Rika's emotions were, for once, totally unguarded. She looked at the man who had rushed to her aid without her usual emotional mask in place. Her eyes betrayed all he needed to see.

A happy warmth blossomed in Marban's chest, the knot in his stomach evaporating. He flashed her a little wink, then turned his attention back to the battle as the Tslavars tried once more to make a move. They were close, and a fair number, but the tide was turning in favor of the human and her space pirate protector.

Rika managed to keep her casting in place as she pulled a slingshot, of all things, from a pouch on her hip.

"Really?" Marban asked. It was such a ridiculous implement to wield in battle, he couldn't help but chuckle. "You must be more concussed than I originally thought."

Rika ignored him, pulling a small, spiked wooden dart from a case on her belt. Marban reached out to examine the utterly ridiculous weapon.

"Don't touch!" Rika chastised him, slapping his hand away. "Just watch."

She loaded the spiked dart into the pouch of the slingshot and took aim. Marban was about to make another wisecrack when she let the dart fly. It would sting, sure. But in battle? It was ridiculous.

The Tslavar she'd aimed for shrieked in pain and fell to the ground, convulsing.

"What in the worlds?" Marban said, truly amazed.

"Made from a special wood given to me by the Kalamani people. Magical plants from this galaxy. Very toxic to people from yours. And apparently, Tslavars are *especially* sensitive to it," Rika said with a grin.

Marban grinned right back at her, adoration in his gaze. This was turning out to be a fascinating, and quite unexpected day.

"Shall we?" he asked, gesturing to the remaining, and now quite hesitant enemy.

"Yeah. Let's finish this," she replied, and the two set to work, slowly clearing the remaining mercenaries from the streets, with the help of a few armed residents, who now felt brave enough to join the fight.

In short order, the pocket of attackers were no more.

CHAPTER FIFTY-ONE

In the safety of the training facility on Chaldra, Bawb, Hunze, and Zilara were surrounded by scores of Wampeh Ghalian come to meet the legendary Geist, as well as receive some of the deadly booty retrieved from the long-lost Ghalian cache.

It was as close to a reunion or family picnic as the secretive order had ever seen. Never were so many of their members present in the same place. But these were exceptional times, and they were about to face off against an exceptional enemy. It was only natural that things might be a bit out of their normal parameters.

The most powerful of the weapons retrieved from the vault on Otsola were distributed to the masters first, well before the others even began to arrive. Handing over a claithe and other incredibly deadly items was something best done in as secure a location as possible.

And while they trusted their brothers and sisters with their lives, the masters had their own set of rules they lived by. Among them, always assume the worst and be prepared for it. It was akin to an adage Charlie had told Bawb once during a particularly trying time as king.

"Expect the worst, hope for the best, prepare for both," the Earthman had said. It was a sentiment Bawb could support.

But now, as the enchanted blades found their way to deserving homes, and slaaps and konuses of great destructive power met their new owners, he was beginning to feel that today would be a day of the best. And it was about time, given the trials and tribulations he and his friends had been through thus far.

Dukaan had been a bit of a shocking sight for the visiting Wampeh. An outsider being allowed into the training facility was an extremely rare occurrence. But this one was cleared by the highest masters.

Then they saw the Ootaki. A woman who was actually a Ghalian herself. It was utterly unprecedented. And the armored vest the Geist wore contained an enormous length of her hair. It was all most unusual.

Fortunately, Hunze had a way with people that applied to deadly assassins as well as average men and women on the street. In no time, she was chatting quite socially with several of the fascinated Wampeh, sharing stories, and even participating in a friendly exchange of martial techniques.

She had decided to leave the vespus blade gifted her by Bawb when they were gathering their prize from the Ghalian vault aboard Kip, not wanting to cause a stir with a non-Wampeh possessing such an item. At least, not until they'd gotten to know her better and were confident in her place among them.

Nearly twenty assassins were casually discussing the new plan for their order when the building abruptly shook to its foundation, despite the decades upon decades of protective spells layered upon it like an enormous jawbreaker of safety.

"What is that?" Dukaan asked. "I thought nothing could get through your shielding here."

"None can," Zilara gasped. "None should be able to."

"Kip, what is going on up there?" the Chithiid asked over his comms.

"There's a huge ship out here is what," the AI replied. "One of Visla Dominus's no doubt. And it's beating the hell out of that building you're in. You need to get out of there."

Bawb and Zilara shared a concerned look as the building rocked violently.

"Everyone, we are abandoning this facility," she called out. "You know what to do."

Without a second's hesitation every last Wampeh sprang into action, gathering everything tied to the order and rushing to a plain wall in the training arena. Zilara stepped to the front of the queue and cast a lengthy and powerful spell the likes of which few had ever heard. And for good reason. This sort of thing simply did not happen.

Except for today.

The wall began to flicker, then dissolve, revealing a short-range portal, powered by the secret cache of powerful Ootaki hair set into the walls of the building itself. An escape route of last resort. Given the likelihood that it was Visla Dominus himself attacking them, it seemed that time had come to employ it.

The portal would only remain open a few minutes at most, the amount of power it required to transport the fleeing assassins only as far as an adjacent town was enormous, and it was being used up at a dangerously fast rate.

The other masters levitated the remaining cases containing the Ghalian wealth of magical power and escorted them through the portal.

"Go with them, Dukaan," Bawb commanded.

"But what about you? The building?" the Chithiid asked as he watched the other Wampeh silently gather their gear, as well as all of the facility's items they could carry, then step through the portal to safety.

"It is just a building. Nothing that cannot be replaced. And we have many other facilities, my friend."

"But how did they find this one? And who has this kind of power?"

Bawb hesitated. "Dominus," he finally said. "Which is why we must flee now. If he's onto our taking up arms against him, we must face him on our terms, not his. Now, go! Have Kip meet us at the portal's exit point. We'll be right behind you."

Dukaan paused a moment, then gathered up his pack and hurried through the portal. Zilara took the remaining pupils, ushering them through, when another massive spell blasted the building. The walls all around them began to crumble, including the one on which the portal had been constructed.

"Go!" Bawb shouted to Zilara.

"Find us," she called back, diving through the portal before the Ootaki hair powering it was crushed by the falling wall.

Bawb called upon the power stored within Hunze's hair inside his vest and began casting with all his might, holding the building up so that they might escape. Hunze, too, did the same, layering her magic with his, and even casting counter-spells at Visla Dominus above as she did. It wasn't going to kill him, but it just might buy them time enough to get clear of the building.

With all of the power she'd absorbed from her recent proximity to the sun's rays as they streamed through the portal to Earth, Hunze had so much power flowing through her, Bawb couldn't help but be in awe of it. And her proficiency with spellcasting was ever growing, her counterattacks gaining in strength as the pair hurried toward the surface egress.

Malalia Maktan, aka Visla Dominus, was already descending to the surface in a small shuttle craft when the counter-spells began to hit. She smiled, her fingers caressing the Magus stone she now wore around her neck. It wouldn't work for her, of course. That much was clear. But chained beside her was Leila, and with her, a risky plan.

Bawb was the first to crawl to freedom, pushing aside a heavy, toppled beam and stepping into the open air. Hunze was just a few steps behind him, casting mighty spells as she moved.

The Geist hurried ahead, scanning for any threats, ensuring a clear path for his love. She was preoccupied with her casting and would be hard pressed to defend herself while doing so.

He quickly dispatched a few Tslavar mercenaries who had taken up positions near the building. They'd hoped to ambush any fleeing Wampeh Ghalian. They should have known better.

Bawb wiped the blood from his blade and turned to check Hunze's progress. That was when he saw something that made even his blood chill.

"Malalia?" he gasped, drawing his wand to deliver a brutal attack, collateral damage be damned.

But there was someone with her. Someone at her side he could not bring himself to harm. Leila.

From her blocked vantage point, Hunze, however, had no idea their friend was there, nor did she know it was Malalia Maktan somehow back from the grave to haunt them. Hunze just scrambled free of the building, firing off her most potent attacks yet as she let the structure behind her collapse.

"Hunze, no!" Bawb called out.

The green stone around Malalia's neck began to glow, and she flashed a cruel smile. Bawb knew all too well what this could mean.

He was not a coward, he was a survivor. There was no way he could possibly stop Malalia if she possessed Leila's Magus stone, even with his wand. So he did the only thing he could do, though it pained him to do so. He turned and ran.

He ran fast, casting defenses behind him with all the power of his wand and the Ootaki hair he carried. He just hoped it would suffice. Hunze also began to run, but unlike Bawb, who had managed to dive into a thick-walled building at the last second, she was unprotected and in the open. He tried to encompass her with his spells, but she was just out of reach.

The Magus stone flared bright, a huge burst of power blasting out, knocking Hunze, and everyone within the spell's reach, to the ground, unconscious as it shook the buildings for miles.

"Nooo!" Leila shrieked, realizing the stone had only reacted because of her proximity, thinking she was the one being attacked.

Malalia pulled her restraints, hurrying her along with her as she rushed to the building Bawb had taken cover in. She kicked in the door, ready to smite him, but he was gone. Somehow, he had quite impossibly managed to protect himself enough to remain unharmed. Or at least, enough to make his escape.

She sent her men out on the off chance they'd find the assassin, but she didn't think it likely. But that didn't concern her at the moment.

"The men don't see him, Visla," a mercenary reported.

"It is of no matter," she cooed, running her fingers through the unconscious Ootaki's golden hair.

The sheer quantity of it was astounding. The same bitch who had given half of it to that troublesome Wampeh. That was probably how he evaded the Magus stone's spell. But this one didn't know that trick, and now she belonged to Malalia.

She plucked a single hair from Hunze's head, intending to sample the tangible power the woman was all but radiating. The hair flashed bright, then went dark, the power vanishing from the strand like an extinguished flame, the energy drifting back into Hunze herself.

This was different. Malalia had never seen its like before. The Ootaki herself was linked inexorably to her hair, and apparently, she knew how to use it. This was troublesome. She couldn't simply harvest her as was her usual protocol. No, this one would have to be kept alive and unshorn. For the time being anyway. And she would have to be kept under deep magical sedation lest she wake and start casting on her own.

Malalia knew she could just gag the woman, but something told her that if the Ootaki was in control of her own power, then there was a very good likelihood she didn't need to speak to cast. And in her experience, it was far better to be safe rather than sorry.

She focused her magic on the unconscious woman, blasting her with another stun spell to ensure the she stayed that way for a good long while.

"Bring her," she commanded, then dragged the teary-eyed Leila back to her ship.

CHAPTER FIFTY-TWO

Far away, in another system entirely, a multi-pronged assault was underway. With the intel forcibly pried from her captured Wampeh blood donor, Visla Dominus had learned much of the plans against her. And with that information, also came the locations of several key elements before Pimbrak somehow managed to cast a stun spell against himself with the tiny fraction of power he still held.

It wouldn't matter. There was plenty of time to force the rest from him when he came around. And Malalia had to admit she admired the spirit he possessed. He'd make a fine meal for a very, very long time.

More importantly, though, she had all the information she needed to set several of her plans in motion. With the revelation about the hidden satellite, and the timing of the next portal opening now made clear to her, one prong of the attack could begin, streaming through the portal and causing chaos and destruction, while the real mission craft jumped away to do their survey.

Then there was the possibility of retrieving some of the lost treasure of the Wampeh Ghalian. It would take some effort to overcome their defenses, but the opportunity of both crushing her enemy, while also gaining many more blood sources to add to her stable was too much to resist. Adding what was sure to be a wealth of powered weapons and artifacts was just icing on that cake.

That attack had gone far better than planned, though there were some complications that had not been foreseen. One was quite surprising, indeed.

She hadn't expected the Wampeh Ghalian to employ her own trick, using a portal to escape. It was clever, she had to admit, and the power it required was massive. But despite her failure to kill and capture the elusive assassins, there was, however, one very unexpected and very welcome surprise. The Ootaki girl who was now lying unconscious in her cell.

How she would ultimately use the woman was still being worked on in conjunction with her greatest strategists. But in the meantime, there was one other prong to her attack plan that should be just about underway in a distant and unnoted solar system.

Charlie and Ara were flying a casual survey of all of the new ships that continued to join their ranks. A great many were not suitable for much of a battle, but their willingness to be a part of the resistance was heartening all the same.

This was a fight against oppression, and whether it was the Council of Twenty, or a Visla going by the name Dominus, those who had lived and breathed free air for generations were not about to fall back into lives of slavery and servitude.

That the unusual man who rode a Zomoki happened to be named Charlie just seemed all the more like providence. Little did they know, he wasn't named after the man who had originally sparked the rebellion that led to their ancestors' freedom; he *was* the man who had done so.

But time travel wasn't exactly the sort of thing that one brought up in casual conversation. Not even among magic-wielding people from another galaxy. So Charlie kept that little tidbit to himself as he personally greeted the captains of every single ship that joined them.

It was that personal connection that caused him to put himself in harm's way so instinctively when the first wave of Tslavar warships jumped into the system.

"Where the hell did they come from?" Charlie wondered as he keyed his skree. "We've been found! Everyone, emergency jump to these coordinates," he transmitted, followed by a quick burst of details.

They'd planned several escape routes should one be required, but until such time as it was actually needed, the exact one was a close-held secret that only Charlie and the pirate captain Rovnik possessed.

"Ships are jumping, Charlie," the captain skreed as his fellow pirates swung into action, engaging the enemy ships.

"Then get going, Rovnik."

"Can't. Not yet. A bunch of the newcomers are having a hard time working up the power to jump. Most don't have powerful Drooks, and Drookonuses are hard to come by. We're going to buy them as much time as we can," the pirate said as he and his comrades flew into the fight.

Charlie spun around and looked back toward his fleet. *"Shit, he's right, Ara. We've got to help them hold the Tslavars back as long as we can."*

"I'll do all I can, Charlie, but if more jump in, we'll be horribly outnumbered."

"I know."

"And we might get cut off as well," she added.

It was an eventuality he was also well aware of. He hoped it wouldn't come to that.

The pirate ships weren't fools. Though they possessed great

firepower, they had their strongest casters and stored magic held back. The enemy *wanted* them to blow their load early. It was then that they'd send in reinforcements to mop up the depleted rebel forces.

But these captains were all veterans of many violent encounters, and they knew full well that this was not a fight they were prepared to engage in. Not fully. Not while on their heels like this. So they would put on a show, using as little of their magic as they could, then jump away as quickly as possible once the slowpoke ships in their fleet had finally managed to make their escape.

As she had feared, the Tslavar ships swarmed Ara, bombarding her from many directions at once. Charlie was casting furiously, his magic strong. But the rigors of battle often throw you a curveball, and today was just one such day, it seemed.

Ara took a hit and was spun abruptly to her left, the force of the impact straining Charlie's harness at the connection point, which, after many battles, had finally had enough.

"Shiiiii—" Charlie exclaimed as he was flung off of Ara's back at speed.

He cast wildly, bombarding the Tslavar ships around him as he spun end over end through space.

"Where are you, Charlie?"

"I'm drifting away from the main body of the ships, I think. I'm spinning. It's hard to tell."

At that instant another dozen ships jumped into the system. The pirates had given the little craft all the cover they could. To remain at this point would be suicide.

"We're jumping. Good luck, everyone," Rovnik said, then he and the other pirates jumped to the rendezvous system.

"I can't reach you, Charlie. There are too many. Can you cast and push yourself this way?" Ara asked.

Charlie assessed the battle around him and made a decision. *"Just go, Ara."*

"I'm not leaving you, Charlie."

"You have to. If you don't go now, they'll capture you too. Or worse. I don't think anyone sees me, so I should be okay,"

"You're floating in space, Charlie," she protested.

"And I'm a space pirate. This is what I do, Ara. If I can't handle a little setback like this, I don't deserve the title. Now hurry up. Jump and meet the others while you still can."

Ara paused. *"I'll find you."*

"Not if I find you first," he replied with a forced chuckle.

A moment later, Ara was gone, leaving Charlie floating in the vacuum, drifting amidst the debris of the ships destroyed in the battle.

Okay, Charlie. You've been in worse situations. Just take a few breaths and figure out your next move. You've got this.

But despite his little pep talk, Charlie couldn't help but have doubts.

CHAPTER FIFTY-THREE

Charlie had been floating quietly in space for about ten minutes, relaxing his body within his space suit as he carefully took inventory of his assets. He wouldn't run out of air for quite some time, and the suit hadn't been damaged when he was torn free of his harness, part of which was still dangling from his waist.

This was a boon, actually. Charlie took the piece and separated it into two segments. He then took one of the two pieces and began spinning it counter to his own spin. It was a difficult calculation to make, but without any other outside items to transfer his energy to, he was stuck with these limited resources.

Hope this works, he thought as he increased the spin in his hands. *One. Two. Three!* He pushed off from the fragment, allowing much of his momentum to be shed in the process. It didn't stop him entirely, but his spin did slow considerably.

Not bad. Not bad at all. Now for one more and I should be able to get close to a stop.

He repeated the process with the final piece of harness, and the action actually did bring him to nearly a stop. It would have to do. With so many Tslavar ships around, any significant use of magic would make him pop out to their casters like a giant radar ping. Or at least, so he speculated, and after the battle they'd just engaged in, he would much rather be safe than sorry.

When it was time to finally use his magic, he had to make it count.

He drifted a while longer, using the occasional piece of floating debris from one of the ships that had come to join their pirate fleet to push off against, sending him floating closer to the enemy ships. He had a plan. It wasn't a pretty one, and it would probably fail, but it beat either eventually suffocating, or being blasted where he sat.

What Charlie was going to do would rival any of the ridiculous feats of his pirate brothers. If he could pull it off, that is.

If he did, his audacious act would rival any tale of counting coup told by the ancient Plains Indians. In fact, in olden days, he'd earn so many eagle feathers he could probably make a whole new bird out of them.

But survival was key.

Well, here goes nothing, he thought, as he pushed off from one last piece of debris, heading straight for his intended target. A small Tslavar assault ship.

It had been a while since he'd participated in a proper pirate raid. Years, in fact. And this time he'd be doing it entirely on his own. Against mercenaries, no less.

"If only Marban could see me now," he mumbled as he activated his on-suit recorder. If he should perish, at least some record of his ridiculous attempt might survive.

Finally allowing himself to use just a teeny, tiny bit of his magic, Charlie finessed his way onto the hull of the Tslavar ship. It was a somewhat familiar design, thank God, and he had a fair knowledge of the basic interior layout.

There would be somewhere in the range of twenty to thirty crew under normal circumstances. That meant he'd have to gain access, then take the ship one passageway at a time, hiding the bodies in adjacent compartments as he went, hoping he didn't miss anyone behind him.

It was sheer madness. No one would ever even consider such a thing. Not against a ship full of armed Tslavar mercenaries. But that was precisely why it *could* work. If his hunch was correct, they'd never see him coming. And if he was wrong, well, it would be a very short-lived effort that would end in a blaze of glory.

He much preferred the former to the latter, for obvious reasons.

"Here we go," he said as he used a focused spell to seal himself inside a tiny force bubble against the hull of the ship, then quickly cut open a small section and slid inside, re-sealing the bulkhead behind him and applying a glamour spell to hide any imperfections in the hasty magical weld.

He'd made it inside without being seen. That was a start at least. Now he just had a few dozen bad hombres to deal with. Piece of cake, he tried to convince himself.

Charlie kept the space suit on in case the fighting got out of hand and the hull was breached. He'd seen that happen before and didn't want to be unprepared for the eventuality. The enchanted blade he carried was a gift from Bawb. Nothing fancy, just a long knife that would cut through just about anything. Today it would be cutting through Tslavar.

The first four mercenaries went down silently, two stunned, and two slain. All were stashed in storage compartments, the traces of blood quickly glamoured. No time for a proper cleanup.

From there it was a methodical approach to the command center. Once there, he would have to wield more magic to take out multiple hostiles at once, but he could worry about that when he got there. For now, he had about fifteen more crew to deal with.

Miraculously, Charlie made it all the way to his destination unscathed, though one Tslavar had surprised him, coming out of a toilet chamber just as he was finishing off one of the man's crewmates with great violence. Charlie had thrown the knife, not really knowing if it would fly true or not. It simply wasn't something he'd trained with. The idea of throwing away a valuable enchanted blade was one that never crossed his mind. But the knife struck home, embedding itself deep in the startled alien's throat.

"I guess the enchantment extends to throwing," he noted, retrieving the blade.

There was no time to waste hiding the bodies. He was so close to the command center, he simply had to rush forward and take it. If there were any stragglers he'd missed, he was sure he'd run into them soon enough. But for now, he had a ship to commandeer.

A low-powered stun spell dropped everyone in the command center the moment Charlie entered it. And good thing it did. He realized the main caster among the crew was wearing a seriously powerful konus.

He quickly stripped the man of the device, as well as taking all magical and otherwise potentially dangerous gear from the downed crew, then bound them securely.

He could have killed them all, but after his experience slaughtering so many Tslavars by accident at the Balamar Wastelands, he had developed and even more profound distaste for death unless absolutely necessary.

Charlie checked the skree console. No incoming. It seemed no one had noticed the surge of magic in the ship.

Excellent.

Now he just had to stash the crew and get this thing moving. The former was relatively straightforward. He just dragged the unconscious mercenaries to a cargo storage compartment, searched it for any possible means of communication or escape, then sealed them inside.

"Now the hard part," he said, setting off in search of the ship's Drooks.

He found them easy enough, but every one of them ignored him when he entered. All wore control collars, and the fear of reprisal kept them ever in check. He had to find a way to bring them around to his side or the ship wouldn't move an inch, and all this would be for naught.

"Hey, the Tslavars are gone. We can do what we want. Let's get out of here," he said.

The Drooks ignored him.

"I said you're safe now. But we have to leave this place, and I mean now."

Again, no reply.

He realized it was time to change things up. To take it up a notch. "Look, do you guys want to be free?" he asked, grabbing the nearest Drook by the collar and casting, forcing his power into the golden band.

It was harder than he anticipated, and the pain in his hand sucked something fierce, but he felt the magical bond weakening in his grip until the collar finally snapped free, falling to the floor.

Fuck, that hurt! And holy shit do I feel drained, he realized. Without Ara nearby to share power with him, he'd pushed himself a bit far in breaking the collar. But there was no time to worry about that. He had to get the Drooks moving.

"You see that? Get us out of here and I'll do the same for all the rest of you. But we have to go *now*!"

The Drooks looked in shock at the broken collar on the

deck, then glanced at one another with uncertainty. Without a word, they made a decision. They turned their gaze to Charlie. It was kind of creepy how they all did it at once, all silent and spooky-like. Then, as one, they smiled.

Again, the creepy factor.

A moment later the ship jumped away.

CHAPTER FIFTY-FOUR

It had been a desperation move. An attempt he really doubted would actually work. But somehow, someway, Charlie's crazy plan had succeeded. With a lot of sweat, and effort.

And blood, of course.

Charlie had laid waste to more than half of the Tslavar crew single-handedly. The other half was unconscious and bound, then locked away in a secure cargo area with no means of escape. Then he scoured the entire craft, just in case he'd missed anyone.

He'd learned early on as a pirate, never, *ever*, assume a ship is clear until you check every last inch of it. And this ship was clear.

The team of Drooks had also surprised him, but in a pleasant way. While he'd expected a bit more reticence, they had been quick to join his cause, jumping away as soon as he'd shown tangible proof of what he was offering them. Freedom.

And now, on a distant world, Charlie struggled to make good on that promise.

"Okay, I need a little break," he said, as yet another of the golden collars broke free and fell to the dirt, leaving the Drook who had been wearing it *truly* free.

It had been a hasty escape, but the casters powering the ship were quite good at their job. And a large enough percentage of them were young enough to still dare dream of freedom, the opportunity for which had just dropped in their laps. They had to at least try.

And now, this odd and unlikely visla was actually *breaking* their sturdy control collars with his bare hands and magic. And he wasn't even uttering his spells aloud. That alone drew attention. That he broke the first few of them without using a konus did as well.

He was an unusual man, of that they were certain. And in short order, a great many of their number were freed. But even after he had eventually begun using the captured konuses taken from the Tslavar crew, it was clear the man was exhausting himself from the effort.

A great deal of Visla Dominus's power had gone into those collars, and no ordinary caster stood a chance of removing them. But Charlie was no ordinary caster.

"Okay, guys. I'm gonna take a break and go scrounge up some grub for us," Charlie informed the Drooks, all of whom were sitting in a circle in the dirt, enjoying the planet's free air.

"Grub?" one asked.

"Food."

"But there is food on our vessel," another noted.

"Well, yeah. But I thought something fresh might hit the spot. You know, free-grown food for a bunch of free Drooks."

A pleased murmur rustled through the men and women. They liked the sound of that.

"Anyway, I need a little time to get my energy levels back up, and this will be a good way to kill two birds with one stone."

"What are you going to kill?"

"It's just a saying. Nevermind. Anyway, I'll be back soon, so, in the meantime, you guys just relax and breathe the free air. When I get back I'll see about getting those last collars off the last of you."

There hadn't been any Ootaki hair aboard the ship—Visla Dominus was gathering every last strand in the galaxy—but Charlie had been able to block the collars' spells well enough with a few carefully modified konuses.

The wearers had to stay close to one another, though. He didn't have enough of them to spread them around. But as more and more Drooks were freed, the number required to stay in each other's proximity was down to just a handful.

"Okay, back in a bit," Charlie said, then trudged off to see what edibles he might find on this planet.

The walk did him a lot of good. At least, it did so far as restoring his energy levels went. He had learned not to tap too far into his power. It was a very important lesson Ara had taught him long ago. The further he drained himself, the harder it was to restore that power. Moderation was key.

But he was also in a hurry. They'd need to rejoin the rest of his fleet as soon as possible. Somehow, the enemy had found their staging area, which meant there had been a compromise to their ranks somewhere. They just needed to figure out who it was to gauge exactly how exposed they had been.

"Mmm, yeah. These should be a nice treat," Charlie said when he discovered a flowering bush covered in sweet berries.

He tested them to ensure they were edible first, of course, using the simple spell Bawb had shown him to gauge their toxicity. Sometimes, the only thing one could find to eat was poisonous. In those situations, it wasn't a question of whether or not it would make you sick, but rather, would it nourish you enough to make the illness worth it.

Charlie hadn't asked for the details of why Bawb knew such

a thing. Given the assassin's lengthy career, there was undoubtedly a reason, and that was good enough for him.

His spirits fell a moment as he assessed his situation. He was on his own. *Truly* on his own, not counting the Drooks, who weren't company so much as the equivalent of a talking team of horses driving him through space. But his friends? They were far away.

It was strange, not feeling Ara at all. Charlie had been close to her for so long that only her absence made him realize how accustomed he'd become to the constant, slight tug of her presence on his power. They were bonded, and they'd been separated now, and by solar systems, no less.

And Leila was still out there, though Pimbrak was going to bring her back to him soon. Having the dapper and deadly assassin working on that for him put his mind at least a little bit at ease knowing someone of his skill was on the job. He wasn't Bawb, of course, but he'd definitely suffice.

Charlie also found himself missing his Wampeh friend. What had started as a union of necessity had blossomed into a deep and fulfilling friendship. And now he was wondering if he'd see his Wampeh pal again.

"Jeez, get it together, Charlie," he muttered to himself. "You've been in worse binds than this."

Amazingly, his little self-pep talk worked, and he resumed his foraging with renewed vigor. A short while later, Charlie had filled a pouch with berries, and had even managed to catch a pair of creatures that somewhat resembled the large hares of Earth. If the hares were covered with bony protrusions and had wicked fangs, that is.

"Hey, guys. I've got us some food," he said as he stepped from the brush back to the clearing beside their stolen ship. "I even caught us some game, which is good, because, boy, am I hungry."

The Drooks just stared, wide-eyed, their gaze flicking past him to the tree line.

"Oh, shi––" was all Charlie managed to say before a Tslavar stun spell knocked him to the ground, unconscious.

CHAPTER FIFTY-FIVE

Charlie's homeworld was faring better against the Tslavar threat than he had been. While he was attacked, chased, and captured, Earth's forces--along with their Urok and Chithiid allies--had broken the enemy's ranks, separating them from one another and neutralizing their threat with great prejudice.

Some of the invading ships did manage to jump away, but they were mostly small craft, and their numbers few. Most had jumped straight to Earth, though a handful of them vanished from the area entirely.

The attackers who had tried to reach Sid's Dark Side base on the moon were in for a nasty surprise. While the craft deployed in a defensive perimeter were not the most robust in the fleet-- those heftier craft being already parked near the portal itself-- the moon's guardians did still have a trick or two up their sleeves.

The biggest was Joshua and his swarm of remote ships. He'd been retooling the system from the safety of his and Freya's hidden hangar on the outskirts of the lunar base when the attack began. Needless to say, his upgrades had been immediately put on hold and his swarm of attack ships thrust into action once again.

He launched his heavily armored core craft and powered up his weapons systems, the swarm coalescing around him into a large, deadly vessel. Joshua then powered into the thick of things, his modified shielding, courtesy of a generous coating of Freya's magical nanites she'd given him, blocking the magical attacks that did somehow make it past his rapidly phasing tech shields.

The Tslavars reacted by spinning off to target the easier prey of the other vessels, hoping to cause as much damage as possible to throw the defensive armada into disarray. Joshua was having none of that.

His weapons systems were a complex array of both the countless railguns and pulse cannons of the small ships interlinked to form his current shape, as well as the much larger battery of cannons mounted on his core craft. Each of them was deadly, and each of them began firing with devastating accuracy.

The mercenary ships quickly peeled off from their attack on the lesser ships and spun into a dive toward Sid and Dark Side base itself.

"Oh no you don't, fucko!" Daisy bellowed as she and Freya crested the outcropping above the base and dropped into position just above its facilities, plasma cannons and railguns all aimed at the incoming ships. It was almost like an old Earth video game, only the stakes were far higher, and there was no replay button.

"Light 'em up, kiddo," Daisy said.

"With pleasure."

Freya logged the locations in space of every single one of their ships in a millisecond, ensuring any missed shot wouldn't keep going and hit one of their own craft, then fired off a blistering assault, the thin, magical nanite coating on her railgun sabots piercing their shielding even faster than Joshua's brute force attack had.

"They're making a run back toward the portal," Joshua called out.

"We see 'em," Daisy replied. "Guess they don't know it's closed already. You got this?"

"Deploying my swarm. Don't worry, they won't lay a finger on Sid's facilities. Now get going."

"See you soon," Freya said.

"I'm counting on it," her AI partner replied as his ships scattered from his core and began tearing through the remaining Tslavar craft.

Freya didn't wait a moment longer, powering her core and warping just ahead of the enemy ships, her weapons firing the moment she flashed into being with a crackling blue around her inky black hull.

The Tslavars tried to peel off and avoid the spray of weapons fire, but her nanite-coated rounds damaged their shields enough before they did so that the other Earth-allied forces were able to target them without a problem.

The larger of the Tslavar ships were being incapacitated one by one as Freya's sabots found their way through the magical shielding. Decompressions had undoubtedly been stopped by magical plugs sealing the air inside, but the raw carnage one of those rounds could do when passing through an object at Mach five-plus was devastating.

Casualties would be great, and morale low. What they had to worry about now, as the tide of battle had finally shifted and was winding down, was the enemy captains scuttling their own ships rather than be captured.

The Uroks seized the opportunity presented by the fallen shields and landed their boarding craft atop the large Tslavar craft, quickly cutting their way inside and charging full speed through the damaged vessel, taking down any who stood in their way. The goal was to overwhelm the command center before any self-destruct sequence could be triggered, and in that they were successful. At least, mostly.

A few ships did abruptly burst apart just as the boarding craft drew near, though whether that was actual suicide or merely a terribly damaged vessel giving up the ghost in the strain of battle was debatable. What did matter, however, was the significant number of ships that actually *had* been captured.

The remaining Tslavar craft that still had the capability jumped away, fleeing in hopes of fighting another day.

"You see that, Freya?" Daisy asked.

"Yeah. But don't worry. I tagged 'em all with tracer markers."

"All of them?"

"I counted a few that got away," Sarah noted, using not just her voice in Daisy's head, but also the neuro link allowing her to speak with Freya.

"Well, I got *most*, at least," Freya clarified. "It'll still be a pain to track them all down, but it's doable."

"Nice job, kiddo."

"Thanks."

"And as for the ones that weren't marked, well, we're just going to have to be on our toes until we find them."

"*If* we find them," Freya corrected. "I have a feeling most of them want nothing to do with us after the ass-whooping they just endured."

Daisy laughed, and Joshua joined in over the comms.

"Hey, Joshua. Glad you're okay, man," Daisy said. "Everything okay down at Dark Side?"

"Fine. We had a few casualties, and quite a lot of damage to the defensive flotilla, but nothing we can't fix. And good news. We captured several Tslavar ships."

"Us too!" Freya chirped. "And it sounds like the attackers down on Earth got their asses handed to them too."

"So I've heard," Joshua replied. "And Daisy, I think you

should know sooner than later that your niece is going to be all right."

Daisy sat bolt upright in her seat. "Ripley's hurt? Get us down there, Freya!"

"On it," the AI ship replied, spinning around and warping to Earth's atmosphere in an instant.

"I said she will be all right," Joshua repeated.

"I appreciate that, Joshua, but I'm not slowing my roll until I see her with my own eyes," Daisy said, worry apparent in her voice. "And where the hell is Arlo?"

"He's fine, Daisy. Marty already sent word that they'd gone to protect Maarl the moment they heard of the attack."

"So he's safe. They're all safe," she said with a relieved sigh.

"They are. And Vince is with them. Apparently, they couldn't just sit by once they picked up Maarl, so they've been hunting down fleeing ground forces from the air, directing your canine friends in the chase."

Daisy could picture it now. Aerial spotters taking all of the attention from the fleeing mercenaries on the ground, all of them unaware of the beasts stalking them on foot. It would be a shitty way to go, but after what just happened, Daisy didn't mind one bit.

"Eddie, you copy?"

"I'm here, Freya," the damaged ship replied.

"Guide us in. We're coming to you."

"Sending a ping now," he said, guiding the stealth ship to his location.

Freya dropped down at a blistering rate, slamming into a low hover just above the ground, her weapons systems ready as she scanned for any sign of hostiles. Ripley had been hurt, and she and Daisy were going to get there as soon as physically possible, and ready for anything.

Daisy jumped out of Freya's open airlock door and raced to her sister and niece. Ripley was standing on somewhat wobbly legs, her clothes bloody, her healing exterior injuries still visible through the rent fabric as the nanites inside her focused on more serious matters. But the Balamar waters were working hard, continuing to heal the wounds even as she watched.

Daisy pulled Sarah, Finn, and Ripley in close and hugged them hard. "I was so worried about you guys," she said, her voice rough with emotion.

"We're okay, Daze," Sarah said, shifting her gaze to look at her miraculously healed kid. "We've just got to get her checked into the med facility."

"Eddie's still recovering. We'll take you," Freya said, prepping for dustoff.

"Thanks, Freya," Sarah said. "And, Daze, you're not going to believe what happened."

CHAPTER FIFTY-SIX

The Tslavars were a tough bunch on a normal day, and this group of prisoners were even more so. Mercenaries tasked with invading another realm and causing as much chaos and damage as possible to disrupt things for the main attack. It was brutal and diabolical. It was also unsurprising.

Visla Dominus ruled the fleet with an iron fist, and these men and women would far rather face capture, or even death, than displease their leader. To do so would likely lead to the latter anyway, and in far less pleasant circumstances.

It had taken a good long while to round up all of the survivors of the scattered battles. Most in space had perished, their ships losing pressure and sucking them into the void or merely suffocating them within their own craft. The disabled ships, however, were another story.

Those vessels contained survivors, and they were quickly gathered up under heavy guard and shipped back down to Earth for sorting and imprisonment, along with the other surviving Tslavars already captured and locked up across the globe. All of them were to be divided into manageable groups and separated from their comrades to provide a housing situation where they felt powerless.

There would be interrogations, of course. Many of them. And after what had just happened, the AIs in charge were in no mood to play nice. Fortunately for the Tslavars, the neuro-stim modifications seemed to be working well enough to cause enhanced pliability among them.

It would save the interrogators a lot of time, not to mention blood and screams. The normally good-natured machines running Earth had finally had enough, and they intended to put an end to this, one way or another.

The interrogation facility serving the greater Los Angeles region was located within the same reinforced building as Cal's top medical facility. It was there that Daisy, Sarah, and Finn stood by, antsy and fidgeting as Cal's best technicians gave Ripley the once-over.

"She's fine," the cyborg doctor told her worried family. Her extremely *famous* family.

She was treating the daughter of two of the brave warriors who had helped save the world, and who was also the niece of the infamous Daisy herself. Needless to say, she took extra care with this particular patient.

"How long until she's able to be discharged, Doc?" Finn asked, his eyes bloodshot from his tearful wait.

"No, you don't understand," the doctor clarified. "I mean she's *fine*. As in, there is absolutely nothing wrong with her at all. Not a scratch. In fact, if I'm not mistaken, even the cavity she had filled has regrown new enamel on the tooth. I tell you, it's a miracle."

Sarah and Daisy shared a look. She'd told her sister what had happened when her nanite hand touched her injured child. How, apparently, Ripley had more of them in her body than any of them had ever expected, and how they reacted in that time of stress to Sarah's own nanite swarm.

More than that, however, was the way the nanites ferried the stored Balamar waters to their brethren, who immediately distributed the healing molecules throughout the teen's body. And now, she was entirely healed and in the best shape of her life. Ripley was right as rain and ready to leave whenever her parents wanted.

Kara and Vee were being checked out in an adjacent exam room. After the battle, it was important the teens received a thorough checkup. It had been a violent affair, and who knew what injuries they might have acquired in the heat of the attack.

Korbin was there as well, standing by, watching with great interest. His niece was physically intact, but mentally she was having a hard time coping with what she'd done on several levels. She had not only killed a man, but she'd done it with magic. *Her* magic. No konus, no slaap. Just her. And it had been a powerful display.

Her uncle watched with carefully assessing eyes, wondering just what else the girl might be capable of, as well as why she had so suddenly grown into her power. If only Amazara was here, the talented healer's insight could help suss out those details.

A little knot formed in his stomach at the thought of her. They'd been friends a long, long time. Briefly something more even longer ago. And now, with the world upside down and far from home, he found himself wishing she was with him. It caught him off guard and was something that would bear consideration if he ever made it back to his galaxy again.

Elsewhere in the facility, a dangerously powerful woman decorated with glowing, magical pigments was getting a very different sort of exam.

Rika's concussion was moderate, but the instability it created in her mind, and thus, the possibility of a weakened hold on her control of her magic, made her a very dangerous patient. As such, she had been placed in the exam room normally used for deadly pathogens or potentially violent aliens.

Machines took samples, while doctors spoke to her over a display. But one person refused to leave her in the room alone. And the scarred pirate hadn't budged an inch since she arrived, watching over her protectively as the machines did their jobs.

Jo arrived a short while after her friend had been brought in. She'd peeled away from combat as soon as she heard Rika was hurt. But what she saw when she rushed into the facility put her mind at ease immediately, as well as placed a happy smile on her face.

Marban, in that moment, reminded her very much of herself on the other occasion of Rika's injury not so long ago. The time she received her lifesaving magical ink. She, too, had stood watch over her friend, keeping vigil, just as he was doing now.

The cyborg's arrival caught Marban's eye. He looked up and locked gazes with Jo for a moment. She smiled and nodded once, then left him to look over the woman who was so important to both of them. Rika was in good hands, and Jo needed to talk to Sergeant Franklin and get some more intel on what was really going on.

Arlo had flown in with his father and Maarl as soon as he heard Ripley was hurt, but by the time he got there, she was up and about, chatty as always. He hugged his cousin hard when he saw her standing on her own two feet.

"Hey, quit it," Ripley griped.

"No way," he said, hugging her tighter. "I'm glad you're okay."

"Yeah, well, I wasn't," she admitted. "But it looks like I've got more of Mom's nanites in me than we ever expected."

"Cool, cool," Arlo replied, looking around the medical facility. "Where are the girls?"

"Wanna see your crush, do ya?" Ripley teased.

"Shut up, Rip. I'm just making sure everyone's all right."

"Uh-huh," she laughed, heading down the hallway. "Come

on, we're all meeting up to get an update from Cal. Kara and Vee will be there too."

Arlo fell in behind her and followed to the nearby conference room where the others had been gathering. Jo and George were discussing tactical options should the alien invaders return, when Cal joined the conversation.

"Hello, all of you. Thanks for joining me. I wanted to give you all an update and get your input before broadcasting globally. So, let's jump right into it. We have stopped the invasion in its tracks. Casualties were moderate on our side, thanks largely to the shielding modifications aided by Korbin and Rika's magical assistance. That alone made a big difference, but Freya's nanite railgun sabots were also particularly effective in our offensive endeavors."

"What about ground forces?" Finn asked. "Rip damn near got killed out there."

"Dad, come on."

"No, it's true. So what can we do to stop them if they make landfall? We're not magic users, and we don't have personal shielding like they do."

"This is true. However, we are learning more about the Tslavar tactics and spell/weapon systems as we speak. We've seen promising results with the new neuro-stim interrogation techniques. In fact, one of the pilots of a captured ship has been quite frank with us. He doesn't possess any top-secret information or tactical revelations, but he has given us details as to the planets and systems being used to stage Dominus's craft, as well as the types of ships and the size of the fleet. At least the part he was embedded with. Apparently, he joined up with them just recently, having just come from a planet called Slafara."

"That's my home!" Kara blurted. "Did he say anything about Visla Palmarian?"

"Actually, he did say that the visla overseeing the planet was quite ill, though he didn't go into details."

Kara rose from her seat. "I have to go. I need to go there, now!"

"Karasalia, you know we can't do that," Korbin said, trying to comfort his niece.

"Korbin is correct. The portal is compromised, and the next opening will have to be incredibly brief, while we try to figure out how Dominus knew its timing."

"But it's my father! Just send me through, then. I'll find my way."

"Kara, it's simply not possible," Sarah said, sympathetic to the girl's plight.

"None of you understand!" the teen yelled, then stormed out of the room.

"Let her go," Korbin said. "And she's right, you know. She does need to get back to her father. As should I. But you are also right that this is not the time. What we must do now is strategize."

Cal agreed, then continued with his briefing, but Arlo couldn't help but think about the violet-skinned girl, wondering if perhaps he could help. But first, he would need to talk to Marty, and in private, because this was his craziest idea yet.

CHAPTER FIFTY-SEVEN

Charlie tasted copper in his mouth. He'd bitten his cheek, apparently, though nothing serious. What troubled him far more was where he'd just woken up. He recognized the ship's design.

"Oh, sonofa.––"

He was back aboard a Tslavar ship, though not exactly the same type as when he'd first started his adventures in this magical galaxy. Captain Tür was long dead, as were all of his friends and foes of that distant time. But that just meant he had *new* asshole captors to deal with.

"Fucking lovely," he grumbled, his head still pounding from the spell that had taken him down while he was in a weakened state.

He knew he was being monitored. It was standard among the Tslavars back when he was a slave, and now that he was a higher-value prisoner, he was certain they were watching and listening even more intently. Sure enough, not more than two minutes had passed since he regained consciousness before a pair of Tslavar guards and their snooty captain strode into his cell.

It was an eerie flashback to his early days with Tuktuk, and Charlie found himself caught in a flash of nostalgia as he remembered his old friend.

"Impressive, what you did," the captain said. "Stealing one of Visla Dominus's ships like that? Quite a feat. And disabling the crew? How many were in your raiding party?"

Charlie was too tired and too beat-up to care at the moment, so he simply told the truth. "Just me," he said.

The captain laughed. "Oh, that's rich. You expect me to believe a single man incapacitated nearly thirty men on his own?"

"You don't have to believe me. Honestly, I really don't give a damn," Charlie said, his pounding headache not making his mood any better.

"Whoever your allies were, rest assured, we shall find them," the captain said with a sneer. "Now, who are you? What is your name?"

"Charlie," he replied, feeling his anger grow.

"Like the rebel? How quaint."

"No. You misunderstand," he said, rising to his feet. "I'm not named *after* the rebel who brought about the destruction of the Council of Twenty. I *am* Charlie."

Power began to crackle from his fingertips. It was a bit showy, but on this occasion, he wanted to scare the bastards a little before smiting them. His power had just begun to flare when a powerful blast around his neck flattened him to the deck.

Charlie pushed up to his elbow, stunned. His fingers went to his neck. Only then did he realize what had happened. He'd been so out of it when he woke that he hadn't even noticed the band around his neck. For the first time in years, he was wearing a control collar.

"Oh, shit," was all he managed to get out before being stunned into unconsciousness once more.

. . .

Charlie hadn't bitten his cheek again, so at least he had that going for him, he grimly mused as he struggled his way back to consciousness.

"How long have I been out?" he muttered, noting the foul dryness in his mouth.

Peeling his eyelids open, he realized it must have been quite a while, because he was no longer in his cell aboard the Tslavar ship. In fact, he wasn't on a ship anymore at all.

Shaking off the aches from the stun spell, Charlie slowly pushed himself up to a sitting position and took in his new surroundings. It was a cell of some sort, that much was obvious. The walls muted all sound, so they had to be quite thick. And the door was equally sturdy, sporting just a tiny slot.

No, the gravity felt different too. He was definitely not on a ship anymore. He was on a planet. The question was, which one?

"Hello? Where am I?" he asked the air.

There was no reply. Just a constant magical weight pressing down on him, keeping his slowly returning power in check. Whoever had him was making absolutely sure he wouldn't be casting. Normally, a control collar would be enough, but with his growing magic, he supposed it was only natural for his captors to be extra careful with him.

But when his power *had* finally returned in full, he would have out of this place, and no stupid control collar would stop him. He could break it off, once he'd recovered. Hell, he'd do it right now if he hadn't been so weak from snapping off all of those Drook collars.

"Oh, shit," he said, as he realized he had failed the poor Drooks.

He had promised them freedom, and a good many had achieved that, at least for a day. But by now they would be wearing collars once again, if not far worse. Having stood up to Visla Dominus, there was a very good possibility that some, if not all of them, were dead.

At least those who still had their control collars on when they were recaptured could possibly use the excuse of being mere slaves and having no choice but to go along, but the others, he feared, might have fared far worse. The thought made him feel sick.

But if they were slaves again, he would find a way to free them once more. He owed them that much at the very least. And if he ever made it back to Earth, he was going to have a nice chat with Cal about designing a portable plasma cutter capable of slicing off control collars. Even the smaller units simply weren't practical for travel, and it seemed like he might actually be needing to do some more cutting of collars before all of this was done.

Slavery had been ended, he thought. A thing of the past, and largely because of his actions a long time ago. But apparently that wasn't the case. Not entirely, at least.

"Well, it looks like I've got one more thing to add to the list," he mused as he paced out his cell, measuring its length and width, as well as how many steps it was to the door from his bed.

He would escape from this place. And when he did, there'd be hell to pay.

CHAPTER FIFTY-EIGHT

Sitting atop the bluffs in Malibu, a teen and his AI buddy went over their plan for the umpteenth time.

"Marty, are you *sure* it'll work?" Arlo asked his best non-human friend. "I mean, that's really soon."

"I'm telling ya, I've got it. I got the timing directly from Zed's push announcement. It went out to everyone in the portal guardian fleet."

"But you're down here with me."

"Well, duh. But I tapped into the relay feed pinging off of Sid's satellite array. Anyway, the next opening is gonna be in an hour, so if you want to try this, we're going to have to go, and I mean really soon."

Arlo knew this was their best chance of sneaking across the portal. And, given the urgency in Kara's voice and the look on her face when she heard about her father, he knew before saying it out loud that he was going to do it.

Arlo was going to cross the portal.

The idea was to deliver a message to her father on Slafara and bring her back a reply. Aside from crossing the portal to provide cover that one time, though, Arlo and Marty had never been anywhere in the distant galaxy. And complicating matters was the issue of warp tech not functioning properly in that magical space.

If you happened to have one of those magical konus thingies with you, it was possible to use it to help guide you, more or less, but he was sadly lacking one. But if he was going to do this thing for Kara, he felt confident she'd get him one. Maybe even from her uncle. He was really powerful, and Arlo almost wanted to ask him to come along, but he knew the adult would almost certainly put the brakes on his plan. And that would not do.

"Hang tight, Marty. I'm going to talk to Kara. Be ready to fly as soon as I'm back."

"I've *been* ready, Arlo. Just hurry."

The teen nodded and headed off to find the violet-skinned girl from another world. Marty had done a scan of the area and located Kara at his cousin's place. Ripley, however, was still going through a battery of tests with Arlo's aunt Sarah and uncle Finn in downtown. Cal was taking no chances with Ripley's health and wanted a full work-up on her done ASAP. Plus he was very curious about her surprisingly robust nanite colony and what it had done.

Korbin had given Kara and Vee a ride back to Ripley's place, then hurried off with a strange chatterbox of a pilot named Tym to finish up some secret new project. Whatever that was all about, it meant that the girls were alone, and that was what he needed.

"Hey," Arlo said to the distressed girl in his uncle's kitchen. "You okay?"

"No, I am most definitely *not* okay," Kara said.

"Yeah. Right. Sorry. Of course you aren't." Arlo shifted uncomfortably on his feet. "Listen, I know you're worried about your dad and want him to know you're safe, but I was thinking, if you can get me one of those konuses, Marty and me, we can help."

Kara wiped her eyes and fixed her gaze on him. Arlo couldn't help but feel a flutter of butterflies in his stomach.

"What do you mean?"

"Well, you have to keep it a secret. And I mean, *really* keep it a secret."

"Keep what a secret, Arlo?" Vee asked.

He paused, then made the decision. "I'll take a message to your dad. Yours too, Vee. If you get me a konus, me and Marty should be able to find our way to Slafara."

"But the portal is closed," Kara protested, though a glint of hope shone in her eyes.

"Marty got the timing. It opens in about forty minutes. So, if you want me to do this, I really need that konus, and soon."

Kara thought for a fraction of a second. "I'm coming with."

"What? No, you stay here, where it's safe."

"We were just attacked here. It's not safe anywhere, and he's my father," she objected. "And besides, I'm far better than any konus," she said, her hands glowing faintly as she channeled her newfound power to them.

"I didn't know you could do that."

"Neither did I. Apparently, there are a lot of things I didn't know I could do."

Arlo thought about it a moment. Just the two of them, alone on a trip? This could get interesting.

"Okay, you can come. Grab whatever you need and meet me in twenty," he said, then rushed back to his ship to get ready.

Twenty minutes later Marty informed him he had company.

"Excellent. Okay, now play it cool, right?" the teen said.

"You worry about *me* playing it cool? Oh, that's funny," Marty shot back. "But I don't think that'll be an issue."

"What do you mean?"

"Okay, we're here. Are you ready to go?" Kara asked as she and Vee stowed their small packs and took a seat.

"Oh, hey, Vee," Arlo said, hiding his disappointment and surprise at her presence.

It looked like there was going to be a third wheel on this little adventure. But if he did good, he could not only impress Kara, but also her best friend. And *that* was a surefire way to a girl's heart. Or so Marty had told him not so long ago in his failed courtship of a classmate.

"Right. So, we're going to have to be really, really fast about this. Like, as soon as we cross over we'll have to warp out of there. Do you think you can have your magic tied in to Marty before we even get there? Just so we're extra ready?"

Kara concentrated and reached out to the ship, feeling his drive systems with her senses. It was a new skill, but she was already getting the hang of it. Or so she thought. Really, they'd have to try it in practice to know for sure. But she wasn't about to put the kibosh on the plan by telling him that.

"Yeah, we'll be ready. I can guide Marty to Slafara when he warps. It's my home, after all. I know it like I know myself." She hoped she was right.

"Cool. All right, then. Strap in and sit tight. We're going to make a quick run to a quiet orbit with a clear shot to the portal's location when it's pulled free."

"You're sure it'll be there?" Vee asked.

"We're sure," Arlo replied. "I trust Marty implicitly. If he says it'll be there, it'll be there. The trick is warping in the moment it's clear of the sun. We know the exact coordinates, so if we do this right, we should warp in and cross over before anyone even knows we're there."

Marty took off in a flash and quickly warped to a nearby spot in space, lining himself up with his destination coordinates. He'd have one chance at this, and he wanted it to go smoothly.

The clock ticked down, and in Arlo's anxiety, time seemed to both take forever but also fly by.

"Thirty seconds," Marty informed them. "Hang tight. This is going to be interesting."

Kara began reaching out with her magic, feeling the ship's power around her. As soon as they crossed over, it would be on her to help guide him to the right system. She was pretty able to link with him in this galaxy, but things might very well feel different back in her own. But, whatever. Her dad needed her, so she'd do the best she could, and that would have to suffice.

"Ten seconds," Marty called out.

Arlo's grip tightened on the arms of his seat. "Here we go."

"Three. Two. One." Marty warped.

The AI ship arrived at the right time, but he was just a little bit farther from the portal than he'd planned. He quickly gunned his drive systems, and a second later was gone, crossed over even before Zed's waiting drone.

"Holy shit! Get us out of here, Marty!" Arlo shouted as they exited the portal.

There was a fleet closing in fast, and it was *massive*.

Marty didn't need to be told twice, and in a crackling blue flash of warp power, they were gone.

CHAPTER FIFTY-NINE

Freya was sitting on the landing pad atop the downtown command center, but she didn't think she'd be staying there much longer. Not with how worried and upset Daisy was.

"He did *what*?" Daisy asked, her anger and concern blending together in a heady mix of dangerous agitation.

"*He warped to the portal, then crossed over,*" Cal repeated. "*Quite an impressive bit of flying, actually. To arrive that close to the portal and time it out so accurately while warping in from within the system is no easy task. That's how they crossed over.*"

"But how was that even possible, Cal? The damn thing is supposed to be on lockdown."

"*It is. Mostly.*"

"Mostly?"

"*Technically, that's not exactly accurate, though we haven't made that bit public information. Only the AI fleet knew of it. And then, only the ones around the portal.*"

"Knew of what, exactly?"

"*We did have to have Rika open the portal one more time to send a drone with a security update for the satellite relay.*"

"Wait, what? Why would you risk opening it again?"

"We have assessed the efficiency and speed of the enemy attack and have come to believe that the crew of the Urok ship that was captured have almost certainly been compromised. And if that's the case, then the invaders are able to read the portal-opening schedule off of the satellite, just like our people can."

Daisy began pacing angrily. "Shit. So you had no choice but to switch to a new protocol that only Charlie and the rest of our guys would know, while keeping the Uroks out of the loop."

"Precisely."

"Well, you're going to have to open it again."

"I'm sorry, but that's not possible."

"Like hell it isn't. Let's go, Freya. Get us up there."

"I told you that you were in trouble, Sis. Boys will do stupid, macho things to impress a girl."

But he should know better than this. I mean, even for Arlo, this is just stupid.

"Teenage hormones, Daze. What can you do?"

Ground his ass until he's twenty-three, that's what.

"Daisy, I've spoken with Korbin. It appears that Karasalia and Vee are nowhere to be found. It seems quite likely that Arlo took them with him."

"Oh, that kid is in so much trouble," she growled.

"I have already begun reaching out to our allies to put together a recovery team. Korbin said he does have one thing he would like to share with us that could make a difference. I should be able to get the others lined up for a strategy session within the hour."

"Nope. There's no time. I'm going now, so you'd better get that portal open," Daisy replied.

The tone in her voice was one Cal was familiar with, and he knew that come hell or high water, that woman was crossing over to get her kid. Fortunately, it seemed that Freya's magically modified nanites were capable of overcoming the issues with their warp systems in that galaxy, though a proper trial hadn't been done yet to verify the theory.

Freya raced skyward in a flash, popping out of the atmosphere and warping to the fleet orbiting the sun in an instant.

"Zed, is Rika still standing by to access the portal?" Daisy transmitted to the waiting fleet's command ship.

"Negative. She went back down to Earth for a follow-up visit with the docs after the last opening, but she's on her way back up now," the AI replied. "But she got pretty banged up in the fight, you know. I'm not sure if her casting again in short order is such a good idea."

"If she can walk, she can cast, and I need that portal open yesterday."

"She's on her way. It'll just take as long as it takes. It seems Marban is bringing her up himself," Zed replied.

"Pirate boy? Great. I'm standing by."

Daisy then proceeded to pace back and forth within Freya's stealthy hull, waiting for the human spell caster to arrive and open the damn portal for her.

"Stop the pacing, Daze. You're giving me a headache."

You don't have a head.

"Precisely. I live in your *head, so if my head's aching, yours must be too. And drink something, will ya? You're getting dehydrated."*

Daisy reluctantly stopped her pacing and forced herself to down an electrolyte pouch and a protein bar.

Better?

"Better," Sarah replied.

Daisy flopped down in her seat, checking the displays to see if they were ready for her yet. They weren't.

"What the hell was that stupid kid thinking?"

"He wasn't, obviously. It's a teenager thing."

"He could get himself killed. Himself and the others."

"The invincibility of youth," Sarah replied with a chuckle. *"You know teens have no fear. At least, not until they experience a bitter taste of the real world."*

"Well, I'm worried he's already got a mouthful on the other side of that portal."

"We'll cross over soon. You know Rika's a pro and won't dick around once she gets here, so just take a breath and chill before you stroke out or something."

"You'll be the first to know if I start smelling toast, Sis," Daisy said, then took a deep breath and focused her energy inward.

She hadn't been spending much time with Fatima's meditative teachings in recent years, but if ever there was a time she could use them, this was it. Sarah was right, she needed to chill the hell out before she blew a gasket.

Finally, Rika and Marban arrived and the human caster began the spell.

"It'll only stay open about ten seconds," she informed Daisy and Freya. "I'm having Jo send you the timeline for the next five subsequent openings. You and you alone have them, so keep 'em close to the vest. Once you're safely back, then we can discuss a proper way to deal with the likely compromise of the satellite."

"Got it," Daisy said. "And Rika, thank you."

"You bet. Okay, here it comes. Portal will clear the sun in ten seconds."

"Weapons hot, kiddo, and be ready to warp as soon as we're clear."

"I'm ready, Daisy," Freya replied.

"Okay, then. Let's do this."

The stealthy ship's engines and warp orb were fully powered, just waiting to release their potential. The moment the portal pulled free, they took off like a shot, blasting through the portal at speed just as it paused and began closing into the sun again.

"She's gone," Zed said. "All we can do now is hope and wait."

On the other side of the portal, Freya popped into the galaxy with her weapons already firing a deadly barrage at the Tslavar ships.

"Punch it!" Daisy commanded.

In an instant, the ship was gone, long before the Tslavar ships could mount a counterattack. All that remained was a crackling blue aura of where she'd just been. Daisy had come to get her kid, and nothing would stand in her way.

CHAPTER SIXTY

After the destruction wrought upon the Wampeh Ghalian stronghold on Otsola, Leila was beside herself. Not only had she been forced to witness the brutal carnage that Malalia had cast upon the building she'd learned of from her drained captive, but also something far worse.

Leila had been forced to watch her own Magus stone be tricked into thinking she was being attacked, the incredibly powerful relic reacting violently. And it was her friends it lashed out at.

Hunze was alive. She'd seen that much as Malalia's men restrained her unconscious body as they took her captive. Bawb, however, was another story. He'd wisely run from the blast, though she knew it must have been impossibly hard for him to do so.

But dead men can't seek revenge, and he was a Wampeh Ghalian. Revenge was a dish best served by his capable hands.

Leila had no real power to speak of on her own. Just an intuitive connection with animals, which was how she became Malalia's father's animalist in the first place. As such, now that she'd been stripped of her Magus stone, she was no longer seen as any sort of a threat whatsoever.

All of these things led to one turn of good luck for Leila. By the time she had the stone taken from her, she'd been in the visla's cells for so long that no one thought to search her. It was a simple mistake the first time, as she was so recently a guest of the house and no one knew exactly why she was being moved to a cell.

After the stone flashed to life, protecting her from any further contact, she'd remained untouched. And now, back in her cell, she would put that to use. Her boots were nothing special. Just boots, or so they seemed. But stitched within the seam was a gift from Charlie, forged with Ara and Bawb's help. A slender, magical rod the length of her palm. Just the right size for easy concealment.

The konus they had selected in making it was not exceptionally powerful—such a degree of magic would likely be detected anyway—but it was more than enough to cast basic spells. It could also help her pick the magical restraining locks keeping her door shut. Or, at least, she hoped so.

Leila had spent enough time in the cell by now to have an idea how they worked, and she'd learned that if she pressed her ear close to the slot, she could hear the faintest traces of hallway noise, if there was any. She leaned in and did just that, pausing thirty seconds, listening for any sound of a guard, or worse.

Nothing.

She stepped back a pace and held the konus rod in her fist, then began slowly, carefully, picking away at the fringes of the magic holding her door shut. It was like trying to dislodge a boulder with a toothpick, but she was confident that all she needed was patience, luck, and time. And the latter she felt she would have in abundance.

. . .

"This is hopeless," she sighed to herself an hour later. It wasn't that she was being impatient, nor that she would not have time, but having now studied the powerful magic holding the door fast, it was apparent that even with a fully powered konus, she would be unable to break the spell holding her prisoner.

It wasn't Malalia's power sealing the room, though. This was Visla Palmarian's. Leila had been around him enough to know the difference. He was an incredibly strong man, and rather than use her own power on things like containment, Malalia had simply commandeered his pre-existing spells and tailored them to her own uses.

Malalia had her trapped, it seemed. But this Leila was not the same woman she had known and bullied back on her father's estate. Nor was she the queen she'd fought on ancient Earth. Leila had friends of great and varied skills, and all had taught her much in their time together. And now it was time to put some of that to use.

Taking a cue from Bawb's bag of tricks, Leila carefully began casting fairly weak binding spells at ankle level. Then, a few paces ahead, she cast the most powerful stun spells she could put in place with the little konus, setting them just above the floor.

It wouldn't be too long a wait. All she had to do now was put on a good show. Acting was never her strong suit, but with her freedom on the line, she was going to do her best to put on an award-worthy performance.

A half hour later a tray of food slid into her cell.

"I need help. I hurt myself," she called out.

"Too bad," a gruff voice replied.

"But I think it might be serious."

"Not my problem," the voice said with a chuckle.

"Mal––Visla Dominus wouldn't be happy if her prisoner isn't kept healthy for her. But I'm sure you can explain it to her and she'll understand."

There was a long pause, then the muted sound of voices conferring among themselves. A moment later the door released and slid open.

She was glad to see there were only three of them. Any more than that and she was pretty sure she wouldn't stand a chance. Even as it was, this would be a serious challenge given her disadvantage.

"It's my wrist. I think I broke it," Leila said, bent over on her bed, cradling her arm, her konus rod held tight in her fist.

"Idiot. What the hell did you do to yourself?" the gruff one asked as he strode into the cell.

To his friends, stacked behind him in the doorway, it just looked like he tripped clumsily as he entered the room. The spells placed at ankle level were subtle things, after all.

Down he fell, but, as planned, his hands each hit the outermost stun spells, numbing them and preventing him from breaking his fall. His face hit the ground hard. Not hard enough to knock a man out, normally. But the strongest of the stun spells was waiting for him and finished the job nicely.

"Durka, get up, you lazy fool," his friends joked.

The downed man didn't move, but just lay there, breathing deep, quite unconscious.

"Oh, you fool. How did you manage this? You'll never hear the end of it," his comrade joked, stepping into the cell, completely unafraid of its unarmed occupant. "Give me a hand with him."

His associate stepped in with him and bent to lift their fallen friend. That was the moment. The opportunity she'd been waiting for.

Leila sprang off her cot and delivered a fierce kick to the nearest man's face, stunning him as his body tumbled backward from the impact. She'd run and played outdoors her whole life, and as a result, her legs were the strongest muscles in her body, as the poor man had just painfully learned.

The poor, weak woman was not so weak after all.

The other guard lurched back, avoiding her follow-up blow.

"You're not injured," he growled.

"No, but you soon will be," she replied.

"Horvath wasn't prepared. But *I* am," he said with a menacing grin.

"So am I," Leila said, casting hard and fast.

The flurry of spells weren't particularly damaging, and the guard had been ready for her to strike. But though he was ready for her, he had been prepared for a *physical* attack. None of them expected her to cast a magical one. She had no power, of that they'd been assured.

The little konus rod wasn't a lot, but it was enough to give her the advantage of surprise, and that would have to be enough.

A quick flurry of Charlie's distracting spells confused the guard. That was what she needed. Leila had the edge, at least for a moment, and she seized it, striking fast and driving her knee into the larger man's outer thigh hard, making the muscle spasm. He dropped a bit lower as a result, just as she threw a wicked elbow to his jaw.

The guard was tough, though, and stunned as he was, he shook it off and lunged for her on unsteady legs. Leila jumped back, throwing a snapping side kick into the face of his slowly rousing companion as she did, ensuring he *stayed* down. The other man whom she'd stunned would be out for at least ten minutes, if not longer.

"I'm going to snap you in two," the remaining guard snarled.

"I highly doubt that," she replied, with an amused laugh that dared him to even try.

The taunt had its intended effect, and the enraged man simply charged at the smaller woman rather than make a careful attack. His overconfidence in his superiority merely because of his size would be his downfall.

Leila pulled all the power she could from the konus, but rather than cast an attacking spell, she used the magical device to pull him toward her even faster, just as she jumped aside. She added a push to the pull as he flew past her, and the combined spells––along with a little kick given on the way––sent him slamming into the wall exceptionally hard.

"Thick skull on this one," Leila mused as he somehow remained upright, though down on one knee.

She grabbed his head and began slamming it into the wall with all the force she could muster. It was ugly and brutal, but effective. Finally, the guard dropped to the floor. He'd live, as would the others, but he would wake with a nasty headache.

Leila stripped the men of their resources, finding a weak konus in one's pouch and a small skree in another's pocket. Other than that, they were of no use to her. Escaping the cell was one thing, but getting free of the building itself would be quite another.

But step one had been achieved, so she crept out of her cell and sealed the door shut. She already knew the binding spells would engage once it closed, as she'd seen happen in her time within. She just hoped the release spell wouldn't work from the inside, and without a konus to power it.

Minimally armed and very much at a disadvantage, Leila quietly snuck off to survey the area properly and find a way out.

CHAPTER SIXTY-ONE

Charlie was sitting in his cell as patiently as he could. His control collar lay in pieces on the floor at his feet. It was a robust one. Far stronger than normally given even high-power prisoners. Whoever had taken possession of him had some idea of the kind of magic he possessed.

But they didn't know he had gained the additional power from his union with Bawb and the sharing of magic with Rika. Those two additional boosts gave him just enough strength to snap the band.

But it had hurt. A lot.

And it had greatly drained him in the process. Fortunately, he'd been afforded enough alone time to focus and meditate, regaining much of his energy. He was still greatly depleted, but at least he was not running on empty. In fact, given his skills and strength, he was confident he was more than ready for whatever fool came to check on him next.

This time he would not be stunned by a collar. *This* time he would blast his way out of there.

At long last, his door began to slide open.

"It's about goddamn time," he said as he casually called up his power, ready to make good on his escape.

His hapless victim strode into the cell. Oh, what a surprise he had in store for them.

"You have no idea who you––" he began, his confident snark cut off in a strangled gulp as his mind registered the impossible sight. "Malalia?"

"Hello, Charlie," she cooed in the most disturbingly sensual way. Said in that exaggerated manner that some would hyperbolically say was because you were so desirable they wanted to eat you alive. In her case, however, it wasn't far from the truth.

"Fuck," Charlie managed to blurt as he realized just how much trouble he was in.

The magic in him surged in an instant. Apparently, the sheer panic that triggered his adrenaline surge also summoned up reserves of magic he didn't know he possessed. A visceral survival instinct. Fight or flight. And with Malalia in the room, there was only one option.

He cast the most violent spells he could in rapid succession. A flurry of deadly magic of multiple styles and origins, including more than a few Wampeh Ghalian tricks he'd learned from his newest friends.

Malalia batted them aside as if the spells were no more than a nuisance. Magic that could have killed or disabled several highly powered casters was a joke to her, and if there'd been any doubt as to just how easy it had been for her to stop his attack, to add insult to injury, she added an amused, and utterly relaxed, chuckle.

She looked at Charlie a moment, then gave him a flirty wink, but the ice in her eyes made her true feelings quite clear. And there was nothing he could do to stop her. Charlie stopped casting, saving what power he had left. He was utterly outmatched, and even at full strength, and with Ara at his side, he doubted they'd be able to stop her.

He took a deep breath, counting to four as he did, forcing himself to calm down. Panic wouldn't help him survive this, nor would his magic. He'd have to rely on his wits.

"I'm sorry about that, Malalia," he said with as relaxed a grin as he could force upon his face. "Old habits, you know."

"Of course, *darling*," she cooed menacingly. "I'd expect no less of you."

An uncomfortable silence hung in the air as the mouse eyed the hungry cat.

"This seems a rather unlikely meeting," Charlie noted. "How, exactly, did you manage to survive? Last I saw, you were sucked through a vortex into what seemed to be empty space."

Malalia grinned. "A fascinating story, I assure you. And one I'm sure you would find most interesting. And perhaps, one day, I'll even share it with you. But that will have to wait. You see, after your little attempt, I find myself feeling rather peckish."

She then smiled at him, her fangs slowly sliding into place. It was a trick he'd seen Bawb do once as an intimidation tactic during an interrogation. Learning you were about to be fed upon was a terrifying thing that loosened a lot of tongues and helped gather much intelligence from frightened captives.

And now he was on the receiving end. The effect was, as he'd known it would be, quite unsettling.

"You're still feeding off of Wampeh? After all this time?"

"Yes. They have a wonderful power that has granted me a very, very long life."

He looked at her more closely. Her skin was perfect, and her hair radiant. In fact, it seemed she hadn't aged a day since he'd last seen her on the battlefield on ancient Earth. However unlikely it may have been, it seemed she'd been able to source the rarest of Wampeh, stealing their power.

"I'll admit, their power seems to have done wonders for you."

"Thank you, Charlie. I do so enjoy my Wampeh meals. But you know what?"

He didn't think he'd like the sound of that *what*.

"For *you*, I'll make an exception," Malalia said, moving close in a flash, her immense power radiating off of her like a heady musk. "We have history, after all. And you have so much more delicious power now," she said, holding him in an iron grip as she forced his head to the side and sank her fangs into his neck.

Charlie felt his legs go weak as his magic was pulled from his body. *So, this is what it feels like,* he mused, utterly unable to speak aloud, let alone break free. He just wondered if she'd drain him entirely or keep him alive to torment at her leisure. In any case, he felt he'd be unconscious soon enough.

"Charlie!" a voice shrieked in horrified distress.

Leila? he thought, unable to voice her name. He really must have been far gone if he'd started hearing things.

But he wasn't. His queen had happened upon the open cell door and peeked inside as she tried to find a means of escape from the tower. What she saw, had both thrilled and horrified her.

Malalia released her grip and let Charlie drop to the ground at her feet, turning and flashing a bloody smile.

Leila didn't hesitate, charging into the cell, ready to fight. Her reaction actually surprised Malalia. This unpowered woman was *actually* foolish enough to attack her? And after she'd taken on even more power, no less?

"Get away from him, you bitch!" Leila shrieked, casting with her stolen konus.

It was almost cute, the futile attempt. But Malalia had other business to attend to. Tormenting the pair would have to wait, but she had all the time in the world to make them both suffer.

Malalia pulled up a powerful spell, designed to hurt as well as stun. She had healers who could repair the damage done, and she wanted Leila to suffer. She cast with malice in her heart, the magic flying true. But then the unexpected happened.

The spell was going to harm Leila, but the woman casting it was still wearing her Magus stone. The reaction was as massive as it was sudden.

Malalia's spell was snuffed out, its power redirected back at its caster and immensely magnified, the stone adding enough power to be utterly deadly for any less powerful being. Malalia found herself knocked flat to the ground, as if pummeled by a giant's fist.

But even then, she wasn't entirely unconscious. Somehow, she managed to keep her eyes open, struggling to regain her equilibrium. Leila rushed forward and snatched her Magus stone from around the dazed woman's neck, then kicked her viciously in the head, making sure she was down.

She tried to strike her again to finish the job once and for all, but found her blows would not land. Apparently, the woman had some sort of safeguard spell in place that protected her from harm should she become incapacitated.

Leila slapped Charlie. "Wake up! We have to go!"

"What?" he managed to say. "Leila? You're actually here?"

She kissed him hard, feeling his pulse and power react as one. He was still weak, no doubt, but she'd given him the motivation he needed to fight back and regain his senses.

"Babe, how—?"

"Later. We have to go."

With her help, he struggled to his feet. His legs were still weak, but he braced himself, arm around her shoulders, and began walking. He looked at Malalia's unconscious form on the ground. Her nose, it seemed, was broken. Whatever Leila had done, he regretted not seeing it.

"Her going down seems to have triggered an alarm," he noted.

"I don't hear it."

"Magic. I can sense it. We're going to have company really soon."

"There's no safe way down. I've been trying to find one, but we're cut off," Leila said.

"Anywhere's better than here," Charlie replied.

"Through there," Leila said, helping him through the nearest corridor.

"Stairs?" Charlie groaned.

The sound of approaching footsteps rang out from below.

"Not down. Up," Leila replied. "The floating gardens. I don't know what we can do from there, but it'll at least buy us some time. And I have this," she said, showing him her stolen skree.

"Small. Not very powerful. And I have no idea who to even call with it," he said.

"We can worry about that once we're outside. Now, come on!"

The couple hurried up the stairs, Charlie's legs regaining a bit of strength as they moved. The gardens were impressive, and had they not been running for their lives, Charlie would have very much liked to spend some time with his lady love taking in the view. But death was on their tail, and it was looking very much like they had nowhere to run.

There were many gardens floating around the building on which they could try to hide, but eventually they'd be caught. Charlie felt the unfamiliar sensation of defeat threatening to overwhelm him, when a strange little rippling blur in the air caught his eye.

"Leila? What's tha—?"

A shimmer ship abruptly appeared. A Tslavar ship.

"Oh, shit," Charlie gasped. "We are so screwed."

A secret fail-safe guard overseeing the gardens? Who would have expected it? No one, obviously, and that was precisely why it would serve its purpose so well. And any second now a team of Tslavar mercenaries would swarm out and haul them back to their cells. And this time they wouldn't be able to escape.

"Hey, Charlie!" Tym said, bounding out of the ship, a pair of pulse rifles in hand. "What are you doing here?"

"Me? What are *you* doing here? You're supposed to be on Earth. And how did you get our captured shimmer ship? I thought it was out of shimmer magic."

"Oh, that. That Korbin fella helped out. Recharged the onboard shimmer power stores. I figured I couldn't very well spend my coin in that other galaxy, and when Cal said he needed someone to fly this thing through to help with something at Slafara, naturally, I was game. But I guess when I added my Drookonus to the jump the Drooks were already casting, I kind of overpowered us and we got here first."

"I didn't know you could do that."

"In a pinch. But some people think it's dangerous, so it's usually frowned upon. Only the most skilled of us can do it. Speaking of skill, things got a bit hairy when I made the run across the portal. Did you see my moves? Best pilot in the galaxy, no matter what Olo says!"

"I saw. And, yes, it was very impressive."

"Legendary. That's what they'll call me. Tymprazagal the Legendary."

"Tym, that's great and all, but can you tell us the rest of this in the air? We've got a pissed off visla and all of her goons about to come charging out here after us."

"What? Oh, crap. Yeah, come on, hop aboard!"

Charlie and Leila raced into the waiting ship and up to the command center. A moment later the ship activated its shimmer as it took off into the sky, its destination unknown to any who may have observed it.

CHAPTER SIXTY-TWO

It had only been an hour or so since the disturbance in the cells after Mareh Palmarian, aka Visla Dominus, aka Malalia Maktan's prisoners had made their unlikely escape, and the chaos inside of the Palmarian estate was at a peak. But the returning Palmarian heir didn't know any of that as she swooped down to her home.

When Kara directed her friends to ignore the open pads on the ground and just land atop the floating gardens of her father's estate, landscaping be damned, Arlo and Marty weren't about to argue. The AI ship quickly settled down as close to the building as possible.

Kara and Vee were out the door in a shot, rushing into the building, Arlo close behind.

"What are you doing up here?" the guard patrolling the staircase asked. He was a visla, Kara was certain. A lower level one, but the traces of power radiating off of him were clear. It was strange, though. She'd never been able to sense these things until recently. Until she was away from home. Until her power began to so abruptly grow.

"Where's Shozzy?" Kara asked the man.

"He's been placed on limited duty," the man replied.

"But he's captain of my father's guards."

"Not at the moment, and the visla has instructed me to personally guard this entrance."

"Entrance? It's to the gardens."

"Yet you entered by it. Proving the point."

Kara knew she didn't like the man the moment she laid eyes on him. His continued attitude only strengthened the feeling.

"Whatever," Kara said, brushing past the man, her friends in tow.

They raced down to her father's chambers, ignoring the guard entirely as she shoved him aside with her powers, not even realizing she was doing it. Vee and Arlo shared a glance, but said nothing.

"Father!" she exclaimed, rushing to his side.

The visla didn't rouse, his chest rising and falling slowly but his eyes not even flickering a hint of awareness.

"Why is he like this? What's going on?" Kara asked, tears welling in her eyes.

She held his hand, but it was limp in her grip. His power was nearly gone. The man whose strength had been such a constant in her life was weaker than even she had ever been.

"How could I have doubted him, Vee? He's so weak. Look at him. There's no way he could have been behind the attack on Earth. What happened to him?"

"Hello, Karasalia," Mareh said, strolling into the room from the adjacent chamber, smiling a pointy-toothed grin.

"You?" Kara gasped, almost falling off her feet with shock.

"Yes, dear. Me."

"You're Dominus?"

"Indeed, I am. Though that's not my true name any more than Mareh is."

Kara and her friends began backing out of the room slowly. This was a deadly cat, and they were very much mice. It didn't need to be stated, it was obvious on a visceral level.

"You needn't run. I assure you, the tower is on lockdown, and I've placed several highly powered guards at all key positions."

"But we got in," Arlo blurted.

"Yes. You got *in*," she replied.

"Oh, crap," he gasped.

"Why, Mareh? My father loved you. I loved you. You were part of our family."

"And a wonderfully powerful family you've been. I've been feeding off you both for so many years. Without the power I took from each of you, I doubt I'd have been able to amass my forces nearly as quickly. And just look at you," Malalia said, reaching out with her power. "Your power is growing so, now that you've been out of my reach for so long. I look forward to making it mine."

"You stay the hell away from her!" Arlo threatened.

"Oh, that's cute. You know what? I think I'll give your little human friend here to my men as a new plaything."

"Like hell you will," a new voice in the room replied with deadly intent.

"Mom?" Arlo said, spinning around.

"Get away from her, Arlo," Daisy said, her sword strapped to her back and a massive, customized, bleeding-edge pulse rifle in her hands. One of Cal's newest experiments, no doubt.

"The heretic is returned? And she's this one's mother, no less? How quaint," Malalia said.

Then, without warning, she cast a powerful killing spell, directing all of its deadly intent at Daisy. It was a massive one. Overpowered for a mere Earth woman, but Malalia was feeling feisty and wanted to make a show of this one's death.

The spell flew true, but dispersed around her harmlessly,

failing to damage so much as a hair on Daisy's head. Both women seemed confused by what had just happened, but Malalia hesitated a split second longer than Daisy did, and that was enough.

The pulse rifle blasted out an enormous charge, catching Malalia square in the chest and sending her crashing through several walls, despite the magical shielding she always had protecting her. At this close range, the weapon seemed more than capable of having an impact on the fight, quite literally.

"Holy shit, Sis. I think you may have had that thing turned all the way up to ten," Sarah commented.

Nah. I had Freya custom mod this one to give it some extra 'oomph,' Daisy replied to her mental ride-along with a little chuckle. *This one goes to eleven.*

Daisy turned her attention to the kids. "I've got a bad feeling that isn't going to stop her for long. Come on!" she commanded.

They took off running, following Daisy up the stairs.

"Daisy, my scans are showing another power user up ahead!" Freya warned.

It was too late, the man was standing ready, apparently keyed in to her pulse weapon by its recent discharge. She fired anyway, but he'd had time to adjust his spells and place multiple layers ahead of himself to disperse the energy.

Daisy shot again, but the man was already moving in, dodging the shot and getting close, fast.

"Arlo!" she called out, tossing him the rifle with one hand, while drawing Stabby with the other.

The bone sword gleamed, even in the lack of outside lighting. It was crackling with power, and from what Kara could sense, it was thirsty for more. The unusual weapon wasn't enchanted, though.

No, as she already knew, the power it possessed was its own, but taken from those it had slain. And the power it currently possessed felt an awful lot like that of the obnoxious visla who'd been guarding the gardens.

The guard casting against them moved in with powerful magic, but Stabby was unsheathed and hungry for a fight. The blade deflected his attacks one after another, confounding the poor man as he tried to wrap his head around how a non-enchanted weapon could possibly do what it seemed to be doing.

He wouldn't have to wonder much longer, though, as the blade plunged through his magic and into his chest, greedily sucking his blood and power from him. Moments later, he dropped to the ground, a lifeless husk.

"Jesus, Mom, what the hell?" Arlo gasped.

"I'll explain later. We've gotta go."

"No. My father is here, and he needs me!" Kara protested. "I'm not leaving him behind."

"We can't go back down there. She's too strong," Vee said.

"I'm not leaving!"

"There's no time for this, Daze," Sarah said.

I know, she replied. "Listen, kid. It's live or die. We'll come back for him, but right now, we have to go."

"I'm not leaving!" Kara protested, a flare of magic crackling from her fingertips.

"I'm so sorry," Daisy said.

"Sorry? Why are you——?" Kara started to say.

Daisy punched her hard and fast, right at the corner of her jaw. Even the toughest of fighters would drop from that blow if they weren't ready for it. Kara dropped in a heap.

"Cover our six, Arlo," Daisy ordered as she threw the girl over her shoulder.

"Mom, what the fuck?"

"Language, Mister."

"Don't 'language' me. You just punched out Kara," he said as he and Vee followed his mom as she raced out onto the gardens.

"No time, Arlo. Shut it and run," she grunted, racing to Freya's waiting shape and scrambling inside.

The teens followed her, their own ride no longer waiting on the surface of the Garden. Instead, Marty was already in the air, hovering nearby, ready to go.

"But we need magic to guide us," Arlo pointed out.

"Freya has it. It's in her nanites. And Marty's warp system has already tied in with hers," Daisy explained as she dropped Kara into a seat and strapped her in. "And you are so grounded when we get home."

"I really don't——" Marty began.

"*Both* of you," Daisy added.

"We're being attached," Freya said.

"Attacked?"

"No, attached. A magical handshake tying into our warp system."

"Weapons hot, Freya!" Daisy shouted in alarm.

"Hey, guys, I see your guns going hot. Don't shoot us," a voice called out over comms.

"How do you have our comms frequency?" Daisy asked. "Hang on, is this Charlie?"

"In the flesh," he replied.

"Where are you?"

"Right next to you, actually," he said, the craft lowering its shimmer for a moment, then raising it again immediately. "Korbin secretly sent Tym through with this ship to help, but he got here before you all and found us instead. We've been waiting to see who would show up. That was quite a performance you put on. But we can talk about that later. I really think we need to get the hell out of here, and I mean like yesterday."

"Ditto," Freya said. "You have a safe warp rally point?"

"Yep. Tym has one in mind, and we're tied in to your warp. Just follow our lead," Charlie said. "Okay, Tym. Punch it!"

A second later the three ships jump/warped away as one, leaving a fuming visla behind on the planet of Slafara.

Malalia was overflowing with rage, her anger manifesting in the form of deadly magic trickling off of her body in rivulets. A holdover from the volatile magic she'd stolen from her husband, no doubt.

She reined in the power when the captain of her surge ship docked atop the gardens and rushed in to his waiting visla. He'd been able to cross into the other galaxy and successfully jump clear of the battle near the sun. And what his speedy survey of the system would tell her was of great interest.

"Visla," he said, eyes lowered as he entered the room.

"What do you have for me?" Malalia asked, her rage slowly coming under control.

"Good news, Visla. We found a suitable world within the system. Uninhabited and unmonitored. A gas giant that is more than capable of hiding our arrival and concealing our forces."

"This is indeed good news," Malalia said, pleased at the little win. After a humiliating defeat like she'd just been handed, she needed one.

"There's more, Visla," he continued.

"Oh? Tell me."

Her captain smiled. It was his good fortune to be the bearer of good news, and she would remember him well for it. "The planet is stormy, but if the portal is placed near enough to the outer reaches of the gaseous mass, it is close enough to the system's sun to receive power from its rays."

A smile grew on Malalia's face. This wasn't just good news, this was great news. She could harvest power for her new portal on this side by pulling it from her enemy's own commandeered one. And now, it seemed, she could also power her portal from the other side, drawing the energy on two fronts.

They wouldn't be able to stop her. Not with an uninterruptible energy source. Not even if they managed to block the power on one end. This was what she'd been waiting for.

All she needed to do now was find a way to create a new portal. And she had an idea.

CHAPTER SIXTY-THREE

Of all the worlds for the oddball pilot to choose, Charlie really couldn't believe the man's choice. Nor could Leila, for that matter. In fact, when he took his stolen Tslavar shimmer ship in for a landing, his two Earth ship friends close behind, they looked at one another with disbelief.

No one else present could have understood what this meant to the couple. Bawb and Ara would, but they were not present as Tym guided them in to land on the overgrown arrival field of Visla Yoral Maktan's long-abandoned estate.

Charlie and Leila stepped out, fingers interlaced as they took in the sight of the crumbling manor at which they'd first met.

The pilot jauntily hopped out of the ship close behind them, followed by his team of free Drooks.

"Plenty of fresh water over at those fountains," he told them. "And there are a whole bunch of fruit trees just over that way. Rest up and enjoy the free air, my friends," he told them.

It dawned on Charlie that since their Tslavar owners had been defeated on Earth, leaving the ship in their former opponent's hands and the Drooks themselves freed from slavery, this was the first time they'd been back to their home galaxy. In that regard, it must have been almost as strange a feeling for them as it was for Charlie and Leila.

Almost.

"Tym, why, exactly, did you choose this, of all places?" Charlie asked as he looked around in wonder.

"Oh, *this* place? It's one of my favorite little secret spots. Quite abandoned, you see, yet close to major shipping hubs."

"But it's been abandoned for centuries. No one's been here," Leila said.

"Well, yes and no. I mean, it *seems* like no one's been here, but then, I take great pains to make sure it looks that way whenever I come here for a stopover. Can't have our best-kept secrets become non-secrets after all, right?"

"And you're not worried about being found out?"

"Why would I? Ever since the fall of the Maktans, anything related to them is pretty much avoided."

"But Malalia Maktan lives," Charlie said, still amazed as the words left his lips. "What? How is that even possible?" Tym replied, confused.

"Believe me, I'm wondering that myself."

"I can help with that," Leila said. "The long and short of it is, she was thrown back to many years after the fall of the Council of Twenty. But she'd stashed wealth and power items before she vanished. Knowing that she could steal Wampeh power and make it her own, she's been sucking them dry ever since, keeping herself young and powerful in the process."

"But that's hundreds of years," Tym gasped.

"And it sounds totally like something that she would do," Charlie replied. "Great, so Visla Dominus is actually Malalia Maktan. And she's been amassing power for *hundreds* of years. Oh, this just keeps getting better. Rika's going to be thrilled."

The trio walked over to the sleek stealth ship to share the information with their allies. Plus, Charlie was looking forward to meeting this Daisy character in person. She was kind of legendary, and from what he'd seen so far, she lived up to the hype.

"Come on in," Freya said as they reached her open door. "The others are inside waiting for Kara to wake up."

"Kara's here?" Leila asked, surprised.

"And Vee," Freya informed her.

Leila eagerly entered the ship, pausing a moment to marvel at the sleek interior. Charlie, as a man from Earth, was even more impressed than the others. This was an engineering marvel the likes of which he'd never seen. And from what he'd learned from Cal, Freya had essentially built herself.

A redheaded woman looked up at the new visitors from her seat beside a groggy, violet-skinned teen. She was holding an ice pack on the girl's jaw, an apologetic look on her face.

Another girl, obviously Ootaki with hair like that, was sitting nearby with what appeared to be a normal Earth boy.

"You must be the infamous Daisy," Charlie said, extending his hand.

"And you must be the equally infamous Charlie," she replied, shaking firmly.

"I'm Leila, and this it Tym," Charlie's queen added.

"Oh, I know that one," Daisy said, nodding toward Tym. "This is Karasalia, and that's Visanya."

"Oh, we know Leila," Vee said.

"And no one calls me that but my dad. Call me Kara."

"And call me Vee."

"Noted," Charlie said.

"And that soon-to-be-grounded one is my kid, Arlo. Say hello, Arlo."

"Hello, Arlo," the teen replied.

Daisy shot him a look that only a mother could pull off.

"*Fine*. Hello, nice to meet you," he said in a far more respectful tone.

"What's with that one?" he asked, noting the daggers Kara's eyes were shooting at Daisy.

"I had to knock her out to get us out of there before that Mareh/Dominus character killed us all. I didn't want to do it, but she left me no choice."

"We could have stayed. We could have saved my father," Kara shot back.

"No, Kara, she's right," Vee interjected. "We could have stayed and been killed. You saw her magic. There was no way we could stop her."

"But *you* did," Kara sniped at Daisy. "That was a *killing* spell she used on you. A powerful one too. How come it didn't do anything to you at all?"

"No idea, kid," Daisy replied. "After all the wizard guys Stabby has killed, maybe he has the power to stop that sort of thing now," she mused.

"Uh, Daisy. Could we chat?" Freya quietly asked.

"Sure, kiddo. What's up?"

"In private."

"After all we've been through? There's no secrets here, Freya. Spit it out."

"Well, okay, but I don't know if you'll like it."

"Only one way to know."

"Right. Okay. So, while you were making your rescue, I was scanning all of the life signs in the vicinity––"

"I didn't need rescuing," Arlo protested.

"Shut up, Arlo," Daisy said with a healthy dose of mom glare. "Go on, Freya."

"Well, something unexpected came up while I was scanning. There was a familial DNA genetic match there with the one called Mareh."

"Her real name's Malalia, by the way," Leila corrected.

"No, that's not possible," Kara said in shock. "Mareh's not my real mom."

"Oh, not your DNA, Kara," Freya said. "I meant Daisy's."

Had there been a glass in Daisy's hand, it would have dropped to the deck and shattered.

"Say what, now?" Sarah gasped in her mind.

"Say what, now?" Daisy echoed, aloud.

"DNA doesn't lie, Daisy. Malalia is apparently your great-great-great-great-great––you get the idea. You're her descendant. Sarah too, of course, seeing as you're sisters," Freya informed her.

"Family," Vee gasped, looking at Kara, who immediately realized what she was thinking.

"Oh my Gods, you're right," Kara said in shock.

"What are you talking about?" Daisy asked, increasingly agitated.

"It's a magic thing. A completely random fluke. A lot of spells won't work on a blood relative. No one knows why, exactly, but it's a well-documented phenomenon," Kara said. "And that would explain why Mar––Malalia couldn't cast against you. At least, not a killing spell."

"But I don't get it," Daisy protested. "She's my age. Younger, even. And she's an alien in another galaxy!"

"Yeah, about that," Charlie said, realizing what this meant, seeing the Gordian threads suddenly untangle. "We kind of had a time travel incident and wound up on Earth a few thousand years ago."

"Time travel?" Freya asked. "Daisy, we time traveled too. Do you think––"

"Freya!" Daisy chastised the AI.

"Oh, right. Sorry," Freya said, brushing her comment aside. "Go on."

But Daisy realized it was too late. Arlo had definitely taken note, and Marty was undoubtedly listening in.

"So, Malalia found a way to use Ootaki hair to power a massive portal through space to pursue us," Charlie said. "Only, she didn't realize what she was tapping into was also a rift in time. And she messed it up and wound up arriving well before us. Needing to get established, she wound up shacking up with a local king. When we finally ran across her in battle, she had just had their child. We never found out what happened to that baby."

"Ask where it was, Daze," Sarah said.

"Right. Where was this?"

"The UK," Charlie replied.

Freya immediately keyed in on what Sarah was getting at. "You have red hair, Daisy. A common trait in the north. And now we know that geographically, it makes sense given your ancestral history. Your genetic line traces back to the offspring of a human and an alien spell-caster."

And other Sarah and I both got itchy from that magic water stuff. A super diluted reaction, Daisy realized.

"Traces of alien DNA," Sarah marveled.

Daisy flopped back down into her seat. Even Kara, who was still mad as hell at her, couldn't help but feel sorry for her. It wasn't every day you realize your darkest enemy is also related.

"Oh, man, I just realized something else," Freya blurted.

"Lord, what now?" Daisy asked with an exasperated sigh.

"It's just, you and Sarah were the first cell lines resistant enough to the Ra'az plague to make an entirely organic body. That's how you came to lead the resistance. Daisy, if it was because of your trace alien genetics, that means that Malalia might actually be the reason we won the war."

"Mind. Blown," Sarah said.

"Me too, Sis."

"Who's she talking to?" Leila asked.

"Her dead/not-dead sister," Freya replied. "I'll explain later."

"Sorry to interrupt," Marty said over Freya's internal comms, "but we have another kind of pressing matter at hand. Freya says the bad guys know the timing of the portal. That means we can't get the new schedule to get back."

"There's a security patch in the works. A new, secret frequency, that we should be able to use at least a few times before the enemy can tap in," Freya said.

"That's assuming the Urok are resisting, of course," Marty replied. "And if they already broke them and got the old code, it's safe to assume they'll get the new one too, if they coerce their techs into helping crack it. They know the protocols."

This *was* a problem, but one Charlie was confident would be worked out. They were alive, and they were safe. For the moment, that was more than enough.

"For now, we stay in this galaxy. We've got a rebel fleet amassing to fight Visla Dominus. And now that we know who we're up against, I have a feeling we'll be able to recruit even more to our side when people learn it's a Maktan they're fighting against."

Tym, for one, was thrilled.

"We're staying? Excellent. In that case, I could use a drink, and I know a quaint little pub on a quiet planet not too far from here. And there's a rather robust underworld presence as well. Perfect to recruit for this sort of thing."

Daisy, shocked as she was, couldn't help but laugh at the ridiculous man's enthusiasm. "You know what? Why not? I could *really* use a drink about now."

"Yeah, me too," Arlo said.

"Don't press your luck," his mom shot back. "You're in enough trouble as it is." She paused a moment. "Come here, I want a few words with you," she said, leading him out of the compartment.

Arlo followed, bracing himself for the tongue-lashing he was likely about to receive. Surprisingly, it was something far different.

"Listen, I know you heard what Freya said about time travel, but you *cannot* mention it to anyone when we get back. Is that clear?"

"So it's true?" he asked, eyes wide.

"I said, is that clear?"

"Yes, ma'am."

"Good. Now, I'm going to have Freya send the details over to Marty, but they're for your eyes only. You're old enough to know the truth about your mom's past, but it absolutely must not go beyond you and Marty. Clear?"

"Clear."

"What are you doing, Daze?" Sarah asked.

Just giving him what he needs to know, Sis. He's about the right age, and we knew this was coming eventually. Who's to say this isn't how it started?

Sarah chuckled inside of her head. *"Poor kid. His life's about to get a whole lot more interesting."*

That it is, Sarah. That it most certainly is.

Daisy and Arlo rejoined the others a few minutes later.

"So, Tym. You were saying you know a pub?" she asked.

"Indeed, I do. A wonderful place I frequent often. And now I can finally spend some of that hard-earned coin. Nothing worse than making a profit and not being able to enjoy it, you know."

"Never had that problem," she replied. "But I'll take your word for it. And it's a safe place for us to lay low while we plan our next steps?"

"The safest."

Charlie leaned in closer. "Then lead the way, my friend," he said. "And Tym?"

"Yes, Charlie?"

The unlikely human caster from a galaxy far, far away smiled wide. "The first round is on you."

EPILOGUE

A tiny portal, no bigger than the smallest ship in Visla Dominus's fleet, sat adjacent to its massive, sun-spewing cousin. But this portal was not destroyed by the burning plasma shooting from the far larger iteration.

In fact, that very solar energy was powering the small amount of Ootaki hair that had been tracked down by Dominus's henchmen. The same hair that was now keeping the little portal open.

In a distant system, quite far away, the other end of that portal ejected a steady stream of pure solar power from Earth's sun. And right in its path, just far enough away to avoid any harm, was a ship.

It wasn't a particularly large one, nor was it overly armed or modified in any special way. But it did possess one thing that Visla Dominus desired. A forward-facing compartment with large window openings in which she could secure her Ootaki captive, feeding massive amounts of the sun's energy into the unconscious woman's hair.

Malalia had tried to cut a few strands by different means, but just as with the lone hair she'd plucked from Hunze's head, every subsequent one taken had reacted the same way, regardless of manner of harvest. They had withered to dull shadows of themselves as the magic they contained rushed back to the slumbering woman's body.

Hunze was the key, and this hair was bound to her. Without the Ootaki woman, her locks were worthless. Perhaps she could willingly gift her hair, as she'd done with her Wampeh lover, but Malalia simply couldn't risk allowing the incredibly powerful woman to wake. Not now. Especially not after supercharging her hair like this with the unusual sun's rays.

If she were to rouse, there was no telling what havoc she might cause. And despite her own immense power, Malalia simply didn't know if Hunze might actually be able to best her. There'd never been an Ootaki caster before, and the power she was able to sense from the unconscious woman was massive. And if her body instinctively hid it, as Malalia did with her own power, there was no telling her true potential.

So no, she would remain unconscious, held that way by a team of casters who would reinforce the layers upon layers of stasis spells keeping her from waking. Even with their skills and powers, though, it was a difficult task. But it was working. She was no closer to waking, so long as they were diligent in their casting.

Malalia walked to Hunze and ran her fingers through the woman's golden hair.

"Such incredible power," she murmured. "And so close I can touch it. *Literally* touch it. Yet for the first time in centuries, I cannot claim it as my own."

The frustration was both maddening but also a rare treat, for Malalia had gone without a true challenge for so many years she almost reveled in her new dilemma. She'd tried to drink from the woman, but the Ootaki magic quickly put a stop to that with an incredibly painful burst of magic that had nearly knocked Malalia to the ground.

Like many creatures of both galaxies, this woman seemed to possess a completely autonomous defense system against that particular type of attack. She likely didn't even know it existed. But then, no one ever bothered trying to drink from Ootaki, as all of their power was in their hair. Normally, anyway.

But it didn't matter. Malalia knew she couldn't rush the process, and patience would reward her far more than haste. The hair on just this one Ootaki's head alone contained enough power to create a modest portal, so long as she was in the presence of the Earth's sun's energy.

And as Malalia's men gathered more to add to the equation, she'd eventually be able to open a *new* portal to that galaxy. To that same system. And as her men had reported, she could position it to receive the sun's rays from that side as well. A double helping of magical power.

Sitting quietly in the chamber with her sleeping captive, Malalia Maktan, aka Visla Dominus, began the slow process of chipping away at Hunze's natural defenses. She had no idea exactly how long it would take, but if she'd been able to remove a Magus stone from its bonded owner, then there was no reason she couldn't likewise claim this woman's hair's power for her own. It would just take time.

Calmly, patiently, Malalia probed and prodded the slumbering Ootaki's magical walls with the gentlest of touch. One day, that power would bend to her will, and at that time, she would have her revenge. At that time, the Earth, and all the worlds in its galaxy, would be hers.

With a calm smile, she sat and worked, knowing that time would come soon enough.

ABOUT THE AUTHOR

A native Californian, Scott Baron was born in Hollywood, which he claims may be the reason for his rather off-kilter sense of humor.

Before taking up residence in Venice Beach, Scott first spent a few years abroad in Florence, Italy before returning home to Los Angeles and settling into the film and television industry, where he has worked as an on-set medic for many years.

Aside from mending boo-boos and owies, and penning books and screenplays, Scott is also involved in indie film and theater scene both in the U.S. and abroad.

ALSO BY SCOTT BARON

Standalone Novels

Living the Good Death

The Clockwork Chimera Series

Daisy's Run

Pushing Daisy

Daisy's Gambit

Chasing Daisy

Daisy's War

The Dragon Mage Series

Bad Luck Charlie

Space Pirate Charlie

Dragon King Charlie

Magic Man Charlie

Star Fighter Charlie

Portal Thief Charlie

Rebel Mage Charlie

Warp Speed Charlie

Odd and Unusual Short Stories:

The Best Laid Plans of Mice: An Anthology

Snow White's Walk of Shame

The Tin Foil Hat Club

Lawyers vs. Demons

The Queen of the Nutters

Lost & Found

Made in United States
North Haven, CT
17 November 2024

60476321R00219